Book One
Women with Wisdom Series

I0639235

Whistling Up the Southwind

A Novel

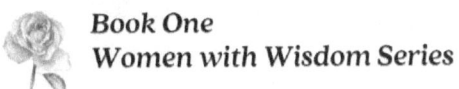

Book One
Women with Wisdom Series

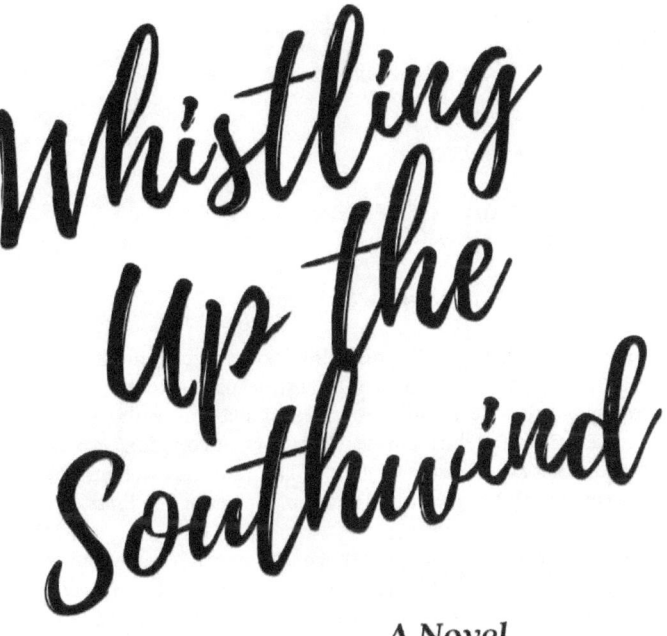

A Novel

Mary Kathleen Mckenna

FLOWER *of* LIFE PRESS

FLOWER *of* LIFE PRESS

Whistling Up The Southwind

Book One of the "Women with Wisdom" Series
By Mary Kathleen McKenna

Published by Flower of Life Press
Astara J. Ashley, *Publisher*
www.FlowerofLifePress.com

For information about special discounts for bulk order purchases,
email support@floweroflifepress.

Cover and Interior Design:
Astara J. Ashley, www.floweroflifepress.com

Library of Congress Control Number:
Available upon request.

ISBN: 979-8-9878275-1-2

DEDICATION

I dedicate this book to my beloved Maine Coon cat Sarabi, who died during the writing of the final edit and layout. She was the matriarch of our family, holding us together with patience.

The first morning after her death, the younger Maine Coon and our elderly Shar-pei, Brandywine Bear, stood in confusion, waiting for her to eat her food and give them the message it was their turn.

That's when I realized the gaping hole in our family she left behind. I expect her to be up in a magical part of the universe with those loved ones who have already departed, guiding us from above.

Sleep well dear one, until we come together again.

PRAISE

"I really enjoyed the well-developed characters in *Whistling Up the Southwind* who spoke to me about the things that were going on in their lives and how it influenced them. The plot seemed so real-life that I felt like the author was telling me her life history. I enjoyed the unusualness of travel in a motorhome—I have never experienced that and found it captivating! I would rank this book up there with others that have had a life-long impact on me."

—June Sadowsky, Geriatric DDS, Avid Reader

"*Whistling up the Southwind* by Mary Kathleen McKenna aka Dr. Kathie Bishop is truly a heart-warming novel about strangers who cross paths. It is a story of three very different women who, during their time together, gain a love for each other and learn to honor the journey each one must take to pursue her own destiny. Mary Kathleen McKenna weaves a narrative that is sometimes hilarious, sometimes heartbreaking, but always inspiring. A must-read!"

—J.J. Caudle, Director of Community Yoga, Dade City, FL

"Thank you for sharing your hard work with me. What an interesting person you created in Granny Rose. I wondered how you were going to get to Oregon and then wondered how you would have Anna Marie return home. At 81 years old, it was worth the read to find out."

—J.G., Reader of the 2007 edition of *Whistling Up the Wind*

Acknowledgments

We are a sum-total of all those who have come into our lives, either briefly or for a longer period of time. There are so many people who have enhanced my life and made my life richer. I can't begin to thank them because it would take an entire book and I would still leave out someone.

I am most grateful for those who supported me during the writing of this book, including my author/mentor friend Kathleen McGowan, my publisher Astara J. Ashley of Flower of Life Press, her editors, and my son V. Eric Pirillo (Vincent Bishop, pen name) who provided his brilliant poetry for the beginning of chapters. I am eternally thankful for my husband Ron Burris who is always supportive of whatever I attempt to achieve. He believes in me far more than I do, and that makes all the difference.

I'm also thankful to my faithful pets who have always loved me and my family with no reservations. Each one has added joy to my life, teaching us all the valuable lessons of giving. My mother, June Bishop, was alive when I first published this book in 2007 under the name Kathie Bishop. Today, I feel her over my shoulder cheering me on in her cautious manner, hesitant to show her pride or emotion, yet feeling the pride all the same.

Cast of Characters

Anna Marie
Main character in all three books in the *Women with Wisdom Series*. Widowed; buys the Southwind motorhome (the wind of new beginnings, transformation); travels to rebuild her life and her courage; 69 at the beginning of the story, seven years before she is 62 and on her Southwind journey.

Ted Golding
Anna Marie's late husband of 3 years; grieving for her husband led Anna Marie to purchase the Southwind.

Jane Golding
Anna Marie's disapproving mother-in-law.

Janet Jonas/Smithers
Anna Marie's mother.

John Smithers
Janet Jonas' husband, Anna Marie's legal/adopted father.

Maya
The Maine Coon Kitten, an adopted stray from a campground in Pennsylvania.

Little Bear
Anna Marie's very loved pug dog.

Circe
The African Grey Parrot, reluctantly adopted by Anna Marie.

Christa
Runaway pregnant teenager (pregnant by an itinerant preacher) with cerebral palsy (minor characteristic, part of who she is).

Granny Rose
A Stowaway on the Southwind near Macon, Georgia; elderly but of unknown age.

Harry (Harry-Jim-Bob)
Granny Rose's third husband, also known as Harry-Jim-Bob; calls Anna Marie in the middle of the night to inform her of Granny Rose's death.

Katy
Anna Marie's oldest child/daughter; married to Clint Clark with three children: Kassidy, Clint Jr., and Jeannie.

Diana
Anna Marie's best friend in Central NY.

Harriet Golding
Ted's mother; Anna Marie's mother-in-law.

Lee Norton
Anna Marie's biological father.

Sergeant George I and II
The ever-helpful two Sergeant Georges, in Macon, Georgia, who support Anna Marie's journey in the Southwind; help the Southwind Gang out of difficulties; they are instrumental in the local newspaper adopting the journeys of the Southwind as front-page stories.

Cassandra
The Administrative Assistant at the Sergeants' police station who answers calls, organizes the police station, and takes care of the Southwind ladies when she is needed.

Sybil
Owner of The Ancient Rose Inn, Sumer, Louisiana.

Prologue

I was adopted before I was born. Throughout my entire life when I have informed anyone of my adoption, the phrase 'before I was born' is important because I don't want people to feel sorry for me—I was very wanted. At the age of four, my parents sat me down to tell me I was adopted, very much loved, and wanted.

I believe I can remember that scene, my father in tears with my mother sitting stoically beside him, the very image of the unemotional Brit while he was the more demonstrable French and Irish descendant. After they finished telling me my story, I got up off my father's lap to ask for dinner and to go outside to play before dinner. I don't know if this is a true memory, or my mother has described this so often to me that it has become my own memory. As a visual person, I play out the memory when I relate this to others as a short movie or documentary.

In my forties, I needed to learn more about my biological family and at the same time, I hoped to expand my knowledge of ancient women's history to restore this to textbooks and common knowledge. I thought both would take me a few months, never realizing how much the pathways of each would intertwine and never totally divide.

My mother helped me by relating the name on my crib in the hospital nursery my parents visited the early morning after they had received the call from the adoption agency I had been born and where to visit. My parents immediately renamed me mentally and emotionally, Kathleen Marie Bishop, permanently removing the name given by my biological grandparents, Mary McKenna.

Or so they thought. I don't believe my mother understood I was legally Mary McKenna until the final court approval exactly one year after my birth. My father may have as she described him publicly crying with happiness when the judge declared me as permanently their daughter.

The judge, according to my mother, pinched my chubby cheeks and admired my plump body, exclaiming I was obviously well-fed and cared for in my first year. Unfortunately for me, growing up in the time of the model of Twiggy as beautiful, I retained the plump body and chubby cheeks throughout my life.

I learned the stories of this time when I was a middle-aged adult. I only learned that my legal name of Mary McKenna was still in place for one year after birth as I rummaged through my mother's legal papers after her death.

I share this story with you to help you understand why I have changed to the pen name of Mary Kathleen McKenna. It represents the combination of the two legal names I held in my early childhood.

Here I am almost thirty years later, passionate about knowing my female ancestors in order to place myself in the context of women's history. I write this as my prologue so you will understand that the basis of my writing is those two passions —ancestry and women's history—and the two winding pathways that have become one. My writing is fictional as are my characters. They are real to me even more so because I find people I meet who are my characters, especially women, and historical figures that match the characters in my books. I find these matches long after I have written the story, confirming to me the importance of sharing their stories with the world.

I write the books in the Women with Wisdom Series as a modern-day tale that doubles as symbolism from women's history. This book and the other two in the Series are always written from both levels. I leave it to you to decide which level — or both—you want to read. My intent is to help to expand your awareness of women's history and that it's often right there in front of us, "for those with eyes to see and ears to hear."

~Mary Kathleen McKenna

"Each friend represents a world in us, a world possibly not born until they arrive, and it is only by this meeting that a new world is born."

–Anais Nin

Chapter One

Beginning the Adventure: The Full Moon of March

The Present

Anna Marie awoke to tears running down her cheeks. Her dream was so real she was not sure if it was a dream or reality. It may have been both.

She dreamt of an RV called the Southwind. She was traveling with a much younger woman who appeared pregnant and a tiny, dynamic older woman along with a kitten, bird, and dog. She looked at the foot of her bed, which was highlighted by the bright rays of the full moon. At the foot of the bed slept Little Bear and Maya curled up next to each other. She knew at least part of her dream was true.

As she tried to bring herself to full awareness, the phone next to her bed rang shrilly. Like most people, Anna Marie hated the sound of the phone in the middle of the night. The best you could hope for was a wrong number by a drunken bar patron and the worst was tragic news.

The voice on the other end of the phone identified himself as Harry. Anna Marie had to pause to consider how she knew Harry or why he would be calling her in the middle of the night.

He related to her, "I'm so sorry to bother you this late at night. Rose insisted I call you immediately. She died a few minutes ago and made me promise that I would call you. She expects you to retrieve the articles she has asked for you to guard for her after her death. She said you and Christa would know what to do?"

The male voice paused, waiting for a response from Anna Marie, which she felt obligated to give. If only she could recall what this was all about and who these people were. She had the feeling this call was directly related to her dream. She couldn't remember how or why.

Anna Marie was now fully awake and said to Harry, "I'm sorry. I've just woken up. Your call came as a shock. You know how it is never easy to get this kind of call in the middle of the night.

She paused and then continued pretending to understand. "Yes, I'll call Christa. Can I call you in the morning after I am more awake, see how you are doing, and let you know my plans?"

She asked for his telephone number, writing it down on the pad she kept on her nightstand. Anna Marie thanked him for calling to give her Rose's wishes. She mentally asked herself who Rose was and why she was called. She hung up confused.

Anna Marie slowly gained consciousness. Realizing the enormity of the call she had just received, the tears on her face from her dream increased. The extreme sorrow was now felt at the loss of Granny Rose. Her dream had been more than a dream. It was a reminder of a special time in her life she had been reliving in her dream. Maybe a premonition of the phone call she just received?

She would not be able to go to sleep again tonight. It was too early in the morning to call Christa on the West Coast. She decided to go make herself a cup of tea and process the telephone call. As she opened the door to her bedroom, her cat "Maya" and dog "Little Bear" looked up, looking outside to get a sense of the time of the day, and curled up back to sleep with sighs of irritation for the disturbance.

The teakettle quickly came to a boil. Anna Marie poured the water into her lovely blue teapot. As she waited for the chamomile tea to steep, she prepared crackers and cheese on one of her antique platters from her grandmother. Once she had the table set and the tea steeped, she sat down. The story behind the dream slowly came back to her…

Seven years earlier

One day in late March, Anna Marie threw her cards down on the table at the Higginsville senior center and said, "I'm done for today. I really don't feel well. I think I'll go home early."

She quickly said her goodbyes; assured her friends it was nothing to worry about and left for her car in the parking lot.

As a 53-year-old early-retired public school teacher's aide, she was heavy set with dark blonde hair laced with silver threads. While attractive, she had always been overweight and wore colorful, stylish clothes to try to compensate for her far from model-sized figure.

She often surprised people with her wit and energy, which she still retained regardless of her age. She was very popular with her friends not only for these traits but also for her kindness and ability to listen. Her late husband Ted and her children were always amazed at how total strangers walked up to her to tell her their life stories. Anna Marie always knew just the right thing to say to these strangers.

She had worked as a Teacher's Aide in the high school with special needs children until her husband's death three years ago. When her husband died, she lost all interest in her job retiring four years after becoming eligible for half-pay retirement. Sometimes she regretted the time she continued to work while her husband was retired. Most days she knew she would have changed nothing about their former lives.

She felt fine. She was thoroughly bored with cards, her life, and grieving. Widowed now for three years, she spent many of her days at the senior center. She could then tolerate the lonely nights. Other days she spent at movies with friends, visiting, or puttering around her large three-bedroom house and gardens. Sometimes she would babysit her four grandchildren—three of her oldest daughter's children and her son's only child. That was becoming increasingly rare, as they were older now and busy with their own lives.

Her middle daughter in Boston was her alternative lifestyle daughter. She lived with her significant other waiting until it was legal for people of the same sex to marry. Remarkably, though she and Ted had once agonized over what they had done wrong for this child, this was the child who was happiest in life and needed her the least. Over the years, Anna Marie called Cynthia when she wanted advice or to go stay with her and her partner, Anita, when she needed a respite from her everyday life. After losing Ted to an unexpected heart attack, she spent a month with them trying to heal. It had been the most peaceful she had felt during the past three years.

As she drove towards her home, she passed a house with a large, well-maintained motor home sitting in the front yard. A 'For Sale' sign was prominently displayed in the window. She had passed this RV and house numerous times before, but for some reason, today she stopped. A balding, chubby man with a wide smile, about her age, came out of the house.

He asked her, "Are you here to look at the RV? It's a real beauty. I hate to sell her. My wife claims we spend too much time on the road and not home with the grandchildren."

In a used salesman-style voice, he told her, "It's worth every penny of the asking price. She's a 1998 Southwind with very low mileage. We bought her new. She's been loved and well cared for in those years."

Anna Marie listened, nodding as he talked, pretending that she understood what he had told her. With surprise, she realized that she was there to look at the RV. Waking up this morning, this would have been the last way she would have thought to spend the day.

The man paused for a breath before beginning again at his record pace, "I'm sorry. My name's Walter Franken. My wife tells me all the time that I talk too much. She says I do not give others an opportunity to say anything. I just assumed you were interested in the Southwind. I get so excited when I talk about her. Are you here to look at the motor home?"

He stopped talking, finally looking at Anna Marie, obviously waiting for an answer.

Anna Marie introduced herself and said, "I did stop to look at the motor home. I'll be honest with you. I know absolutely nothing about RVs but..."

She stopped, wondering how much to say to Walter. Could she tell him about her loneliness or her need to change her life before she went insane? How the grieving consumes most breaths, making it painful to breathe or think even after three years? How staying numb has been the only way she survives every day?

She didn't know how to tell a total stranger let alone a friend about the dream last night of her beloved husband, Ted. He told her in that dream that it was time for her to live again.

The dream had been so real with Ted apologetic, telling her that they had clung to each other far too long in their lifetime of love and companionship. He was releasing her to build a new life for herself. He told her he would always be there, watching out for her. He wanted her to be happy.

She realized that one of the reasons she stopped was the name of the motor home, the "Southwind". From her reading of ancient history, she knew that the south was considered the direction for the reawakening of desires and energy. In high school, she had loved history and had hoped to go on to college to become a history teacher. Girls in her town were not expected to go to college. After World War II, it was expected that the men returning home from war would work and women marry those men to raise a family. Ted, returning home from the Korean War, was ten years older than 16-year-old Anna Marie.

She never regretted marrying Ted at a very young age. She kept up her love of history by reading every moment she could find time over the years. Unfortunately, even her joy in reading and learning had been disrupted by her sadness. If there was anything she now needed, it was to reawaken her life and desires. The journey back to her life and herself could be through this motor home named the Southwind.

Walter stood quietly, waiting for her to answer.

She couldn't tell him everything she was thinking but she was able to say, "I'm widowed and need to move on with my life. Maybe this Southwind is the way to do that. Can you show me the motor home and explain some of the features?"

He had patiently waited for her to finish telling him her thoughts and to answer his question. Anna Marie did not know that this was very uncharacteristic of Walter as he talked almost all the time during his waking hours. Sometimes, to his wife's irritation, he talked in his sleep.

Walter's wife had long ago stopped listening to him. He appreciated a new person to talk with who might listen. He had given her as much quiet as he could give her. Somehow, Anna Marie felt instantly comfortable with Walter. She thought she could probably share some of her deepest feelings of loneliness without Walter making fun of her.

Walter nodded and proudly showed her the motor home kitchen, dining area, sleeping areas, bathroom, and the slide-outs in the living room and bedroom. He kept up a running monologue of every feature of the motor home. Anna Marie was particularly impressed with the pastel colors of the living areas, the large storage areas under the motor home, and the leather seats on the couch. As he described each area, excitement built in his voice. It was obvious that he really did love this Southwind.

"Would you like to take her out for a drive?" he asked.

She was so impressed that he trusted her enough to do this with his beloved motor home and for taking her seriously that she said, "Yes, I would."

Walter directed her into the driver's seat while he calmly took the passenger seat.

Once she had the RV on the road with a few false starts and jerky motions, she began to feel comfortable with the size and driving of the motor home. Walter's patient explanations of how to gauge the width and turning of the Southwind helped Anna Marie develop confidence in her driving a vehicle as large as a bus.

Walter asked, "Doesn't she hold to the road like a dream? My wife and I had some wonderful trips with her. I am sure going to hate to part with her. I have a sense that you and she are meant to be together."

Walter looked closely at Anna Marie with a wistful and sympathetic look. She was surprised that Walter was so astute over her need to change. Probably without realizing it, he had given her just the kind of encouragement she needed right now.

Thirty minutes later they were back at Walter's house. Anna Marie proudly parked the motor home in its original position and climbed out as though she had been doing this all her life. She felt like she had just flown her first solo flight. For the first time in a long while, she felt good about herself and life.

Walter showed her a few more features of the motor home, encouraging any questions Anna Marie might have.

"Of course, if you were to buy the Southwind, I would be happy to show you all the features, walk you through everything you need to know, and even give you some driving lessons. We could do some trial set-ups with me giving you tips," he said.

He paused to take a small breath, "It is not that hard to do once you get the hang of it. It does help to have someone give you tips. My wife could do it when she wanted to, which wasn't very often. She really has never liked this Southwind."

They discussed the negotiable price. Amazingly, within another half hour, Anna Marie wrote a check for a down payment on the agreed-upon price.

Instead of going straight home, Anna Marie went directly to the bank for a loan for the Southwind. She decided she did not want to take that much out of her IRA or empty out her savings account. She, like most older adults, never could predict what the future would bring. She also did not want to give her family a chance to talk her out of the purchase. Quickly applying for the loan made the most sense.

On the way home from the bank, she stopped to buy her favorite ice cream, Heavenly Hash, to celebrate her spontaneous purchase. She thought to herself that she had never had a slim figure anyway, so what were a few more calories? She also stopped at AAA for maps and books of several adjoining states. She talked to them about how to plan for a trip with a motor home. She left AAA with a pile of information to help her with her planning.

On the way home, Anna Marie found herself whistling for the first time since she was a young teenager. She had not felt this good in years and the whistle came out spontaneously without her even thinking about it. She practiced her whistling for a few minutes, laughing with sheer joy that she still could whistle.

She heard her mother saying to her, "Anna Marie, young girls who whistle and hens that crow will come to a bad end."

Since Anna Marie was now sixty-one with no major catastrophes, she thought that her mother's dire forecast was not likely to come true. She continued to whistle.

She whistled as she opened the door to Little Bear, her pug dog, who greeted her at the door with her usual exuberance and obvious joy at Anna Marie coming home. Little Bear stopped to listen to the whistling. She cocked her head in question as Anna Marie realized that Little Bear had never heard this sound from her before.

She hugged Little Bear extra hard to let her know that this was a happy sound. Anna Marie fed Little Bear, gave her fresh water, and then opened the mail.

Thinking about who would be the child most supportive of her spontaneous purchase, she first called Cynthia. Cynthia wasn't home but her significant other Anita was home. Anna

Marie explained to Anita why she was calling. Anita was extremely enthusiastic, congratulating Anna Marie on her important decision.

Anita exclaimed, "Cynthia and I have been so worried about you these last few years. I think this will be wonderful for you. You will be starting a whole new life. I hope that Cynthia and I will be welcome to join you in your Southwind during one of your trips?"

She added, "It's nothing we've ever done. It sounds like it will be very adventurous. I'll have Cynthia call you when she gets in. She's interviewing at one of the schools here to teach a couple of continuing education art courses. I know she'll be excited for you."

Anna Marie thought, as she had so frequently over the last few years, what a nice person Anita was and how well-matched they were as a couple. They each seemed to care for and about each other. They had built a wonderful life in an old loft they had rehabilitated on the North Side of Boston.

She said to Anita, "I don't know my full plans. When I have them finalized I will let you both know. Of course, you are welcome."

Anna Marie next called her eldest daughter to begin the difficult job of explaining why she had made such a spontaneous choice. She was still not quite prepared for the very harsh, negative reaction from Katy, even though that was often Katy's response to her mother's choices.

When Katy answered the phone Anna Marie said, "Hi hon. Are the kids home from school yet?"

After talking about the grandkids and Katy's day, Anna Marie announced, "I've just purchased a motor home. It's called the Southwind. I'm going to take a long trip with it. I think across the country. I still need to map out my route."

She decided the best way to approach this was to be straightforward and just tell Katy. She knew that this was far more than a trip she was taking. She didn't know how best to describe it even to herself yet, let alone her eldest daughter who could be difficult. Katy was her model perfect beautiful daughter, who spent a lifetime acting neglected no matter the situation once the other two siblings were born.

After moments of stunned silence, her daughter Katy stuttered, "Did you say you just bought a motor home? I couldn't have heard you right."

Anna Marie assured her that she did hear her right. Ignoring the sarcasm in her daughter's voice, she excitedly described her new purchase.

She told her daughter, who was unusually quiet; "I'm not sure exactly when I will leave. It will be after Jeannie's birthday. I will probably go sometime in early or late April. That will give me enough time to pack and get ready. The winter snow should be over in the mountains by then. Walter tells me most of the campgrounds are open by early spring, especially in the south. Some are open all year, according to Walter."

Anna Marie was proud of the way she sounded. Almost like she knew what she was doing with a 37-foot motor home.

Jeannie was Katy's five-year-old daughter, her youngest and the one who looked the most like Katy. She was Anna Marie's favorite when she allowed herself to have a favorite grandchild. At that moment she decided Jeannie was going to be the first grandchild she tried to teach to whistle. She regretted that she had never tried to teach Katy or Erin, her son. Now that she thought about it, Cynthia had been her only child who whistled with absolutely no lessons or encouragement from Anna Marie.

Katy exclaimed, "Now, I know you have lost your mind. What would Dad have said? You can't just take off to who knows where on your own. I assume it is you alone. Do you have a boyfriend that I don't know about? Who is this Walter you mentioned?"

Anna Marie responded impatiently, "No, I don't have any boyfriend. Walter is the former owner of my Southwind. I'm going alone. If your father wanted to comment on my purchases or decisions, I think he should have stayed alive to do so!"

Katy spoke angrily, "Mom, I know you still miss Dad terribly, but this is no way to get over his death. You legally have three days to back out of a major purchase. Call whatever his name is you bought it from. Get any money you put into it back."

Anna Marie had lost patience by now.

She replied firmly, "It is 'she,' not an 'it'!"

Anna Marie was amazed at how attached and defensive she had already become of the Southwind. The motor home had begun to take on a life of its own.

Anna Marie continued, "I have no intention of backing out or getting my money back."

Katy sniffled and asked, "How long are you going to be gone? You do have grandchildren who need you. Respectable grandmothers don't go across the country willy-nilly like this, especially this time of the year when they will be out of school shortly after you leave. They always spend some time with you over the summer."

She paused, sniffling louder on the phone, "You know, Clint and I go to his college reunion in July every year. We count on you to take the kids then. Why don't you wait until school is out and go up to the lake for a few days with the kids if you insist on keeping this…?"

Anna Marie angrily interrupted her, "She's called the Southwind. Since when did you get so holier than thou? I haven't seen any rulebooks lately on how to be a good grandmother. I hardly think they will even miss their grandmother they are all so busy with camp, their friends, and their sports during the summer."

"Which they should be," she added not to appear as though she were complaining.

As much as she loved her grandchildren, she found it very difficult to be in their lives when their parents requested or out of their lives when it was apparent she would only be perceived as an interfering grandparent. They couldn't fill her life. They saw her as an extension of themselves without awareness of a person underneath. She had been used to this as a parent. It was even more frustrating to her as a grandparent. Why were the people she loved the most the ones who knew her the least while loving her despite not knowing what was important to her?

Still trying to win this argument, Katy said, "Well, what will the great-grandmothers think? They will be very disappointed in you. I'm going to be the person they complain to, like what I say makes any difference to you."

Anna Marie laughed and responded, "They have both had many years of practice. My purchase will come as little surprise or disappointment to them."

Anna Marie's mother loved her. Despite her love for her, she made it apparent Anna Marie was not exactly what she had hoped for in a daughter. She was 81 and living in an apartment that was an extension of different levels of assisted living.

Her mother-in-law still lived on her own in the family home of fifty-five years. She had never liked Anna Marie. Throughout her marriage to her son Ted, she made it apparent that she only tolerated his chosen wife. She was the mother of her adored grandchildren and the wife of her only child with that relationship making it necessary to maintain contact with her. She had threatened many times over the years to disown Ted and Anna Marie because of many things she thought out loud to Ted about Anna Marie's latest wrong action.

Anna Marie always thought it was her orneriness that kept her going. Her mother-in-law would likely outlive her by many years. She had long ago written off any inheritance from her in-laws. Anna Marie felt very sorry for her mother-in-law, who didn't even know how little the inheritance mattered to Anna Marie or had made a difference to Ted when he was alive.

Anna Marie knew that these were frequently empty threats. Though recently her mother-in-law had indicated she was still deciding how to split the inheritance amongst the grandchildren rather than including Anna Marie in the will.

Cynthia had, of course, already been threatened with removal if "she didn't wake up and live like everyone else with a husband and children."

Most of the time, Anna Marie felt she was trying to protect her children from their grandmother's cruelty. She hated this type of manipulative behavior. Often, she had all she could do to protect herself, let alone her adult children.

Katy made one more attempt. "Well, what about Little Bear? She can't go an entire summer without you."

Anna Marie realized she hadn't thought all the details out yet.

Her automatic response, which turned out to be the correct response, was, "Of course Little Bear is going with me. There is air conditioning in the Southwind. I can leave her when I want to visit something or stop to eat. There is plenty of room for her to be comfortable in the motor home. I'm sure she'll love it. Little Bear loves to travel. This will be an adventure for her, too."

Anna Marie paused, "I guess I'm not really going alone after all. Little Bear will be great company. I'll take your father's car. That way, I can leave the motor home at campgrounds during the day for Little Bear if I visit someplace that does not accept pets."

Anna Marie was actually very surprised at herself because Ted's car was under a tarp in the garage. She had not been able to even look at it since his death. It was almost as though another being had taken over her mind, thinking and talking for her. Maybe Ted really had visited her in her dream last night?

Katy said, "The kids are coming in the door. We will have to talk about this more later. I need to be the adult and talk some sense into you. You do know that I need you, too. I'm only concerned about your well-being. Clint is out of town so often on business. I look forward to your visits when he is away from home."

Anna Marie reminded Katy of all her friends and her work life. Katy was an elementary school teacher. Katy had a huge group of friends who partied together, took care of each other's children, and were there for each other when they needed support. Anna Marie finally hung up the phone after promising to come for dinner at Katy's house Thursday night. She promised to be open to talking more about her intended journey, even though Anna Marie was more determined than she had been before her conversation with Katy to take her trip on her own with the Southwind.

After that call, Anna Marie thought it was best to get all the responses out of the way at once. She next called her son and daughter-in-law. They were "somewhat concerned" about her decision. It was obvious they thought some form of dementia or mental illness had set in. They apparently were humoring her until this passed.

Her son Erin asked her if she was feeling well or if she needed a physical. Anna Marie assured him she was feeling fine, in fact, the best she had felt in three years.

He said, "Grandma is going to be very angry. You don't visit her enough now, as it is. How could you even think of leaving her here while you take off for some unknown place?"

Erin had always been his maternal Grandmother's favorite. The two of them often decided what Anna Marie should be doing or not doing.

Anna Marie reminded Erin that his grandmother was busy with her friends and activities that she barely had time for her anyway. Erin grudgingly gave in for the moment. Anna Marie could tell that she would hear more arguments from him in the future.

After that conversation, Anna Marie called her mother. She decided not to call her mother-in-law. Word of mouth would be soon enough for her mother-in-law to learn of her plans. They barely talked to each other from one month to the next anyway. It could be a few months before she realized Anna Marie wasn't home. She may have left and returned before her mother-in-law noticed her missing.

Her mother answered after several rings. As soon as she heard her mother's voice, she was sixteen again, apologizing for deciding without her.

Surprisingly, her mother was supportive of this decision.

She said, "Anna Marie, I have not liked the way you have acted the past couple of years. I know you miss Ted, but life does go on. You noticed my life went on after your father died. If this is what it takes for your life to go on, then more power to you! I wish I were younger and healthier. I would go with you if I could."

Her mother sounded wistful, "You make sure to call me often and send postcards along the way. I can remember when the kids were young, you and Ted took those wonderful trips. The kids took turns sending your father and me postcards. Every day we'd look forward to the mail. It felt like we were taking a trip with you. It will be great to have those postcards again."

Anna Marie's father was her stepfather. Her biological father had never been in her life or even knew about her existence, according to her mother. Her mother had been very young when she became pregnant with Anna Marie. She lived at home with Anna Marie's grandmother until she met John, Anna Marie's stepfather.

Anna Marie was only two when her mother and stepfather married. John had been a loving father to Anna Marie in every way possible. They rarely acknowledged over the years that he was her stepfather rather than her biological father. Because of her mother's complications with the birth of Anna Marie, her parents were not able to have any more children. Anna Marie had been an only child. John adored Anna Marie and always appeared proud of everything she did.

Ted and her stepfather were the two men in her life that supported her absolutely. With both gone, there was an emptiness she was not able to fill. Anna Marie was not sure if she would ever be able to fill that void. She thought the Southwind might be the key to healing.

After she completed her calls to her family, Anna Marie called her best friend Diana. Diana was Anna Marie's friend since their children were young. Diana was widowed at a very young age and never remarried. She was a single Mom long before it was common to be a single Mom. Diana's son was as close to Anna

Marie as her own son. Anna Marie's children considered Diana an aunt, often talking to her when they were not comfortable going to Ted or Anna Marie.

They talked for a few minutes, catching up on the latest news. Then Anna Marie made her announcement. Diana was silent for a minute.

Diana quietly said, "I think this is great if you think you can manage this on your own. I will miss you dearly, though. I hope you won't be gone for too long. I'd come with you if you would let me. I don't want to leave home in the spring with my first grandchild so close to delivery. I'm hoping they will let me help with some of the care after the birth while my daughter-in-law is recovering."

Anna Marie gave her some details of her thoughts on how long and where she would be going. She admitted honestly to Diana that she hadn't really thought this all the way through, yet. After this last supportive and positive call, Anna Marie took a break, ate her dinner, and started making plans for her trip.

Just before falling asleep, Cynthia called.

She said, "Mom, I'm sorry for calling too late. I was so excited for you about your news that I wanted to call and congratulate you. We're happy for you!"

Cynthia updated her on her job interview and the art classes she'd be teaching. Anna Marie was pleased with the positive reaction from both Cynthia and Anita.

When Anna Marie hung up the phone, she wished for Ted so she could tell him what a good job they had done raising their three children. Each one had become a very happy adult in their way. Somehow, Anna Marie suspected Ted knew. That night Anna Marie slept through the entire night without waking up. She was more rested in the morning than she had been in years.

The next few days were jam-packed with Anna Marie finalizing the loan, deciding details with Walter for training sessions before finally taking the Southwind, and making a to-do list for her trip. She debated over how best to deal with the bills and mail. She really didn't want to hand that over to one of her children. Yet she didn't want to fall behind on payments.

She planned with the Central New York Utility Company to go on a budget plan so that she would know the amount to send each month. She was also able to reduce her phone bill to a minimum vacation mode amount without losing the phone number that she had for over forty years. She found that she could obtain her bill for her cell phone by calling an 800 number. All other bills she had were the same each month. There were few of those as she and Ted had been able to pay off their house early. Anna Marie had only one credit card with no charges on it. She could pay the balance off each month if she were to use the card on her trip.

She was fortunate that her pensions, IRA payments, and Social Security were already direct deposited. She would need to learn how to use ATM machines and cards. She was determined that she would learn so that she didn't need to carry large amounts of cash or have someone else access her money for her. Like many of her generation, she avoided using ATMs. Now was a good time to get over her reluctance.

She started a list of what she hoped to accomplish on the trip. Number one was to have sex one more time before she died. Anna Marie was astonished that she was able to write this down. She felt some embarrassment over number one on her list, but she didn't plan to share her list with anyone else, especially her children. Intimacy had always been a wonderful part of her relationship with Ted. It was something she missed dearly because it brought them closer together.

Anna Marie couldn't imagine marrying again. One more time before she died, she'd like to feel that freedom of self, to feel desirable again to someone. This was going to be a difficult goal to achieve, as the only man she had ever been with in her life or felt comfortable enough to share herself with was Ted. She had difficulty thinking about being intimate with anyone else.

She started to erase number one off the list, instead saying determinedly to herself, "This is about changing my life and living again! I'm going to leave it on in case the opportunity arises."

Number two was to travel spontaneously without a set itinerary. This would be different from how she had traveled before or lived her life. She had always been a list maker relying on lists as she grew older to make sure she didn't forget something important. Anna Marie laughed to herself as she realized the irony of placing spontaneity on her List.

Number three was to laugh at least two times a day, something she had done very little of in the past three years.

The fourth on the list was to find her biological father. In the past five years, she had become very interested in genealogical searches and learning about the paternal side of her family since she knew so little about her father, extended family, or paternal ancestors. She had narrowed this search to a small town in Georgia, hoping to visit this town to learn more about her biological father and to meet him if he was still living. She had the last known address. She gathered all the important papers she needed for this trip, including his possible address, in a folder for later on her trip.

Anna Marie assumed that she would continue to add to this list. This was the opposite of spontaneity. Anna Marie knew she could only change a little at a time and felt good about this small amount of progress. She didn't want to cause too much internal trauma. It felt good to write down the list as it made the trip real. She had already laughed more in the past two days than she had in three years, even if only at herself.

Anna Marie thought, "Maybe I will not be such a bad traveling companion after all."

The next few weeks were fun days, with Diana helping her with shopping and packing for her trip. Anna Marie, who had always been a collector and saver of everything, tried to limit what she took, attempting to adjust to her smaller living space in the Southwind.

Every item had to be considered before it was packed in a

suitcase or set aside to load into the Southwind. Diana was very skilled at this with less emotional attachment to Anna Marie's objects or even her personal items. Diana and Anna Marie laughed a lot, with some items bringing back memories of shared experiences.

A few times, Diana commented that Anna Marie was almost her old self.

Once during the sorting, Diana hugged Anna Marie, saying, "I've missed you. It's good to have you back."

Many days after Ted's death, Diana sat by Anna Marie's side, listening to her and warming the tea when it became cold. Diana had forced Anna Marie to eat on a few occasions.

Anna Marie had joked with Diana, "The least you could do is let me lose weight from grieving. You aren't even going to let me have that one comfort."

Now, with the purchase of the Southwind and plans for a new beginning, she accepted Diana's offer to help clean out some of Ted's personal items, including clothing. Anna Marie had been unable to do this before. Right after his funeral, she addressed the issue by moving into one of the children's old bedrooms.

Before the cleaning out when one of her children or Diana suggested it was time to donate or throw out at least some of Ted's things, Anna Marie changed the topic or told the requestor, "It was not yet time."

While it was difficult to let go, with Diana's help, she laughed and cried at the memories some of the items gave her, the process soothing.

A few things, like his worn and well-loved sweater, Anna Marie hung back up in a spare closet, saying, "This is a piece of Ted I have to keep."

Diana understood and did not try to talk Anna Marie out of keeping any of the items. When they were done, they had four large full garbage bags to throw out and five boxes to go to the Salvation Army. Another box had some items like an old army watch and assorted jewelry she planned to give to her children as keepsakes from their father.

By the end of the day, Anna Marie felt relieved she had accomplished this very difficult task with Diana's help. They chose their favorite restaurant for dinner to celebrate the accomplishment.

Walter scheduled several days of practice runs with Anna Marie. One day, Anna Marie packed a picnic lunch. They drove the New York State Thruway to Seneca Lake for a day trip. On the Thruway, Anna Marie kept the Southwind to a speed of 58 miles per hour, the speed that was most effective for gas mileage, according to Walter.

As Anna Marie carefully drove, cars sped by, pulling close in front of her, impatient due to her slower speed.

One car pulled in extremely close, causing Anna Marie to brake, exclaiming to Walter, "I think these drivers do not have as much fear of me as they should."

Walter laughed for miles after that. The laughter helped Anna Marie relax while driving.

Three days after her big purchase, Anna Marie decided it was time to do something about Ted's car. Even though she had told Katy that she was planning to take Ted's car, pretending it was an easy thing to do, she had dreaded the moment of pulling off the tarp. Since it had been sitting idle for three years, it likely needed servicing. She planned to ask for advice from Walter or another expert on how best to tow the car.

Anna Marie turned the light on in the garage and walked slowly to the car. She carefully uncovered the bright red Jaguar convertible. This was Ted's last car, purchased a few months before his death. The leather seats were hardly used, the odometer read 777 miles. They had planned their first trip in Ted's pride and joy on the day he had his heart attack. He died three days later.

Erin covered the car after the funeral at Anna Marie's request. Her intent had been to sell the car, though she had never had the will. Instead, she left it sitting in the garage waiting for the day when she developed the courage to sell.

After removing the tarp, Anna Marie opened the door and sat in the driver's seat. The car had been sitting so long that it smelled musty. There were no remaining smells of Ted. The tears ran down Anna Marie's face as she pictured Ted's beaming face on the day they bought the car. Both loved cars and driving, especially wandering over unexplored roads.

The Jaguar had been purchased through Ted's Deferred Compensation from teaching. The car was their gift to Ted for retirement after forty years teaching high school history. She remembered how concerned he was that she would like the car as much as he did. Maybe he had a premonition that this would become her car?

She married Ted when she was only seventeen and freshly graduated from high school. Ted was nine years older and a returning war hero. He went back to school on the GI Bill to become a high school history teacher. A cousin of Anna Marie's introduced them. It was love at first sight despite the age difference. Both loved historical stories of people's lives, the outdoors, and cars.

They never stopped talking when they were together. Ted told her so many fascinating stories of the war and Europe, where he had been located. One of their goals was to go to Europe together. They planned their dream trip to Europe for the following year after Ted's death for a time. They thought they would be able to afford the extra, frivolous expense. If Anna Marie had any regrets, it was that they had never made this trip. Unfortunately, life, not enough money, and responsibilities to their family always prevented them.

Anna Marie thought of a poem she read once by an elderly woman who regretted she had not laughed and danced more during her life. She wished she had taken those words to heart during Ted's life. She was now determined to make up for lost time for the remainder of her own life. She owed Ted her grieving, also owing herself a rebuilt, exciting life.

Anna Marie and Ted eloped after two months of dating, a

day after Anna Marie turned seventeen so they could legally be married without her parents' permission. They knew both families would likely not approve of their marriage and felt they could not bear to wait years for the approval of their families. Ted had seen too much horror in the war to wait for normal life to start. He wanted a wife, home, and family quickly to forget the pictures of death that sometimes came back to him in the middle of the night.

Anna Marie didn't know what to do with her life at a time when society did not expect women to have careers. Ted was a dream come true. It seemed and was a perfect match.

Her parents had been surprisingly supportive when they returned from the small, impromptu wedding in Tennessee. They were told Anna Marie was visiting with the cousin who introduced them. They were shocked when Ted and she returned to tell them their news. Her parents wanted reassurance that she was happy with her decision, even though she was so young. Once given that reassurance, they accepted Ted as a member of their family without contesting the legality of the marriage.

Anna Marie suspected they thought she was pregnant, even though she had not been. They had waited until their wedding night to make love to each other, with their oldest daughter Katy born fifteen months after their wedding ceremony.

Ted's family, on the other hand, demanded the couple get an immediate annulment of their marriage. Ted's mother felt that Anna Marie was too young and not 'right' for her son. She did not speak to them for months as Anna Marie's parents helped them clean and renovate the small cottage Ted had purchased with the money he saved from his wartime service.

After a few months, when Anna Marie became pregnant with Katy, Ted's mother called a truce but never truly got over Ted marrying Anna Marie without her permission. Over the years, Anna Marie stayed far away from her mother-in-law. She tried not to argue with her mother-in-law when they were together for the occasional family gatherings, not an easy act as her mother-in-law held some racist and sexist views that were hard to hear. On the way home from family events, Anna Marie was often in the uncomfortable position of explaining to her children why their grandmother's views were not opinions she wanted her children to repeat.

Anna Marie heard the garage door open as she sat in the car reviewing long-forgotten memories. She looked up to see Erin in the doorway. He appeared surprised to see her sitting in his dad's car. Without saying anything, he walked around to the passenger side, sitting in the passenger seat quietly.

He gently asked, "What are you doing, Mom?"

He waited a few seconds for her to respond. When she didn't, he asked, "You really miss Dad, don't you?"

Anna Marie nodded and said, "Taking the tarp off this car is one of the hardest things I have done. It's time to take the car out from mothballs. I'm planning on towing this car with me on my trip. Your Dad would want me to do that. He'd be happy to know the Jaguar was still being driven as he loved this car."

She hesitated, then continued knowing Erin would understand, "It was a small piece of him I couldn't sell. It makes sense to take it with me now. Would you mind helping me get it serviced and figure out how to best tow it?"

Erin said, "Of course, Mom. That is if you are still determined to take this trip of yours." Anna Marie could tell he had finally given up on persuading her to cancel her trip and was now resigned to being helpful.

"We'll call Mack; I'm sure he'll know how to safely tow this car. We'll have him check it all over and make sure it is safe to drive after it sat for so long," Erin assured her.

Anna Marie thanked him and asked, "Would you like one or two of your favorite chocolate chip cookies? I just happen to have a few for you."

Anna Marie was an excellent cook, one of the reasons she never lost weight since she sampled her latest creations. She usually had freshly baked cookies in the cookie jar for her children and grandchildren.

Anna Marie had already carefully packaged and arranged herbs from her garden and spices for her trip, as she couldn't imagine being without them. Over the years, she learned from her mother and other women how to use the herbs she grew so lovingly in her garden for healing and cooking. She had also attended courses at their local BOCES on cooking and healing with herbs.

She mentally added to her list, "*Number 6: Learn more about the herbs used for cooking and healing in other parts of the country.*"

While she made coffee and set the table with small pink Depression glass plates, Erin called Mack. Mack was the mechanic their whole family had used for so many years. He was like a member of the family. He agreed to come the next day, start the car and take it to his garage. He suggested that since the car was rear-wheel drive, it would be easy to tow with a tow bar and offered to buy the necessary parts.

Anna Marie certainly didn't know enough to argue with him, agreeing that sounded like the best way to tow the car. The next day Mack came taking the car for all the needed adjustments and equipment for towing. Anna Marie called Walter to let him know Mack was stopping by his house to check out the towing gear already on the RV.

Two weeks after Anna Marie's purchase of the Southwind, Walter delivered it to her house. They had made many practice trips, enjoyed each other's company, and shared memories they normally did not tell most people. Anna Marie already found the freedom of the road allowed her to leave her comfort zone to share thoughts with Walter. She hoped this continued throughout her travel.

A few times, they set up at a local park with a picnic lunch "so that Anna Marie could get the hang of what it was like."

The last day Walter arrived with the Southwind, asking her to take a short drive with him one last time in his cherished motor home. When they arrived back at Anna Marie's house, Walter handed Anna Marie the keys asking her to drive him back home.

He was very quiet on the drive to his house. Anna Marie suspected that he was saddened over saying goodbye to the Southwind.

She patted him on the shoulder when she stopped at his house, thanking him for all his kindness with the lessons on the Southwind. She gave him her cell number in case he needed to contact her with any information on the Southwind while she was on her trip.

As he got out of the Southwind he said sadly, "I'm going to miss my home away from home. I really liked the fun we had together in the past weeks. You're a natural at this. Take care of yourself, Anna Marie. I will be thinking of you."

He waved wistfully as she pulled away from his house, Anna Marie proudly driving solo for the first time and wishing she had an audience to see her newly learned skill.

Anna Marie attended Jeannie's birthday party as promised, which was held by Katy two days before the start of her trip. Katy and Erin reluctantly understood that she really was going on this journey. They at least outwardly attempted to be less negative than they had been originally.

She promised to stay in constant touch with them and to quit her trip at any time if she felt she couldn't do it alone. Anna Marie thought little white lies were okay when they hurt no one and they made people feel better. She had no intention of quitting this trip. In fact, the more it was suggested, the more determined she became to see this through to whatever end there might be.

In the last days, Anna Marie moved from room to room in the house to make sure she had packed everything needed. She also checked to make sure that the house would be safe while she was gone. This was the house she and Ted lived in all their married life. Originally a small cottage, over the years they added rooms, a second floor, sheds, a gazebo, and gardens. It was now quite large, probably too large for Anna Marie, but it had become part of her. She was not willing to give it up if she could take care of the house on her own.

She lovingly touched antique pieces of furniture, pictures

from celebrations past, and her collections of baskets. Each object brought a memory to her and a feeling of comfort. She found it harder than expected to say goodbye to the house, her friends, and family even if only for a short time. She still knew she had made the right decision. While she was afraid, she was also excited about the possibilities. Anna Marie looked forward to being on her own for the first time in her life. She left her parent's house as a very young adult to marry Ted and eventually lived in a house full of children, their friends, and extended family.

As she checked each room, she came to her craft room that had been Katy's room as a child. After Katy left home for college and then marriage, Anna Marie converted the room into a space for her weaving, rug making, and needlework. This was the hardest room in the house to leave. She still had not decided which projects to take with her, leaving that complicated decision until last.

She had not worked on any weaving since Ted's death. Some energy or emotion was now drawing her back to the weaving. She knew there was little room in the Southwind for the large loom. The smaller tabletop loom could fit easily under the RV so she could bring it out on the round folding table she planned to use when sitting outside.

She also selected a needlepoint chair cover pattern that had been left undone for many years along with a rug that she could work on with the handheld frame. She picked up a few more needlepoint projects, thinking she wanted to be prepared in case she finished the other projects since they took up little room in the Southwind. She packed the projects into a large traveling bag, a gift from Diana years ago.

She carried those along with the loom and the wool for the rug-making to the Southwind. The needlepoint chair cover she placed inside the Southwind, storing the rest underneath to work on later during the trip. She looked forward to establishing a pattern of traveling and stopping when she wanted. There were no lists as to where she had to travel or her final destinations, a major change from her former need to plan. She knew the direction she planned to travel and that she wanted to return home before the winter snow began in upstate New York. Otherwise, her journey might be guided by the stars, the weather, or her current whim.

The last night before the start of her trip, her two children who lived nearby and all of her grandchildren came to say goodbye with small travel gifts, including a calling card for the cell phone she had to promise to use frequently. Up until then, Anna Marie had avoided cell phones, enjoying the space of time out of contact with others.

Diana stopped over with a new book on herbs for Anna Marie and a hug for encouragement. Cynthia and Anita had sent a gas card for her to use on her travels along with thirteen deep red roses, each one with a small card indicating how each rose represented something positive they expected Anna Marie to gain from her new adventure.

In a few short weeks, Anna Marie thought with pride, she had everything planned, packed, and arranged to begin a new life for herself.

That night she fell asleep, excited about the prospects ahead of her.

⁓⚬⁓

The Present

Anna Marie sighed with relief that her dream was based on real-life events. She could now remember why Harry had called her in the middle of the night. At 60, Anna Marie was always glad that she had not experienced significant memory loss. The memories continued to flood her mind as she heard Little Bear and Maya waking up above her.

Each yesterday has brought me here.
Tomorrow's bounty is wonderfully unclear.
A new beginning to appreciate the past,
Staying here would only make life
slip by too fast.

–By permission of Vincent Bishop, author's son

CHAPTER TWO

THE JOURNEY OF SEEKING SELF

The Present

Anna Marie finished her tea and snack. The sun rose, peaking over the eastern edge of the earth. Maya and Little Bear were at her feet waiting for their morning breakfast. Anna Marie tied Little Bear out on her line while she prepared the hungry pug's breakfast and opened a can of cat food for Maya.

After they were settled, she went upstairs to take a shower, changing into clothes for what was likely to be a long day. As she looked outside the bathroom window, she saw reflected in the early morning beams of sunlight a newly woven spider's web. The web sparkled from the evening dew and reminded Anna Marie of early mornings at campgrounds on her first Southwind journey.

She wondered the morning she bought the Southwind and began her planned trip if she would have noticed the spider webs spun overnight. Did she have any idea on that day what the Fates had in store for her? She recalled vaguely that day had started as a start for her new life.

The memories continued to come back…

Seven years earlier

All the goodbyes were said the previous evening. Little Bear and Anna Marie checked out the house one last time, both exhibiting signs of excitement and apprehension at the same time. Anna Marie planned to only drive to Pennsylvania for the first part of her trip and to stay for at least a week. She felt that would help her gain confidence in her ability to do this alone and give her some experience before traveling on unfamiliar roads.

She planned to spend some time alone at her reserved campground, deep in the Poconos but not far off I81, figuring out her next stops and general direction. She remained determined to be as flexible as possible. No deadlines for the entire summer and no straight lines of travel other than to usually go in the directions south to west to north to east. Those directions meant good luck to her, even though the directions would likely look very strange if mapped out.

By 6:30 a.m., they were on the road. Little Bear sat in the front seat, proudly wearing the new bright blue visor cap Anna Marie had purchased for her. She appeared to be studying the map, hoping to be a help on this monumental journey for both. Anna Marie wondered how much she understood about this journey. Instead of taking her usual morning nap, Bear seemed determined to stay alert. Anna Marie reached over and gave her a pat on the side, again appreciative of her companionship and loyalty. Little Bear had often been the crutch that helped Anna Marie through long, lonely nights after Ted's death.

Anna Marie was dressed in a jean skirt with a bright red sweater and a jean blazer. Typical for Anna Marie, as her friends and family could not imagine her without a hat, she had a bright red floppy hat to match her sweater. One of the most difficult decisions had been which hats to bring and which ones to leave behind. She had a huge collection of hats and limited space in the RV.

She had carefully selected five of her favorites, placing the four she was not wearing in a large hatbox in the storage compartment over the dining room table. She knew it was likely that she would purchase at least one more hat on her trip and thought the five varying colors would do for a start.

She started up the engine, waved goodbye to her house, and they were on their way. The initial tension quickly changed to excitement and thrill that she, Anna Marie Golding was doing something so adventurous, daring, and fun. She carefully maneuvered the Southwind through the narrow village streets, onto the county road, which led to the New York State Thruway. Once on the Thruway, Anna Marie breathed a sigh of relief that she had made it to the major highway with no mishaps. In a short time, they were on Interstate 81, traveling south.

The road gave way underneath their wheels, quickly finding a rhythm of traveling that suited both occupants; an hour or two of driving and then rest stops. Little Bear loved the new smells and took advantage of each stop for as long as she could, responding to the new energy in Anna Marie. The two of them ran along the walking paths at the stops, exhilarated by their adventure, no need to be anyplace other than they chose, and new surroundings.

The day had begun overcast and threatening rain. The further south they traveled the brighter it became. By 10:00 o'clock, the sun was out, and the dew on the grass drying. It promised to be a perfect late April day.

By noon, they entered Pennsylvania. Anna Marie decided to have lunch at a rest stop at the top of a mountain with wonderful views. It was the first meal she made for the two of them aboard the Southwind. It was surprisingly fun. She even set up the awning on the side of the Southwind and brought out their dishes along with her chair for sitting. She had purchased a new folding table for her and a new dish for Little Bear, making this first meal a celebration.

Little Bear ate only a little, preferring to watch people and sniff the smells. Anna Marie suspected that in the evening when they stopped for the night, Little Bear would relax and eat more. Fellow travelers stopped to greet Little Bear. Anna Marie soon found that her traveling companion helped her make friends easily. It would be this way for the rest of their journey together.

After lunch, Anna Marie checked the car to be sure it was still secure on the tow bar and then walked Little Bear one more time. After settling Little Bear in the Southwind, she decided to use the public restroom to postpone for as long as possible her need to dump the black water holding tank. She was quickly reminded why she hated public restrooms.

She wondered for the umpteenth time about the male inventor who thought two sheets of toilet paper at a time from the dispenser were sufficient for women. She often imagined them sitting around a boardroom discussing how to save money by using toilet paper dispensers that did not allow you to take more than two small sheets at a time. As she headed back to the Southwind, she wondered if the same men had been responsible for the development of mammogram technology.

In an uncharacteristic sign of protest, Anna Marie took off her pantyhose while in the ladies' room and stuffed them in her purse. She was determined she was never again going to put up with pantyhose that crept down around her ankles, even though the package claimed it would fit someone her size.

"From now on," she thought, "I'm going to be comfortable and only wear socks, knee highs, or nothing at all on warm days. No more 'droopy-pantyhose syndrome' for me!"

She felt particularly rebellious and free as she and Little Bear entered the highway again after their lunch stop.

Anna Marie had selected a campground hidden within the Poconos with many amenities, including a lake with paddleboats, a pool, and hiking trails. It sounded very peaceful but also safe, as it was listed as a "Family campground." She hoped she would not be the only person traveling alone. Even if she were, she felt she would blend into the campgrounds. This early in the year, it was not likely there would be many families traveling. While school was still in session, she assumed it would be mostly older people like herself.

The early afternoon went by fast. In what felt like only a few minutes they were driving into the campgrounds she had reserved for the week. It had not been located too far off Interstate 81. The roads had not been difficult for her to maneuver the large RV. She was enjoying herself and the challenge.

It felt good to think of other things besides herself and her loss. It was also good to have people respond to her as an older woman rather than "the widow." She had felt almost as though she was expected to play a part. Even on those days when she could have laughed or smiled, she was unsure how others would perceive her return to her old self. She had been afraid she would appear disrespectful to Ted's memory. With strangers and her new life none of that mattered. The spring flowers on the side of the roads seemed to be symbolic of her rebirth.

It was simple to register at the campground office. As soon as she explained she had never camped in a RV or set one up on her own before, the young clerk was extremely helpful. He drove his small jeep in front of her to help her find her spot. He stayed to direct her into the space, advising her of the best way to position the Southwind and showing her where the hook-ups were. He had to leave to get back to the office as he expected a few more campers to check in. He advised her he would check on her before leaving his shift for the day.

After hooking up in a short period of time and connecting Little Bear's lead, Anna Marie set up the table and chairs under the side awning. She also placed a pitcher of flowers on the table, given to her as a going-away present by Erin and Bonnie, her daughter-in-law, along with the vase of roses from Cynthia and Anita. She hung the sign that Kate had painted, "the Southwind, Anna Marie, and Little Bear Golding."

She carefully brought out the folding table and loom from under the Southwind. Anna Marie placed those under the awning as well. She checked to make sure there was a small tarp near to cover the loom should it start raining. She selected the wool thread she wanted to start weaving with, determined that she would add to the weaving every day somehow in a way that would give her memories of where she had been.

It felt settled and almost like home. Little Bear had smelled every blade of grass she could reach. Anna Marie thought it was time to explore the campgrounds before making supper for both. The walk felt good. The air was crisp but the sun warm enough that they both built up a sweat. Anna Marie thought at this rate she might lose a few pounds and Little Bear would certainly be in good shape.

Upon returning to the Southwind, Anna Marie decided to use the shower for the first time before preparing dinner. She thought it best to leave Little Bear inside for safety reasons when she showered as she was unsure what wild animals there could be in these mountains. Little Bear quickly sprawled across the couch in what was to become her favorite place in the RV. Anna Marie found the small shower a challenge but still felt refreshed from her shower. She changed into a comfortable silk jogging suit.

Dinner was a small steak grilled over her new portable grill with vegetables and ice cream for dessert. She shared a small piece of the steak with Little Bear, mixing it in carefully with Little Bear's food. They had never fed Little Bear people food when Ted was alive. Anna Marie thought this was Little Bear's vacation, too, and a little would not hurt her.

She poured herself a glass of red wine from Argentina that she had chilled in the refrigerator and turned the water on for tea after the meal. As they were eating, Frank, the very helpful young man from the office, returned to check on her. He accepted her offer of food and a beer, sitting with them for more than an hour telling Anna Marie about his girlfriend, jobs, business school classes, and his grandmother who had died in the past year.

After an hour that flew by, he said, "I'll check back with you tomorrow to make sure you and Little Bear are doing okay.

Thanks for dinner and the beer."

Anna Marie thanked him for the help and the company on her first night on her own.

After dinner, Little Bear and she sat outside. Anna Marie lit a candle and slowly sipped her tea, savoring the warmth and taste. By the lake she could hear the peepers croaking. She could tell it was high mating season, as the night was full of these sounds. She had not been this close to seeing the Milky Way in years and was thrilled when she spotted shooting stars flaming across the night sky.

Little Bear crawled onto her lap, underneath the cozy woven lap robe she had brought with her. It was as though the sky was putting on a show just for them. They watched the three-quarter moon creep across the sky in her never-ending cycle. Anna Marie felt like she was a young child again, experiencing all this for the first time.

Her son Erin and his wife Bonnie were both reporters for a small city newspaper near Higginsville. Erin was her sensitive child and the one she shared a love of writing. Their only child, Ted Jr., called Teddy by his family, was also a writer and sensitive like his parents. He had found a lovely diary with a hand-painted cover at a local craft fair. He gave it to his grandmother for her trip and asked her to write about her travels.

She took out this diary and began a tradition that she continued for the trip, tracking the moon in the sky along with some major events with her thoughts of the day. She silently sent a thank you to Teddy for reminding her of this simple pleasure in life. After one more walk for Little Bear, they both settled down for the best night's sleep in months.

The next day Anna Marie rented a paddleboat from Frank. Frank found a tiny child's safety vest that fit Little Bear. Little Bear appeared to feel very important as Anna Marie and Frank positioned it on her. Anna Marie assured Frank that she had a cell phone with her for emergencies.

Frank asked her, "Would you mind if I brought my grandfather over to meet you tonight? He has been so lonely since my grandmother died. I have tried to get him to go camping but he just sits in the house, watching out the window."

Anna Marie tried to be tactful, "Frank, I don't think I could handle that yet. I'm still getting over losing my Ted. I'm not ready to meet anyone."

Frank said, "Oh, Anna Marie, I didn't mean anything like that. I just wanted him to see someone close to his age who was living her life. We'll bring pizza and beer. I could tell him I feel sorry for you but it's really to get him out of the house. Please?"

With deep reservation, Anna Marie agreed to the two of them coming for dinner.

As she settled in the paddleboat, Frank added, "Would you mind if I bring my girlfriend, too? I don't get much time off from my three jobs or classes. This is my one free evening this week."

Wondering what she was getting herself into, Anna Marie agreed.

Anna Marie and Little Bear thoroughly enjoyed the paddleboat ride. After an hour she headed back to shore when the cell phone rang.

Anna Marie answered to hear a loud voice say, "Anna Marie, it's Walter. I'm not getting you at a bad time, am I?"

Anna Marie hesitated, as it took her a few minutes to remember who Walter was.

She answered, "Well, I guess not, Walter. I'm in the middle of the lake with Little Bear. Other than that, it's an okay time."

Walter said, "Oh," and then paused with a long silence.

Anna Marie finally asked, "Was there something you wanted, Walter?"

She could hear a sniffling coming from Walter over the line.

The stuttering Walter answered her, "Anna Marie, I need to talk. My wife has left me. She said that I am not paying attention to her anymore and we have nothing in common. Can you imagine that? Nothing in common after forty-five years of marriage! She has left me for that darn Iggy. He's president of our

Senior Club. She thinks he's so wonderful but he's just a smooth-talking ladies' man."

Walter paused and sniffed again.

"Anna Marie, I don't know what to do. I've never cooked for myself or washed clothes. The nights stretch out in front of me. I don't even want to go to the Senior Club because I'll see my wife swooning over that man. What should I do?"

Anna Marie didn't quite know how to answer him. Partly she wanted to laugh over the idea of Iggy, the ladies' man at the Senior Center. She stifled the laugh as she did not want to hurt Walter's feelings.

She answered, "I don't know what you can do except put one foot in front of the other and keep living every day. I'm sorry to hear about your wife, Walter. Maybe you have a male friend you can talk to or go to a therapist for help?"

Walter snorted and said, "I'm not going to a therapist. That's for pansies or those New Age people, not for me. Anna Marie, I really miss the Southwind. That was something that always made me feel good, the freedom of the road and the fun at the campgrounds. Can I come and join you for a few days?"

Anna Marie answered quickly with no hesitation, "Walter, I don't think that is a very good idea. What would your wife think or others if they knew about it? I don't want to give people the wrong idea. It might only make things worse between you and your wife. Even though we are only friends, it would appear otherwise."

Walter pleaded, "Anna Marie, please. I'll use the pull-out bed in the living room, and I won't get in your way. I'll be quiet, and I'll pay for the nights at the campgrounds. I'll pay for groceries, gas, whatever you want. I'll tell people that I'm going to visit my brother. No one will ever know. Please Anna Marie. I don't think I'm going to get over my wife otherwise."

Anna Marie wondered how she had become everybody's lifesaver these days or why she could never say no.

She remembered a quote from a trainer on taking care of

yourself as a caregiver, "The word NO is a full sentence." She personally had never learned to make the answer "No" firm enough.

She said, "Walter, think about it overnight. If you still feel the same way tomorrow, we'll talk about options. I bet if you sleep on it you'll realize it's not a good idea."

Walter asked, "Where are you?"

Anna Marie gave him the name of the campgrounds and told him it was in Pennsylvania. After she gave that information, she realized that was the second mistake she had made today; the first was answering the cell phone.

Anna Marie emphasized, "You are not to come here until we talk again tomorrow. Right, Walter?"

Walter ignored the question and said, "Anna Marie, someone is at the door. We'll talk again later."

He quickly hung up the phone before Anna Marie could repeat her request another time.

Anna Marie said to Little Bear, "I seem to be picking up needy people left and right. I hope we're not going to have company join us tomorrow."

They docked the paddleboat. Frank, who appeared to be waiting for them, pulled it up onto the shore. He reminded Anna Marie of the night's arrangements and told Anna Marie they would be there about 5:30.

Frank added, "Grandpa can't eat any later than that. My girlfriend is bringing him right here after she is out of work. Do you think you could make some of your steak and potatoes? Even though I'll order pizza and Iris is bringing beer, Grandpa can't eat that stuff. He has a real sensitive stomach, you know."

Anna Marie agreed to prepare steak and potatoes for Grandpa. She and Little Bear took the long way back to the campsite so that Little Bear could get as many smells out of her system as possible. Anna Marie also wanted to see if there were any new campers in the campground. A few had driven in. They waved as Anna Marie and Little Bear walked by. A couple with license plates from Maine came over to pet Little Bear and to introduce themselves to Anna Marie along with their dog Calloway.

As Anna Marie approached the Southwind, she heard a sound like the meowing of a young kitten. She looked around the RV for the originator of the sound. Sitting next to the RV on a bush was a skinny black bird, making the sound and holding her wing to her side. Anna Marie slowly approached the bird, leaving Little Bear on her lead by the table so as not to frighten the bird.

The bird did not appear to be afraid of Anna Marie. She allowed her to gently touch the wing that the little bird protected. Anna Marie could see that there was some injury to the wing.

She softly said to the bird, "You stay here. I will get something to clean your wing that should help you."

Anna Marie went into the RV to her medicine cabinet and found the salve mixed from lavender and mother's tongue with oil. She was grateful she had brought her herbal mixtures along. The mixtures were already needed on this trip. She found a washcloth and filled the sink with warm water. After considering the situation for a moment, she decided to see if she could bring the little bird inside to do a thorough job cleaning the wounded wing.

Little Bear intensely watched the bird, protecting the bird from any enemies who might harm the bird further. Anna Marie again approached the bird slowly and reached out her hand for the bird. The bird walked carefully onto Anna Marie's hand and sat perched there as Anna Marie carried it into the Southwind.

Little Bear followed along behind her, and Anna Marie detached her lead before shutting the door to the RV. She washed the bird tenderly, quietly uttering assurances. This seemed to keep the bird calm as she washed the wound and applied the salve to the wound.

Anna Marie could almost feel the little bird's release from pain.

She said to the bird, "I think you would be better off staying inside with us tonight so that no creatures can harm you while your wing is healing. I'm only trying to take care of you. As soon as the wing is healed, I'll release you back to your outside home."

The bird cocked her head, appearing to understand what Anna Marie was saying. The bird made a cooing noise that sounded like a dove. Anna Marie wondered if this was some form of mockingbird. Later she would read that this was a relative to the mockingbird called a Catbird, known to make at least thirty different sounds and able to imitate sounds from other animals or people.

Anna Marie found her sewing basket and removed the sewing items from the basket. She placed a soft guest towel in the container. She also found a little dish in which she placed water. Anna Marie settled the basket in a box with the bird in it on the front passenger's seat. She found another tiny dish in which she placed cut-up green grapes. The bird looked over her surroundings in the box and quickly curled up in the basket. The Catbird was soon fast asleep in total trust that Anna Marie would take care of her.

Anna Marie gave Little Bear some fresh water, which she drank with great enjoyment. She found Little Bear's treats and gave her one of those while she busily prepared a tray of cheese and crackers and baked cookies for the company coming that night. She shook her head as she wondered how many more living things she was going to collect on this journey. But she also realized that much of her life had been collecting people and animals, so this really was a return to her old self of connecting with others.

After the cookies were out of the oven, she laid down for a brief nap waking up in time to take a shower before her company arrived. The bird was awake but sat quietly in her box, watching the activity. It looked as though the bird may have drunk some water as there was water on the end of her beak. Anna Marie thought that was a good sign of recovery. She checked the towel to make sure it was still clean enough for the little bird and wiped away a small stain.

Little Bear opened her eyes for a few moments and then went back to sleep. Anna Marie cleaned the wing of the bird another time and reapplied the salve on the wing. The little bird carefully drank some more water, took a few pecks of the grapes, and then also went back to sleep. Anna Marie waited for her company outside after first waking Little Bear for a quick walk, rearranging the flowers in her pitcher and adding a candle to the table.

She looked over the table setting. She thought it looked very welcoming and pretty. She remembered the small dinner parties she and Ted gave for their friends. She realized that she had not entertained in this way since Ted's death. It felt good.

Anna Marie sat quietly reading until Frank's old car pulled up to the Southwind. He honked the horn and waved. In the front seat of the car was a young lady with striped hair, numerous body piercings, and tattoos on both arms. She argued with the man sitting in the backseat who refused to get out of the car.

The young lady said, "Now, Grandpa, stop being so stubborn and get out of the car. I'm sure there will be more to eat than pizza and antipasto."

The man answered her gruffly, "I am not your grandpa. I don't know why you and Frank insisted on my coming here. I don't need to meet some pathetic widow. I would rather eat in my own house."

Anna Marie thought, "This is already not working out well. I changed the role of grieving wife for pathetic widow. Great advances I am making for myself."

She decided to try to help the situation and joined the young lady trying to get grandpa to leave the car. Frank stood back to the side, obviously afraid to enter into the argument and looking very sad. Anna Marie felt sorry for Frank who really had his heart in the right place, even if others could not see that.

Anna Marie put out her hand to the young lady and said, "Hi. You must be Frank's girlfriend. I'm Anna Marie."

The girl nodded and said, "Yes, I'm Irisa."

Anna Marie turned to the man sitting in the back seat of the car with his arms folded, ready to hit anyone who came too close.

She said, "You must be Frank's grandfather. He has told me so much about you. I know how horrible it is when your family tries to interfere in your life and make decisions for you. I can understand why you're upset. You know how families are."

Anna Marie winked, wondering to herself where this performance was coming from. She would have preferred to have dinner alone with Little Bear and her new bird friend.

"I grilled a steak for you and me with mashed potatoes and vegetables. I didn't think either of us would want pizza. I can't digest those kinds of foods like I used to. It would be nice for me to have someone closer to my own age for dinner."

The man was quiet for a minute and then looked at Anna Marie like they were longtime co-conspirators.

He winked back and said, "These kids do so want to meddle in your life. In my day, youngsters minded their own business. They didn't butt into their grandparents' lives. They also knew how to dress and act."

Frank's grandfather looked glaringly at Irisa and Frank. Irisa attempted to ignore the grandfather by petting Little Bear. Frank also pretended he was hundreds of miles away from them.

"It would be nice to have a steak dinner. If they had told me that in the first place, I wouldn't have been so angry. My name is Terence; by the way, not Grandpa as everyone seems to choose to address me."

He gave Irisa another dirty look before getting out of the car, following Anna Marie to the chairs set up by the folding table.

Anna Marie settled Terence, Irisa, and Frank at the table.

She went inside to get coffee for Terence as his response to a glass of wine was, "I've never drank alcohol before in my life and I'm not going to start now. I hope you are not serving one of those French kinds after what those people have done to us. Ungrateful people! Pardon my French but they just get me so angry. I fought in France during World War II and they ought to appreciate everything we've done for them. Whose business is it anyway if we want to blow up that horrible desert country?"

Anna Marie was relieved to be able to leave his ramblings behind and began to appreciate the prospect of later tonight being alone again. She wondered how Frank had turned out to be such a thoughtful person. Maybe his parents were like Frank rather than Terence? This felt like it was going to be a long evening.

She brought out the tray of cheese and crackers along with coffee for Terence.

"Black, two spoons of sugar-not those fake kind-and very hot, thank you!"

Terence dived into the crackers and cheese as though he hadn't seen food in weeks. Frank brought out bottles of beer for Irisa and himself. Beer seemed to be okay for Terence as he rapidly cleaned off the tray of cheese and crackers and ignored their beverage choice.

Frank fired up the grill for Anna Marie as she poured herself a glass of wine. It was Chilean rather than French. She figured it best not to even go there so she put the bottle back in the refrigerator. Who knew what Chileans might have done to anger Terence in the past?

With the cup of coffee and his stomach half filled with cheese and crackers, Terence became a much pleasanter dinner companion. He and Frank both talked about fond memories of Frank's grandmother. They related story after story of Frank's childhood. Terence had been a miner and had many stories to tell of his adventures underground. He knew some of the Pennsylvania coal miners who had been stuck underground for many days with the nation cheering for their safety.

Anna Marie talked about Ted without feeling sad, a first since his death. She told them all about her tentative plans for her trip and how upset her family had been about this trip. Each nodded sympathetically, including Terence who mellowed with each cup of coffee and bite to eat.

Little Bear, doing her part to make the evening pleasant,

curled up at Terence's feet. Every few minutes Terence quietly reached down to pet her.

The steaks on the grill smelled wonderful. The kids decided they'd have steak along with Anna Marie and Terence. Anna Marie added a couple more steaks to the grill, grateful she had extra in the freezer. She placed the antipasto Frank had brought into a large salad bowl.

Anna Marie made a mental note to herself to replace the steaks the next time she shopped for groceries, realizing for the first time how small the freezer was in the Southwind. She found she had to do lots of improvising in her new kitchen and had begun a running list of things she needed to stock in her kitchen for her cross-country adventure. It was finally becoming real to her as she slowly built confidence in her capability to travel in the Southwind alone.

It began to cool off, so Frank started a fire in the large fireplace at the campsite. Anna Marie cut up the pizza into small slices as a side for the steak, potatoes, and corn. Everyone ate with great pleasure. Anna Marie was into her second glass of wine. This much to drink was unusual for her but with all the food and not driving anywhere for a few days, it helped make Terence's company tolerable.

The unlimited coffee and food continued to tame Terence. Anna Marie understood that some of his orneriness was a cover for his loneliness and sadness. Not that she would ever share some of his political views, but she realized that she needed to listen to and learn from people as they each had a story to tell.

At about 9:00 o'clock, Terence looked at his watch as he cleaned up his second serving of cookies. Anna Marie wondered how much he had been eating living on his own. She offered to make up a "to-go" package of food for him.

She told him, "I can't eat all these leftovers myself. It's not good for me anyway. You would be doing me a favor."

Terence agreed, "Sure, I could see how a woman alone would not want to eat this much, especially as you look like you don't need any extra food. I'll take it out of your hands to help you out. It is getting quite late, and my dog is not used to being alone this long."

Terence looked to see that Frank and Irisa were busy talking to each other.

He hesitantly continued, "You know, Anna Marie, you're a nice woman but not my type. I don't want you to get your hopes up about me. I'm afraid Frank may have encouraged you to think I might be interested."

Anna Marie tried not to laugh and answered as seriously as she could, "I understand. I'm not ready to date yet, either. I may never be. I appreciate your being open with me. I'm only going to be here for a few more days. You're welcome to dinner with Frank whenever the two of you want. Frank has been wonderfully helpful to me. He made my first camp stop great. He's helped me build confidence that I can do this. Your coming to dinner helped, too. Thank you." She surprised herself with her ability to keep a straight face as she talked to Terence. She was also astonished that she did mean most of what she said.

Frank and Irisa helped Anna Marie clean up while Terence loaded his food into the back seat of the car. As they cleaned up the leftovers, Frank noticed a car driving around the campground. It appeared to be lost. Frank felt he should check up on it even though he was officially off duty. He was gone a few minutes. When he walked back to the campsite, the car followed slowly behind him.

Frank, puzzled, said, "Anna Marie, I've found a friend who is looking for you. I didn't realize you had someone joining you. I thought you said you were camping alone?"

Anna Marie answered, "I am. I don't know what friend you are talking about."

As she said this, she had a strange premonition that she did know who this "friend" was.

The car stopped next to the campsite and out of the car stepped Walter.

He held up his hands and said, "Anna Marie, before you get upset with me, I just had to come."

He looked to the others and said, "This is not how it looks. We are just friends. I was the previous owner of the Southwind. My wife just left me. Anna Marie offered the Southwind for me to stay a few days until I figure out how to go on from here."

Terence stared at her with an open mouth. Anna Marie did not want to know his thoughts.

She loudly protested that she hadn't offered Walter to stay a few days and then realized this was probably a futile discussion.

She turned to Frank and asked, "Frank, are there any cabins or RVs in the campgrounds for rent? I think Walter would be more comfortable with a space of his own. So would I."

Frank indicated there were cabins for rent on the other side of the lake. He offered to take Walter to the office to make those arrangements. Walter looked longingly at the Southwind but didn't seem to have much fight left in him. He must have realized that he was outnumbered in his argument. He quietly followed Frank to the office while Irisa and Terence waited for him by the Southwind.

Anna Marie tried not to be as upset as she was that Walter had taken it upon himself to just come here without talking to her first as they had agreed upon. Though as she thought about it, only she had agreed to wait until tomorrow. Walter had listened and then changed the subject. She should have realized what he was up to. She thought she might as well figure out how to make the best of this, make lemonade out of lemons as her mother always said.

Frank soon came back without Walter. He explained that he had settled Walter in his cabin. Walter would be over after he had dropped his luggage off and arranged his cabin.

Frank said, "I hope you have some leftovers. As Walter mentioned, he drove straight here without stopping. He wanted to arrive here before it was too late at night and didn't want to scare you by showing up late. He seems a very nice man, Anna Marie." This was said as a question and not a comment.

Anna Marie said, "He's a very nice man who is married. I barely know him other than spending time with him to learn how to drive the Southwind. Thank you for finding a cabin and taking him to the cabin. It makes it much easier for me this way. I'm sure when Walter regains his senses, he will understand that, too."

Frank's grandfather and girlfriend waited for him in his car.

He kissed Anna Marie on her cheek and said, "Thank you, Anna Marie. This is the first time Grandpa has smiled and talked about anything other than Grandma. Please excuse his gruff ways; he doesn't mean it. He's just lonely and scared."

Anna Marie told Frank, "I understand completely. Thank you for helping me to realize that I can do this alone. This will be an adventure of meeting people. You've helped me remember what adventures are like and how much fun it is to make new friends."

Frank drove off waving. Anna Marie walked Little Bear to the end of the road and back.

At the Southwind she checked on the bird still sleeping quietly and then heated up some of the food remaining from dinner. In a few minutes, there was a knock at the door and Walter's face appeared through the screen door.

"Anna Marie, I hope you are not angry with me. I just didn't know what else to do. And now that I have my own cabin it will be simpler for you."

He looked longingly at the bedroom in the back and said, "Though I've had my best sleeping nights here in the Southwind."

Anna Marie quickly responded, "You're not going to sleep in the Southwind while I own it."

She softened her voice and added, "It's fine for you to visit. I don't want your wife or anyone else thinking we are having an affair. I've warmed some supper for you. Why don't you sit down and eat something."

She offered him a glass of wine, which he drank while he ate. She made a last cup of tea for herself and sat across from him while he hungrily ate.

Even though she was angry with him for ignoring her request, she found she was happy to see a familiar face. It was so easy to talk to Walter that she soon gave him a minute-by-minute update of her time since she had left home. She realized this was one of the things she missed most about Ted, someone to talk to in the evening and share the day's happenings. Even though she was sure Ted often nodded and pretended to listen, there was that sharing of the small daily occurrences of life that make up a marriage.

After a couple of hours of quietly talking with each other over the wine, tea, and food, Walter stood up and said, "Thank you Anna Marie. I know you didn't want me to come but already I feel better. You are such a good listener. You make me believe I am not this horrible boring person my wife says I am. Can I come over in the morning? I'll even bring breakfast."

They set a time for breakfast. Walter gently hugged her like a precious, breakable object before going back to his cabin.

After checking on the stage of the moon and writing in her diary, Little Bear, the bird, and Anna Marie quickly settled down for the night. Each slept through the night. They all woke up a little after dawn, totally refreshed from their night's sleep.

Anna Marie noticed that the almost full moon was still in the sky. It would be another hour before it was no longer visible. She realized she was losing track of dates and time with a new pattern of days emerging based on the moon's cycles. She checked the calendar and saw that it was April 30. Somehow the realization that May Eve was going to be a full moon sent shivers up her spine. Anna Marie had a sense this day and night was going to portend change and excitement.

The bird moved around in her box and appeared quite restless. Anna Marie checked the wing and found that amazingly the wound was almost healed. The little bird experimented with the wing and seemed to be just as surprised that the wing was feeling better. Anna Marie couldn't get over how little fear the bird had of her or Little Bear. She thought it was time to try the bird outside again. She placed the bird in the box outside while she and Little Bear took their first morning walk.

When Anna Marie came back, she fed the animals and showered. Little Bear curled up on her favorite sleeping place while Anna Marie showered. The bird sat contently on one of the outside chairs. She had flown a little bit while they were walking. The little bird made meowing sounds every so often and then experimented with other sounds that sounded like a dog barking or a human crying.

Walter was at the door when Anna Marie came out from her shower. Fortunately, she had her robe with her and asked him to wait a few more minutes while she dressed. He set up breakfast on the table outside with Egg sandwiches, orange juice, coffee, and cappuccino for Anna Marie. Anna Marie was surprised he remembered that she liked cappuccino in the morning instead of tea.

He said, "It's mint chocolate; I took a chance that you would like it."

Anna Marie thanked him as tears came to her eyes. This was the flavor that Ted knew she loved. He had often driven miles out of his way just to get it for her.

Anna Marie shook her head, wiped off the tears dropping to her cheeks, and thought, "It's the small things that get me. I'll be doing just fine, not thinking about Ted at all, and then something like this will remind me."

Walter had a pile of brochures for ideas of how to spend their day together. He assured her he was open to trying anything.

He emphasized, "I'll prove that I am not as boring as my wife says I am."

They selected a visit to a miner's museum, which neither of them had ever been to before, and an art museum of local artists that sounded interesting. Both individually decided that the day was going to be a special one for fun and a time to set aside their grieving.

The last brochure was a celebration of "May-Day Eve" with a

bonfire, music, and fireworks. Both agreed they loved fireworks and music. They each thought what a great way to celebrate the arrival of May and their own beginnings.

As they made plans and finished their breakfast, the little bird practiced flying, with Little Bear cheering her on. Every time she flew a little further, Little Bear wagged her tail with an excited yelp. Soon the little bird sat on the branches overhead and looked down at them with Little Bear practically hopping up and down in excitement.

Anna Marie settled Little Bear with her food and opened the windows for a breeze. It was early enough in the year that she did not have to worry about air conditioning, especially in this shady campsite. She left more grape pieces and water outside for the little bird in case she still needed some food.

She felt an almost adolescent excitement as Walter arrived, opening the passenger door for her. They started on their day of exploration.

Each of the sites they had selected to see was easy to find and well worth the visit. They had lunch at a Cracker Barrel, which again brought tears to Anna Marie as Ted loved to stop at Cracker Barrels when they traveled. She often joked with him that this was his idea of a romantic dinner. This was the first time she had eaten at one since his death. Being with Walter made it easier for her.

Throughout the day, both talked to each other as though they had known each other for lifetimes and could share their innermost thoughts. Walter talked more about his adult children and past work, and less about his wife. To Anna Marie, this was a good sign of small progress.

At about four o'clock, they went back to the Southwind to spend some time with Little Bear before going to the "May-Day Eve" celebration. Walter returned to his cabin to shower and change while Anna Marie changed and prepared a light dinner for the two of them.

The little bird was nowhere to be found. She felt somewhat

saddened by the loss. At least she and Little Bear had helped nurse it back to health. She poured Walter and herself a glass of wine, sipping the wine while waiting for him to return.

She played a Yanni CD as she waited. This was another first since Ted's death as they had attended several Yanni concerts together. She could not listen to Yanni previously without bursting into tears.

Walter had changed into a sport coat and Dockers from his earlier jeans and t-shirt. When Anna Marie saw his new appearance and the flowers he presented, her heart skipped a beat. She thanked him for his thoughtfulness. She did everything possible not to remind him of his wife at that moment while kissing him on the cheek. Walter smiled and said nothing.

They sat outside, slowly eating their dinner while Little Bear took advantage of the opportunity to revisit every smell around the RV. Ted had always disliked the outdoors. Anna Marie had not eaten these many meals outside in years. She wondered if Ted would have liked the Southwind.

They walked Little Bear around the campgrounds before settling her in the RV. Anna Marie reminded herself this was only Walter, who was temporarily separated from his wife; she was not a young schoolgirl in love.

As the day wore on and the full moon began to rise in the sky before sunset, it became harder and harder to remember this. There was electricity in the air that built throughout the day.

Anna Marie couldn't explain her feelings for this man that she hadn't much liked a few days ago. She felt as though a spell was being placed over her and she was losing control of her senses. Walter, too, appeared to be dazed.

Halfway through their walk, he reached for her hand. She let him hold her hand. Little Bear seemed not to mind Walter's intrusion. They settled Little Bear in the RV. Anna Marie refreshed the water for her bird in case she returned.

Walter again opened the passenger door for her. He kissed her on the head after she was seated.

Anna Marie thought, "Maybe tonight's ceremony was not a good idea."

She started to tell Walter this. But he concentrated on backing the car out, not paying much attention to her. She decided that it would be okay. It was a public celebration, after all, and they were two reasonable adults, not teenagers.

On the road, Walter again reached for her hand. Anna Marie let him hold it all the way to the city park where the celebration was held. He helped her out of the car like a delicate young flower rather than an overweight old lady. Anna Marie felt years melting away, especially as she smelled the growing bonfire, saw the rising full moon, the fireflies in the fields amongst the rising mist, and felt Walter's arm around her.

They brought the folding chairs out of Walter's trunk. They found a spot on a small hill that overlooked the band shell, bonfire, and the fireworks that would be displayed after total dark. Anna Marie thought the fireflies combined with the stars starting to appear were enough of a fire show without the man-made ones. Thousands of people were placing chairs around the park. It was a little chilly and Walter had thought to bring a blanket to place over the two of them.

He said, "My wife is always cold. I never go anywhere without a blanket. It comes in handy."

The band concert began with some of the strangest and truly magical music Anna Marie had ever heard. In the background was an erotic drumbeat that never took over the music. She thought the music must be something Oriental or Middle Eastern as there was a combination of sounds and instruments she had never heard. How strange that she was in the middle of mining Pennsylvania listening to one of the most magnificent concerts she had ever heard—by a municipal orchestra, no less.

Walter and she spoke little, both mesmerized by the sound and the night surrounding them. He placed his hand on her thigh and she put her hand over his squeezing it every so often when the orchestra made an incredible sound.

At intermission, Walter bought them both hot chocolate in plastic cups, which they drank like it was an exotic new beverage. Both were afraid to look at each other. When they did, sparks appeared to flow from their eyes to the bonfire and back. Anna Marie shivered less from the cold and more from the fear of what was happening between to two mature adults.

She realized that even though she had decided her number one goal was to have sex *one more time* before she died, Ted was the only man she had ever made love to. How could she even be thinking such thoughts, especially with a man she had only known briefly and who was still legally married?

She wanted to stop whatever was happening but every time she looked to Walter to say something, the sparks flew between them, and she changed her mind. He was so kind and gentle in the middle of a magical night that had them both out of control. She decided to relax more and worry less—what was to be would be.

The music started up again with the same magical quality. Occasionally, the music sounded a little familiar, coming from her ancient and subconscious past. Anna Marie noticed couples who danced slowly with each other in slow sensual movements. Small children danced to the music, also taken by the underlying beat and energy of the night. The bonfire reached a crescendo at the same time as the music.

With the last note of the concert, the crowd broke out in a spontaneous cheer that lasted a few minutes until overhead the fireworks display erupted in a plethora of colors and shapes. Mesmerized, Walter and Anna Marie stood up at the same moment to watch. Walter put his arm around her tightly and kissed her on the cheek again.

She turned to smile at him and found his lips in front of her so that their first kiss was natural with no awkwardness. Overhead the fireworks popped, boomed, and sizzled. Instead of cheering at the end, the crowd quietly drifted off to their cars. Those in attendance obviously didn't want this magical evening to end.

Couples and families walked with arms wrapped around each other in their own safe cocoons.

Back at the campsite, Anna Marie and Walter quietly walked Little Bear around the lake while they watched the shooting stars and full moon. There were few fireflies now. The mist made it appear they were walking above the ground and in a world of their own. The sky did not want to let go of the magical night and continued to give a performance of its own.

The sparking electricity in the air was added to by the dew reflecting the moonlight as it lay on the grass. The ground glittered beneath them as they walked.

Anna Marie whistled, making a sound that she did not even know she could. She felt electricity in her body that she had not experienced in years. Walter floated beside her. Little Bear also seemed to be conscious of the magic in the air. She refrained from her usual sniffing and quietly walked along beside them.

Once at the campsite again, little needed to be said between them. Walter helped Anna Marie up the steps. He warmed the tea while Anna Marie fed Little Bear. Little Bear ate quickly and then curled up in her favorite place with a contented sigh that all was right with her world tonight. She accepted Walter as a member of the Southwind family, comfortable that he was there with them.

Walter and Anna Marie sipped their tea, saying little. Every so often, Walter placed his hand over Anna Marie's, rubbing it gently and seductively. When the tea was finished, they simultaneously placed their dishes in the sink. Anna Marie took Walter's hand, leading him purposefully back to her bedroom, turning off the lights as they walked back.

She thought, "I didn't really expect I would meet my goal number one so quickly and so magically. I guess this was meant to be the first part of my adventure."

Walter and she fit together like lovers of many years. They each knew each other's needs. Their individual years of experience added to their pleasure with each other. Fireworks continued in the sky overhead and within the Southwind, reawakening desires that they had long forgotten existed.

They fell asleep curled around each other, enjoying the warmth and companionship. Later in the night, Little Bear curled up beside them. The three slept soundly through the night.

Anna Marie woke in the morning to the sound of a kitten crying outside the Southwind. She had to think about where she was and then felt the bed next to her. The bed was still warm. She was alone in bed. She breathed a sigh of relief as memories of the previous night came back to her. She felt her face blushing from her own bizarre behavior the night before.

In the early morning sun with only a faint full moon left in the sky, Anna Marie wondered what had gotten into her. She had never in her life behaved in such a way, especially with a man who was practically a stranger. It was like something or someone else had taken over her body and mind along with Walter's. She wondered where he was and if the two of them would be able to face each other "the morning after."

She laughed to herself as she thought, "Well, at least I won't have to worry about an unwanted pregnancy. There is some advantage to being old."

The sound of meowing outside became louder and more desperate. She wondered if the bird had returned with a re-injured wing. Little Bear sat at the door, cocking her head to question what creature could be making that sound this early in the morning, disturbing her sleep. After all, Little Bear had been up later than usual last night, too, as his part of the bed had been occupied by a new man in Anna Marie's life.

On the table was a note Anna Marie assumed was from Walter but the sound outside was so desperate, she thought it best to check on the source of the sound before reading the note.

Outside under the table was the scruffiest-looking kitten Anna Marie had ever seen. She assumed it was gray. It was likely a Maine Coon Cat, a favorite breed of Anna Marie's. The kitten looked like it had not eaten in days and could use a good bath. Against her better judgment, Anna Marie approached the kitten.

She had the feeling this was another living creature she would assume responsibility for in a very short time.

Little Bear watched as Anna Marie picked the kitten up to bring her inside. She hoped that she would not give any diseases to Little Bear. She knew that she needed to warm and feed the kitten if it was to survive.

She found a towel washing the kitten with warm water with no resistance from the poor little thing. She also heated some condensed milk she had for baking, remembering the days when her children were young. They had frequently brought home stray animals like this.

As the kitten lapped greedily from the saucer, Anna Marie took Little Bear outside for a short walk. She then prepared Little Bear's breakfast while she put water on for tea. After setting the table, fixing herself a light breakfast of an English muffin, and making a warm cozy place for their latest addition, she read Walter's note.

Anna Marie,

Thank you for such a lovely night reminding me how to feel like a man again. I now realize what has been missing from my marriage. I am going back to fight for my wife. I hope that I have not hurt you in any way. I will always be grateful for our night together of such fabulous sex. I will call you and let you know what is happening with my wife and me. Thank you again for your understanding.

p.s. It would probably be best if no one other than us knows what happened last night.

Anna Marie couldn't have agreed more. She was surprised at how relieved she was. She did not want her grand adventure to end this soon. A developing relationship could have meant the end of her independence. She also did not want a repeat of last night, especially with Walter. He was a lovely man, but it was time for her to be alone in her life, learning who she was all over again without a man to define her or limit her new adventure.

The kitten poked at Anna Marie, trying to get up on Anna Marie's lap. Picking her up, she noticed how cute the little thing was once it had eaten and was clean. Long grey hair stuck out around her tiny body while gentle orange-gold eyes looked at Anna Marie gratefully. She purred as Anna Marie stroked her fur, trying to think of an appropriate name for her new addition to her family. She knew this little one was meant to stay with Little Bear and her to share their great adventure.

After thinking for a few minutes, she stumbled on the name "Maya," thinking this name of a Hindu Goddess was perfect.

There was a knock at the door. Anna Marie carefully placed the kitten in her warm bed. Food, attention, and warmth helped the little one quickly doze off for a much-needed nap.

Frank stood at the door. He had been off the day before which was just as well, as he had no idea of all that had transpired between Anna Marie and Walter.

Frank said, "I just wanted to thank you for the other night and to make sure you were okay. Your friend Walter seems to have left in a hurry." Unable to hold back his excitement, Frank continued, "I have some news to tell you."

Anna Marie invited him in for coffee, showed him Maya, and added, "Walter thought he should go back and try to patch up his marriage. I'm spending today planning the next part of my trip. I think it is time for me to move on. What's the news you have to tell me?"

Frank literally glowed as he said, "Irisa and I are getting married in the fall. Your visit with Grandpa helped so much that he called some of his fishing buddies in Florida. They have invited him to come down. He's decided to look for a trailer home there. He wants Irisa and me to have the old family home 'as long as we are married.' Irisa said yes and we both have you to thank for this. I know I've only known you for three days, but you have changed my life."

Frank approached Anna Marie, gesturing a hug which Anna

Marie returned enthusiastically. "I will really miss you, Anna Marie. Can I call you? Will you send me postcards to let me know how you are doing or if you need anything from me? Irisa and I hope that you and Little Bear will come back for our wedding?"

Anna Marie congratulated him, gave him a big hug, and assured him nothing would get in her way of coming back for their wedding. They talked for a few minutes more and then Frank returned to his work.

The rest of the day was very quiet with walks around the lake for Little Bear and a trip to the grocery store to stock up for the next phase of the journey. She planned on leaving very early in the morning before Frank was on, so after his shift, they shared one more beer, a few stories, and then hugged goodbye. Anna Marie thanked Frank for starting out her journey perfectly.

Before leaving home, Anna Marie had cards made up with her cell phone number on it, plus her name and Little Bear's name, and the address, "The Southwind, somewhere in the United States." She had purchased 100 cards with a goal of meeting at least that many people to share a card with. She gave Frank three: for himself, Irisa, and his grandfather. That left 97 to go. They hugged again, promising to stay in touch frequently.

Maya had eaten enough throughout the day to make up for the days that she had gone without. She had already begun a routine of eating, sleeping, playing, and then the same all over again. She chased the new catnip mouse Anna Marie had found for her around the Southwind. Little Bear attempted to steal the mouse away. Maya clung to her new toy teasingly.

Anna Marie was reminded how wonderful it was to have young beings around as she observed the pure pleasure they showed when playing. Anna Marie had picked up litter at the grocery store so that Maya would not have to go outside anymore. Maya was already litter trained. Anna Marie thought she was a very bright kitten, learning and following directions quickly. She hoped she would be a natural traveler like Little Bear.

After an evening of play, now three companions went to bed

right after dark to be able to wake up at five am for the next part of their journey.

In the morning, Anna Marie connected the Jaguar to the Southwind. She heard a sound of meowing that was not coming from Maya. Looking up in the majestic tree overhead, she saw the healed Catbird. The bird appeared to say thank you and acknowledge that she had brought the gift of Maya to Anna Marie.

Anna Marie waved and said, "Thank you, little bird. I will take good care of her. You stay safe."

The bird flew off. Anna Marie climbed back into the Southwind with Little Bear and Maya sitting in the passenger's seat, ready for their next adventures, too.

The Present

Anna Marie sipped her tea, thinking about Walter's death last year. She was glad she and he had their one magical night together. She was sure that night had helped him and his wife live out their last days happily together. She was always amazed at how the puzzle of life invariably fit together into a beautiful spiral pattern connecting the past and present. Anna Marie was thankful she had this past to think about with the connection to her present and future.

She also thought back to Irisa and Frank's very simple wedding she had attended the winter after her first Southwind trip. She still heard from the couple. Christmas and birthday cards sent throughout each year. They had two children and now owned the campgrounds she had stayed at in Pennsylvania. She was determined to visit them next summer.

Suddenly remembering something, she ran to her desk in the den. There in the top drawer of her desk were the remaining

Southwind cards. There were 24 of them left as she had handed out many along the way, then had forgotten about them as she progressed into her journey. She had become so engrossed in her quest in the Southwind, she had forgotten the cards. She placed them in her purse with a new goal of handing out the rest to her next new friends. She was determined to remember the lessons of the Southwind.

*"Life engenders life. Energy creates energy.
It is by spending it on oneself that one
becomes rich."*

—Sarah Bernhardt

CHAPTER THREE

FINDING CHRIST: THE NEW MOON

The Present

N ow that it was later in the morning, Anna Marie called Christa. It was very early on the West Coast. She did not want to miss Christa as she remembered Christa usually left early for college or her job. She wanted as much time as possible to make their plans for the trip to New Orleans, hoping that Christa could make the trip with her.

The phone rang crisply in Christa's apartment. Anna Marie could picture the cozy rooms she had visited a couple of years ago to meet Christa's soon-to-be husband and visit with Christa for long, wonderful hours. Their wedding was scheduled for the upcoming summer.

Anna Marie planned on staying a week in Oregon and another week traveling by train round trip with stops along the way. This was a dream trip she had always imagined. Her journey on the Southwind had given her the courage to go alone. She also wondered if she should reconsider her decision and take the Southwind instead, thinking it best to wait to make the final decision. She couldn't predict the outcome of her trip to New Orleans or the next change in her life. The purchase of her RV continued to change her life for the better, even though sometimes she wished for more time in her cozy home.

A very sleepy voice answered on the other end of the call.

Anna Marie recognized it as Christa and said, "Christa, this is Anna Marie. I'm sorry to bother you this early in the morning your time. Harry called me last night to inform me that Granny Rose has died. Her last directions to him were to call me. She hoped you and I could go to Louisiana to retrieve the box Granny Rose left to me for caretaking until the next person was identified. I wanted to give you enough time to make plans."

The voice on the other end said, "That's okay, Anna Marie. You could have called even earlier."

She hesitated, apparently taking in what Anna Marie had told her and then asked, "Is Harry okay? How about you, Anna Marie? It has taken me a minute to wake up and understand why you are calling. I can't imagine a world without Granny Rose."

Anna Marie could hear the tears in Christa's voice.

"Granny Rose was in so many ways bigger than life. Though we were together only a short time, meeting her changed my life. Our lives will likely change without her. I always thought she was my example of how to live life to its fullest, just like you. You are both my earth mothers."

A suppressed sob ended Christa's ability to talk.

It was a relief to hear the sweet melodious voice on the other end of the phone. Anna Marie realized how much she missed being with Christa the last few years. She was again transported back in time…

Seven years earlier

Anna Marie parked the Southwind at the campsite indicated by the older man showing her to the site. She was in Virginia near the Skyway Caverns, right outside a small town located not far from I-81. She had parked and hooked up the RV on her own, feeling very proud of herself for her accomplishment of hooking up with no help. She felt as though she had been accomplishing this all her life. For a reward, she and Little Bear walked into town for ice cream at the little diner they had noticed when driving into the campground.

Before leaving, they had left a special treat out for Maya, who was catching some of the last rays of sun in the back window of the RV. She was resting after a hard afternoon of chasing a fly around the Southwind. When Anna Marie yelled at her to stop, she waited for Anna Marie to turn away, swatting at the fly again. Little Bear joined her in abusing the fly. Anna Marie stopped their play as she would two spoiled children, afraid they would knock over something in the limited space the three shared.

It had taken her twice as long to hook up the Southwind because of the disciplining of her two "children." She had given up even trying for a while so that she could watch them for the sheer joy of their activity. Anna Marie thought there was much to be learned from pets and children for their outwardly expressed joyfulness.

After ordering her favorite cone and a dish of vanilla ice cream for Little Bear with a bone in the middle as a special treat on the menu for dogs, Anna Marie found a picnic table in the shade. She tried to read the newest novel by a favorite author she carried in her bag but found watching and listening to the sounds of the small town far more interesting. She was amazed how quickly she had adjusted to this life of a wanderer without long-term roots causing her to feel content with her life.

Deep in these thoughts, it took many moments for her to be aware of the young girl sitting at the next picnic table crying. In fact, it was Little Bear's nudging of her leg that made her pay attention to their neighbor.

Anna Marie said to Little Bear, "I guess you are trying to tell me there is someone who needs us?"

Little Bear wagged her tail, pulling Anna Marie towards the next table. She picked up her book and Little Bear's treat along with her own ice cream. She walked over to the table with the crying girl.

Anna Marie said as they approached the table, "I'm Anna Marie, and this is my friend Little Bear. We're feeling lonely and could really use some company. Would you mind if we joined you?"

Little Bear licked the young girl's hand as she patted Little Bear with her other hand. Anna Marie handed her a Kleenex from her fanny pack. The young girl wiped away her remaining tears. Little Bear's face was covered with ice cream as she had not had time yet to wipe off her face with her paws. The girl laughed despite her obvious sadness. She motioned for Anna Marie to sit down at the picnic table.

As Anna Marie settled herself with the ice cream, she spoke gently to the young girl.

"We are from Upstate New York on an adventure cross-country in my new-to-me RV. We're having fun but sometimes it gets kind of lonely. I appreciate you letting us join you. Little Bear always loves meeting new friends."

Anna Marie waited for the young girl to say something while carefully observing her. Next to the girl was a large backpack. She was dressed in clean jeans, sandals, and a tee shirt with a peace symbol. Her lovely long strawberry blonde hair accented her face and slender body with curves rather than the more current trend of ultra-skinny. Her eyes, the window to her soul, were soft green and had a quality of innocence along with some mischief—or perhaps intelligence—thrown in.

Anna Marie immediately liked this girl, feeling a quick connection to her, an experience that had happened only a few times before.

The girl shyly said, "I am Christa Lane. It is nice to meet you and Little Bear. I'm a little lonely myself."

She paused and Anna Marie waited for her to say more.

She didn't, so Anna Marie asked, "Do you live here?"

At that question, Christa began crying again. She shook her head to indicate no. Anna Marie waited while she cried harder and Little Bear jumped on the picnic table bench to nuzzle in closer to the crying girl. Unfortunately, Little Bear had been eating her ice cream again, and Christa's jeans were now white from the ice cream.

Anna Marie said, "Oh, dear. Little Bear got you good this time. I'm sorry. Sometimes she is lacking in social graces. Are you here camping or staying with your family?"

Christa stopped crying to wipe off her jeans and answered, "It's okay. Little Bear means well, I'm sure. No, I'm here by myself and I don't really have any place to stay or anyone to go to that I know here."

She began crying again.

Anna Marie thought about the innocent-looking girl and decided to take another risk that was becoming so common on this trip.

"Have you eaten dinner yet? How would you like to come back with Little Bear and me for dinner at the Southwind? Hopefully, our ice cream has not spoiled our appetites. You could tell us your story over our meal."

Christa looked relieved, knowing she did not have any idea where to go next anyway.

She also had developed an immediate liking for and trust of Anna Marie with her adorable Little Bear.

She answered Anna Marie, "I'd love to if you don't mind. I haven't figured out what to do. I'd have some time to plan. I have only a few dollars left on me. I really didn't want to spend it all on eating. I wanted to leave money for a phone call if I needed to make one."

She paused, realized what she had said and then added, "But I'd be happy to pay you for my dinner."

Anna Marie responded, "Of course not. Little Bear and I wouldn't hear of it."

Christa hesitated again and then asked, "Anna Marie, before we go, can you tell me what the Southwind is?"

Anna Marie explained the name was for her RV, giving her a brief explanation regarding the recent purchase of the motorhome.

Christa walked alongside Anna Marie and Little Bear and

displayed a slight limp.

She stopped walking, pointing to her left leg, "I have Cerebral Palsy. It's very minor and only really bothers me when I am this tired. It doesn't mean I am delayed or anything. It's just that I can't walk as fast as others. I'm used to it and hope you don't find it embarrassing. I learn as fast as anyone else."

"Why would I be embarrassed? You are a lovely young lady and I'm proud to be walking with you. I can already see that you have outside beauty. But even more important, you have a special shine from inside which is the best kind of beauty. I am honored that you are willing to keep us company for dinner," Anna Marie responded. "I was a Teacher's Aide in the high school with children with all kinds of disabilities. Let us know if we need to slow down. It is early yet for dinner."

Anna Marie wondered what kind of encounters Christa must have had in her life to feel she needed to explain her condition. From her own experiences in high school, she could imagine the cruelty Christa experienced as she was growing up. She was now even more interested in Christa's story, realizing that at least half the fun of this trip was meeting new people and learning their stories.

As they walked back to the RV together, Christa told her story. She was eighteen years old, from Portland, Oregon, and had left her home against her parent's wishes after high school graduation to go on a "missionary trip." The trip was on a bus with 15 other young people on a religious outing. The group leader of 'The Saviors of People' (SAP), was a 38-year-old named James. James immediately "adopted" Christa as his favorite disciple on the first night of their trip, placing his sleeping bag next to Christa.

Over the next couple of months, he often asked her to share the sleeping bag so that both would be warm while teaching her "more about God and godliness." Christa was a virgin, had rarely dated, and attended a small religious school with little experience or knowledge of sex. Her period had not come for the past two months, she was often nauseous, and her breasts hurt. She told this to one of the other girls on the missionary trip who reported this to James against Christa's wishes. Christa thought the other girl was jealous of James' attention to her. James had been furious, at the next small town told Christa to leave the missionary trip right away.

Before getting off the bus, James told everyone to look at Christa closely as the face of a sinner. It was because of her sinfulness that she had to leave the trip and go out on her own "as though in the wilderness to smite her demons."

This had happened last night. Christa spent the night sleeping on the grass behind the ice cream parlor, hoping no one would see her. She planned to eventually gather up enough courage to call her parents.

By the time Christa finished her story, they were back at the campgrounds. Anna Marie immediately made a cup of weak tea with Chamomile and toast for Christa while she busily prepared dinner for all of them.

Maya came out from her sunny sleeping place to meet Christa. She curled up on Christa's lap to resume her sleep, still exhausted from her afternoon play. Little Bear fell asleep at Christa's feet, making it obvious they both trusted Christa. Christa pet one or the other every few minutes, appearing to help calm Christa.

As Anna Marie set the table and made dinner, she talked gently to Christa, telling her how she had found Maya. She told of her adventures at her first campground, including the happy ending of Frank and Irisa. She intentionally left out the episode with Walter, thinking that was not one of her finer moments. She amazingly had no regrets while preferring to keep it her secret memory.

Noticing Christa more comfortable in the Southwind, she asked, "Would you like to use my cell phone to call your parents, honey?"

Christa shook her head softly. "They were so angry at me I haven't been able to call them. I can hear them say I told you so, blaming me for everything. I can't face them yet even if I don't know what else to do other than go home. I have less than ten dollars left. I can't live on that. I've thought about finding a job, but I don't have a telephone number or place to sleep for anyone to contact me."

Anna Marie thought that eating while getting to know Christa was the best thing to do at the moment for both. At first, they ate quietly along with Little Bear whose ice cream treat did not spoil her appetite.

Maya left Christa's lap when the soup, bread, and salad were placed on the table to eat her small dish of kitten canned food Anna Marie found in the campground store. She finished her food and went back to lay on Anna Marie's bed.

Once Christa had eaten some of her meal, Anna Marie shared her own story. She left little out including the pain with the need to begin her life again. She told Christa about her dream of Ted telling her to go on with her life in his familiar voice. She had told no one else about the dream.

She also shared with Christa her reasons for buying the Southwind and the symbolism of her trip. She told of her other intent to find her biological father from her 'To Do' list. She explained some of the items on her 'To Do' list, purposefully leaving out number one on the list, telling herself that had already been achieved.

Christa quietly listened as she enthusiastically ate her meal. It was obvious she was very hungry. As she ate, a rosy color returned to her face. Even her eyes sparkled with no further crying. Occasionally, she asked a question, but most of the time she listened. Little Bear curled up next to Maya as the sun set behind low-hanging clouds.

It was very peaceful in the campgrounds. It was midweek and early in the season with very few campers. Occasionally, voices from the few other campers or smoke from one of the campfires drifted across into the Southwind, adding tranquility and contentment to the moment for all the occupants.

The two women, feeling as though they had known each other for a lifetime, cleaned up the dinner dishes. Christa volunteered to do the dishes before leaving for town, saying this very wistfully, knowing she had no place to go.

Anna Marie suggested instead, "It is too late for you to make any major decisions tonight. Why don't you stay with me and be the first person on this journey to use the foldout bed in the dining area? We can talk more tomorrow about your options. I planned to stay here a few days anyway and explore the area. I'll wash the dishes and make up your bed while you take Little Bear for her last walk."

The look of relief on Christa's face was unmistakable.

She responded, "That would be wonderful, Anna Marie. You don't think Little Bear would mind me taking her for a walk or staying with you?"

Little Bear heard the word "walk" and carried her lead, kept next to her dish, to Christa's feet.

Anna Marie laughed and said, "I think Little Bear has answered for herself. We would love to have you stay with us while we help you figure out what to do next."

While Christa took Little Bear for her walk around the campgrounds, Anna Marie dried the dishes, put on the teakettle for a last cup of tea, and made-up Christa's bed. When they returned, both looked happy but tired from their walk.

Anna Marie gave warm milk to Christa, cookies for both of them, and a cup of tea for herself on the picnic table next to the RV. They ate their snack and talked quietly about small things in life, the day-to-day events or thoughts that friends share with each other. It was apparent Christa was exhausted. The stars and moon climbed higher into the sky. Saying goodnight to each other in Waldon style, they each fell quickly asleep.

In the morning, Christa showered and changed her clothes. Anna Marie was up a few minutes before Christa and already had breakfast on the picnic table by the time Christa finished showering and dressing. She also had a chance to set up her weaving. She resolved that she would spend at least a few minutes every day on her weaving when she was stopped for more than a day at a time. Little Bear already had her morning walk and ate her breakfast alongside Maya in the RV.

Anna Marie suggested to Christa, "Before you make any decisions, how about we find a clinic in the area and determine if you are pregnant or not?"

Since neither had used the word the night before, it was somewhat of a shock to Christa. A part of her had to know this was a strong likelihood. Christa had pushed the thought to the back of her mind, too afraid of the implications for the next stage of her life.

Christa asked, "Would you come with me? I'm afraid to go alone. I've never even had an examination like that from my doctor at home. I don't know what they will do to me.

"Of course," she added. "I did have my mandated Sex Education in school but the teachers, many of them nuns, were too embarrassed to talk about it. The class turned out to be little more than just 'say no' to sex."

"I wish I had known what sex to say no to," she commented wistfully.

Anna Marie explained some of the procedures. She also clarified they would check her out for any sexually transmitted diseases she may have contracted from James.

Christa looked surprised and asked, "But James is so holy. You don't think he has done this with other girls, do you?"

Anna Marie answered angrily, "Without a doubt, honey. He may even have been having intercourse with other girls on your missionary trip. I suspect he looks for innocent young girls like you. This has not been the first time he has left some young girl on the side of the road. There are men like James who prey on young girls like you. These men get you to trust them, then take advantage of that trust. They blame the young women for their own sexuality and cruelty. Unfortunately, too many women have experienced men like James."

After settling Little Bear and Maya for a few hours of sleep, Anna Marie and Christa drove the car to the office to look in the Yellow Pages for clinics. They found a Planned Parenthood in a nearby city. Anna Marie phoned for directions to the clinic.

It was a quiet day at the clinic. They were soon seen by the Nurse Practitioner. Anna Marie was particularly glad that there was no one demonstrating outside this small-town clinic, as that would have frightened Christa even more.

After explaining their reason for being there, arrangements were made for blood work and a physical examination. Staff at the clinic must have assumed that Anna Marie was Christa's mother, as there were no questions asked about their relationship.

Anna Marie thought it was best to let them continue to assume that relationship. She wasn't sure what the laws were for sharing confidential information or for abortions in Virginia. Christa needed her by her side.

After an hour of tests and examinations, they were asked to wait for the test results. The Nurse Practitioner called them back in her office and asked them to sit down.

"Mrs. Lane, your daughter is pregnant. We did not find any diseases. It looks at this point as though Christa is healthy. I'm estimating about two months along with a due date maybe around the first part of November or possibly earlier. Of course, you both have a decision to make. I don't know what Christa's personal circumstances are, if the father is still in her life, or if at her age she wants to keep this baby. Whatever decision is made, it should be made soon as abortions are much easier for the woman when performed in the first trimester of the pregnancy."

The Nurse Practitioner handed Christa a pile of papers as she explained, "Here are some pamphlets with information that should help you make a decision that is right for you. I want Christa to take these samples of vitamins, as they are good both for Mom and the fetus. You can buy others in the future at any grocery store or drug store, but make sure you use a brand name that has all the essential vitamins and minerals that Christa needs. If she decides not to keep the baby, she will need to build up her own reserves. In the meantime, we want to do everything possible to keep Christa healthy as she makes her decision, hopefully with help from her family."

Anna Marie and Christa left the clinic, saying little, each deep in her own thoughts as to what to do next. Outside the clinic, a few right-to-lifers demonstrated with signs that read "*Murderer of children*" and "*Sinners who take life, repent.*" They attempted to block the pathway of Anna Marie and Christa, shouting at them to not murder their children for the sake of Jesus. One particularly mean-looking man shouted, "Be born again and find your savior. Don't take life. Only God has the right to do that. Harlot! Whore!"

Anna Marie took Christa's arm, guiding her firmly past the small group to the parked car. Christa looked terrified. Anna Marie was angry these people could impose more sorrow and guilt on top of her already existing emotions. It was especially angering since it was under the guise of religion that caused Christa's pregnancy.

Anna Marie settled Christa in the car and said, "It's okay, honey. They think they are doing the right thing. They have no idea what you are going through. Their shouting and their signs say more about their issues than who you are. This is where the adage '*Walk a mile* in *my moccasins*' is applicable."

Christa didn't say anything, staring straight ahead. She clung to the side of the door hoping she might wake up from this bad dream by holding the door handle hard enough.

As they drove back to the campgrounds, Anna Marie suggested, "I think you should at least contact your parents and let them know where you are. They are probably worried about you, especially if anyone from your missionary group contacted them to let them know you have left the group."

Christa was silent for a few minutes and then asked, "Anna Marie can I stay with you for a while? I won't be in your way. I will clean, do our laundry, take Little Bear for walks, anything you need me to do. Please? I need to be with you until I figure out what I should do. Please!"

They pulled up in front of the Southwind. Anna Marie heard Little Bear barking a greeting to them.

She thought about Christa's request for a few minutes and didn't respond to her as she unlocked the Southwind and reached for Little Bear's lead. She certainly seemed to be picking up companionship along the way without even trying. If this had been one of her daughters, she would have wanted someone like herself to take care of her.

Christa watched anxiously from the side, appearing afraid to move thinking that might cause a negative decision.

Anna Marie nodded and said, "On one condition. You call your parents. Let them know you are with me, and that you are doing okay. You should give them my cell number so they can feel free to contact you at any time. This will probably only be for a few days until you decide what you want to do."

Christa wrapped Anna Marie in a huge bear hug, laughing and crying at the same time. Anna Marie realized she had been hugged more in the past week than she had in years, a nice benefit from this trip, something she had missed the most from Ted who was a hugging type of person.

Christa said, "Thank you, Anna Marie. You won't regret it, I promise. Only one thing, I have not decided whether to keep the baby or not. I don't want to tell them yet. It would be one more hurt. They don't need to know until I decide. I want this to be my decision, not theirs."

Anna Marie agreed, handing her the cell phone for the call. Christa went inside the Southwind. Anna Marie heard bits and pieces of the conversation.

In a few minutes, Christa was back outside speaking into the phone, "She's right here. I'll let you talk to her. You'll realize she's a nice lady. I'm perfectly safe with her and she likes my company."

She turned away as she said quietly into the phone, "She was lonely until I turned up. I think she needs me with her."

Anna Marie laughed to herself since being lonely was the last thing she was on this trip.

Christa handed Anna Marie the phone as she said to her, "Please talk to her and assure her that I'm safe with you. Please tell her I will be a great help to you on this trip."

She whispered, "I told her I needed to stay with you because you are lonely. It would help if you said something similar."

Christa looked at Anna Marie with a pleading expression.

Anna Marie took the phone from Christa and said, "Hello. I'm Anna Marie Golding. Christa is very safe with me. I could use some company."

She explained to Christa's Mom how she came to be in Virginia. She told her she would be willing to give her some references from home to know Christa was safe. At first, Christa's mother sounded very cold towards Anna Marie. Anna Marie told her about needing to get over her grieving and how upset her family was with her for taking this trip in the Southwind. Christa's mother slowly seemed to become more sympathetic. She sounded appreciative that Christa was with an older woman who was also a mother.

She asked Anna Marie if there was anything Christa needed.

Anna Marie responded, "She should have some money for clothes, food, or the small things that young girls always need. I don't expect her to split any expenses, but I think she would feel better about being with me if she did not need to ask for money from me for her own purchases."

Christa's mother agreed to send her money every few weeks if Christa would call to let them know how she was doing and she was safe. They figured out how best to get the money to Christa and a reasonable amount for her.

Christa's Mom said, "We didn't want her to go off with that SAP group. I just knew there was something funny about that older man leading them. I have a feeling there is something you are both not telling me. Hopefully, Christa will be able to tell me over time."

She sighed, continuing, "We really hoped she would go to college. Money was so tight here with my husband laid off from his job. Then trying to take care of her twin brothers took most of my time. And you know she has a disability, so we didn't know if she would be accepted at a college even though her grades were good. Maybe you will be able to talk her into coming back home and going to college. We'll find some way to afford it for her."

Anna Marie assured her she would do what she could. Anna Marie gave the phone back to Christa. Christa and her mother talked a few minutes more and then hung up.

Christa said to Anna Marie, "Thank you. That was not as bad as I thought it was going to be. She knows something isn't right. I can't tell her until I know what I want to do. I'm afraid I'm in no situation to take care of a baby. I can't make the decision yet not to have it. At least I have some time to think about it, thanks to you."

Christa hugged Anna Marie again, asking to take Little Bear for a walk. Anna Marie told her to go for the walk as she would like some quiet time to work on her weaving or to read. She had a bag full of books and hoped to start reading again.

She thought she might be able to sell some of them when she finished reading at used bookstores along the way to purchase others. So far, she had almost no time to read or weave. It would be a treat to do both for an hour or so. She had to play with Maya for a few minutes, as Maya obviously felt left out of the walks and attention.

When Little Bear and Christa returned from their long walk, she asked Anna Marie about the weaving. Anna Marie demonstrated how to use the loom. She asked Christa to pick out the colors for this project. Christa mentioned she had always wanted to learn needlepoint, so Anna Marie found a needlepoint of a vase of flowers underneath the RV that she had not started yet and gave to Christa. The two worked alongside each other for a few hours, enjoying the quiet companionship and respite from the worries of life.

Anna Marie and Christa decided to stay in the campgrounds for a few more days before traveling on. The days were lovely spring days, with Virginia in full bloom. Each day took on a pattern of relaxation and time separate from the rest of the world. They explored the Shenandoah Valley, small historical museums, and even some of the caves, despite Anna Marie's fear of going far underground.

Anna Marie knew this journey was also about conquering old fears. It was easier with Christa at her side. Both believed they were meant to be together at this time in their lives. The difference in ages didn't seem to matter— they could talk for hours about the simplest pleasures of life.

Both spent time with Little Bear and Maya. They took Maya to a local Veterinarian for shots. They also found a collar that allowed her to be outside with them during meals so she would not feel so left out.

As the Veterinarian examined Maya, she asked, "Tell me again how you found this little one."

Anna Marie explained how she found the little kitten looking lost and disheveled next to her RV.

The Veterinarian listened and then shook her head said, "That's strange. I'm almost positive this is a purebred Maine Coon Cat. Those are usually expensive to buy. People don't just let them wander away. You didn't see other kittens or the mother anywhere around?"

Anna Marie explained how she had asked at the various campsites and the office. No one knew of any kittens at the campsite or any houses within walking distance of the campground. The Veterinarian responded, "Well, the good news is she is very healthy. I suspect only about 6 to 7 weeks old, which is also unusual for her to be able to survive away from her mother at that young age. She could not have been away from her mother very long. Quite strange!"

They left the Veterinarian's Office wondering about Maya's story. They knew it was likely they would only be able to guess.

They were pleased she had survived to give such pleasure.

Both Little Bear and Maya enjoyed the pattern of the days, as well. Maya slowly filled out into a lovely young long-haired kitten with a unique personality. Early in the morning, to wake everyone up, she would run from one end of the Southwind to the other, sliding whenever possible on the small rug next to the sink.

Little Bear sighed with an expression that said, "Kids do the darnedest things."

Occasionally, Maya climbed up on Anna Marie or Christa's lap and stared into their eyes.

One day, Anna Marie laughingly asked Maya, "Are you looking to see if you knew us in another life?"

Maya glared back at her as she asked this, scaring Anna Marie with the intensity of the stare. While Maya was a typical kitten, she also appeared to understand everything that was said to her and had, at times, a strange maturity about her. An old soul like her mother would have described a child with that kind of stare.

In between exploring the valley and maintaining the Southwind, the women worked on their individual projects, read, played with the animals, or shopped for small necessary items. Christa's mother sent the money as promised via Western Telegraph along with a form to fill out with Christa's signature so her mother could open an ATM account for her with bi-weekly deposits.

Christa was relieved to receive the money and immediately offered to pay Anna Marie for her room and board. They reached an agreement that Christa would buy and prepare one meal a week, along with being responsible for the care of the animals and assisting with cleaning. Anna Marie did not want her to feel she was a charity case or lose pride in herself. She thought this would be the best way to prevent that from happening.

One night the campgrounds sponsored a karaoke party. They went to the entertainment despite it being something neither would have done in their previous lives. They became so involved in the party that they sang a duet together of "I got you, Babe."

Anna Marie was amazed to find someone of Christa's generation who loved Cher almost as much as she did.

The ladies were so good together that they received a standing ovation from the small audience in attendance. They had to sing the song two more times due to the number of requests for encores. Both laughed all the way back to the Southwind. As they had a last cup of tea together for the night, Little Bear and Maya watched them both, obviously thinking they were acting strange, which caused Anna Marie and Christa to laugh even harder.

They met a couple in the campgrounds who had lived together for seven years. They told the ladies they planned to finally marry while they were in Virginia. All the people in the campgrounds were invited to their impromptu wedding, including Little Bear who enjoyed it as much as the 27 other campers.

Maya looked upset when she saw Little Bear in her new cap bought especially for the occasion. She pouted going back in the corner looking lonely. Anna Marie decided she would have to find a special toy or hat for Maya the next day as her feelings seemed to be easily hurt. Even though the event was spontaneous, with a quick gathering of campers, it was a beautiful wedding. Both Anna Marie and Christa cried throughout the ceremony.

Afterwards, one of the campers played guitar and sang requested songs while the campers shared covered dishes brought to the wedding. The couple poured wine and beer liberally. The campers became an extended family for the night, thinking how fortunate they had been to be there for this special occasion.

Another night Christa shyly told Anna Marie it was her birthday. Anna Marie baked little round honey and oatcakes for her, a tradition she had for her own family birthdays along with Christa's favorite meal Baked Southern Fried Chicken. They invited some friends from the campground, including the newlywed couple, to dinner. Everyone sang Happy Birthday and spent the night around the campfire talking. Anna Marie passed some of her cards to her new friends, making the remaining number 86.

Christa seemed the happiest she had been since Anna Marie met her. She thanked Anna Marie enthusiastically for the nicest birthday in many years. Little Bear enjoyed all the company. However, both she and Maya seemed glad when everyone left. Within minutes, both curled up for a peaceful sleep.

Anna Marie noticed Christa had put on a little weight. She hoped Christa was thinking about what was best for her to do with her future. She hesitated to bring it up as she thought that Christa needed time for healing. Anna Marie knew it was Christa's decision to make on her own without input from others who would not be responsible for her decision.

Anna Marie promised her family she would stay in constant touch by phone. Initially, she called either her son, daughters, Diana, or mother every other day. Now she stretched calls out to about every four days. Whomever she called updated the others on Anna Marie's journey.

She gave some details of her experiences intentionally leaving out Walter and other incidences that likely would make her family uncomfortable. She felt she needed to tell them about Christa and debated for a few nights how best to tell them without them worrying about her. Deciding it best to break the news slowly, she first introduced them to the idea of Christa as someone she had just met without informing them that she was staying with Anna Marie.

After a few calls, she broke the news carefully to Katy, knowing she would be the most difficult to persuade.

She said, "Katy, remember Christa, I told you about meeting? I've talked with her parents, and we've decided it would be best for her to stay with me for a while before choosing when she wants to return home. She is company for me. You don't need to worry so much about my being alone."

Katy was livid. She angrily told Anna Marie, "Mom, I really think it's time you come home. You can't travel around the country with strangers who are out to take advantage of you. If you had waited, one of your grandchildren could have gone with you for an extended weekend to a campground near us. You would get this all out of your system without so much risk."

Anna Marie responded, "I am not just getting something out of my system. I am living my life in the way that I want. I am happy for the first time since your father died. You should be proud of me for not sitting home waiting to die or for each of you to entertain me. I am an adult, raised you kids, and certainly know when I am going to be harmed or not. Christa is a lovely young lady who needs me right now."

Anna Marie paused and then continued, "And if I were to be honest, I need her, too. For the first time in a long time, someone needs me who is not related to me or wants little more than my company. She doesn't feel sorry for me as you all do. It feels good not to be pitied. I hope I have taught you children that life is about making connections. That is partly what I am doing, besides connecting back to my old self that I needed to find again."

Katy said, obviously in tears, "I need to go now. I'll talk to you later. I do love you, Mom. We are just two very different people."

She hung up the phone in a way that did not sound very pleasant.

Later that night, Anna Marie received a call from her son and Mother, both concerned for her welfare and about "that girl you have picked up." Anna Marie thought it best not to argue as she was getting nowhere. She casually changed the subject to the weather. She guessed they would get over it in time. She thought it was not her responsibility to make them accept her choices as long as those choices were not hurting them.

Since she couldn't think of any way that Christa's traveling with her was hurting them, she determined to no longer argue or worry about their comments.

The next call came from Diana. Anna Marie assumed her family thought if all else failed, Diana would be able to persuade Anna Marie of the errors of her ways. Instead, Diana listened to Christa's story and then agreed with Anna Marie that this was the best thing for both Anna Marie and Christa right now.

Diana assured Anna Marie, "Don't worry, Anna Marie. I'll find a way to calm your family. They have invited me for a cookout on the weekend. Probably to complain about you, but I'll use it as an opportunity to help them understand why this is good for you at this moment in time."

Anna Marie thanked her. She was relieved that Diana understood why this was important and was on her side.

When she called Cynthia to tell her, Anita again answered the phone. Since Cynthia had not returned from her teaching job, Anna Marie told Anita, who thought it was wonderful for both Anna Marie and Christa. Later that evening Cynthia called her back to ask if she and Anita could come to the campground for a long weekend to meet Christa, promising to rent their own camping equipment.

Anna Marie agreed it would be great to see both. Cynthia asked her to reserve a campsite close by their campsite. This early in the season Anna Marie was able to reserve a campsite directly across from the Southwind.

Christa and Anna Marie excitedly prepared for their weekend visitors by cleaning the Southwind from top to bottom, making out grocery lists for needed supplies, and a menu of foods while their visitors were there. Anna Marie could tell Little Bear was anxious with all the activity, wondering what was happening next.

Anna Marie attempted to reassure her by explaining the activity. She could never be sure how much Little Bear understood. To appease her, they bought her a new cap with 'Virginia is for Lovers' written on the visor. This time she made sure to buy a hat for Maya, which Maya wore proudly around the Southwind.

The time flew by quickly with the planning and preparations. Before Anna Marie knew it, she was hugging Cynthia and Anita as they got out of their huge SUV. They explained they had rented the SUV for the trip so they could sleep inside the vehicle rather than out in the open if it should rain or become colder.

Anna Marie introduced them to Christa, who stood shyly back by the Southwind. Anita shook Christa's hand, patted her hard on the back, and then looked at her intently.

She asked in her booming voice, "Have you been taking good care of my mother-in-law?"

Christa nodded and looked to Anna Marie for support, appearing a little confused by the greeting.

Anna Marie thought Anita was quite a picture to adjust to, dressed in her jeans with suspenders, plaid shirt, and hair cropped so close to her head she looked almost bald except for the bright red streaks through her hair. It was hard to imagine that she was a successful and wealthy artist.

Cynthia, Anna Marie's daughter, was as tiny as Anita was large, with very delicate features. She wore skin-tight leather pants and a lacy turquoise blouse. Anna Marie was afraid the pants were going to rip open when Cynthia bent over.

Cynthia admonished Anita, "You're scaring the poor girl. Give her time to get to know us."

She patted Christa on the shoulder and said, "My Mom has told me so much about you. I'm glad you've been able to keep each other company. I look forward to getting to know you. I hope you don't mind us barging in like this?"

Suddenly Anna Marie realized that Cynthia and Anita thought she and Christa were a couple.

She laughed to herself thinking, "Maybe I should have told them about Walter. I'll have to clear up this misunderstanding before they leave."

She also hoped they had not expressed this thought to anyone else in the family. She'd likely have more visitors in a short period of time if Cynthia or Anita shared their impression. She didn't need Katy or Erin to be more upset than they already were. She had come to accept Cynthia and Anita's lifestyle. She knew it was just not one of her choosing.

The next few days together were wonderful. The four ladies explored areas of the countryside, taking some lovely hikes to waterfalls in dense forests. Anna Marie had never known she could be athletic. She noticed that for the first time in her life, without dieting, her jeans were loose. She thought it likely she might have to buy new jeans if she kept losing weight. Feeling the best she had in years, knowing she looked healthy, and was enjoying the company of those around her gave her joy. Anna Marie spontaneously walked into a beauty shop a few days before and had a new shorter hairstyle that matched her new life.

One night, as she came out of the Southwind with cheese and crackers, she overheard Christa confiding her pregnancy to Cynthia and Anita. Anna Marie ducked back into the Southwind so as not to disturb the conversation.

She heard Christa share with them the very difficult decision she had to make, "I just can't bring myself to make the decision to end a life. But I don't know if I am ready to be a good mother. I keep going back and forth with those two thoughts."

Anita said to her, "It is a decision you must make for yourself as only you will be responsible for that child. You need to decide if you are ready to give that child a good life. Whatever decision you make will be right for you and best for the fetus. You could also decide to have the baby adopted as there are families like ours who are anxious to have children. Not deciding is making a decision. You will need to make it soon before it is not healthy for you to have an abortion."

Cynthia added some supportive words to Anita's comments, telling Christa, "No matter what you decide, we will all love you and support you. You have a family in all of us. We'll be there for you when you need us. We're so glad you are with my mother. You are good to each other. We at first thought you two might be a couple like us. We realize now that you are more like mother and daughter or friends from two different generations."

Cynthia added, "It is not taking a life when it is a fetus. It may be saving a life. Consider your options and who you can count on to help with your decision."

Anna Marie wondered once again what she had done to raise

such an understanding and loving daughter. Cynthia had gone through a very rough period waiting for her family to accept her lifestyle. Yet, she remained a thoughtful person with great values and caring for others in her life.

In some ways, she wondered if Katy might be jealous of Cynthia's life, as it appeared that she had no worries or responsibilities.

As there was silence outside, she thought it was a good time to join three women with her cup of tea.

Christa had been silent. Once Anna Marie was seated, she said, "Do you know what I am most afraid of if I decide to keep my baby?"

She looked to the three ladies for an answer but all three remained quiet, each shaking her head to indicate no.

Christa continued, "I'm concerned that my baby will be shunned, will be labeled illegitimate because she doesn't have a father."

Cynthia angrily responded, "Our society has it all wrong. In many cultures of the world, there is no such thing as being illegitimate. Every child the mother decides to have is wanted. How could there be a concept of illegitimate when a child is wanted? Of course, those societies also understand that it is each woman's decision if she can bring a child into the world based on available resources. Are there enough to sustain this child's life considering who else in her life she needs to feed and nurture."

Anna Marie added, "Cynthia's right, there are still many cultures of the world who do not even consider the idea of illegitimate. For thousands of years, the decision to give birth was made by the mother with support from her female relatives. With patriarchy, that decision-making power has been taken away. Even when it is legal, often the woman is made to feel sinful, evil."

Anna Marie thought about her many readings on women's history and health.

She shared with the others, "It has only been since the late

1800s in the United States that the concept of illegitimacy came about. In the late 1800s, men attempted to monopolize the medical care traditionally the responsibility of women. They wanted to remove the decision to give birth from women as well as destroy the community midwives. Illegitimacy was related to children as the property of the father and a way to protect the line of inheritance for the father.

"There was no way to be sure who the father was before DNA testing. The Latin word for family means all the people owned by the patriarch, including wives, slaves, and children."

Anna Marie recalled the shock she felt when she read this definition of the word 'familial.'

Anita responded, "There are still cultures within the United States that do not accept this idea of illegitimate. For example, when I worked in graduate school with the black community in Boston, they told me from their perspective every child was a wanted child. There was no such thing as illegitimacy.

"This discussion begs the main issue. Will Christa's child be seen as different from others because she does not have a father in the picture? Does it matter if the child has a quality of life or will this impact her quality of life? Can Christa provide food, shelter, and love?"

"I was an illegitimate child," Anna Marie related. "Cynthia's grandmother made the difficult decision to keep me in a time when unwed mothers and their children were condemned and shunned. My mother had to leave her town to live in a home in the Midwest for unwed mothers like her. She talked very little about her experiences except to say it was the loneliest time of her life.

She'd look at me with love in her eyes and say, 'It was worth every minute of it because I had you.'

Anna Marie continued, "She later married my stepfather who was every bit a good father to me. She raised me by herself for a couple of years before her marriage. Her parents never forgave her for that. While she lived with them, they reminded her frequently of her 'big mistake.' After she married my stepfather, her family accepted her again."

She added, "I have not suffered in my life for her decision as far as I remember. I was loved and cherished. I think I am probably stronger because my life was not a picture-perfect life. My mother did suffer. She never finished high school and was only able to work in low-paying jobs. My grandmother reminded her of her inability to give her child a good life or be able to pay for the necessities."

Anna Marie added, "I think times have changed. I understand your concern. There will be some people who may think 'illegitimate' when they see your baby. I recommend your decision be based on can you give this baby a decent life and plenty of love. Will you be able to feed and clothe this baby? Can you develop your life so that you do not live in poverty the rest of your life because of your decision to have this child? Who will be your support to help you do this at your young age?"

Anita and Cynthia both reinforced, "Our family will be there for you if you are concerned about your own family. We will do whatever you need, including having you come live with us if you need a home."

Anita and Cynthia looked wistfully at each other.

Cynthia said, "That is my only regret, that we cannot have children together. We're hoping the laws will change soon so we will be allowed to marry. Adoption will then be made easier for us. Otherwise, we may need to adopt from another country when there are so many children in this country who need a good life."

Christa listened intently. She looked up at the stars and moon overhead. Everyone was silent for many minutes as they observed the sky overhead.

Christa said, "Look, the moon has a ring around it."

They all looked up overhead, realizing Christa was changing the emotional intensity of the discussion.

As they looked, she said, "I don't know that I have ever felt so supported in my life. I love each of you although I have only known you for a brief time. Thank you, Anna Marie, for taking me into your life and letting me meet your family. No matter what decision I make, you will have helped me make that decision. You give me the courage to know that it will be the right decision for me."

Anna Marie, thinking it would be a good idea to give Christa time alone, said, "You're welcome, Christa. I'm glad I made the choice to take this trip, as a result met you at a time when we needed each other."

She yawned and continued, "I don't know about the rest of you, but I'm tired. I'm going to bed."

The others indicated they were, too. Christa quickly took Little Bear for a short last walk of the night. Soon all of them were deep in each of her dreams as clouds moved over the moon to cover it. The frogs in the woods around provided a cacophony of sounds with a distant wolf occasionally adding to the music of the peaceful night.

The next day, as Cynthia and Anita packed their SUV in the falling light rain, Anna Marie and Christa watched with sadness. Even the animals seemed subdued. They had enjoyed the extra attention, already missing their guests. Goodbye hugs were given to each of the animals.

Anna Marie said, "I'm not sure where we're going next. I'll keep you informed of where we are. I hope you can join us other times in our journey."

Cynthia and Anita both promised they'd visit again. They hoped to be able to join them soon, wherever they were, for more hiking and time together.

Cynthia said, "You know how much I love Wyoming and the Grand Tetons. Maybe if you go there, we could join you for a few days?"

Anna Marie agreed that could be a possibility and would keep them updated on her plans.

Christa and Anna Marie waved as they drove away.

Anna Marie stated as they went back to the Southwind, "I think it is time for us to go on with our journey. It already seems too quiet here for us. Let's get out the maps and brochures to decide where we want to go next."

With the maps and AAA books out in front of them they chose Tennessee. Neither had visited there before and it was an easy drive from Virginia. Anna Marie found it fun to have someone pour over the AAA books and maps with her. They prepared everything that night, including attaching the Jaguar back on to the Southwind, so they could start early in the morning.

As they drove away from the campsite in the early morning mist, they wondered what adventures the next part of their journey would give them. Both were deep in thought pondering what decision Christa would make or how that decision would affect her life.

Anna Marie said as they drove out of the campground, "Christa, whatever you decide will be right for you. Let's just enjoy today and see what this day and night brings. Until we reach Tennessee, we will only bring it up if you want to discuss your thoughts."

Christa nodded with a smile. Little Bear climbed up on her lap so she could see where they were going next.

Christa placed the visor cap hanging over the mirror on Little Bear's head asserting, "I think that is what Little Bear is telling us, too."

With that, they both began to sing, 'I've got you, babe!"

For the next few miles, they laughed with the joy of being silly and for having this day together, along with the anticipation of their next adventure.

The Present

Anna Marie thought how close she had come to Christa and her own family because of her first Southwind journey. Sometimes it seemed that distance created a closeness that could not be gained any other way.

Little Bear, sitting at her side, reminded her that it was time to refresh her water and a treat. Anna Marie hugged Little Bear tightly.

Little Bear wagged her tail as Anna Marie ran the water and handed her the treat.

As above so below.
The rose mirrors the stars.
Intricate, the path of a soul,
Finding meaning beyond the scars.

–By permission of Vincent Bishop, author's son

CHAPTER FOUR

MEETING GRANNY ROSE

The Present

The phone rang, startling Anna Marie who was deep in thought. It was Christa, letting her know she was planning to travel to Sumer, Louisiana and needed further information to complete her plans.

Christa asked, after enthusiastically greeting Anna Marie, "How soon do you want to go? Is there a memorial service first? Should we do that before going to Louisiana? You probably told me all this before. In my defense, I was half asleep and in shock when you called."

Anna Marie responded, "No, Granny Rose distinctly told Harry that we were to retrieve the box first, then he'd plan a service for her. She was very adamant about that. I hope we can arrange flights out tomorrow. Do you think you can schedule a flight that soon? We promised we'd do what Granny Rose asked us to do. I know she is watching from above to make sure we follow her wishes exactly. You know how ornery Granny Rose could be in life so you can imagine her wrath in death if we don't keep our promise. She'd understand if you can't join me but not if I didn't go."

Christa laughed, "Yes, I can just picture her. Hands on hips, trying to look six feet tall instead of not quite five feet with an expression on her face that we better not mess with her."

Christa, sorrowfully asked, "Anna Marie, I truly loved her and will miss her. Do you think she really is close by?"

Anna Marie assured Christa that Granny Rose could not be very far away. Granny Rose would likely watch over them because she loved all of the Southwind Gang.

Tenderly, Anna Marie added, "I loved Granny Rose too. I feel a piece of me has been lost. I'm hoping she is close by watching us to make sure we don't mess this up."

Christa promised she would call back after finalizing her flights and hung up the phone.

Anna Marie packed a small bag, gathering up the belongings she would need for her trip to Louisiana. She knew she was partially doing this to keep herself from thinking too much about their loss.

She mentally made a list of things to do including calling her children to see who was able to keep Little Bear and Maya while she made this journey for Granny Rose. As she gathered up her toiletries and a couple of simple outfits that would pack easily, she found herself back in the Southwind on an early May spring day.

Seven years earlier

Anna Marie stopped at the entrance of the campground. They were someplace in Georgia, staying in the current campground for two days, now very anxious to move on to their next chosen site. This had been a noisy site with a bunch of teenagers who were celebrating their upcoming high school graduation. The bottle smashing in the middle of the night had scared all the occupants of the Southwind.

Each of the Southwind passengers breathed a sigh of relief when about four that morning all the teenagers had apparently finally fallen asleep or home to sleep off hangovers. Christa and Anna Marie waited, each with a cup of hot tea, for the sun to rise so they could be on their way, away from this campsite that had been so unpleasant.

They had hurriedly packed up the Southwind with relief. Anna Marie drove the Southwind to the office so that she could report some problems with their campsite along with the unwillingness of the security staff to do anything about the underage drinking and noise.

As they stopped, Little Bear anxiously pawed at the door and ran back to Christa to let her know she was expected to take her for another walk before they were on the road for hours.

Anna Marie suggested, "Why don't you take her for another walk while I report the hook-up problems and lack of help from the staff in quieting down our partiers. I shouldn't be too long but long enough to give Little Bear some last-minute exercise. I think our partiers are sleeping it off or have gone home, so you should be safe."

Christa quickly put on Little Bear's collar with Little Bear's anxious assistance. This was the last opportunity at this site for Little Bear to smell the area. Anna Marie waved to them as she stepped out of the Southwind.

She hesitated for a minute, debating whether to lock the door. Christa hadn't taken her key, and Anna Marie did not think either would be gone that long. She hoped to be able to watch the RV from the office window.

Inside the office, Anna Marie impatiently waited behind two other people who appeared to be purchasing the campgrounds. Or maybe unhappy campers due to the partying the night before. She watched the minute hand on the clock moving first 15, then 20 minutes. She thought about going out to check on the RV but assumed by now Christa and Little Bear must be back from their walk.

Maya also acted as a watch cat. She would likely hear her if there were any problems in the Southwind. She didn't want to lose her place in line, or this could be the entire day wasted.

As she crept closer to the front of the line, her cell phone rang. She answered the phone to hear an increasingly familiar male voice, "Anna Marie, it's Walter. Did I catch you at a bad time? I thought early in the morning would be a good time to call."

Anna Marie wasn't sure how to answer that question, wanting to admit it was a bad time to call while not hurting Walter's easily offended feelings.

She said instead, "Hi, Walter. I can talk for a few minutes. I'm in line to check out and may need to cut the call short if my turn comes up. I've been waiting over half an hour and hoping to be on the road soon."

Walter responded, "Well, I won't keep you too long. I just wanted to see how you were doing and to let you know how well I'm doing. Anna Marie, my wife and I had great sex for the first time in years. It's all thanks to you, Anna Marie. She is no longer talking about Iggy, her crush from the Senior Center. She says I'm head over heels better than him. She wants to know what happened to change me. I haven't told her anything about us."

Anna Marie stepped out of line, afraid someone might hear this conversation.

She spoke admonishingly into the phone, "Walter, this is not a good time to be talking about this. And there is no such thing as a good time. I guarantee your wife would not be happy that you are talking about your private life with me. Walter, I need to get back in line again. Can we talk another day?"

Walter said somewhat apologetically, "Sure. Sure, Anna Marie. I just wanted to update you on my progress and to thank you again. I'll try to call at a better time next time I call."

Anna Marie whispered into the phone, "Walter, it would probably be a better idea for you if you didn't call me so often. Suppose your wife were to find out? That could upset her and break you apart again."

Anna Marie looked around to make sure no one was listening to their conversation. Her face and neck were bright red, wanting to crawl under something with nothing obviously available to her at the moment.

Walter did his usual ignoring of Anna Marie's comments,

"Anna Marie, you have a safe trip. I'll call you again in a few days, maybe in the evening at a better time. I will likely have new updates."

Anna Marie literally heard the 'wink, wink' from Walter.

He added, "It's hard to keep track of what time zone you're in. In a few days you will likely be lonely. I hope you are not angry at me for going back to my wife. You do understand, don't you? I didn't mean to have sex and leave you. I felt I needed to try to work it out with my wife. Too many years invested in that relationship to let it go."

Anna Marie responded impatiently, "No, Walter, I am not angry with you. And I am not lonely. I have more company than I ever counted on."

They both said goodbye. Anna Marie put the phone back in her purse. She stepped back into line behind a couple that came in after her, quietly waiting her turn, attempting not to bring any more attention to herself.

About an hour later, Anna Marie walked out of the office. As she approached the parked RV, Christa and Little Bear came up the hill on the other side of the road.

Anna Marie asked anxiously, "You're just getting back now?"

Christa responded, "Little Bear really seemed to need to follow her smells this morning. I saw there was a line inside the office. I knew you would call us when you were finished. We were both enjoying the peace and quiet this morning."

Anna Marie looked around inside the Southwind.

Not seeing anything out of place other than Maya looking very irritated at all three of them, she said, "Well, everything looks okay so nothing lost but a few minutes of travel time. Maya is feeling left out. Please, give her some treats before we leave."

Christa did that, also slipping a second bone to Little Bear. Christa took her place in the passenger's seat. They were quickly on the main highway back to the expressway.

It felt good to be on the move again. It was an exceptionally sunny and clear day with a light breeze and low humidity.

Anna Marie and Christa had realized on their first day of travel together they were very compatible traveling companions, both setting a similar pace and an interest in trying new experiences.

As they rode on that bright sunny morning, both Anna Marie and Christa sang songs from the 1960s and 70s on the radio station they found the night before. Anna Marie was amazed how many songs from previous generations her own children had loved. Apparently, this next generation to which Christa belonged was still listening to the same songs.

A few times, Anna Marie looked back at both Maya and Little Bear lying on the floor facing her bed in the back of the RV without moving or making a sound. This was not their usual place for travel. Since they were quiet, Anna Marie assumed it must be a game the two were playing with each other.

She thought, "Maybe Maya is still feeling left out from this morning and is letting Little Bear know it."

She wished she could read their minds or understand their communication better.

They made one short rest stop before lunch trying to make up for the lost hour of travel in the morning.

At lunchtime, Anna Marie suggested, "Let's stop at a fast-food place rather than make lunch. That way we can make the time up we lost this morning and be at our next stop before it is dark. I don't feel confident enough of my skills to hook up the RV in the dark."

Christa agreed.

They stopped for only a short lunch break. After quickly walking Little Bear, who was surprisingly reluctant to leave the RV, they drove on. Because the traffic was light and it was a clear day they made excellent time, putting many miles behind them and the noisy campground of the night before. At five o'clock, they pulled into the next selected campground. They were soon checked in and hooked up at their site.

This was a small, quiet campground with few people around. Both ladies were extremely pleased with the quiet after the previous evening. Since it was midweek with few other campers, they were fortunate to be next to a pond with a lovely sitting area. As Anna Marie set the table with flowers placing the sign next to the Southwind she noticed a small gray-black bird overhead chirping a meow.

She shook her head, thinking it could not be the Catbird again, wondering, "If it was the Catbird, what's in store for us now? The Southwind is getting a little crowded. I can't imagine adding another being. I hope I am wrong on the appearance of this bird every time another creature joins me on my journey. I hope this time it's only a strange coincidence."

It was Christa's turn to make dinner. She baked a chicken casserole and mixed a salad with a glass of wine for Anna Marie and homemade peach iced tea for her. Anna Marie was amazed at what a good cook Christa turned out to be. She always looked forward to Christa's turn for dinner or lunch. She also liked to watch Christa fold laundry. This was a task Anna Marie always struggled with, often finding clothes more wrinkled after she had folded them than before.

She frequently thought she was an imposter of a housewife and mother with other women of her generation far more comfortable with the required skills. She wondered if she had been born in her children's generation with their choices if she would have been a housewife or even a mother at all, as none of the expected skills came naturally to her. She would have much rather been reading a book, working with her children with disabilities as a Special Education Assistant, or planting in her herb garden than cleaning the kitchen.

Anna Marie walked Little Bear around the campground while Christa prepared dinner. They took a little longer than usual as the few people there wanted to be introduced to Little Bear. Little Bear seemed exceptionally restless, not as anxious to stop and meet people as usual. The new friends did not seem to notice. One couple wanted to know where she had traveled from while sharing some of their own travel experiences.

Little Bear grew increasingly impatient, finally barking at Anna Marie to go back to the Southwind. Anna Marie made her apologies. She walked back to the Southwind, wondering what had gotten into Little Bear who usually liked the attention of new friends.

As Anna Marie and Little Bear entered the Southwind, Christa put the finishing touches on the dinner lighting the candle on the table. Christa dished the food out of the pans as they both heard a loud noise coming from the back of the RV, sounding like something passing gas underneath Anna Marie's bed. A very foul odor emitted into the dining area with both Little Bear and Maya rushing to the back of the RV before the two ladies responded.

Christa and Anna Marie looked at each other. Anna Marie grabbed a knife and Christa grabbed the broom out of the closet without saying a word. A look of fear passed between the two of them. Both walked quickly to the back of the RV, joining the animals already next to the bed.

Anna Marie attempted to sound as threatening and forceful as possible, "Whoever or whatever is there, come out now! We have you covered!"

There was a moment of silence, then a rustling sound from underneath the bed.

The bed slowly lifted.

They heard a cracking, raspy voice, "Damn, I knew I should not have eaten that piece of pizza. Too much garlic always gives me gas. I can barely move as it's just too cramped under here."

Anna Marie lifted the bed up the rest of the way. From under the bed came a wizened face with long, grey hair sticking out wildly all over the head thus making the head appear pointed. She had hundreds of wrinkles, and mischievous faded blue eyes.

Without realizing it, Anna Marie instantly relaxed her grip on the knife. Christa moved back and lowered the broom. Little Bear licked the arm of the strange-looking person. Maya, appearing unafraid, watched the movements of the person curiously.

Anna Marie asked as the creature, an elderly woman, stepped over the edge of the bed, "What in the world are you doing under there? Who are you? Where did you come from? Why are you in my RV?"

The woman stared back at Anna Marie, appearing lost in space, with a confused look on her face.

Christa softly said, "I think you are frightening her, Anna Marie."

Anna Marie exclaimed, "I'm frightening her! She is the one crawling out from under my bed."

Christa admonished, "Anna Marie, why don't you let me ask the questions?"

Anna Marie paused, thinking she did feel a little out of control.

She wondered why Christa was not more upset and then said, "Okay."

The little old woman, who weighed about 80 pounds if even that, stood about 4'10" when she straightened herself. She looked to be at least ninety.

The new unwanted Southwind passenger angrily asked, "What are you two doing in my home?"

Christa said, "You may be confused. This is Anna Marie's RV, the Southwind. You're in her home on wheels."

The woman scratched her head and said, "Oh, that's why it has been moving so much. I just came here to get away from those men who were after me."

Christa asked, "Who were those men?"

The strange woman responded, "They claim they are my sons. I don't recall my sons looking like that. These were old men. My sons are young. Plus, these were very nasty men. My sons were always well-behaved. They tried to make me go to that big place on the hill. The one they call "Resting home for angels."

She sputtered indignantly, "I'm not an angel and I don't need to rest. No one ever called me an angel before in my life so why start now? They might as well bury me alive as put me in that place."

Anna Marie and Christa looked at each other, still not quite comprehending how this woman was in their home.

Christa asked, "Anna Marie don't you think we could go sit down at the table? Our meals are getting cold and it's a little cramped back here with all of us in the same place at the same time. I bet our new friend might be hungry, too. If we sit and eat together, we might be able to get to the bottom of this."

Anna Marie nodded, somewhat in a daze as Christa inquired, "Do you have a name?" The lady thought for a minute and said, "Everyone calls me Granny. I guess that's my name."

She hesitated a moment and then sadly added, "I used to be called Rose. But nobody has called me that in years. I don't know why everyone calls me Granny. I can't be everybody's Granny."

Christa replied, "We'll call you Granny Rose even though you're not our Granny. That's if it is okay with you?" '

Granny Rose nodded. Anna Marie gave Christa a warning look. She wondered why she was so worried about this strange person's name. Anna Marie thought she should be more worried about what she was doing in the RV in the first place or how they were going to get this lady out of the Southwind.

The three of them, with the animals trailing behind, walked back to the dining area in a Congo line.

Christa suggested, "It is such a lovely night. Why don't we move everything out to the picnic table? We can bring the candles. It will be more comfortable as we listen to Granny Rose's explanation."

Christa handed Granny Rose a place setting, adding the chicken casserole and salad to the dish. The other two ladies picked up their food and drinks from the table. Soon they were settled at the picnic table with Little Bear contently sitting next to Granny Rose.

Anna Marie was surprised at how comfortable Little Bear was with Granny Rose, especially given that she had been hiding under the bed. Now she knew why the animals were watching the bed so intently. She wondered why they were not disturbed by the presence of this strange creature appearing before them. She had hoped they both were better at watching the RV than that.

Christa gently asked Granny Rose as they ate their meal, "Can you tell us more how you came to be under Anna Marie's bed?"

Granny Rose responded, slurping up the chicken casserole as she spoke, "I was just trying to get away from those men and thought this was my house. They're trying to take me away from my house. I am not going with them."

She was quiet a moment and then asked, "This house moves?"

As Anna Marie and Christa nodded, Granny Rose said, in between huge mouthfuls of food, "Well, there's my answer. If I am moving, they can't take me to that place. I'll stay with all of you, and we'll move together."

She looked around at the two women, Little Bear, and to the screened doorway where Maya sat watching. Granny Rose appeared to be very satisfied with her solution to her problem. Anna Marie did not look or feel quite as happy with the idea.

Anna Marie quickly said, "I am sure your family is very worried about you. You can't just stay with us out of the blue. We need to contact them to come and get you."

Anna Marie thought about the possible delays while waiting for the family to arrive, not pleased with this latest development.

Christa said to Anna Marie, "Can you walk with me and Little Bear while Granny Rose finishes eating?"

Granny Rose, busy eating her second helping of chicken casserole, seemed content to let them go while she continued to eat. Christa's voice made it apparent that she expected Anna Marie to follow her as she picked up Little Bear's lead and walked toward the path around the pond.

Anna Marie, who didn't want to ignore this new, assertive Christa followed behind.

Christa said, once they were safely out of Granny Rose's hearing, "We need to take her. I think her sons were trying to put her in a nursing home. My grandmother was in a nursing home. She died there because of the lack of care. She wasn't washed every day and cried for us to take her home when we visited. I was in school. My mother was working, with the twins still very young, so we couldn't bring her home. My stepfather also stopped my mother from visiting the nursing home claiming she took too much time away from the care of his sons and the house. We visited when he was away."

Christa paused, remembering vividly that difficult time. "Both my mother and I left the nursing home crying every time we visited. I hated to go because it was painful for us. Yet we didn't want to leave her without visitors at the mercy of strangers. When she died, we were relieved that all of us were spared any more pain. We felt guilty as though we willed her death. We had so few options. I think she would have lived longer if we could have found a way to keep her home with us. We can't let that happen to Granny Rose."

Anna Marie forcefully responded, "First of all, we barely know Granny Rose. We don't know if she was going to be placed in a nursing home. She may have already been in a nursing home or escaped from a mental institution. Why, she might be a criminal. She appears to me to be showing signs of dementia and is probably not even able to tell us what is going on."

She paused for a response from Christa, waiting for agreement with her comment.

The hoped-for response didn't come, so she continued her argument, "There is something very strange about her. She thought this was her house, for goodness' sake. Secondly, we could be charged with kidnapping. We can't just pick up every stray we run across."

Christa argued softly but firmly, "Maya and I were strays. Suppose you hadn't taken us in? You didn't know any more about us than you do Granny Rose. What would have happened to us if you hadn't trusted us and taken us in?"

She looked at Anna Marie, begging her with her eyes and words, "I have a sense that Granny Rose is supposed to be with us. She needs us right now. For some reason, we need her. You have taught me to trust my instincts. It is not just chance she found us. Please, Anna Marie. We can't leave her here on her own or ask her to go someplace else. Where would she go?"

Anna Marie looked closely at Christa and thought proudly how much she had changed in the few weeks she had been with them. Her cheeks were rosy colored, her breasts much fuller. She looked like the picture of an expectant young mother, even though she had not yet made the decision to become a mother.

With the money her parents had sent, she bought new shorts and a loose-fitting white top she could wear for some time if she did continue with the pregnancy. She also had her hair trimmed neatly around her head so her natural curls framed her face. With the bleaching from the sun, the style created a halo effect.

Anna Marie thought there was an easy way out of this without upsetting Christa any further or making herself look cruel.

"I'll tell you what. I'll call the police in the county we stayed in last night to find out if they have a missing person's report. We will then have Granny Rose's family or staff members from her nursing home or mental hospital come and get her. If there is no missing person, she can stay with us until we figure out who she is and where her family is so they can come and get her. We're not going to leave her at the side of the road."

While Anna Marie knew that was the best solution, she regretted making it. She had hoped for a quiet couple of days exploring the area.

Christa smiled and said, "That sounds fair."

Anna Marie thought that by tomorrow, they would have Granny Rose safe with her family or nursing home. Then they could go on to their visits in this area and then on to their next planned stop. Everybody else would be happy, even if Granny Rose wasn't.

She thought, "How many creatures can I take on as my responsibility? It isn't fair. This was supposed to be my journey to heal myself, not every living being I find along the way."

Instead of expressing these thoughts to Christa, Anna Marie

suggested, "Why don't you sit with Granny Rose to learn more about her? I will go to the office to find out the county we were in last night and use the cell phone to talk to the county police there."

At the office, Anna Marie had difficulty getting information from the clerk, who spoke very little English. He was involved in what appeared to be an amorous conversation on the telephone and very irritated by Anna Marie's interruption.

He finally gave her the telephone book, motioning her to go to the other side of the office so he could continue with his phone flirtation. Anna Marie tried to ignore his obscene gestures as he talked animatedly into the phone.

After flipping through the telephone book, Anna Marie decided to try 'Information.'

The automated operator came on asking for the city and state. Since Anna Marie did not know the city, she stayed on the line for help from a living person rather than a recording. This person also had difficulty with English but after ten minutes, she had the number to the State Police in the central part of Georgia, assuming that must be where Granny Rose came on board to the Southwind.

The Georgia State Police checked their missing person's file finding no one who came even close to the description of Granny Rose. They gave her the number to the Sheriff's office in Macon County, the county they had camped in the previous night.

The man who answered the phone sounded rushed, like he was not having a good day. He asked her several times to repeat her request and if she was sure she had the correct number, almost accusing her of being a crank caller.

Finally, the man on the other end connected her grudgingly to Sergeant George, who listened patiently to Anna Marie's request for help. He explained that he had no reports of a missing elderly lady at the moment but would watch for any that came into them in the future.

Sympathetically he asked, "Can you call back regularly so that as soon as we have a report of a missing person, we can check it with your description? Now, how did you say we could get in touch with you? What's your address?"

Anna Marie explained to Sergeant George, "We are in an RV with no permanent address. I can give you my cell phone. In the meantime, what do you suggest I do with this strange woman in my RV?"

Sergeant George did not respond on the other end.

Anna Marie became more exasperated by the moment as she had naively thought this would be simple.

She tried again, "I can't keep some strange lady with me until you have a missing person's report. Suppose there never is one. I'm supposed to be going on to eventually arrive in Oregon. I can't sit here waiting for someone to realize an elderly lady is missing. What would you recommend I do?"

Sergeant George advised, "I guess you find the closest nursing home. See if you can get her admitted. It's on your conscience if you want to leave her at a strange campground. I wouldn't do that if I were you. You'll have to decide what you can live with, lady."

Anna Marie protested, "I didn't cause this. I'm just trying to be a Good Samaritan and find her home or family. I can't keep picking up strangers to house them in my RV!" Sergeant George asked suspiciously, "Are you in the habit of finding strangers to travel with you? Maybe you have a problem and need some help. What other strangers have you picked up recently? You're not kidnapping people as you travel, are you? There was a woman in Florida a few years ago who picked up male hitchhikers and killed them for sport. Should I be sending someone to interview you for any other missing persons?"

Anna Marie thought it best not to tell him about Christa, and Maya didn't count. She could tell this conversation was going nowhere, and could get her in serious trouble so she gave up for now.

Anna Marie responded carefully, "That was an expression I used because I was so upset. I'm certainly not a kidnapper or serial killer. I'm just an older woman traveling across the country in my motorhome, finding a strange woman stowed aboard."

She hoped that would help her appear normal. All she needed was the Georgia police to call her own family. They might have her committed.

She hurriedly countered, "Thank you for your help. I will keep in constant touch with you in case you do get a report of a missing person who matches my lady. In the meantime, I'll figure out how best to keep her safe."

She gave the Sergeant her cell phone number and thanked him again.

Anna Marie already dreaded the conversation with her family about the latest addition to her nest. She knew she needed to creatively come up with a way to tell them without sounding like the target for every person on the road in need of a home.

She held imaginary conversations with each of them as she walked slowly back to the Southwind. She also mentally rearranged the Southwind to fit one more person aboard, hopefully only for a few days.

Granny Rose and Christa were sharing a cup of tea outside of the Southwind when she returned. Anna Marie taught Christa this habit of tea with company, for healing, or relaxation. Christa had adopted it wholeheartedly.

Anna Marie thought Christa seemed as if she had been raised on tea rather than Portland coffee. She shared the latest information from her phone call while Christa poured Anna Marie a cup of tea from the steeping pot.

Christa, making sure that Granny Rose could not hear them, implored, "Anna Marie, you would be the first person to tell me that this is what is meant to be at this moment. For some reason, Granny Rose found us and needs us. Maybe we need her without realizing it. She will enrich our lives in some way; I can feel it."

She paused, then added what she hoped was a persuasive comment.

"You promised we could keep her if we couldn't find her

home. There are few options other than to put her on the street. I can't imagine you can do that to a helpless old lady."

They both looked over at Granny Rose, who pretended not to listen. When she realized she was being observed, her expression changed to look as pitiful as possible. They could see one tear run down her face. Anna Marie wondered how much this behavior was an act and how much was real.

She was ashamed of herself when she realized how cynical she was becoming. She blamed her attitude on the voices of caution from Katy and Erin in her head. It felt better to blame someone else.

Granny Rose said to the two of them, giving up the pretense of not listening to them, "You can put a helpless old lady out on the street. I'll understand. I can hitchhike to someplace else where old, frail ladies are welcome. They don't appear to care here. Hopefully, there are no muggers of old people around here. I'll just take my things from under your bed and be on my way."

She struggled for a few minutes to get out of her chair. Instead of standing up, she settled back down further in her chair, waiting for Anna Marie's response.

Christa looked at Anna Marie, obviously very taken by the old lady and determined to win this argument.

She said angrily and forcefully, "You can't break your promise to me. If you do, I'll never forgive you. I can go with Granny Rose if you find having us around is disrupting your precious plans. I'm sure the two of us can do fine on our own."

She walked over to Granny Rose and put her arm around her, ready to defend her from anyone who wanted to take her away. Granny Rose put her head on Christa's shoulder and stuck her tongue out at Anna Marie so that Christa could not see her doing it. Granny Rose had decided that Christa was the one to champion her cause.

Little Bear moved protectively closer to the two women as Maya looked anxiously on from the door of the Southwind. Maya scratched at the screen to be let out.

Absentmindedly, Anna Marie hooked Maya's collar to the outside lead attached to the table as she considered what to say next. Anna Marie knew she was losing this battle rapidly. She didn't want to give in so soon. She remembered when her children were young, giving in too quickly led to further problems. She couldn't imagine what problems were going to be in store for her now.

She tried desperately to win Christa over to her side of the argument. "Christa, she is not a helpless old lady. There is probably a family someplace desperately looking for her. We have an obligation to help them find her."

She looked at Christa, who had not changed her mind. Granny Rose burrowed even further into Christa's shoulder.

Anna Marie thought it looked like an act giving up her losing battle for the moment, "I guess you're right; we have no option other than to keep her with us. I'm sorry I upset you both. I really was trying to do what was right for Granny Rose, not just me."

She looked directly at Christa, "You are not a problem to me or disrupting my plans. I've grown to love having you with me. You are like a daughter to me. We'll figure out how to take care of Granny Rose together and how to find her home. I will need your help explaining my latest addition to my family."

Christa quietly and apologetically said, "Thank you, Anna Marie. I'll do everything I can to help. I know you didn't bargain for all this responsibility on your journey. I'll try hard to make you not regret it. You've taught me to trust my senses. I have a strong instinct that Granny Rose is meant to be with us."

She added, "Be thankful Granny Rose found us, not someone who would put her on the side of the road or hurt her. I will find a way to help you tell your family."

She grinned and added, "I'll volunteer to call Cynthia and Anita to let them know. You can tell the others."

Anna Marie gently and teasingly cuffed her on her shoulder and said, "Thanks. I can do that for myself. As you well know, the others are who I am most worried about telling about Granny

Rose. Maybe if I rehearse in front of the mirror before calling. Or maybe I should turn off my cell phone until I figure the best way to break the news to them or wait until I return home after our travels, whichever comes first."

The rest of the evening passed quietly with Granny Rose finding one of the folding rocking chairs, adopting it as her own, promptly falling asleep with loud snores breaking the silence.

Anna Marie worked on her weaving, choosing a deep burgundy color reminding her of Granny Rose, as the color of royalty.

Christa worked quietly on her needlepoint. Occasionally, Christa looked at Granny Rose sleeping in her rocking chair, smiling lovingly at her. She had covered her with one of Anna Marie's woven lap robes, making Granny Rose look the picture of an ancient woman of wisdom.

Anna Marie wondered about the instant love Christa felt for Granny Rose. She was jealous that Christa did not look at her in the same way. After all, she had been the one to save Christa from Pennsylvania by helping her travel back home while she made her personal decision on whether to have the baby or not.

Even Little Bear and Maya seemed to have immediately taken to this lady. If Anna Marie were to be totally honest, she was a little resentful that Granny Rose was accepted by her family so easily.

Granny Rose woke up shortly before bedtime. Christa asked her to walk with her and Little Bear one more time. Again, Anna Marie was intentionally left out, not understanding fully how she became the pariah, perceived as dangerous or to be ignored.

When they returned, she overheard Christa telling Granny Rose, "I haven't decided if I should keep the baby or not. How did you know I was pregnant? I don't think I look it yet."

Granny Rose answered, "I've always been able to tell when a woman is pregnant, even if she is only a few days along. It's a special skill I have. You do need to make your decision quickly as you will be too far along for your own health otherwise. I'd guess you're close to two months?"

Christa nodded as Granny Rose continued sounding very rational, "This is a decision thousands of generations of women have had to make based on the resources the mother has available to her, the likelihood of the baby born safely and healthy, and the number of children she may already have. I do know natural ways to stop the pregnancy if that is what you decide to do. They should be done within the next few weeks to be safe for you."

They both looked up to see Anna Marie staring at them with an open mouth. Anna Marie wondered how this woman seemed to go in and out of dementia-like behavior. She thought once again most of the behavior was an act put on for her benefit.

Christa climbed inside the Southwind with Little Bear to give her water and to make Granny Rose's bed from the dining room table, leaving Anna Marie and Granny Rose glaring at each other. Christa pretended to be unaware that there was a confrontation pending between the two older women and chose to leave them to work it out between themselves.

Anna Marie angrily said, "I don't know what you are up to. You are not fooling me. You may have fooled poor, helpless Christa, not me."

Granny Rose placed her hands on her hips, stood up on her tiptoes to make herself closer to Anna Marie's height, and glared into her eyes. In front of Anna Marie's eyes, she seemed to grow large and lose twenty years.

Granny Rose stated firmly, "That is not a 'helpless Christa.' She is a bright young lady who can take care of herself and unlike you, she cares about people. I am not up to anything other than to get away from my home where my sons are trying to place me in a nursing home. Not because I can't take care of myself but because they want my assets. They can have my assets. I am not going into that nursing home, whatever I have to do.

She paused for breath and then continued. "I'll tell you what. Since I am such a burden on you, just get me to the next state. I am far enough away from my sons that they can't find me. I will sneak away in the middle of the night. Christa doesn't need to know it is you making me leave. That way, you can still look good to Christa. I can get far away from my sons. I don't want to be with someone who doesn't want me around. That's just another kind of prison and doesn't give me any freedom or peace. Do we have a deal?"

Anna Marie nodded, mentally calculating how many days it would take to get to the next state to get rid of this menace disrupting the peace she had worked so hard to achieve. She had promised Christa that they would stay at this campsite for a few days to restock their supplies and to explore some of the historical sites of the area.

She also wanted to do some research on her father to pinpoint exactly where he lived now as the last address she had for him was in Georgia. That meant they couldn't leave until the end of the week. With another few days of driving, by some time next week they could be rid of this Granny Rose, unless her family miraculously appeared for her. Anna Marie was becoming increasingly convinced this woman was more than able to take care of herself with her helplessness an act that she put on in convenient moments.

Anna Marie said, "Okay. I'll call a truce with you for now. I've promised Christa to stay here for a few days. After that, we can go on to the next state. You can quietly disappear then, just the way you suddenly appeared. That way, no one will be hurt, and you have gotten your way. In the meantime, don't let Christa get attached to you any more than she already is."

Granny Rose answered, "You've got a deal. But I'm not some animal that you can just leave by the side of the road and forget about. I think you are not learning all that you should be from your journey away from Ted and grieving."

Anna Marie looked at her, shocked, "How did you know about Ted? Did Christa tell you about me already?"

Granny Rose peered into Anna Marie's eyes and said mysteriously, "No, Christa does not have to tell me anything about you, Maria Anne Golding. I know who you are and can see inside your heart to your soul. For some reason, you have decided to take your loss and anger out on me. You have yet to learn to enjoy those things that just happen to you in life or to see the beauty in all that is."

She paused. "You think you own Christa, Little Bear, and Maya. You thought you owned Ted and take his death as a personal affront to you. That was instead of valuing your time together enjoying something most people don't have in a lifetime."

Granny Rose continued, seeming to build up her anger, becoming more formidable and younger as she spoke, "You miss the beauty in yourself and in me because you think older women are dispensable to society. You took this journey under false pretenses of courage and adventure when you really were running away. This will become your journey when you learn that you can't run from your loss. Instead, you must embrace it. You have not learned that death and loss are part of life. That is what connects us to our past and future. You have let your grief become your cause and your excuse for everything, including hating me."

Granny Rose pointed to herself and said, "One of the reasons you hate me is your worry that I am a picture of what you will be in not too many years. What you don't understand is that I am beauty and wisdom. I am what you should want to become. I can help you learn to accept your loss, along with enjoying the beauty that is all around you, including your own aging. You remember that Maria Anne as you try to pass judgment on others, trying to get rid of me."

Anna Marie felt like she had been slapped and walked away from the Southwind towards the pond. She cried so hard she could hardly see to walk. She felt the hard ground underneath her, using that as her instinctive guide.

She heard Christa call to her, then from a foggy distance Granny Rose tell Christa, "You have to let her go. Only she can take this part of her journey. She will be back. Let's go inside and get ready for bed. I also have some things under the bed that I need to unpack."

Anna Marie couldn't see them as the two women took each other's hand, led Maya and Little Bear back into the Southwind. They added some of Granny Rose's personal possessions to the Southwind's decorations, blending naturally into the decorations already there as though the objects had been there from the beginning.

Anna Marie found a bench next to the pond, gratefully sitting down. As she thought over Granny Rose's words, she realized there was much truth to what she had said. She did fear Granny Rose's wrinkles. She was trying to run away from her own aging and grief instead of embracing them as painful but beautiful experiences.

She looked up at the sky overhead, noticing that the moon was in its "resting stage," not visible tonight. She realized that she hadn't made her diary entry yet, wanting to note this disappearance of the moon. In two more days, the moon would reappear and begin the cycle of the past millions of years. This reminder helped Anna Marie understand, as did her ancestors, that the cycle of life and death continued, each feeding the other.

Anna Marie thought maybe Christa was right. Granny Rose was meant to be with them for a reason. Anna Marie reluctantly began to sense the reason. She was disappointed in herself for her reaction to Granny Rose, especially of her jealousy as her other traveling companions accepted Granny Rose so readily.

She walked slowly back to the Southwind, somehow feeling as though she had chosen a new path, a new direction on this journey of adventure and discovery. She would accept Granny Rose for now and learn from her, only until they reached the next state.

Christa and Granny Rose were sound asleep when she entered the Southwind. Maya was curled up next to Granny Rose. Anna Marie wondered if she would return to her side tonight.

Little Bear was already curled up on Anna Marie's bed. Little Bear and Anna Marie settled for the night after Anna Marie entered her brief notations from the day in her diary. She left a night light on so they could see.

Early in the morning, Maya joined her on her bed, starting a routine of sharing part of the night with Granny Rose, equal time with Christa, and the early morning hours with Anna Marie.

It was lightly raining in the morning as the ladies silently prepared breakfast while making a list of needed supplies. Granny Rose and Christa tiptoed around Anna Marie, apparently afraid of another outburst from her.

Anna Marie took a deep breath and said, "Look, I was wrong in my reaction to Granny Rose yesterday. I'm sorry. Let's make the most of this time together."

Mentally, she still counted down the days until Granny Rose would be gone. She was determined in the meantime not to ruin her or Christa's days.

The days at this campground flew by with Granny Rose settling into their routines as though she had always been with them. Anna Marie and Granny Rose avoided each other as much as possible in the small space of the Southwind. Christa and Granny Rose did some of the shopping, leaving Anna Marie to relative quiet in the Southwind while they picked up supplies.

Granny Rose had added items she wanted to the list. Anna Marie reluctantly agreed with Christa to purchase the requested items when they were at the store, wondering how she was going to be able to support all the occupants of the RV. When she had calculated expenses she had not counted on the additional traveling companions, each with her own needs.

She was grateful for her and Ted's pensions, making a mental note to transfer some of the funds from her IRA to her bank account for easier access. She thought it might be wise to start buying the mega-states' lotteries since her traveling family kept growing.

Granny Rose had been particularly interested in Anna Marie's herbs growing in the small window. Anna Marie overheard Granny Rose ask Christa if they could stop at a local Agway to add some herbs to the window garden.

The herbs had been struggling to survive in the limited light of the Southwind. Granny Rose pruned them, placing them in a container to move outside on the table. They were now thriving. Anna Marie wondered why she had not thought to do that and placed another check mark next to the resentments she had built against Granny Rose.

When Granny Rose and Christa returned from their shopping expedition, Granny Rose added a few more herbs to the plants on the table with a new watering can for the herbs.

"All purchased with my money. Christa seems to think that it's Granny Rose doing all this," thought Anna Marie resentfully as she observed the two women planting the additional herbs into their new clay pots, talking like longtime friends.

Anna Marie found the local historical society, spending one afternoon searching for information on her father through the filed deeds and wills. She found very little in the written documentation. The volunteer at the society remembered a family by her father's name.

The volunteer recalled, "They lived here for about ten years, down in that old house by the railroad tracks. You can't miss it when you go by. It stands all alone, looking like it has been abandoned. It has looked that way for years, even when the large Norton family lived there. I don't know if anyone lives there today."

She paused and continued, "I think they moved to Alabama. From what I remember, the father Norton was an alcoholic. He was always chasing some dream or another woman besides his wife. His wife was a worse alcoholic than he was. I think they left for him to go work with oil wells or some foolish idea he had. He always thought he would get rich quick with some scheme or another."

Anna Marie thanked her for the information, determined

that Alabama would be where they traveled next. Whatever she had to do, she was going to find out what happened to her father and if she had any brothers or sisters.

That night the three ladies discussed packing up and traveling to Alabama.

Anna Marie said, "I'd like to get there soon so I can keep researching for my father. We can pack up and be on the road the next day with just an overnight stopover."

Granny Rose looked at Anna Marie and smiled while shaking her head, reading Anna Marie's unspoken thoughts.

Christa innocently agreed with Anna Marie's plans pulling out the maps for their next portion of the trip along with AAA books on places to stay and visit along the way.

She asked Granny Rose, "Is there any place here you would like to visit or see?"

Granny Rose shook her head and answered, "No, wherever you want to go. I'm just along for the ride."

Rose looked at Anna Marie and said, "Just get me to the next state. Then we'll all be happy."

Christa looked puzzled, sensing an undercurrent that she was left out of understanding. Finding no answer to what or why she was left out, she looked back at the maps in front of her.

The next morning, Christa and Anna Marie spent some time by the pool in the campground reading and enjoying the warm sun. The afternoon was spent putting everything back into its place in the Southwind so they could be on the road early the following day.

Granny Rose talked to the herb garden as she placed the plants back in the Southwind, reassuring them they would soon be outside again after they arrived at their next stop. Anna Marie noticed that the plants almost seemed to sigh with relief. Anna Marie thought this woman was causing her to lose her mind.

Already, Granny Rose had gained weight, her hair was in place, and she looked pretty, unlike the unkempt appearance from the first day. Christa had purchased a purple blouse and a jean skirt for Granny with her own spending money. She wore the new outfit naturally with pride.

The morning was very foggy. Due to the reduced visibility, their travel was very slow. Anna Marie felt a rumbling in one of her tires and pulled over at the next rest stop to see what was causing the noise.

She noticed something sticking out from the left front tire. It looked like someone had tried to puncture the tire. She suspected Granny Rose, who stood to one side watching Anna Marie's reaction to the tire.

Christa looked closely at the map to see the next turnoff from the expressway. It was a small town. There was a campsite with a service center advertised in the AAA book. Anna Marie decided it was worth the risk to try to get to that campsite for repairs since the tire did not seem to be punctured all the way through yet.

Traveling thirty miles an hour, they were able to get to the service center and campsite in less than an hour without any obvious further damage to the tire or Southwind.

The service center was extremely busy.

A young male service attendant took a quick look at the tire and said, "Wow, how did you do that, lady?"

Anna Marie responded angrily, "It's not something I did. It just happened."

He laughed and said, "Well, you know what they say just happens. From the looks of it, you had better check in to the campsite for a few days as those are unusual size tires. We will need to order one from Houston. If all goes well, we can have a new tire by Friday for you."

Anna Marie asked, "Can't you do any better than that? What about repairing the tire?"

He answered, "It's your life, lady. We can't get to it until at least tomorrow morning. You'll need to stay one night here anyway. I can't guarantee the repair will work. My advice is to buy a new tire. You can park the RV at the campground, and we can repair or replace the tire there. Your choice!"

Granny Rose grinned foolishly as Anna Marie looked increasingly frustrated. Christa looked concerned.

She turned back to the man and said, "Fix it as soon as you can. I will be over at the campsite and will check back in later today to see if you can get to my tire. Will it be safe to set up the RV at the site in the meantime?"

He assured her it would be safe and easy.

Anna Marie walked back to the Southwind, giving Granny Rose a look that could have killed a less hardy person.

Christa saw the look and Granny Rose's smirk, trying to unsuccessfully hold back a giggle. All three climbed back into the RV as Anna Marie drove it to the office to check in for the night.

Later that day, Anna Marie was told by the service center that they would get to her Southwind first thing in the morning.

That night was very peaceful. Rather than cook, they had dinner at a small local restaurant, which turned out to be quite good, and then came back to the Southwind for tea. Granny Rose quickly put the tea on to boil, cutting a small stem off one of her new herbs to blend into the tea mixture.

Anna Marie had to admit that it tasted wonderful with honey added as a sweetener. She broke down to compliment Granny Rose on her tea mix. Granny Rose nodded silently to acknowledge the compliment.

After the tea, the ladies worked quietly on their crafts while Granny told stories from her years living in Georgia. Anna Marie couldn't help laughing along with Christa. She would not admit even to herself that she enjoyed the night with Granny Rose.

At the end of the evening, Granny Rose turned to Anna Marie and said, "Maria Anne, you always had an ornery streak. No matter what I did, it would make you even more stubborn."

Anna Marie looked at Christa behind Granny Rose's back.

Both shrugged their shoulders to say, "Just a moment of confusion. Must be the dementia making her confused."

In the morning, after an early breakfast, Anna Marie thought she was the first in line at the service center.

The man at the counter shook his head and said, "Lady, there are ten vehicles in front of you. You'll have to wait your turn. Why didn't you reserve a time yesterday?"

Anna Marie answered, now very frustrated, "The man I talked to never told me that I needed to do that. I thought he had reserved the first spot of the day. Can you give me a time sometime early today?"

The man looking at the sheet of paper in front of him said, "The best I can do is tomorrow at three o'clock."

Anna Marie angrily replied, "If I had known that, we could have ordered the tire. That means we have to stay here for at least two more days. Will the repair even work?"

The man shrugged and asked, "Do you want the appointment or not?"

Anna Marie had very few options. She asked him to put her name on the paper for the three o'clock appointment tomorrow.

She left the service station frustrated with the delay wondering how much Granny Rose had to do with this delay. She couldn't prove it or think of any way that Granny Rose could have interfered with the appointment.

The day was a lovely June day. She meant to make the most of it despite the delay. The three ladies spent the day with the top down on the car, exploring the very rural and beautiful southwest Georgia.

They found a small lake with a seafood restaurant. Lunch was a freshly fried fish and hush puppies, favorites of all three of the ladies. For dessert, they each had pecan pie with rich vanilla ice cream. Anna Marie wondered how Granny Rose was able to eat with such relish, never gaining more weight than was healthy for her. She also never seemed to be bothered with acid reflux, a condition Anna Marie tried to avoid unsuccessfully.

That night they ate outside, leftovers from lunch with fresh vegetables purchased at a farmers' market that day. Anna Marie had two glasses of peach wine she bought in Georgia. Granny

Rose drank a local beer from a microbrewery in the area. Christa had her favorite peach iced tea.

Anna Marie was strangely at peace with the world and her traveling companions, including Granny Rose. Occasionally, a night bird called out from the woods behind the lake, but little else disturbed the sound of crickets.

Anna Marie attributed her peacefulness to the two glasses of wine. She left Christa and Granny Rose to clean up, falling asleep in her bed as the quarter moon rose in the sky.

Christa and Granny Rose stayed up with the animals, talking for hours. Their laughter from Granny Rose's stories drifted into the back window of the Southwind.

A few hours later, Anna Marie got up to use the bathroom and observed Christa and Granny Rose with their heads together, laughing over some shared joke. As soon as they saw Anna Marie, they both stopped laughing and looked guilty, trying to cover their laughter with their hands.

Anna Marie noticed another bottle of beer next to Granny Rose. "Don't you think you've had enough for one evening?" she asked.

Granny Rose answered sarcastically, "Yes, dear."

Christa broke into uncontrollable laughter.

Anna Marie grunted, quickly returning to her reason for getting up to use the bathroom. Her previous peace from earlier was now destroyed. She lay awake for hours listening to the sounds of Christa and Granny Rose enjoying each other's company, finally falling asleep long after her traveling companions were both asleep.

The next day, Christa took clothes to the small laundry while Granny Rose and Anna Marie scrubbed down the inside and outside of the Southwind with an herb mixture of a mint and thyme. Anna Marie tried not to like the smell, but finally gave in by complimenting Granny Rose on her herbal mixture.

"How do you know to come up with all these herbal mixtures?" she asked.

Granny Rose answered, "My mother and grandmothers taught me how to grow and use herbs. You should have learned when you were younger, too. I didn't know I would have such little time with you."

Anna Marie shrugged her shoulders at the nonsense Granny Rose uttered, thinking how easily she seemed to go in and out of dementia-like behavior.

Close to three o'clock, Anna Marie walked over to the service station, hoping to direct the mechanics to the Southwind. It was hectic, as usual. Anna Marie waited impatiently for someone to pay attention to her.

Finally, the mechanic from the day before asked grumpily, "Can I help you, lady? You can see we are busy."

She responded, "Yes, I can see that. I am here for my three o'clock appointment. I came early to direct you to my campsite."

The man looked angrily at the book on the front desk.

"What's your name?" he asked.

Anna Marie gave him her name, trying to wait patiently as the man leafed through the appointment book.

After a few pages he said, "Ah! You are mistaken. Your appointment is not until Friday."

Anna Marie said angrily, "No, you gave me an appointment for today. I need to have you make the repair. I'll pay you extra, if necessary. I really need to be on my way."

The man peered threateningly into Anna Marie's eyes emphasizing, "I said your appointment is on Friday. It has nothing to do with money. You can take your big city bribery elsewhere if you don't want to wait."

Anna Marie took a couple of deep breaths trying to remain calm.

She knew he was her only hope to resolve this quickly, "I apologize," she said. "I didn't mean to be rude to you. I was trying to help you understand how important it was to me to continue on my trip."

She breathed a huge sigh, thinking of her Yoga exercises on breathing.

"Can you suggest anything else I can do to hurry this along? Are there other service stations for RVs in the area?"

The man looked at her, not won over by her apology. "Do you think we would have this much work if there were other places? The next closest place is 50 miles away. If you think you can make your tire last that long…otherwise, you'll have to wait until Friday."

Anna Marie continued with her breathing exercise. She brushed her bangs out of her eyes, searching her mind for other options.

Realizing she had few choices other than placating this cranky man, she said, "Okay. If by any chance you get any cancellations, you'll be sure to put me in that spot to repair my tire?"

He nodded, still not won over, though obviously glad to be able to get back to the car he was working on and away from Anna Marie.

Anna Marie said, "Goodbye. Please keep me in mind." He waved absentmindedly to her.

At the Southwind, Granny Rose baked peach pies. Anna Marie could smell the pies as she approached. She reluctantly looked forward to a glass of iced tea and Rose's freshly baked peach pie.

Granny Rose removed the pies from the small oven and said, "Maria Anne, you're back just in time. You always loved your peach pies fresh out of the oven. Sit at the picnic table and I'll bring a piece to you. Christa is walking Little Bear and should be back in a moment."

Anna Marie wondered if Granny Rose thought she was playing house mother or that she could convince her of her value by her baking. She was more determined than ever to make every effort not to like the pie or to compliment Granny Rose.

Christa joined the two ladies at the picnic table while Little Bear went inside with Maya for water and a brief nap. Anna

Marie suspected they often curled up together when no one was looking. She chuckled at how cute they both were. The ladies ate quietly, savoring the smell and taste of the pie.

Christa asked, "Any luck at the service station?"

Anna Marie updated the two ladies on the most recent incident.

Granny Rose looked at Anna Marie and asked, "It really means a lot to you to be able to travel soon?"

Anna Marie nodded, thinking that Granny Rose should already know this.

Granny Rose left the table going inside the Southwind. She came out in a few minutes with her apron removed, hair freshly combed, and carrying the still-warm second peach pie.

"I'll take care of this for us. Just wait here," she announced.

She was gone for a little less than a half hour while Christa and Granny Rose sipped their iced tea, wondering what Granny Rose was up to now. As they waited for Granny Rose to return, Anna Marie almost admitted part of her need to travel to the next state, deciding against the admission, knowing it would upset Christa.

They looked up to see Granny Rose with her large floppy straw hat, sitting in the middle of the front seat of the Service Station repair truck, directing the two men in the front seat with her to the Southwind. The truck stopped in front of the motor home and the mechanic who had been rude to Anna Marie got out of the vehicle.

He gently helped Granny Rose down from the front seat as though she were a precious gem. Granny Rose thanked him, pointing the two men to the tire on the RV.

"These kind gentlemen found it in their hearts to work on our tire this afternoon so we can get to the funeral of my dear sister," she said, winking at Anna Marie and Christa.

"I suggested they come back for dinner after they are finished at the shop as these poor boys rarely get a good home-cooked meal. Their mother died last year. You ladies need to help me cook up a feast."

Anna Marie looked at "these poor boys" thinking they were not much younger than she was and wondering how Granny Rose could have talked them into repairing the tire today. She had attempted for days to do the same thing. She thought she should be happy with this latest development since it would get them on the road the next day. Instead, she mentally added Granny Rose's success to her list of reasons to be angry with Granny Rose. She did not belong with them.

The tire was quickly repaired and "the poor boys" left, assuring the ladies they would be back later for dinner.

Granny Rose busied herself in the kitchen, mixing a chicken stew of various unknown ingredients, rolls from scratch, peeling potatoes, and pie dough for a couple more pies. She directed Christa and Granny Rose with orders they could not refuse—neither chose to ignore her requests.

"Why are you preparing enough for an army?" Anna Marie asked Granny Rose.

Granny Rose responded, "Because the boys are inviting a few of their friends. They also suggested bringing their neighbors who have a bluegrass band. I thought a celebration for our tire was in order. We're going to have an old-fashioned hoedown tonight."

Anna Marie looked around the Southwind and the campsite and asked, "How are we feeding more than three people with our supplies? There isn't much room here for a hoedown, whatever that may be. Don't you think you might have asked me first before inviting half the town to come here?"

She sniffled, resenting the whiny sound of her own voice, "This is my Southwind, after all. You both seem to have forgotten that."

Christa and Granny Rose appeared not to hear her or chose to ignore her complaining. They discussed how they could make the food stretch further, ignoring her presence at their side.

Granny Rose suggested to Anna Marie, "Why don't you go pin a note in the office, inviting others in the campground to our hoe-down? That way they won't resent the noise. You can stop on the way and invite campers that you see. Suggest whoever comes to bring a covered dish or beverage. I'm not sure how many people will come. The universe usually answers the call when people are welcomed into your home."

Anna Marie shook her head, "Didn't you hear a word I said?"

Both Christa and Granny Rose ignored Anna Marie. After a few minutes of waiting for a response, Anna Marie gave in. Following Granny Rose's directions seemed the easier route to take.

"Tonight will be a celebration. Granny Rose will be gone soon, and I can get through it," she thought.

If she were at all honest with herself, an "old-fashioned hoe-down" sounded like fun anyway.

Anna Marie sulked off to do as directed. She soon realized she was getting into the spirit of the coming party. Everyone she met responded positively to the invitation, agreeing to bring additional food to the Hoe-down.

Anna Marie could see that the Hoe-down was growing by leaps and bounds. Fortunately, she had placed some money in her pocket. She walked to the small grocery store outside the campsite to pick up snack foods that would help make the food go further.

When she mentioned to the clerk at the counter, who also appeared to own the store, why she was buying the food, he asked wistfully, "Would you mind if my wife and I join you? I'd be happy to bring a keg of beer. My wife makes a fabulous macaroni and cheese that could feed fifty. We haven't been to a hoe-down in years."

Anna Marie couldn't say no. She mentally added a few more people to her list of potential attendees. She had the feeling this was going to be a night to remember.

When Anna Marie arrived back at the campsite, it looked like a transformed place. Lights were strung from tree to tree to their moving home. The table had been pushed to the side with new tables added. Already the tables were beginning to fill with food that looked enough to feed the large crowd expected.

Anna Marie asked Christa and Granny Rose, who were both scurrying around the campsite, "Where did all the food, lights, and tables come from?"

Christa and Granny Rose mumbled an answer that remained totally mysterious to Anna Marie. She decided to go in and dress for this party since everything seemed under control or totally out of her control at least.

Anna Marie dressed for the hoe-down in a red plaid shirt and jean skirt that swirled around the middle of her legs, a gift she had bought for herself to reward her recent weight loss.

People arrived carrying food and drinks. The bluegrass band set up and tuned their instruments to add to the festive ambiance.

Anna Marie knew she had a choice of ruining the evening with her mood of anger or joining the spontaneous party. She smartly chose the latter, greeting guests as they arrived. She introduced the arrivals to Southwind occupants and pointed out the remaining places to set the food.

Christa joined her in greeting their guests, directing them to the beverages at the side of the Southwind. Granny Rose came out carrying platters and plates of food Anna Marie didn't know they had.

The store owner arrived with large packages of paper cups, plates, and plastic utensils and the promised macaroni and cheese baked by his wife. Even the supplies seemed to be growing rapidly and meeting the needs of the continually expanding crowd.

Granny Rose and Christa both changed quickly into jean outfits that fit the theme of the night, each looking lovely in her own way. They had taken time to put on Little Bear's most recently purchased plaid hat and a checkered bandanna for Maya, though they had thought it best to have the animals view the party from inside to avoid injury by the continually enlarging crowd. From the expressions on the pets' faces as they watched with their noses pressed against the screen, it was apparent that watching from a close but safe distance was fine with them.

Soon there were at least fifty people in the small campsite, spilling out into the next campsite and the dirt road around the area. Campers on both sides joined in the fun setting up tables of their own, adding to the already plentiful food and beverages.

Anna Marie lost count of the numbers. The band was in full swing. Gradually, after enough food and drink, more people joined the dancing with Granny Rose leading some of the calls while encouraging bystanders to join in the dancing. Christa took turns dancing and joining different small groups of people, seeming to love every minute of the hoedown.

Anna Marie danced energetically with total strangers, becoming their friends for the evening. Occasionally, Anna Marie stopped dancing to eat and drink. She found the local beer which she rarely drank quite refreshing.

As the evening wore on, she spontaneously hugged both Granny Rose and Christa, grateful for this wonderful hoe-down, the joining of strangers to become friends.

The moon slowly soared into the sky. People drifted away to their campsites or home, thanking the three ladies for the wonderful evening. The band played one last song, 'Goodnight Ladies'. Everyone remaining sang along to the song as they gathered up their leftovers. Anna Marie handed out her cards to people who asked to stay in contact with her.

The three ladies decided to wait until morning to clean up the rest of the campsite, joining the animals in the Southwind who were safely snuggled in their favorite sleeping places.

Anna Marie fell asleep, dreaming of the little lady Granny Rose who joined them recently. In her dream, she wondered why she had been angry with Rose. On this night, all seemed right with her world.

The gentle snores of Granny Rose fit perfectly with the other sounds in the Southwind. Anna Marie planned to mention her change of heart to Granny Rose in the morning. This decision helped her sleep soundly through the night.

The Present

Anna Marie finished packing the last of her toiletries. She looked out the window for Little Bear, sleeping in the sun on the back doorstep, noticing another spider web on the side of the house. Sunlight glistened through the web, creating diamonds across it. She knew she should clean the side of the house deciding instead to leave that for another day so as not to destroy the hard work of the little spider.

She shook her head, knowing she had been permanently changed by her Southwind experiences, especially by Granny Rose. It was the spontaneous meeting of people that made her adventure the joy it became, not the visiting of landmarks along the way. She hoped to never forget that connections with others were what made each life precious. Silently she sent a thank you to Granny Rose above.

"Each friend represents a world in us, a world possibly not born until they arrive, and it is only by this meeting that a new world is born."

—Anais Nin

FINDING ANNA MARIE'S FATHER: THE SECOND FULL MOON OF THE JOURNEY

The Present

The phone rang, Christa's voice on the other end when Anna Marie answered.

"Anna Marie, I have arranged a flight to New Orleans for early tomorrow morning. I know we didn't talk about it, but I remember Granny Rose wanting me to bring Maria Anne with us. I made reservations for her to come with me. Is that okay?" she said.

Anna Marie answered, "I'm sorry I wasn't clearer earlier when I talked with you. Of course, Granny Rose expected the three of us to go together. I should have reminded you of that promise. I haven't been thinking very clearly since the phone call last night. I find myself daydreaming back to the Southwind instead of being in the present."

Christa exclaimed, "I'm having the same problem. It's almost as though we are back there instead of now. I need to actively concentrate to accomplish anything as I feel like I am in two different places and times at the same moment. It's a strange feeling. Scheduling the flights was an overwhelming task as I couldn't focus on the calendar or the choices."

Anna Marie agreed she had the same problem scheduling and planning for care of her pets.

"Maria Anne picked up on my strange mood and behavior. Maria Anne refused to go to school today, telling me she needed to be with her Mama. She has been doing dishes and prepared breakfast for us, instinctively knowing I can't do it today." Christa explained.

She's so mature," Christa continued, "What a sweetheart I have for a daughter. Anna Marie, I keep going back to the night of the storm. That was a turning point for me. I often wonder if I would have made different decisions if it weren't for that night."

Anna Marie drifted back to seven years before, in the same time warp Christa described…

Seven years earlier

The morning after the hoedown, the ladies worked quietly alongside each other, cleaning the mess at the campsite from the night before. There was a new camaraderie between the three of them, with Anna Marie no longer feeling like the person left out.

Anna Marie intended to tell Granny Rose she was welcome to stay with them for as long as she needed. Each of the ladies was in such good spirits, she felt it was unnecessary to say what could be assumed.

Christa appeared relieved at the new relationship, even the animals sensing the change. Anna Marie whistled as they worked together, trying new keys she had never attempted in the past.

When the cleaning was finished, Anna Marie suggested they go back to the restaurant they had eaten at a few days before. After that, she thought they could sit down and plan out the next part of the trip, now with the purpose of finding her father rather than getting freed of Granny Rose.

Lunch was pleasant as they were able to sit out on the deck. The waitress, the wife of one of the mechanics, had been at the impromptu party the night before. She thanked them for the evening before by giving each of them a slice of fresh peach pie, not quite as good as Granny Rose's but close.

Back at the Southwind, they packed up, making plans for an early morning on the road. Anna Marie hoped the tire would last with no further unplanned detours. She now knew this detour was meant to help her accept Granny Rose. She was glad for last night's party and sense of community, all thanks to Granny Rose.

The following morning was misty, with feathery clouds floating across the roads and hovering above the tall RV. They were able to leave as early as planned, stopping for short breaks for Little Bear or lunch. With no unexpected interruptions or delays, their morning was uneventful.

After hours of travel, they crossed into the State of Alabama. Late in the afternoon, they arrived at the next planned campsite, only intending to stay one night. Anna Marie hoped to go on to the area suggested by her resource where she thought she might find her father. At least she hoped to gain further information about him, knowing she may not find anything related to her father.

They only partially settled the Southwind, leaving the car connected to the RV overnight for an early departure in the morning. Anna Marie thought back to the few short days ago when crossing the state line meant leaving Granny Rose behind. She was shocked at how much she had already grown to admire this curious lady. She was glad she had worked the relationship out, as it felt so natural for all of them to be traveling together.

She thought, "Christa was right; this was what was meant to be. We all need each other for some reason. The Southwind would be empty without Granny Rose and her stories."

The herbs would also miss her dearly. Each time they stopped, Granny Rose talked to the herbs, assuring them that they would soon be outside in the sun again. Even for this brief stop-over, she had quickly set all the herbs out on the picnic table at the campsite, not an easy task as the numbers and types of herbs grew at every stop.

Sometimes neighborly campers shared one of their favorite herbs with Granny Rose. Occasionally she found unusual basils or thymes at local farmer's markets. Anna Marie always wondered how she was able to purchase the herbs as Anna Marie had never seen any money cross hands.

Anna Marie cooked a light dinner, which Christa ate heartily. Granny Rose uncharacteristically picked at the food, throwing most of the meal away. Anna Marie hoped Granny Rose was not coming down with something.

Christa and Anna Marie worked on their smaller craft projects, watching the moon slowly rise overhead, crossing paths with the setting sun. Granny Rose rocked in her chair with a book on her lap without moving a page. Soon all three and the pets settled down for the night, looking forward to the next part of their journey.

Or so Anna Marie thought as she fell into a deep sleep.

Before the sun was fully up, Anna Marie found herself shaken awake by a frantic Christa.

"Anna Marie, wake up! Wake up! Granny Rose is gone and so are her objects. Even a couple of her new herbs are missing. I'm afraid something terrible has happened to her."

Christa stared at Anna Marie, obviously in a panic, "Why would she be gone? I got up to use the bathroom, noticing her bed was empty, and her belongings missing. Even stranger, both Little Bear and Maya are sitting at the door, sadly looking out."

Anna Marie shook off the last bit of sleepiness to listen to what Christa was saying.

She hesitated for a moment and said, "I think I know what happened. Let's try to find her first, then I'll explain. She can't be very far away. If we take too much time right now, we could lose any trace of her. Get dressed and we'll walk Little Bear quickly. She may want to go with us. Her sense of smell could be helpful."

Christa dressed quickly, as did Anna Marie. Little Bear insisted on going with them. They left Maya behind looking even more dejected than usual. It took only minutes to take the Jaguar off the tow bar as the followed the campground road, the only pathway out of the camping area. Christa had a map in front of her with some details of the area.

Anna Marie said, "We will need to follow our instincts as to which direction she may have headed. In the middle of the night, she was likely to be on the road. It would be very hard for her to walk in the woods or fields at night without any obvious paths. We'll just keep trying different roads and directions until we see something that looks like a pathway off the road."

Christa asked Anna Marie, "Why would she have left? She seemed so happy here with us. I thought we were a family."

Anna Marie answered regretfully, "It's my fault, Christa. You know how unhappy I was with her joining us at the beginning. She and I worked out a truce in which she was going to leave in the middle of the night once we crossed state lines. We didn't want you to know why she left."

Christa looked at Anna Marie in absolute shock.

"Why would you plan this together without me? I didn't have any say?"

"I am to blame. I didn't want you to know I asked her to leave. I was being selfish while I pretended it was best for everyone."

Christa said, "Let's pay attention to the road and possible pathways. I am too angry with you right now to talk about it. Save it for after we find Granny Rose. Maybe then I can forgive you."

Anna Marie tried to explain further. "I, like you, have come to enjoy having her with us. I assumed she knew that. I didn't think to tell her when I should have. I thought she knew I had grown to appreciate having her with us. I'm sorry, Christa. If I hadn't been so miserable to begin with and had accepted her as you did, we wouldn't be searching for her now. I'm sure we'll find Granny Rose and bring her back home."

Anna Marie hoped she was right. Even though she tried to sound reassuring to Christa, she realized all the possibilities. Granny Rose might have climbed aboard someone else's RV or car. She could have been attacked by a wild animal at night and lying by the road in pain.

She promised herself she would never react so negatively to someone like this again. She'd take the time to get to know each person before making judgments. She practiced positive visualization, a technique she had learned from her Yoga instructor at the Senior Center, hoping the positive images would help them find their friend.

Anna Marie and Christa drove up and down the country roads around the campsite for hours. They drove through surrounding small towns awakening as the sun rose higher in the East. They stopped to ask the few people if they had seen an older lady wandering the road, probably looking lost.

No one reported seeing Granny Rose nor could they find any sign of her. Anna Marie felt like she couldn't breathe, afraid of the implications of what may have happened to Rose. None of the possibilities looked positive, and she knew she was fully responsible for the dangerous situation her companion was now in.

Close to seven o'clock, Anna Marie suggested, "Christa, let's go back to the campsite and have breakfast. Then let's start all over again, thinking out what makes sense as to what direction she would have gone. Maybe we haven't used Little Bear enough to help us. After all, she and Maya likely saw Granny Rose leave."

Christa agreed reluctantly. Anna Marie could see she was holding back tears and trying to hide her fear for Granny Rose's safety. She hadn't yet verbally blamed Anna Marie. She wondered if Christa would also decide to leave the Southwind because of Anna Marie's foolish mistake.

Each of the ladies silently ate toast with freshly brewed tea. After washing their faces to freshen up, they both stood at the door of the Southwind pondering where to look next.

Anna Marie said, "Little Bear, we need you and Maya to help us. Can either of you help us find Granny Rose so that we can bring her back home?"

Little Bear and Maya, who were both outside on their leads,

looked at Anna Marie intently as she asked them this question. They then looked at each other in silent communication. Little Bear jumped up and down, barking, and strained in a direction towards the field behind the Southwind.

Maya appeared to pick up her paw and point in the same direction as Little Bear. Anna Marie and Christa intensely watched Little Bear and Maya.

Anna Marie said, "I think Little Bear and Maya are telling us that she didn't go on the road. I think she left here to go to the field behind us. We should change into hiking shoes and long pants so we can follow Little Bear. Maya you are going to have to stay back here and wait for us to return, as it is not safe for you to hike with us."

Christa looked dazed, obviously holding back her worry as much as possible.

Maya, in clear understanding of Anna Marie, walked back to the door of the Southwind waiting for Anna Marie to open the door.

Both ladies quickly changed as Little Bear waited impatiently outside the Southwind. Maya settled in the front seat to watch them for as long as she could. Little Bear jumped up and down when the ladies came out of the RV, straining at her lead to be off in the direction that she and Maya had earlier indicated.

Anna Marie locked the RV and Jaguar. She and Christa followed behind Little Bear, giving her a slack lead so that she could use the smells to help lead the way to Granny Rose.

Little Bear led them to a partially dry stream bed behind the Southwind. She stopped and sniffed the ground around her, looking back to Christa and Anna Marie to make sure they were following her. She confidently led them for the next two hours, stopping to sniff the ground before proceeding.

They crossed back and forth over the stream bed where it was either very dry or the stones were high enough to serve as stepping-stones. Anna Marie wondered if she placed far too much confidence in Little Bear. She realized they had few options left if they wanted to find Granny Rose.

Little Bear seemed so sure that she was going in the right direction that Anna Marie had a strange sense Little Bear would lead them successfully to Granny Rose.

After another hour, Anna Marie began to wish they had brought water and something to eat. She glanced over at Christa; her face was bright red and she looked exhausted. When Anna Maire tried to suggest resting, Christa waved her away, continuing to follow Little Bear who was anxiously barking at them to keep up with her.

Anna Marie ignored Christa's reluctance to rest, requesting Little Bear come back and sit down with them for a short time. Little Bear looked ahead as though she expected to see Granny Rose. She walked back reluctantly, slowing her pace the closer she got to the now-sitting ladies.

Suddenly, Little Bear froze in her tracks, holding perfectly still. Anna Marie, now really frustrated with Little Bear, walked toward her, stopping immediately as well,

Christa asked anxiously, "What's the matter?"

Anna Marie responded while attempting to move as little as possible. "Don't move, Christa. Stay exactly where you are. Right next to Little Bear is a rattlesnake that looks ready to strike Little Bear. I don't know what to do. I do know that sudden moves are the worst thing we can do."

All stiffened for what felt like hours but in real-time, it was only a few minutes. Anna Marie knew that a rattlesnake bite for Little Bear would be deadly. She was so small and venom usually worked too quickly to have time to go back to the campsite for help.

She desperately tried to think what to do to save Little Bear when she heard a whistling sound from behind the large boulder ahead. The sound then grew to a crackling. From behind the boulder flew a grayish blue-black bird that looked very much like the Catbird, following them previously on their journey.

The Catbird flew to the snake, landing behind the snake, making large crackling sounds as she moved rhythmically back and forth.

The snake looked at Little Bear, then turned towards the bird, finding new and more irritating prey to strike. The bird danced back and forth, moving a little further away each time with the snake following. The snake looked hypnotized by the movement of the Catbird. The Catbird led the snake to the boulder, then behind the boulder, where both disappeared.

Anna Marie, Christa, and Little Bear remained frozen in space for more agonizing minutes, none of them sure they had really seen or knew what just happened to save them.

Anna Marie whispered to the air, "Thank you, little one. You keep bringing good things our way. I'm sorry I doubted you in the past."

Anna Marie called to Little Bear, who came gratefully back into Anna Marie's arms as Christa hugged both.

Anna Marie asked her, "Are you okay, Christa? You look so hot and tired."

Christa softly answered, "I'm fine, just worried about Granny Rose and wondering if we are *ever* going to find her."

Anna Marie said, "Christa, you don't know how sorry I am that I caused this to happen. You were right about her. I was angry and jealous. One of the things that I was most jealous of was how quickly you became close to her. I think that made me resent her more. She was also more competent at things like growing herbs than I was. It all seemed to come naturally to her."

Christa responded, "Don't you know how much I love you, Anna Marie? I appreciate all that you have done for me. I have room enough in my heart for Granny Rose and you. Loving her doesn't take away from my love for you. We have a Native American tribe near us in Oregon whose matriarchs teach that when you give love, it comes back seven times to make your heart that much larger."

She tightly hugged Anna Marie, still holding Little Bear close to her side, "I know you didn't mean to cause Granny to run away."

Anna Marie exclaimed, "You and Granny Rose have become my family. Regardless of what happens later in life, you will remain two very treasured people in my life. When I add other people in my life to love, that will only increase my love for both of you, Little Bear, and Maya. Each of those loves increases my heart by seven. Thank you for the reminder and your forgiveness."

Anna Marie visualized an ever-expanding heart. She hoped that expansion would continue to include Granny Rose's love.

Christa asked Anna Marie, "Can you please stop talking about Granny Rose as though she is in the past-tense? I think that is what makes it harder for us to find her. Little Bear can follow her because she believes she will find her. We both need to believe that with Little Bear."

The three sat quietly together, touching each other to reassure themselves that each was still safely here and grateful for the moment. Anna Marie thought about Christa's comments and realized that she was right. She sat visualizing Granny Rose, looking well and standing in front of them in her new jean skirt.

In the back of Anna Marie's mind, she smelled smoke, wondering if that was also part of her visualization, even if it was a different sense. She found herself in a trance-like state, removed from her surroundings while viewing from overhead. She tried to bring herself back to awareness but something kept her from returning to full consciousness.

She became fully alert when Little Bear and Christa tugged at her arm, gently shaking her.

Christa impatiently called, "Anna Marie, please wake up. There is someone or something behind that boulder ahead. Smoke is rising over the rock; we need to go look. I didn't want to go without you or leave you here by yourself."

Anna Marie wondered how much time she had lost in her trance. She hurriedly got up to follow Little Bear and Christa. Christa looked refreshed, her face not as red as previously.

Anna Marie cautioned, "Be very careful. This is the direction of the rattlesnake and bird. We don't need to walk into a rattlesnake nest after just being saved from one."

They walked along the worn trail leading to the boulder. The boulder seemed to reflect sunlight, glitters glowing from the rock.

Anna Marie pondered aloud, "This is an old trail. I wonder what it was used for before now and how long ago."

Christa said, "From the looks of it, it's been used for hundreds of years. I wouldn't be surprised if we find arrowheads or other remnants from the people who used it previously. It has a good feeling about it, even with our experience of the rattlesnake."

Anna Marie thought again about how mature and knowledgeable Christa had become, far beyond her age.

They cautiously approached the boulder following the trail behind the boulder. Anna Marie examined the surface of the ground, hoping not to see any movements of snakes. Fortunately, there was no movement or rattling sounds that might indicate a snake was nearby.

As they walked around to the other side of the boulder, they noticed that the streambed was full of water. A small waterfall with a pleasant valley appeared before them, filling the area with laughter from the falling water. A short distance down the path was another boulder. Smoke rose from behind this boulder, filling the air with swirls moving in the same rhythm as the bird's dance a short time ago.

Anna Marie commented to her companions, "Look at how beautiful the valley is below. Who would have thought that stream had enough water to become a waterfall. And there is something strange about that boulder."

Christa responded, "You're right. If you look closely at the rock, it looks like the face of an old woman. "

They both noted that the top of the rock was extremely smooth, worn down from what looked like years of use. All over the rock were carvings of spider webs, creating the face of an ancient woman wrinkled from years of experience and knowledge.

They looked to see if the Catbird and snake were close by, hoping to not see the serpent. No trees or bushes grew in the area, surprising with the water so close by.

Anna Marie stopped walking and commented, "Listen to the sound of the wind here. It sounds like someone humming in harmony with the bubbling water."

Christa listened with Anna Marie, "I don't think that is the wind. It sounds more like a human humming from behind the rock. At least I hope it is human."

The three cautiously approached the rock peering behind the rock to see a woman sitting with her back to them. All around the woman were freshly cut herbs. A pot of herbs like the pots in the Southwind was placed close beside the body. The sounds of humming came from the creature as she rocked back and forth.

They stood watching the vision, looking for clues as to what they were seeing. As the vision became clearer, they hoped it was more than a vision.

A familiar voice said without turning around, "It's about time you got here. A person could starve to death waiting for you two to arrive."

Christa ran to the woman and shouted, "Granny Rose. Little Bear found you."

She hugged her, tears tightly streaming down her face.

She buried her face into Granny Rose, sobbing, "Oh, Granny Rose, I was afraid we wouldn't find you in time."

Granny Rose held her tightly, still rocking and humming. The two rocked together as Anna Marie watched from the side. Little Bear joined the two ladies, trying to get in the middle of them, barking excitedly as she jumped up and down.

Anna Marie didn't know whether to be angry at what this woman had just put them through or grateful for finding her. Relief seemed the most appropriate emotion. Anna Marie joined the huddle to hug all of them.

Granny Rose said, "It's about time you came to your senses and came off your high horse Maria Anne. I've sprained my ankle. You ladies are going to need to help me back to the campsite. I hope that won't take too long. I'm hungry and thirsty.

I wouldn't be if you had found me earlier. It's a good thing I can take care of myself."

Granny Rose let out a huge grunt, exhibiting her contempt for the lack of promptness by her companions. She then sniffled loudly.

Instead of asking any questions or commenting on how hungry and thirsty they were, as well, Anna Marie saved the questions until after she had figured out how to get them all safely back to the campsite.

Responding to Granny Rose, Anna Marie commented, "We've come to take you home and that's all that matters. I missed you as much as Christa. I can't imagine the Southwind without you with us."

Granny Rose smiled and gracefully didn't say anything else. She looked strangely like the wise old woman drawn into the boulder beside them.

Overhead they heard the Catbird again and looked in the direction of the sound. To one side stood a tree with dead limbs, unnoticed previously. Anna Marie approached the tree broking off a large limb just about the height of Granny Rose's armpit. She silently thanked the tree and the Catbird for their assistance.

She and Christa helped Granny Rose up, attempting to fit the limb underneath Granny Rose's armpit. The limb fit perfectly under Granny Rose's as though designed for this purpose.

Anna Marie directed, "We'll get on each side of you and help support you. Place some of your weight on the crutch. Little Bear can lead the way. Hopefully, we can be back in a few short hours."

Granny Rose pointed to her herbs, indicating for Anna Marie and Christa to pick up the ones in the pots while keeping the others spread out in their circle as a gift to the earth. Anna Marie wondered if the circle of herbs had protected Granny Rose while they were searching for her. She planned to look up any symbolism for circular herbal protections.

While the journey back was exhausting, it was uneventful.

The travelers were so relieved at the successful outcome of their search, none complained or regretted the exhaustion.

At the Southwind, Anna Marie settled Granny Rose on the couch, putting a pillow under the ankle to elevate it. Granny Rose looked extremely exhausted, uncharacteristically not protesting Anna Marie's caregiving. Christa hurriedly prepared chicken soup for all of them, after getting fresh water and food for both Little Bear and Maya.

Maya greeted the returning friends with cat joy, kissing Little Bear on the nose, sensing that Little Bear was the heroine of this adventure.

The chamomile tea and soup, along with large glasses of spring water, satisfied the three ladies' hunger and thirst. All ate quietly while Anna Marie determined how best to treat Granny Rose's ankle.

After eating, Anna Marie asked Christa to bring warm water and fresh towels along with clean clothes for Granny Rose. Together they cleaned and changed Granny Rose, who was remarkably cooperative.

The ankle was swollen and discolored, though no bones appeared to be broken. Anna Marie asked Granny Rose if she knew which herbs they grew that might help hasten the healing process. Granny Rose gratefully gave Anna Marie a recipe she thought would help at least ease some of the pain.

The rest of the afternoon was spent in a long, restful nap for every creature of the home. The next day each of the ladies shared their version of what had happened. Anna Marie apologized for suggesting that Granny Rose was not welcome with them, emphasizing Granny Rose was welcome for as long as she wanted to stay.

She did add, "I feel I need to keep contacting the Sergeants so that we know what your sons are doing or if anyone is looking for you. Is that okay with you, Granny Rose?"

Granny Rose reluctantly nodded yes, and the subject was dropped.

Later in the day, Anna Marie left the others in the Southwind to "run an important errand." When she returned, she had a small sign to hang underneath the larger sign Katy had made for her with the words *Christa, Maya, and Granny Rose, the Southwind, somewhere in the USA.*

She explained, "This is to let you know you are residents of the Southwind for as long as you want or need to be. You are part of the Southwind family."

Granny Rose uncharacteristically wiped away a tear from her eye. Christa hugged Anna Marie. Maya watched out of the corner of her eyes, appearing uninterested but obviously knowing she had been included in this honor.

While Anna Marie had intended to move to another campsite, she now realized that her search for her father could be conducted from the current campsite. The Southwind was prepared for a longer stay. A routine developed with each woman taking a turn for meals, pet care, and cleaning. Anna Marie spent days at the local library researching her father, finally finding a possible recent address for him.

The evening of her discovery, she announced to the others in the Southwind that she had located what she thought was the last address for her father. She planned to leave early in the morning to attempt to find him. Everyone sensed what a difficult emotional time this could be for Anna Marie. They spent the evening quietly with their crafts, discussing Anna Marie's decision to meet her father.

Before she left in the morning, she wrote a note cautioning Christa not to do any heavy lifting or movement today, advising her to take it easy. All the occupants slept soundly in the cozy home as she locked up from the outside. She hoped Christa and Granny Rose felt better today. Christa had not looked well the night before. Anna Marie worried about her as she followed the road over the bumps and curves. Anna Marie thought maybe the seven days straight of temperatures over one hundred and the emotional search for Granny Rose had worn both down.

Even with the air conditioning full blast, the little car was warm. Anna Marie decided not to take down the convertible roof because of the heat. Anna swept away sweat from her forehead and wondered if it was the heat or fear of what she might find that made her feel so hot and anxious.

Her mother had given her the name and minimal information about her biological father to start her search. That was all her mother would talk about the man her mother claimed was her biological father.

She had mentioned his family had been very unhappy about their relationship, if it could have been called that from her mother's description. Anna Marie's mother kept it a secret from her family until her pregnancy became obvious. Her biological father walked away from her the night she informed him she was pregnant. Over the years, her mother always reassured her she was loved and wanted without needing her biological father's family in her life.

Her mother told her to 'let sleeping dogs lie,' and maybe that is what she should be doing now. Anna Marie thought how sad it was that so many people, her in-laws included, spent too much time thinking people were not good enough for their son or daughter. Families might be happier if people took the time to get to know each new family member, including them in their family at the beginning.

While her mother understood Anna Marie's need to know more about her genetic Dad, she had not been happy about Anna Marie's search. This was obviously a painful memory of her life she had long ago tried to leave behind.

When Anna Marie thought about the man who later married her mother, legally adopting Anna Marie, she remembered how caring and thoughtful he was to Anna Marie. Warm emotions came to her as she thought about is lifelong support of her. Her mother frequently protested "his spoiling of her."

She had no regrets about her life and loved her real father dearly, but there was still a piece of her missing that she needed to discover. Not knowing half of her ancestry, she had often made up her heritage, celebrating St. Patrick's Day or other ethnic holidays even though it may not have been her actual ethnic heritage. Her mother was German and English; her legal father was Irish and French.

The miles passed under her tires. She continued to wish herself back at the RV with her family. She reminded herself the reason she was doing this search was to learn more about the other generations before him, especially her female ancestors, to understand her full heritage.

She thought about the book she was currently reading, *Composing a Life* by Margaret Mead's daughter, Catherine Batson. The book reminded her that no matter the age, women were always creating and evolving their lives, trying to find attachments from the past to the present and future. This present moment was a gift to her composition of life.

She thought it important to gain this information to share with her children and grandchildren. They would have more of the pieces of the puzzle of their own ancestry and could do with that information what they wanted. Anna Marie visualized writing down the knowledge she learned about her father in her diary and giving that to her three children as part of their legacy.

The road had been only slightly covered in the early morning mist. The mist gave Anna Marie the impression she was the only person awake in this corner of the world. After hours of driving, the sun now brightly lighting the path ahead, she found a dirt road matching the directions provided by the search she had conducted at the library.

Anna Marie stopped at a Seven-Eleven store amazingly located on the corner of the turn to the dirt road to ask for further information on the drive ahead. She hoped the address she found from the clues given to her in Georgia and the internet search was recent, taking a deep breath to settle her anxiety before entering the store.

The Clerk at the counter gave her more detailed directions,

assuring her she was going in the right direction. She was thankful for the additional tips, as she could never have found her way to the next road otherwise. The directions she found in her research left her sitting in the middle of the last town.

She traveled along a single lane country road, praying she didn't meet any oncoming traffic. A row of unkempt trailers stood in front of her, strangely in a line replicating military attention. Anna Marie looked for the number forty-seven.

The number 47 was on the middle trailer, the number seven hanging precariously from the side of the trailer. Garbage was strewn around the trailer, a goat grazing on the side of the trailer, and at least four unlicensed cars as lawn decorations. She was surprised someone bothered to number the trailers, except possibly for mail delivery. Hopefully, there were not too many daughters like her searching for their fathers.

She parked the car on the side of the dirt road, as she was afraid to park on the lawn, possibly causing a flat tire from all the debris which included glass and metal. She didn't know how she could change a tire on her own and was not confident AAA or cell phone coverage was available here. She locked her purse in the trunk so she wouldn't have to carry anything other than keys into the trailer. The door of the trailer was hanging unsteadily on one hinge, imitating the angle of the number seven. The goat looked up, must have thought she was less tasty than the little remaining grass, and went back to his grazing.

Afraid to knock as she might take the door off the one hinge, Anna Marie yelled, "Hello? Is anybody home?"

There was no response, so she tried again, "Hello, I'm looking for Lee Norton. Is anybody here?"

She heard rustling from the back of the trailer. The voice grumbled about being woken at this hour of the day. It was 11 a.m. so she had thought this was a reasonable time to visit.

The noise increased as a man lumbered towards her with a horrible stench of yesterday's beer and garlic, looking like he hadn't bathed in weeks. Anna Marie hoped with all her heart that this was not her father.

As the man approached her, she stepped back from the door, both to get away from the increasing smell and out of fear of his anger with her for disrupting his sleep. The closer he came, the more she realized he could not be her father, as he was too young, maybe about her age.

He mumbled, "I'm Lee Norton. Are you another one of those do-gooder social workers, or are you a bill collector? If you are the first, I'm eating and taking care of myself. If you are a bill collector, I have no money for you. Get out of here while you still can get."

Anna Marie answered, "No, I am neither of those. My mother was a friend of Lee Norton's. She asked me to look him up while I was in this area. Though I don't think you would be old enough to be my mother's age?"

Anna Marie thought that this was another appropriate place for a white lie. Her mother would never know she had lied about her interest in the man she had tried to forget. It wasn't totally a lie; at one time, her mother was a friend of Lee Norton.

The disheveled man looked at her with bloodshot eyes, "Where did your mother know Lee Norton?"

Anna Marie explained she was from Higginsville, a small town in Upstate New York near Syracuse.

The man grunted and said, "You are probably looking for my father. He lived in New York years ago before getting my mother pregnant. He doesn't live here anymore. One of those so-called social workers had him placed in a nursing home claiming I was spending his social security check and not taking proper care of him. She accused me of drinking his money away. It's great for me as I didn't want to take care of the complaining idiot anymore."

Shocked, Anna Marie realized she was probably talking to her half-brother, a very unpleasant thought. She looked at him closer, not finding any similarities. The perception of looking nothing like this man might have been wishful thinking. Or the similarities may have been hidden behind the unkempt and dirty appearance?

She had a fleeting thought that this could have been her family and her life. Not for the first time, she thought how grateful she was for the life her mother and father had given her.

"I'll give you the directions to the nursing home if you want to find him. If you go, I won't have to visit him for another week or so. If I can remember the directions, that is. You don't happen to have any cigs or money on you for cigarettes, do you? That might help my memory come back."

Lee Norton leeringly looked at Anna Marie as he asked for the money. Anna Marie pulled out five dollars and change she had placed in her pocket when she decided not to carry the purse into the trailer.

She handed the money to him, explaining, "This is all I have on me. It's yours if it helps your memory."

He hurriedly put the money in his pocket, "Yes, the directions are slowly coming back to me."

He gave her directions to a town about ten miles away.

As she turned to leave, he said, "Wait. Don't I know you from someplace? You look awfully familiar."

Anna Marie responded, thankfully, "No, we have never met. People often mistake me for someone else. I must have that kind of appearance. Thanks for your help."

As she approached her car, she took a deep breath, realizing that she had barely been able to breathe in the trailer or around the man who was likely her half-brother. This journey did not turn out so well up to this point. She wondered if it would be a good time to go back to the Southwind without seeking out her biological father any further.

She thought, "This may be one piece of me that I should have best ignored."

She hesitated for a moment, deciding that since she had come this far, she might as well keep going.

The directions were surprisingly good. A half-hour later,

she stood in front of the nursing home called *Wanderers Rest*. Anna Marie thought it sounded more like a humane society for animals than a home for older people.

She wondered who was responsible for coming up with some of these ridiculous names. Did it make older people want to stay in the nursing home more because of the name? Or was it to appease the family members to feel less guilty about needing to place a family member in a nursing home? She took a deep breath, glancing at her watch, wishing this were over before she entered the front door.

The switchboard operator, without any questions, gave her the number and directions to Lee Norton's room. She had been on the phone with someone having an argument. It was obvious she was glad to get rid of Anna Marie quickly, motioning for her to follow an aide coming down the hall.

The operator said to the aide, "This lady is here to see Lee Norton. Please take her to his room on your way."

The aide gestured for Anna Marie to follow her, leading her down the hallways looking depressingly the same. They stopped in front of a room at the end of the last hallway.

A man sat in an overstuffed chair, apparently watching birds at the feeder outside his window.

The aide said in a monotone voice, "Mr. Norton, you have a visitor."

The man looked up, staring through watery blue eyes, shaking hands bouncing on his lap. Anna Marie's first thought was Parkinson's disease before she realized that she was probably looking at her biological father.

The aide left the room and the man asked, "Do I know you?"

She answered, "No, but I think you knew my mother."

She thought, laughing to herself, "In a biblical sense, with me as a result."

She said to the man, "My mother is Janet Smithers, ah, Jonas before she married. I'm traveling through here. She wanted me to stop and say hello if I could find you. I stopped at your son's trailer. He gave me directions to here."

Anna Marie realized this was a very weak story. It was the one she would have to stay with at this point, as she couldn't think of another reason to give him for her being here other than the truth of their possible relationship.

The man sat quietly, then said, "I haven't heard that name in years. How is your mother?"

Anna Marie responded, "Well, thank you. She is still active and enjoying life."

He commented, "Obviously she married? From the looks of you, I take it, well? You certainly have never missed any meals. Janet was always thin and beautiful when I knew her. You must take after your father."

Anna Marie tried to ignore the comment. Tears sprang automatically to her eyes from years of worrying about her weight and reacting to similar insults. She already agreed with her half-brother's comment about "the idiot," stronger language that she normally used coming to her mind replacing the word idiot.

The man rambled on, talking to the room rather than Anna Marie as long-lost memories came back to him. Every few seconds, he wiped the drool off his chin with an obviously well-used handkerchief.

He said in his rambling way, "Janet and I became quite a hot item in our day. We could never get enough of each other. She was a few years younger than I was, from the other side of town. She lived in the Catholic side of town while we were in the Baptist community. My family was very unhappy that I was dating one of those. I don't think her family ever knew about me."

He paused to blow his nose, then continued, "My family wanted me to marry another Baptist, and I did. We found out later that she was a second cousin with a drinking problem. I had at least three kids by her by then. She had five while we were married. Only three looked anything like me. I took care of them all because she was usually at a bar someplace or passed out in the bedroom. She did sober up for Sundays and church events.

That was about all."

The man wiped away more drool, "My wife was always pregnant, between her bouts of drinking. Eventually, the children were able to take care of themselves. The son you met is the one I am most sure is mine. He turned out to be the best of the bunch. I sometimes wonder how my life would have been different if I had married your mother. She was a great piece, willing to run away with me, just so we could be together."

Anna Marie turned bright red at that comment, turning to leave, saying, "I think I've made a mistake in coming here. I don't need to hear you talk about my mother this way."

With her hand on the door, the man who was most likely her father said pleadingly, "Just like your mother. She was always sensitive, crying at the drop of a hat. I'm sorry. You're right. I get so few visitors these days, I forget my manners."

He took a deep breath, deprived of oxygen, then coughed violently.

When the coughing stopped, he said, "That was rude of me. You may not realize that I did love your mother. I've never loved anyone else like her since. I was too afraid of my family, with no courage to go against their wishes. Your mother read me poetry, showing me another world I never knew then or since. It was much more than just sex. I was a young man and certainly enjoyed that part of it. I think she made me believe that I could do anything in life. I ran away from her expectations of me as much as fear of my parents."

He paused, coughed again, and then continued, "It was more than family. My friends thought she was stuck up. She wouldn't party with them and didn't want to spend any time with them. She was a dreamer, that one, while my friends were real. Poetry won't make you laugh or feed your family. It sure made me see another part of life."

Anna Marie heard another side of her mother she had never known. She took her hand off the door and turned around to listen more intently.

"I met the woman I married at a Baptist social. Little did my family know she would go with me to the church basement doing about anything a man could possibly want. If you weren't so sensitive, I'd describe some of the things she did. Then you'd understand why I left your mother. Poetry couldn't measure up to the wild sex with my wife. That was the only thing that lasted in our marriage. Usually, she was so drunk she didn't know what she was doing. I suspect she learned something from the other men she was with besides me. Probably doing it for a pitcher of beer since she never worked. I tried to keep money out of her hands so the kids could eat and have clothes for school."

He paused in deep thought.

Then he said, "I did stay with your mother for as long as I could after I met my future wife. She cried every time I tried to break it off. My other girlfriend became pregnant. I knew she was the one my family would accept. I told your mother one night. I've never seen anyone cry as hard as she did. I'll never forget that look on her face when I walked away from her. She called me back. I stopped listening and walked away into the other life waiting for me. She called to me, trying to tell me something, but I had to leave her right then and there or I may not have had to courage to leave."

He noted, "I married my wife a few weeks after that. I never saw your mother again. We came down south shortly after to live near my wife's cousins, where I could find work in one of the cotton mills. We moved here to work in the oil wells a couple of years later. I've never been back to New York."

Mr. Norton coughed violently again. With a shaky finger, he pointed to the pitcher of water on the stand beside his bed. Anna Marie poured a glass of water from the pitcher, handing it to him. Her hands were not much steadier than his.

With trembling hands, he drank the water. Finally, the coughing let up. He wiped his mouth off with the back of his hand, gasping for breath. Anna Marie was grateful his breathing returned to normal as she didn't want to watch him go into convulsions in front of her.

Anna Marie understood the man she met in the trailer was likely the offspring of that union he just mentioned. There appeared to be more half-siblings she would never want to meet as her half-brother was enough of a shock. She knew already she had no desire to meet them or learn more than what she had already learned. She also knew that her mother's life, as well as hers, had been the better for this break-up, as neither could have had a better man in their lives than John Smithers.

Anna Marie thought, "It is surprising the turns life takes, often leading you to a better life than you could have imagined. It is as though there is a woven pattern for each of us to follow without knowing it exists or at least options of good paths to take. Perhaps that was why Mom had to meet this despicable man so I could be born. Maybe I was a lost soul that needed to come from this union of the two of them."

The man, obviously happy to have an unexpected audience for his memories, continued with his story, "Your mother left town shortly after that, from what I heard. I was told she had received a scholarship to go away to the state college. She was always a smart woman. I was glad to hear she had left that two-bit town. Never had any grudges against her. It's not her fault she loved me so much. It's hard to see now; I was handsome in those days. Women used to follow me around, begging for attention. Your mother was not the only girl in town that wanted me."

He looked down at his gut bulging over his belt and then rubbed his bald head.

He regretfully said, "I was especially good-looking in my army uniform. Of course, I never got to wear it very long as I flunked boot camp. They sent me home with a dishonorable discharge. I told everyone I was home on an extended leave. They believed me for a while. I take it your mother came back to town after college?"

Anna Marie nodded, too stunned to say anything.

She thought about the single mom who took care of her infant daughter going back to college to try to earn a degree. When she met John Smithers, they both fell head over heels in love with each other. Her mother never took another course after that. Anna Marie wondered if she regretted that. For the first time, she understood some of her mother's disappointment in Anna Marie's not going on to college after high school and her obvious pride in her grandchildren's degrees.

A Nurse's Aide came into the room.

She looked briefly at Anna Marie as she said, "Mr. Norton, it's time for your tests. I'm sorry, your father will be gone for an hour or more. You can stay and wait for him or come back later."

Anna Marie felt as though she had been struck by lightning. She didn't know how to respond.

The man, drool still running down his face, looked at her slowly up and down, sucked in his breath, and then smiled. Anna Marie could not look at him, as both the drool and man sickened her.

He shook his head, contemplating the Aide's comment, "So that's how it turned out. I should have known. My wife was always pregnant, drunk, or not. I guess I was more a man than I ever realized. I wonder how many other babies I left behind."

Anna Marie, getting her speech back, firmly said to the aide, "He's not my father. I'm just here visiting him."

She thought at the same time she answered the Aide, "No, you were not more of a man than you thought but less. My father was the real man, taking responsibility for a child that was not his and raising me as though I was."

The Nurse's Aide said, "I'm sorry. You look so much like him, I thought you must be one of his daughters. The offer to stay still stands. Mr. Norton doesn't get many visitors; I'm sure he would like you to stay."

Anna Marie shook her head, explaining she needed to get back to her home. The Southwind would be an especially welcome sight tonight, along with Christa, Granny Rose, Maya, and Little Bear, her family waiting for her.

As the Aide helped Mr. Norton into his wheelchair, he turned to Anna Marie to say, "I never knew. It might have made a difference. I don't know what I could have done. You were still probably both better off it turned out the way it did. Maybe more poetry in my life might have been good for me, though. Say 'hi' to your mother and tell her for me that she did a great job."

The Aide wheeled him down the hall as he turned once more to look at Anna Marie, waving shakily to her as they went through double doors closing behind them. Anna Marie suspected this was the one and only time she would see her biological father. She was relieved she had survived this one-time meeting.

Anna Marie wandered dazed out of the nursing home. She drove back to the campsite in the same daze, hardly remembering how she got back to the site. Christa and Granny Rose sat next to Little Bear on her line next to the RV. Both were quietly talking and drinking iced tea as Anna Marie drove up to the site.

Anna Marie stopped the car but did not get out immediately to let the flow of tears run down her face. She could barely see anything around her and waited for the flood to ease up. Not only had she been hugged more on this journey than previously in her life, but she had cried more, too—emotions somehow easier to express around her new companions.

Christa and Granny Rose came over to the car.

Christa commented worriedly, "Anna Marie, are you okay? Did you find him?"

Anna Marie cried harder, sobs subsiding then returning faster than before. She shook her head to try to indicate she was okay even though she obviously wasn't. She did not know why she was so upset but couldn't stop the tears. She continued to cry, not able to answer Christa's questions.

Granny Rose patted her on the back and repeated many times, "That's okay, Maria Anne. It will be all right. Momma's here to help you."

Christa paid too much attention to Anna Marie to notice, while Anna Marie did not hear the words of Granny Rose. Instead, she paid attention to her soothing touch.

Christa and Granny Rose helped Anna Marie inside the

Southwind to the table where iced tea with lemon and honey was already poured into Anna Marie's favorite glass. Little Bear sat at her feet. Maya tried to climb on Anna Marie's shoulder to soothe her, as well.

Anna Marie calmed down enough to tell them her morning experiences. Maya settled down on Anna Marie's lap while all quietly sipped the tea listening to the soothing sounds of the air conditioning.

Anna Marie looked at her adopted family around her thinking how different the Southwind was before they each joined her. She couldn't imagine how she would have gotten through this day if she had an empty RV to come back to after meeting the man who was her biological father.

Christa had a wonderful, scrubbed look, even "glowing' as pregnant women were often described. Granny Rose's eyes looked less vacant, and she had put on a few pounds in the past couple of weeks. Maya's fur sparkled from the care Maya and Christa gave it daily. She was a chubby, cuddly kitten with a mind of her own attached to the loving family around her. She and Little Bear had an amazing relationship. Maya was the boss, often putting Little Bear in her place.

Anna Marie knew her pets and the ladies with her were more her family than the man she had just met. Family was far more than who fathered you or sometimes even who raised you. Anna Marie knew she had no complaints about her childhood and her true parents.

Anna Marie told them her story of the morning along with how she felt about meeting the man his son had described as the "idiot." She explained how rudely he had talked about her mother up until the end when he realized Anna Marie was his daughter after the Aide called her his daughter.

As she talked, she told them stories of her childhood and the love she had received from her mother and the gentle man who was her true father.

She related to them her memory of her fifth birthday, "It was that evening my father took me on his lap telling me he had adopted me because he loved me and my mother so much. He cried as he told me this. My mother told me years later that I hugged him nonchalantly, giving him the impression, this was last year's news."

"I climbed off his lap to play with my new puppy, a birthday present from my dad. Mom later told me how Dad was so pleased that I accepted him easily as my father, never hesitating to call him Dad. They had both agonized for years deciding how to best tell me without any lasting trauma. They laughed that the trauma was apparently their own and not mine. Maybe knowing you are loved and secure is more important to a child than who the biological parents are?"

As the day became evening, Anna Marie told one story after another to the two ladies and two pets. Granny Rose and Christa prepared a light meal while Anna Marie continued with her stories.

"My father was always there for me, every concert with out-of-tune voices, every graduation, and every special occasion. The only other person who loved me so unconditionally was my husband. He'd get the same look on his face, like he couldn't get enough of me. It was a look of amazement at his luck in life, extra pounds, gray hairs and all."

Anna Marie related all of this with great nostalgia and gratefulness for her past life.

Christa said wistfully, "I wish I had that. My stepfather was there though busy working, with my stepbrothers, or out golfing with his friends. I think I embarrassed him because I limped and sometimes stuttered. My mother was put in a situation to have to defend me, trying to make my relationship with my stepfather.

"When we were out in public, I felt the rest of the family didn't want to walk with me or claim me as part of their family. I excelled in school, but I could tell my parents hated to go to the parent's conferences with the "Special Class Teacher." No matter what I did for attention, it was never right, never good enough."

Anna Marie realized, with a start, that she had forgotten that Christa had a "disability." While Christa, of course, still walked with a limp, favoring one side, Anna Marie never paid attention to the walk or limp. Christa was beautiful to her.

It was not Christa's physical beauty that Anna Marie paid attention, though she was a very pretty young woman, it was the gentleness that made her forget about the limp. It was also that Christa was able to do so many things to help and was great company.

Granny Rose patted Christa's hand, "It is the girls that carry on the generations and give life. Often fathers don't realize that or care to remember. Mothers know though sometimes others around make them forget. My only girl was Maria Anne. I feel she has finally come back to me through both of you."

Both Anna Marie and Christa looked at Granny Rose with surprise. This was probably the most lucid comment she had ever made and then had followed it up with something that made no sense whatsoever. Neither knew quite what to say so they didn't respond to the comment, hoping she would tell them more. She didn't and neither wanted to push her further to share more of her story.

In an hour, dinner was ready. They sat down to a candlelight dinner. Christa had picked wildflowers on her afternoon walk with Little Bear. She looked a little less tired than she had been this morning. The hot, humid day was cooling down with a light breeze bringing in soft showers, possibly adding to Christa's look of contentment.

They ate quietly. As they ate, what had been a light breeze became a strong wind, threatening clouds rolled in, and lightning bolts shot across the sky. They turned on a local television channel to hear the weather warnings for high winds and flooding in their locality.

Little Bear ran outside quickly for her last walk. Everyone settled down swiftly, hoping for the forecasts to be inaccurate.

Within an hour, the Southwind rocked back and forth as

the trees and branches crashed down around them. All four, including Maya, and Little Bear gave up on sleep. They sat in the front end of the RV, huddled together, attempting to sleep sitting up.

As the wind continued, Christa became increasingly restless making frequent trips to the bathroom, returning with a disturbed look on her face each time.

After her sixth trip, she came out of the bathroom with a very worried expression, relating to the ladies observing her, "Anna Marie and Granny Rose, I'm scared. I have horrible cramps. The last time I peed there was some spotting of blood. I'm afraid I'm losing the baby. What should I do?"

She started to cry. Anna Marie suggested she sit down on the sofa with her feet up. Granny Rose brought pillows from the back of the RV to raise Christa's feet.

Christa said as she settled on the sofa, "I don't want to lose this baby. I know I've been back and forth on my decision. But I have come to love this growing child inside of me, maybe because she also is connected to both of you. I am ready to take care of her, especially with the help from my friends if my mother can't. I need your help now not lose this baby."

Anna Marie picked up her cell phone, explaining, "I'm calling 911 for an ambulance. I'm sure you're fine but let's not take any chances."

Anna Marie let the phone ring on the other end for many minutes. She wondered if the high winds caused the cell phone towers to go down.

Granny Rose sat next to Christa, rocking her gently and singing a lullaby in a language unknown to Christa or Anna Marie.

Gradually, Christa appeared calmer.

Anna Marie indicated, "I'm going to the office to call from there. It may be there is just bad reception for the cell phone at this campsite."

Outside the Southwind, Anna Marie struggled to walk. The

wind blew so hard she was barely able to stay upright. All around her branches and trees fell or bent to the ground.

After a few minutes of the struggle to walk and too many close calls from falling branches, Anna Marie practically crawled back to the RV. The door ripped open as she clung to the handle, trying not to let it blow away in the vicious winds.

Anna Marie caught it before it blew off its hinges. She pulled the door shut behind, relieved to be back inside out of the storm. The Southwind rocked back and forth, still providing more shelter than outside in the storm.

Inside the RV, Granny Rose had prepared a warm glass of milk mixed with honey for Christa. Christa drank the milk with tears running down her face from apparent agony and fear. She sipped the milk, calming her, reducing the tears and look of fear. She allowed Granny Rose to rock her gently as she continued to hum her strange lullaby.

Anna Marie informed them, "It's too dangerous to be out there. I can't get to the office with all the debris from the wind flying around. We'll have to wait for the storm to end, then I'll try again."

To lend evidence to Anna Marie's statement a large tree limb hit the ground next to the Southwind, shaking the ground beneath. All five occupants of the RV jumped, the wind howling louder.

Anna Marie, trying to distract the others, poured cranberry juice from the refrigerator suggesting Christa drink the juice after the milk.

Christa laughed asking, "Are you two trying to fatten me up or make me have to run to the bathroom even more?"

Despite her protestations, she drank the cranberry juice after she finished the honeyed milk. She made faces as the contrast of the acidic juice to the sweetened milk was obviously very bitter. She settled back into Granny Rose's soothing arms. Granny Rose sang her lullaby, continuing to rock Christa along with the swaying of the protective home.

Anna Marie sat down at the end of the couch, wishing to be rocked, as well. Maya curled up next to Christa and Little Bear jumped on Anna Marie's lap, helping ease Anna Marie's anxiety. Anna Marie spoke soothingly to Christa, gently rubbing her feet as she spoke.

The sounds outside made the Southwind feel even more like a cocoon of safety. They each thought the Southwind would protect them from harm, like a great earth mother holding her children within her arms. Anna Marie closed her eyes and pictured this mother, the Southwind, hoping that this image would help protect each of them.

At one point, they could see lightning illuminate the entire sky followed by an immediate thunderclap so loud Anna Marie was afraid they would lose their hearing. A tree next to them caught on fire from a direct lightning hit, an acid smell of destruction seeping into the Southwind.

Rain and hail hit the roof and sides of the Southwind from all directions as the storm swirled around them looking for a place to land. Whenever the thunder became louder, Granny Rose increased her volume of humming to help them forget the threatening weather.

Anna Marie was not sure how much Granny Rose understood what was going on or even if she realized that Christa was pregnant. Regardless, she was very appreciative of Granny Rose's soothing presence. She silently thanked Christa for talking her into agreeing to Granny Rose staying with them and for the goddess who brought her back to them despite Anna Marie's cruelty and stupidity.

Gradually, the storm started to subside. As the wind became gentle, all the occupants fell asleep, including Christa who had been soothed to sleep by her friends. Waking later in the night, Anna Marie covered Christa and Granny Rose with a blanket while she and the two animals went back to her bedroom for what little time remained in the night. Everyone slept soundly for the few hours of the night remaining.

The sun was high in the sky when the companions woke to the glistening day. It was a beautiful clear day, much cooler than it had been for the last few days with little humidity.

Anna Marie walked Little Bear close to the RV. It was obvious they were not going very far as all around them trees and branches lay across the roads and campsites. Miraculously, none of the neighboring campers had suffered any serious damage to their RVs. The next-door campers waved to Anna Marie and Little Bear, giving a high five sign for surviving the storm without harm.

Anna Marie believed that the Southwind had magically protected them from harm, including the potential for Christa's miscarriage. Christa no longer seemed to be in pain. She commented after her last trip to the bathroom that she no longer spotted blood or felt the pressure she had during the previous evening. Anna Marie could see the look of relief on her face.

Around them, crews came in to pick up the trees and branches from last night's storm. They heard chainsaws and trucks in the distance, indicating widespread damage in the area.

Anna Marie told Christa and Granny Rose, "Once the roads are cleared, I think we should take Christa to a doctor or clinic to have her checked out."

Christa and Granny Rose agreed.

Later in the morning, the area looked clear enough for them to attempt to drive to the closest town. The television station had returned to the air with the news reporter commenting that while there was significant damage and injuries from the storm, most roads were now open to traffic.

Leaving the animals to guard the Southwind, the women slowly made their way in the Jaguar to the next town. When they had briefly stopped at the office, the clerk gave them the name of a clinic in town.

At the clinic, there was a long line of people, some of whom were injured from the previous night's storm. They listened to the stories people told of tragedies from the night before, including a trailer turned over by the strong wind with three people seriously injured. Several local towns had been devastated by tornadoes that had touched down in those towns.

Anna Marie said to the two ladies with her, "I guess we were lucky after all. Especially with all the trees around us, we could have had serious injury to ourselves or the Southwind."

Both Christa and Granny Rose agreed. Christa was very tired and somewhat in a daze. She responded only minimally to the conversation.

After an hour of waiting, the three ladies were called into an examination room. A Nurse Practitioner came in and introduced herself to the ladies waiting.

She asked, "Which one of you or are all of you here to see me?"

Anna Marie indicated Christa and said, "Christa is pregnant. During the storm last night, she had lots of cramping along with spotting of blood. She seems to be better this morning. We were worried she was losing the baby. She's not very far along and this is her first…"

Anna Marie stopped. She didn't know how much to tell the Nurse Practitioner or if she should admit that Christa was not even sure she wanted this baby until last night.

The Nurse Practitioner asked Christa, "Would you take off your top and leave only your underpants on for me? There is a gown here for you to put on."

The Nurse Practitioner turned to Anna Marie and Granny Rose and asked them to leave.

Christa fearfully asked, "Please, no, they are my family. Can't they stay with me? I would feel better if they were both here with me."

The Nurse Practitioner answered her, "It's your call. I'll just leave the room while you undress and get on the table. I'll be back in a few minutes."

Christa undressed, put on the unattractive gray gown, and sat on the examination table, looking like a lost little girl. The look in her eyes was one of pure fear. Anna Marie wondered if it was because she thought she had lost the baby or because she was afraid, she had not and still had a major decision to make.

Anna Marie patted Christa's arm and said, "It will be okay, honey. We're both here with you, and whatever happens, we will be by your side. The examination will not hurt and it's better if we know."

Christa nodded and stared into space, waiting for the Nurse Practitioner to return.

When the Nurse Practitioner returned, Granny Rose and Anna Marie stood to the side of the small room. As she examined Christa's pelvis and uterine area, she explained gently to Christa what she was doing and why. Christa looked less fearful as the examination went on and she quietly answered the questions about how much blood she had lost and how she felt now.

After the examination, the Nurse Practitioner turned slightly so that she could face all three ladies and said, "I don't think she has lost the baby. I need to have a urine test and some blood work. I suspect she had a kidney infection. She appears much better now. What did you do during the storm as she was experiencing her symptoms?"

Anna Marie explained about the milk and honey Granny Rose gave her and the cranberry juice she made Christa drink. She also told the Nurse Practitioner that they just held each other through the storm and tried to stay calm, which worked for all three of them.

The Nurse Practitioner assured them, "I think you stopped the kidney infection from getting worse if my guess is right. Sometimes, this early in a pregnancy, a kidney infection can cause a spontaneous abortion, so you did exactly the right thing."

She turned to Christa and asked, "How old are you, honey?"

Christa answered, "I turned eighteen a few weeks ago."

The Nurse Practitioner then asked, "I take it you are not married. Have you decided to keep this baby?"

Anna Marie held her breath, as she had avoided asking

Christa this very question this morning. She knew that Christa needed to make her decision soon for her own safety and health. Christa looked at Anna Marie and Granny Rose.

Granny Rose stood quietly to the side, listening to the conversation.

When Christa looked to her, she smiled broadly and said, "That's my girl! Isn't she beautiful? They are both beautiful girls!"

Granny Rose had first looked at Christa and now referred to Anna Marie.

Granny Rose turned back to the Nurse Practitioner and said, "This beautiful girl is going to have another beautiful girl soon. I can already see her. We all worked together last night to save her child."

Christa smiled back and looked at the Nurse Practitioner.

She said to her, "I have never wanted anything so much in my life. Last night I was terrified that I would lose my baby. Until then, I didn't realize how much I wanted this baby or how awful I would feel if I lost her. I already love her and would have done anything last night to prevent losing her."

Christa spoke to Granny Rose and Anna Marie, "This baby is part of each one of us."

The Nurse Practitioner nodded and said, "I want you to take a few more tests including the urine test. Then we'll go from there."

She instructed Christa on where to go for each of the tests and said that she would be back to read the results when they were complete. The tests and waiting for the results seemed to take forever as the ladies waited for the Nurse Practitioner to return.

When she came in the door holding papers in her hand, she smiled and said, "I have good news for you. You have not lost the baby. I don't think any harm has been done to the baby. From the urine test, you did have a urinary tract infection. I want you to sleep at night with your feet higher than your head, drink lots of water, and continue to drink cranberry juice. I will give you an antibiotic that has been tested on pregnant women and has no known side effects for the baby. You are both going to be fine."

Anna Marie caught Granny Rose's hand and squeezed it while Granny Rose did what looked like an old-fashioned jig.

Christa softly said to the Nurse Practitioner, "Thank you."

Back at the Southwind, the ladies celebrated Christa's health and decision with a quiet cup of tea while the evening breezes blew through the Southwind over the sleeping Maya and Little Bear. Anna Marie looked around at her growing Southwind family and realized she was the most content she had been in years.

That night she dreamt of Ted who told her, "Good job, Anna Marie. You are living your life to its fullest. I can feel your happiness and I am happy for you. I love you."

Anna Marie slept soundly for the rest of the night, comforted by the thought of Ted's love and her companions sleeping peacefully around her in the Southwind.

Mounds remain when the tale is buried.
Unearthed when the stars align.
Holy land where her hands once
Covered that which is divine.

–By permission of Vincent Bishop, author's son

CHAPTER SIX

CONTINUING THE JOURNEY:
THE NEW MOON

The Present

Anna Marie called her list of family members. She was saddened as she realized that her mother and mother-in-law were no longer on her 'to call' list as both had died within a few months of each other last year. In the past, they would have been on her list to call. Maybe not her mother-in-law Jane, if she were to be totally honest with herself. They both would probably have raised objections to another strange journey for something they didn't understand.

Anna Marie had come to understand it was out of fear for herself and their reluctance to have her so far away that caused her family's fear, especially her mother's. They both relied on her for help with everyday concerns, even though her mother-in-law would rarely have admitted it to Anna Marie.

It was pure trust in Granny Rose to believe that a safety deposit box existed in Sumer, Louisiana. Anna Marie thought how strange it was that the voices of all the significant people of her life stayed with her even after their death, continuing to add a dimension to her life that would be absent without them.

Even her mother-in-law, who had often made her question herself, helped make her a more critical decision-maker. Jane had helped her appreciate those people in her life that loved her and were not resentful of her very existence. She wondered if this was part of aging, living in her past more frequently, or a product of increased wisdom by understanding the connection of her past life and people to her present self.

After calls to Diane, Katy, Erin, and Cynthia and leaving messages on their voicemail, she made herself another cup of tea and sat at her kitchen table to create the list of the arrangements she needed to make for her trip, including canceling mail, newspapers, and the small tasks of life. She thought of her list of many years for the Southwind journey. She realized she had never physically crossed off her accomplishments for that list though she had often reviewed the list mentally.

Her mind drifted back to the days and weeks following Christa's decision to keep the baby. Little Bear and Maya settled in a sunny corner of the kitchen for a morning nap while Anna Marie recalled her past journey.

Frantically, she suddenly remembered that she had not uncovered Circe's cage and ran onto the side porch. As she ran, she glanced at her watch, noting it was only 9:30 a.m., even though it felt much later than that.

She could hear Circe's anger underneath the cover and quickly removed it. Circe ruffled her feathers and gave a squawk to let Anna Marie know that she was very upset at being forgotten.

The large demanding African Grey Parrot screeched, "Bad Maria Anne!"

Anna Marie said to Circe, "I'm sorry little big one. With Granny Rose's death, I've just not been functioning well. I'll get you some fresh water and fruit to make up for my poor memory."

Circe nodded her head in forgiveness of Anna Marie and asked, "Granny Rose? Granny Rose here?"

Anna Marie responded that she was not, quickly fetching the promised food and water for Circe. She brought Circe inside to the sunny corner of the kitchen while she finished her tea. She realized she had not planned yet for Circe's care while she was gone, adding that to her mental list of things to do.

Circe pecked at her food and then screeched, "Want Granny Rose! Want Granny Rose!" Anna Marie talked soothingly to Circe, feeling somewhat foolish as she gently tried to explain

Granny Rose's death to Circe. In many ways, Circe had been Granny Rose's pet, but they had all decided Anna Marie would be better able to care for Circe. They also had not wanted to split up Maya, Little Bear, and Circe, who had developed a tight bond of companionship. Circe calmed down, pecked at some more of her food and then put her head underneath her wing mourning the loss of her friend.

After this near tragedy was averted, Anna Marie settled back with her list and her memories.

Circe leaned over the cage trying to get Maya's attention, who gave Circe a passing glance and one feeble swipe at the bird before settling down deeper into her nap, "Pretty Kitty, pretty Maya. Want Granny Rose?" The exchange between her two pets and Circe's demand for Granny Rose brought so many memories flooding back.

Seven years earlier

The days flew by for all five of them in wonderful routines of discovery. Sometimes they spent a few days at a campground and other times just a night to get to the next place they all agreed they wanted to visit sooner. In the evenings, they often studied their maps to determine the next campground and destination. Once they found a destination, they looked through the travel books and brochures to choose what they each wanted to visit.

Sometimes Granny Rose participated in the conversation and planning; other times, she appeared confused as she sat in her favorite chair, drifting off into a world that was not shared with anyone else. Her favorite chair was a rocking lawn chair they bought at a flea market, giving Anna Marie back her own rocking chair. She hummed when she rocked, a tune that neither Anna Marie nor Christa recognized.

Occasionally, they asked her questions. She responded with an answer that appeared to have nothing to do with the question. Christa and Anna Marie looked sadly at each other when this happened, assuming this was dementia-related. They then hugged her or patted her on the arm to reassure her of their presence.

Anna Marie thought how differently she felt about this mysterious woman from just a few weeks ago and how right Christa had been about their needing her with them. They found out that Granny Rose was a quilter, purchasing supplies for her so that she could quilt in the evenings along with Anna Marie's weaving and Christa's needlepoint. Most evenings were very peaceful with the three ladies each lost in their crafts, the animals napping by their side or watching serenely as the ladies worked on their individual projects. Some evenings Anna Marie and Christa read from Anna Marie's vast collection of books while Granny Rose worked on her quilting or slept in her chair.

One of the routines they developed was searching for the state line to see who could spot the next state first. They all heaved a big sigh every time a state line was crossed and then laughed like young children. Since they often took detours, a state line would sometimes be crossed two or three times in a day. They kept a chart of who spotted the state line first, with the weekly winner choosing a dinner of her choice for the other two to cook.

This custom came about because Anna Marie shared with them the story of Erin as a little boy who loved to travel. Anna Marie's family did not go on their usual trip one summer because Ted taught summer school that summer, as they needed the extra money to replace the roof on the house. That Christmas, they visited with Ted's aunt in Maryland.

When they crossed into Pennsylvania, Erin, seven at the time, heaved a huge sigh of relief and asked, "Doesn't it feel good to be in another state?"

Since then, Anna Marie's whole family could not pass a state crossing without heaving a huge sigh of relief in remembrance of that precious moment. Both Christa and Granny Rose loved the story, having fun with each state line. It made the travel itself more fun, providing them with a shared tradition. Anna Marie was constantly reminded that half the fun of travel was the journey, meeting people along the way, and not just reaching the destination.

Once a day, or every other day, Anna Marie called the police station near where they assumed Granny Rose joined the Southwind. She talked to either of the Sergeant Georges as they were now on a first-name basis. The Sergeants and their police officers had pinned markers on a map where the ladies in the traveling home were located when Anna Marie called, enjoying the frequent updates on their adventures.

The Sergeants informed Anna Marie that their travels were now the talk of their town, with even a newspaper reporter interviewing the Sergeants about the ladies in the Southwind. Anna Marie gave the men permission to give her cell phone number to the reporter, semi-hoping the publicity might give them a lead to Granny Rose's family.

The reporter called Anna Marie to add to the feature story scheduled for publication in the next Sunday edition of the travel section of the Rome County Gazette. The reporter had a picture of a Southwind motor home she found on the Internet. She asked if she could visit the ladies to take some pictures of her own for her next article and promised to send the Sunday article. Anna Marie agreed to a visit from the reporter when they were settled in Wyoming where they planned to stay at least one week. She was a little anxious about the publicity but felt it might help them find Granny Rose's family. Anna Marie wasn't even sure any longer that finding Granny Rose's family was in Granny Rose's best interest.

So far, every time they talked, there was no information on a missing older lady with possible dementia who might or might not be called Rose. That made Anna Marie wonder how actively her family was looking for Granny Rose. Granny Rose may have been right about the sons only wanting her money and other assets.

One of the good things that came out of the phone calls was that Anna Marie had come to know about both of the George's families. She, too, looked forward to the telephone calls even though they were non-productive in terms of information about Granny Rose. Anna Marie was increasing her extended family without little effort.

If she missed a few days without calling, when she did call, either George would tell her how worried they had been and to make sure "their ladies" didn't hesitate to call if they needed assistance. They promised they could get one of their fellow police officers to wherever they were in a few minutes time. "Professional courtesy" was the term the Sergeants used, and it somehow seemed they were more safe and secure because of the Sergeants. She thought how only a few weeks ago they had appeared to be rude and uncaring men. Now they were offering to help in whatever way they could along with obvious concern for their safety, even including the entire town in the stories of their travel.

She remembered an expression her mother liked to use, "You can never tell a book by its cover." She felt that was appropriate for the many experiences and people she was meeting on this quest for a new life. She had already made a new life for herself, even if not quite the one she had expected. Like much in life, it really was turning out better than she could have imagined.

At one campground they met a young homeless man, Jack Linton. He was traveling to return home to his family in California. His traveling companion was a lovely appearing but cantankerous African Grey Parrot, Circe, who enjoyed sitting on his shoulder and visiting with the ladies, especially in the quiet time of the evening. Jack arrived at dinnertime every day, asking if they had any work for him, and then settling Circe on one of the tables outside as he did small jobs the ladies made up for him. They thought Jack might be intellectually disabled or mentally ill. Each of the Southwind occupants had developed a fondness for him and his grouchy bird.

On the last day, the ladies planned to be in that campground, Jack came to visit much earlier in the day.

He approached Anna Marie hesitantly and asked, "Anna Marie, I really want to go home but I have no money. Can I sell you Circe for $50 to buy a bus ticket home? Circe really loves all of you and I can't afford her anyway. I have all I can do to feed myself."

Anna Marie answered anxiously, "Jack, we are running out of room in the Southwind. How about if I give you $75 and you keep Circe? I can give you my card with my home address. When you are able you can pay me back."

Jack shook his head and said, "I don't think they would let me take Circe on the bus. I know my parents will not let me keep her. They already have too many mouths to feed. I think Circe would be better off with you."

Anna Marie asserted, "We have no room left but I want to help you. How about I give you $100 and that could buy a place for Circe on the bus, too?"

Jack vehemently shook his head, almost in tears now, "Anna Marie, Circe belongs with you. I just know it. I've never seen her as happy as she is when she is here."

Anna Marie looked at Circe who watched Anna Marie out of one eye while pretending to look elsewhere. As Circe never looked particularly happy at any time Anna Marie saw her, she wondered how despondent she must be at other times. She looked at Jack, just as she heard a Catbird in the distance by the pond.

Sensing it was useless to argue with the Catbird nearby, she said to Jack, "I'll give you $115. That's all the cash I have on me right now. But you have to find a way to come and take Circe when you get back home."

Jack carefully and hesitantly hugged Anna Marie thanking her many times. He brushed away the tears in his eyes.

Anna Marie suggested, "Stay for dinner with us tonight for one last time. I'll give you the money when you leave tonight. You can leave Circe with us overnight, so in case she's not happy with us, you can change your mind in the morning before you go."

Jack nodded his head and gave Anna Marie another hesitant hug.

Anna Marie walked inside the Southwind to relate to Christa her arrangement with Jack, whose turn it was to make dinner and to set another plate for Jack.

Christa had listened to the conversation between Anna Marie and Jack. She laughed when Anna Marie came inside.

"Anna Marie, you are the only person I know who negotiates up, instead of down and still ends up with something she really doesn't want in the first place. I'll make room for Circe. We should go to the pet store this afternoon before dinner and buy Circe a cage to keep her safe, along with her favorite bird food. Maybe a book on how to care for an African Grey Parrot, as I don't think any one of us knows much about this type of bird. It sounds like you will need an ATM visit."

Anna Marie failed to see the humor, but Christa continued to laugh. That night Circe joined them on their journey. After Jack slipped away from dinner, they never heard from him again. Circe remained a permanent resident of the Southwind, adding noise to the already busy motor home.

One day, at a campground in Arkansas, Anna Marie called excitedly to Granny Rose to look at the beautiful bird soaring overhead. Granny Rose had her back to Anna Marie, making no response whatsoever to Anna Marie. Anna Marie wondered if the dementia was getting worse and then thought to try something. She whistled to Granny Rose, but still no response. Little Bear woke up from her nap in the sunny window to see why Anna Marie was whistling. She went back to sleep when she saw no obvious reason or at least one that interested her.

Anna Marie walked over to Granny Rose standing in front of her.

She said slowly, "Granny, look at the beautiful bird overhead."

Granny responded, "Why are you talking so idiotically to me?"

She turned to look up in the sky, "Where? What kind of bird do you think it is? Oh, I see it. I'll bet it's an Osprey. They have a distinct way of flying that is different than any other kind of bird. We used to have a lot of them by the lake we lived on in Georgia."

Anna Marie was surprised that Granny Rose could immediately identify the bird. Then suddenly, a light bulb went off in her head.

She moved behind Granny Rose, saying, "I think you are right. It is beautiful."

No response from Granny Rose.

She moved in front of her again, looked directly at her as she spoke and said, "You're right. It is a beautiful bird. It's large enough to be an Osprey."

Granny Rose responded, "Of course I'm right. I know my birds. I would take my boys and you, Maria Anne, on bird-watching hikes. I could identify any bird that I saw. The boys never took to it. I wish that I had been able to teach you Maria Anne. You left me too soon. That just adds to the many regrets I have about my time with you."

Irritated, she added, "Will you stand still while you talk instead of hopping back and forth behind me?"

Anna Marie ignored the last reference to her as Maria Anne, assuming that Granny Rose was in one of her "senior moments," and asked Granny Rose, "Have you had your hearing tested recently that you remember?"

Granny Rose answered, "No, dear. I left my hearing aids back where I came from, as they were very uncomfortable. I figured I'd hear what I wanted to hear. It gives me an excuse to ignore what I don't want to hear."

Anna Marie laughed and said, "I think we should have your hearing tested again at a clinic. We'll find hearing aids that is not so uncomfortable so you could hear what we say and talk with us. That is, if we are people you want to hear? You could also hear Little Bear, Circe, or Maya when they needed you. You could still shut off the hearing aids when you were tired of listening to us or the noises around."

Granny Rose responded, "Well, all right Maria Anne if you think that's best. It would be nice to hear what you and Christa are saying more often. Though I don't need my hearing to talk to the animals. We can communicate with each other without words. If you don't get angry with me if I do turn them off when you are talking. I get tired of listening to noise. I like my quiet every so often. The silence gives me time to think and to reflect on those memories. I would like to hear more sounds of nature. It would be nice to hear the songs of the birds again."

Granny Rose continued to turn Anna Marie's name around. Anna Marie had been unable to change her habit of doing this. She thought that after Granny Rose had new hearing aids maybe they could talk about why she was mixing her name with someone else in her past life. Granny Rose seemed determined to call her Maria Anne no matter how many times she had corrected her. She also seemed sure that she had known her from a long time ago rather than for a short time.

Anna Marie suspected she confused her with someone else, maybe even her own daughter. She had never mentioned any other children than her sons. She thought her daughter's name might be similar and that led to some of the confusion, especially if she did have dementia. Anna Marie hoped the hearing aids would correct this apparent confusion.

The next day Anna Marie found a clinic from a list in the campground office. She and Granny Rose left early in the morning to be one of the first at the clinic while Christa stayed back with the pets. Christa grew larger every day and Anna Marie was a little concerned that Christa was maintaining water. She would make sure to give Christa tea with lemon each night. If that didn't work, they needed to take her to a local clinic for medicine. She decided first to take care of Granny Rose and then Christa.

They were seen very quickly at the clinic because of their early morning arrival. The paperwork was somewhat confusing to complete, as initially, Granny Rose claimed not to remember her Social Security Number. After some discussion with Granny Rose, Anna Marie was able to get her to "remember" the number so that she could receive the Medicare benefits for which she was obviously eligible.

Granny Rose mysteriously pulled a card out from her little purse that she always carried with her and handed it to the clerk without letting Anna Marie see the card. She placed the card back just as carefully, not allowing Anna Marie even a glimpse at the information on the card.

Anna Marie did not know if the number she gave was accurate or if the card had Medicare information on it. Since the receptionist was satisfied with it, Anna Marie decided to just pretend everything was okay. She jotted down the Social Security number given to the receptionist to ask Erin to do an Internet search for Granny Rose using that number, placing the slip of paper in her purse. Anna Marie wondered if they would be able to get new hearing aids for Granny Rose.

The Nurse did find significant wax in Granny Rose's ears, and removed the wax, stating, "You really need to watch the build-up of wax. Try warming water and oil for the ear canal. That will prevent the build-up. Unfortunately, this build-up is very common in older people and is one of the main causes of loss of hearing. We'll do a hearing test after the wax has been removed so we can get a more accurate test."

The hearing test demonstrated a significant loss of hearing. They were referred to the audiologist connected to the clinic for further testing and fitting for hearing aids. Granny Rose tried several different types and settled on the one that was most comfortable for her. The audiologist told them there would be several days to wait for approval of the hearing aid from Medicare. They would be called when the approval process was complete.

Anna Marie was relieved they had already decided to stay at this campsite for a few days. They could extend their stay until they were able to get the hearing aids for Granny Rose while they explored the area.

Back at the campsite, Christa rested from her walk with Little Bear. She read through the many local pamphlets they had gathered from the front office while waiting for Anna Marie and Granny Rose to return from the clinic visit.

After pouring each a glass of iced tea with mint and honey, she said to Anna Marie, "Anna Marie, while you were out, Katy called. She sounded distraught and said she needed to talk to you as soon as possible. I asked her if there was anything I could do for her, but she just said, 'I need to talk with my mother.'"

Anna Marie had left the cell phone with Christa because of her concern for Christa's weight gain from water retention and wanted her to be able to call for assistance if needed.

She took the iced tea outside with the cell phone sitting under the awning while speed-dialing her daughter's number. It was rare that Katy called this time of the day, and she was concerned something had happened to one of her grandchildren. Katy picked up on the second ring, making Anna Marie think she had been anxiously waiting for this call. As soon as she heard her mother's voice, Katy broke into sobs on the phone.

Anna Marie waited patiently for her to stop crying before asking, "What's wrong, Katy?"

Anna Marie had a sick feeling in the pit of her stomach, dreading what Katy was going to say but was in no way prepared for Katy's response.

Katy said, in between sobs that began to subside, "Mom, can I come out and stay with you for a few days? I need to think it over if I am going to stay with Clint. I found out he's had an affair with his assistant at work who accompanies him on business trips. He tells me our marriage is over but that's only after I found out about the affair. I happened to read some e-mail messages from her. And the worst of it is he has given me some kind of STD, which is how I thought to look at his e-mail."

Katy cried harder again and stopped talking. Anna Marie wished she were there with Katy at that moment so she could hug her, make her a cup of tea, and listen to her as she talked about her feelings.

Anna Marie softly suggested to Katy, "Honey, why don't you hang up the phone and make yourself a cup of tea? You should cry as hard as you want while the water is boiling and then tell yourself to stop crying after the tea has steeped in the teapot. I'll call back in twenty minutes to give you time to have your tea next to you and a box of Kleenex by your side. Then we can talk for as long as you want. And of course, you can come out with us for a few days while you think this out. In fact, I would have suggested if you hadn't already asked. Now go get your tea."

Anna Marie sipped her iced tea as she waited for twenty minutes to pass. The others in the Southwind did not come out, sensing Anna Marie needed this time with Katy.

It was a quiet, overcast day, though overhead, Anna Marie could hear the Catbird. She shook her head, wondering if she was now imagining this sound all the time. She thought that Catbirds could not be native to all the states she had been in since Pennsylvania. She also didn't know if the Catbirds were portents of good news or bad news, as both had happened when she heard the Catbird. Thinking back on all the times she had heard the Catbird on this trip made her realize that on balance the bird brought good people or creatures to her.

She thought about Katy and Clint as she sat listening to the sounds around her. Katy met Clint in college, marrying in Katy and Clint's senior year of college. They planned to wait until they were both out of college. An age-old story, Katy became pregnant. They pushed the wedding date up so that the baby would be born to married parents in a permanent relationship. That allowed them to live in the family complex and finish college together, as well as receive more financial assistance.

Anna Marie always thought Clint was good for her sometimes very difficult daughter as he was very soft-spoken with a calm demeanor. Now she wondered about Clint and what hidden secrets he may hide. She knew that Katy was not always easy to live with, but she was beautiful, a wonderful mother, and extremely hard-working in the house as well as in her middle school teaching. She seemed to worship Clint, often hanging onto his every word.

Long ago, Anna Marie asked Katy not to share their more intimate problems with her, not wanting to be the interfering mother-in-law. She knew in this situation she was likely to learn far more than she wanted to hear.

After twenty minutes, she pressed the speed dial for Katy's number. Katy answered the phone and already sounded much calmer.

She said, "Thanks, Mom. As strange as it sounds, that worked. I think I can talk about it now. But please don't mind if I start crying again."

Katy talked for thirty minutes with no time in between for Anna Marie to say much except small utterances like "oh, my" or "I'm sorry dear" to indicate she was listening. While occasionally Katy sniffled or cried a little bit, she was now under control enough to be able to talk.

She said, "I think I've repeated this at least twenty times to my friends. It still feels like a nightmare that I'm going to wake up from at any minute. I never thought Clint would do this to me. My friends and I thought we had the perfect marriage. Mom, I haven't told anyone else but I'm back to my old eating patterns and bulimia again."

Anna Marie heard this with a sinking heart, as she knew her daughter had worked hard to overcome this disease.

Anna Marie asked, "Would you be able to come out for a few days? What about the children?"

Katy said, "Clint has agreed to take a few days off and stay with them so that I can come out to visit with you. He's at the point where he claims he'll do anything to save our marriage. Now he's apologetic! I don't know if it's savable. I do know I need to get away for a few days to think about what to do next. I have personal leave I can take from work. I never thought I'd be saying this, but thank goodness you are doing your trip so I can join you. I know I have not been very supportive of you about your trip. I'm sorry for that."

They talked briefly, discussing arrangements for Katy.

Katy said, "I'll call you when I know my flights and times. I'm sorry to bother you, Mom. I know you have your own plans and other people with you who may not be thrilled with my coming out to visit."

Anna Marie assured her, "You will be amazed how supportive both Christa and Granny Rose will be. I'm thrilled to have the opportunity for them to meet you and you to meet them. I'm bringing together people and pets I love. I wish it could have been under better circumstances. We're waiting for approval for new hearing aids for Granny Rose, which is going to be difficult. I don't know if she gave them the correct Social Security number or Medicare information. We're going to be camping here for a while as we wait for the approval or disapproval. You are not bothering any travel plans at all."

Anna Marie paused and then continued, "Besides, part of this trip was to be spontaneous. You coming here to visit is a spontaneous moment we are all going to enjoy. Call me anytime, honey. I do need to warn you I have an addition of a kitten called Maya and the most recent is Circe, an obnoxious but lovable African Grey Parrot. I didn't mention those to you before. You need to be prepared that there is a lot of activity and creatures living in my Southwind with me. It's a little crowded but wonderful."

She added hastily, "There is plenty of room for you."

Anna Marie hung up and went inside to explain to Christa and Granny Rose the call from Katy. They discussed how to make her welcome and where it would be best for her to sleep, deciding to prepare the dining room table into a bed at night for her.

Anna Marie also reluctantly offered, still less willing to give up her own space, "If that doesn't work, then she can share my bed with me for a few days."

Hours later, Katy called back with plans to fly out the next morning and stay for at least five days, careful to do a Saturday night stay so that her airfare was cheaper.

Anna Marie phoned the clinic after this call to check on Granny Rose's hearing aids. The receptionist was quite flustered, asking if she could call back after she found the paperwork. Anna Marie wondered if they would be able to get the hearing aids for Granny Rose as Anna Marie could not afford the hearing aids on her own and support their travel as well with all the additional mouths she had to feed.

That night the ladies scrubbed the Southwind from top to bottom. Christa walked to the Laundromat in the campgrounds to wash the extra set of sheets, taking Little Bear with her for companionship. Anna Marie made a list of grocery items to buy on the way to the airport to pick up Katy. She thought of some of Katy's favorite foods and added them to the list, knowing that food can be a comfort during difficult times. She hoped she could help Katy stop using food as a poison to her body again.

As they prepared for Katy's arrival, Anna Marie pictured the little girl Katy had been lovely, extremely sensitive, and easily brought to tears. Anna Marie remembered one Christmas when Katy insisted on buying the scrawniest-looking tree in the lot because she was worried no one else would buy the tree and the "tree would be hurt that no one loved it." She remembered the strange polite looks her women's group who attended a Christmas tea gave the tree until Anna Marie explained the choice. Anna Marie, a typical mother, wondered how she had contributed to Katy's emotions frequently so close to the surface and her problems with eating. She knew she did not have her own problems with weight and her own appearance resolved, thinking that may have contributed to Katy's eating challenges.

The next morning was rainy with clouds hanging close to the ground. Anna Marie hoped Katy's plane would not be delayed due to the weather. Little Bear rode with Anna Marie to the airport while the rest stayed back to finalize the preparations for their guest and to give the mother and daughter time alone. Granny Rose and Christa were excited, if a little apprehensive, about meeting Katy. Maya and Circe seemed to catch that excitement.

Anna Marie left the Southwind with Maya sitting in front of Circe's cage, batting with halfhearted attempts at the cage with her paw as Circe repeated over and over, "Pretty, Maya. Pretty, Kitty," followed by uproarious and somewhat lecherous laughter. She wondered about Circe's previous owner or owners. Occasionally, Circe screeched out the worst set of four-letter words Anna Marie had ever heard. The words were often for no apparent reason except maybe to get attention from one of the ladies.

Anna Marie was grateful for the rain so Little Bear could accompany her to the airport and wait in the car, which would remain cool enough in this weather to be safe for Little Bear. Little Bear was dressed in one of her new hats, wearing it proudly, obviously aware that they were meeting an important visitor.

Anna Marie waited at the entrance to the terminal, as she was not allowed to enter any further due to security measures. She watched the entrance for her daughter, anxiously shifting from one foot to another as she saw a lovely blonde middle-aged woman walk forcefully out of the entrance. Anna Marie realized with a start that this was her daughter.

Katy had always been 'model' beautiful, but Anna Marie had forgotten over this summer how beautiful she actually was. Even her obvious distress over her marital problems added to her beauty rather than detracting from it. Anna Marie noticed others pausing to look at this beautiful woman. Unfortunately, some of her price for meeting society's definition of beauty had been her eating disorder.

Katy spotted her mother, running to her, picking up the bag she had placed down at her side as she looked for her mother. Katy hugged her mother tightly and then held her at arm's length to look at her with grateful eyes.

She said admiringly, "Mom, you look ravishing. You've lost weight and done something different with your hair. This trip is obviously agreeing with you."

Anna Marie laughed and cried at the same time as Katy did the same while they firmly hugged each other.

Anna Marie said, "I was thinking the same thing about you. Not to say having problems with Clint makes you more beautiful. I think I had forgotten how lovely you are."

Anna Marie realized that she and Katy would never have shared their thoughts like this in the past. This trip of separation from each other had already helped their relationship.

Little Bear greeted Katy by jumping up and quickly settling on her lap for the drive back to the campground. Once at the campground, Little Bear pulled at Katy, wanting to introduce Katy to all her new friends, while Anna Marie unloaded Katy's bag from the trunk of the car. Anna Marie followed behind as Little Bear approached first Granny Rose, then Christa, and finally over to Maya and Circe, who were next to each other on the table. Little Bear stopped in front of each and barked.

Granny Rose cackled.

Christa laughed, taking Katy's hand, and said, "Katy, we've all heard so much about you. We're glad you can join us. You can see that your mother has generously opened her home to all of us. We will be eternally grateful to her for saving each one of us in different ways."

Iced tea and homemade blueberry muffins were quickly placed on the table as everyone crowded around to talk about Katy's flight to get to know each other a little better. At first, it was awkward, but the animal's constant attempt for attention and antics soon had all four of the ladies laughing and sharing some recent experiences.

Anna Marie thought it was best for Katy to decide when she wanted to discuss her reasons for joining them and with whom she wanted to share her story. After this snack, which Anna Marie noticed Katy ate almost none but at least drank the iced tea with honey, Christa and Granny Rose found excuses to leave the mother and daughter alone. The animals settled down for a mid-morning nap. Anna Marie and Katy sat quietly across from each other while Anna Marie patiently waited for Katy to talk.

Katy said, "Mom, I'm already tired of this whole thing. Can we not talk about Clint and me at all right now? I would like at least a few hours to be myself again so that I can think rationally."

Anna Marie agreed and then suggested, "We've found a wonderful state park near here where they rent canoes. Since the weather has cleared, let's rent a canoe and take a picnic lunch with us."

Katy agreed enthusiastically, as canoeing was something she had always enjoyed as a child during the family camping trips. Anna Marie made room in one of her closets for Katy's few clothes and both changed quickly, looking forward to time on the water.

Within a short time, they were in the canoe with a picnic lunch at their feet, slowly paddling down a very calm river in the park. It was a quiet day with few breezes. Both women remained deep in their personal thoughts, speaking only to point out some unusual scenery or bird. Anna Marie told Katy about her unusual experiences with the Catbird.

Lunch by the side of the river was also very quiet as both ladies ate hungrily of the quickly made lunch. Anna Marie was glad to see Katy eat as enthusiastically as she was eating. She vowed to observe her for any signs of purging later in the day.

The sun was warm by the side of the river, with the water lazily passing them by. They both fell asleep for a short nap, waking up rested, at peace with the world.

Katy reached over for Anna Marie's hand as they gradually woke up from the nap and said, "Thank you, Mom. I needed some time like this. I've been so involved with child rearing, teaching, and trying to be a good wife that I've forgotten some of the simple pleasures that I used to enjoy. Clint has never liked camping or canoeing. I gave it up a long time ago. No matter what happens, I'm going to start doing some of these kinds of things that I enjoy again. How do we lose ourselves as people when we become adults? Mom, did you do that?"

Anna Marie answered honestly, "Yes, I did, Katy. That's one of the reasons I needed to take this trip, to find myself again and to stop playing the part of the grieving widow or overbearing Mom. I thought your generation would be better at keeping yourself intact while you nurtured others and pursued your careers. I can see you have fallen into the same trap. I haven't figured out how to be attached to others and still find time to be me."

She hesitated, and then added, "Even on this trip I have let others kind of take over my home so that I have little time to think about my own needs. Maybe as women, it's important for us to give to others, especially our time. I think we need to find a balance of ourselves separate from the others we love. I don't have the answers to that except to grow old and grab alone time as you go. Unfortunately, by the time you can have that alone time, there is too much of it and too many people you love that you have lost along the way."

Katy listened, silently nodding in agreement.

She said, "I think Clint partly had an affair because I lost who I am. That made me less interesting to him. I'm not making excuses for his bad choices but I am trying to think what part I may have played in this. How do I go back and start over, Mom? I don't know what the right decisions are for me. I must consider my children even if Clint didn't. I always hoped to have the perfect marriage like you and Dad."

Anna Marie shook her head and said, "Your father and I didn't have a perfect marriage. We grew to love each other as best friends over time. We had some really difficult times in the beginning. He almost left me after you were born as he thought he wasn't ready for all of the responsibility. After the war, he thought family was all he wanted. Then suddenly, there were three mouths to feed and no time for fun. I also changed after you were born. He'd tell me all I ever thought about was baby care.

She explained, "You didn't divorce in those days, so we just lived day after day doing what we had to do to raise a family. Your Grandmother Golding hated me. She did everything she could to try to talk your father out of staying with me, including threatening to disown him even back then."

Katy laughed and said, "Grandma Golding is still threatening to disown each one of us when we make her unhappy. If I decide to divorce Clint, I'm sure she'll threaten to disown me for that. She claims she has already taken Cynthia out of her will. I used to think Cynthia was wrong in her lifestyle. I now realize this was her way of being herself and her right to be herself. Maybe she was able to keep herself by her life choices? I wish I had been more understanding of her need to be who she was. It was not my business and I should have accepted her for who she was. I hope she can forgive me."

Anna Marie suggested, "One of the things you can do is mend your differences with your sister. I think you'll find she and Anita are understanding and amazing women. They would be supportive of whatever choices you make."

Katy asked, "Why did or does Grandma Golding dislike you?"

Anna Marie answered, "I'm not sure. I think I was not who she pictured should be with your father. It may in part be because he refused to move back near her. I think she is just angry about her life, disappointed in her own choices. She's used me as the scapegoat. Maybe she wished her life was more like mine or she thought Ted would stay near her and marry a woman she chose for him. She did spend a lot of energy over the past years being angry at me."

Anna Marie asked, "Do you have any sense if you want to divorce Clint or if you want to try to make a go of it yet?"

Katy said, "I can't imagine my life without Clint, especially trying to raise three children on my own, financially and emotionally. But I don't know how I can ever forgive him. And now I have a sexually transmitted disease because of his choice, not mine. That doesn't seem fair." Anna Marie agreed, "It isn't fair. Life often isn't fair. I don't know how to change our lack of control over some of events that happen to us. I guess my best advice is to spend a few days with us, finding who you are again. While you are here, think about how you can go back home and take that person back with you. You'll need to make some changes. Maybe more time for you away from the kids and Clint? What interests have you left behind because of being married, like camping and canoeing? If you decide to stay with Clint, then I suggest counseling. I wish we'd had the option of counseling in my day. That was considered only for people who were very mentally ill or in institutions."

They were both silent for a few minutes, then Anna Marie added, "After that, it is just putting one foot in front of the other to live each day until some of the pain subsides. I think your father had an affair in our early years of marriage. I was too afraid to ask him. During that period, he went out for drinks every night and came home late at night smelling of perfume. That's one of the reasons there is several years difference in age between you and Cynthia as for a couple of years we did not touch each other."

She thought back to that horrible time.

She added, "I'm not even sure if he was having an affair. He wasn't sleeping much during that time due to flashbacks from the war. I think he spent those years reliving his war experiences and didn't feel he deserved to live while his other buddies died around him. I tried to get him to go talk to someone at the Veterans Administration. He felt crying about the war when he came home pretty much physically unscathed was unmanly. Then when he finally agreed to talk with someone, there was no such program available anymore from the VA. I guess they all thought it was unmanly to react to the horrors of war. Fewer people paid attention to those who came home from the Korean War, and most didn't think PTSD existed, including the VA and politicians who funded the programs."

"After one huge fight, your father agreed to give up drinking and going out at night. Somehow, we patched it up, he started talking about the war to me, and then over time we matured into our relationship. An elderly neighbor also taught me some forms of natural birth control so we could be intimate without fearing we would have a child every year. He became my best friend but that was many years later with a lot of work from both of us."

Anna Marie could remember this painful past as though it were yesterday.

As the sun dropped slowly beneath the trees, mosquitoes began to bite, both deciding it was time to take the canoe back. They quietly paddled the canoe to the rental place, each deep in her thoughts and memories, continuing in this peaceful silence until they were back at the Southwind. They could smell wonderful aromas of food floating in the air causing sudden hunger for the delicious food waiting for them.

After quick showers and changing into clean clothes, they joined Christa and Granny Rose, who had set the table and prepared a feast for all of them to celebrate Katy's joining them. Katy ate as heartily as everyone else. Anna Marie observed a rosy glow coming back to her complexion.

There was much laughter and talk throughout the meal on the small pleasures of life as well as some of the larger political issues of the day. Granny Rose told one story after another, keeping all laughing so hard they cried. Anna Marie worried a couple of times she would pee her pants from laughing so hard, one of the "joys of aging" she occasionally experienced.

Anna Marie wondered how Granny Rose was able to tell her stories without revealing anything about her past life or real identity. At these moments, Granny Rose did not appear to have dementia at all, looking much younger than she did when she first joined the trip. Anna Marie continued to puzzle over who Granny Rose was, how old she was, or why she had come to be with them.

That evening Katy asked for Anna Marie's cell phone to call Cynthia. She talked for a long time and finally hung up, smiling from the call.

"You were right, Mom. Cynthia and Anita are neat people. They have invited me to come out to Boston for Anita's art show opening. I think I'll take Cassandra with me. She would enjoy the trip to Boston and seeing her aunt's art exhibit. It would be good for both of us," she said to Anna Marie.

Cassandra was Katy's middle daughter, who appeared to have some artistic ability of her own. Prior to this, Katy had not wanted her children "exposed" to their aunt's lifestyle. Anna Marie was pleased, wishing she had encouraged this contact sooner.

Katy yawned, "If you don't mind, I'm exhausted from our day and the early rising. I'm going to bed. Can one of you tell me where that would be?"

All the ladies were equally tired from the excitement of Katy's arrival and agreed they, too, would like to go to sleep early. The half-moon was barely in the sky as the occupants of the Southwind fell soundly asleep, each comfortable in their space on the Southwind.

The days with Katy flew by, with all the members of the Southwind enjoying the visit thoroughly. Too soon, Anna Marie drove Katy back to the airport. Anna Marie overheard Katy share her reason for visiting them with both Granny Rose and Christa. Each had given advice from their own experiences. Anna Marie thought it was probably the silent support Katy had received from each of the travelers that was most healing. Anna Marie hoped it was also visiting with three strong women from different generations that helped her to think what would be best for her.

Both were silent until they reached the airport.

Katy said wistfully, "Mom, there has been one good thing to come out of all of this. I discovered you as a person. That is almost worth all the hurt. I wonder how many children ever realize the person behind their parents. I am so lucky to have you and am glad that you didn't listen to me about your trip this summer."

Anna Marie parked the car and carried Katy's bag as they

walked into the terminal with their arms around each other. The plane was on time for a change. With the time needed for security precautions, Katy was instantly hugging Anna Marie goodbye as both women cried openly.

Anna Marie waved from behind the TSA check-in as she watched her beautiful daughter walking away. She had put on a few pounds during her visit. With relief, Anna Marie thankfully noted she had seen no signs of her eating disorder. Anna Marie walked back to her car slowly, waiting from the parking lot until she saw Katy's plane take off from the tiny airport.

Anna Marie quietly sent a prayer to her daughter, "Be kind to you, honey. Please find time for laughter, love, and joy amid your life."

At the Southwind, Christa and Granny Rose rearranged the RV. When Anna Marie returned, missing her daughter, she was once again reminded how glad she was for the companionship she had gained on this trip.

She immediately called the Clinic, hoping for some news on the hearing aids. The young-sounding receptionist was flustered and apologetic after Anna Marie explained they were being delayed on their journey and really needed an answer soon.

She suggested, "For some reason, we seem to keep losing your information. I don't know what is going wrong. We are usually very organized and have people in their hearing aids usually in less than three days."

The receptionist laughed and said, "It is almost as though there are Gremlins who keep losing or messing up the paperwork. It's not fair to you. Why don't you come in tomorrow and we'll let your mother try out one of our hearing aids? I don't know what the mix-up is. We'll get it straightened out so that you can continue your trip."

Anna Marie felt somewhat guilty as she hung up the phone, as she knew it was likely they hadn't given the clinic Granny Rose's correct Medicare information, let alone the likelihood that it was not her correct Social Security Number.

They spent the day exploring one of the local touristy arts and crafts areas of the region and then planning their next adventure when they returned home. Early the following morning, Granny Rose and Anna Marie waited at the door of the clinic before opening hours, hoping for some miraculous news on the hearing aids approval.

Granny Rose seemed less anxious about the approval, suggesting to Anna Marie, "Maria Anne stop worrying about this. It will turn out okay. I will have my hearing aids today. You have always been such a worrier! You'd think this journey would help you relax more."

Sure enough, when they were escorted back to the fitting room, the receptionist assured them that the paperwork had finally been cleared. A few minutes later, Granny Rose was called into the office for her new hearing aids fitting.

The helpful woman shook her head, "It's strange…right after I talked with you, I received a message on the computer stating there had been a one-number mix-up in numbers that had been cleared and we could give your mother the hearing aids with full coverage. Not even a deductible which is unusual. After your long wait and the inconvenience to you, I'm not going to say anything."

Back at the Southwind, Granny Rose proudly demonstrated the hearing aids to Christa and the apparently interested animals.

She said teasingly, "When I am tired of listening to you, I will just shut you off!"

After that, she rocked in her chair for hours until lunch, stating the names of the various birds she could hear again. Anna Marie was grateful this had worked out and could already see more appropriate responses from Granny Rose when they questioned her.

Anna Marie announced at lunch, "Tomorrow, we are going on to Wyoming. I'll call Anita and Cynthia tonight to let them know. Maybe they can make plans to join us. I also must warn you; Erin is talking about bringing his family out for a visit us so we may have a full house and even more activity."

They spent the afternoon napping and preparing the Southwind for the next stage of the journey. It was a warm, hazy morning as they left the campsite. Anna Marie said goodbye to the campsite as she drove the RV out of the campground, towing the Jaguar behind them.

She always had a hard time saying goodbye to any experience or person, making each campsite, except for the Macon site, a temporary home with new friends at every stop. She hoped this experience of frequently saying goodbye would help her in the future with accepting losses or changes. She did find that sharing goodbyes with her friends made the goodbyes easier and the journey more fun.

Little Bear came to Anna Marie for one more hug, settling in the back of the RV with Maya for a morning nap as the travelers continued their journey.

The Present, Higginsville, NY

Anna Marie had asked her son Erin to check out the Social Security number Granny Rose had given them. Erin tried to find the number at the time of their trip with no results other than the number was no longer active. Anna Marie had to assume, as she sipped her tea, that this would be another part of the mystery of Granny Rose that she might never learn.

She sighed, realizing that sometimes mysteries were not meant to be solved.

She writes on sacred stone with a light gleaming in her eye.
Time a concept only important to you and I.
The Peace found within is now something she must share.
Connections made, she smiles and laughs with a shedding tear.

–By permission of Vincent Bishop, author's son

CHAPTER SEVEN

THE GRAND TETONS
AND THE GREAT ARREST

The Present, Higginsville, NY

Anna Marie woke up, startled; she had fallen asleep over her iced tea. She hoped it was because of the missed sleep the night before, not because she was growing old with more frequent naps needed. In the past, she had needed nine hours of sleep at night, so the five hours the previous evening was not enough for her to feel rested. Her pets all napped around her appearing peaceful, as they often had in the Southwind before.

She walked out to the porch, stretching out on the lounge chair to allow herself the luxury of a nap and the time to remember her Southwind days. She soon drifted off into a deep sleep with memories from the Southwind, not all of them peaceful.

Seven years earlier

The first day after leaving the Arkansas site passed uneventfully, as did the next two weeks of traveling. They stopped at tourist spots or sites of interest to one of the passengers, never following a straight-line path slowing down their travel. All the travelers now knew that it was the journey and not the arrival that mattered. None of them had any deadlines or reason to hurry, other than a desire to be in Oregon, Christa's home, before the birth of her daughter. The birth was expected in 3 months, leaving them plenty of time for travel together.

It was the most freeing feeling Anna Marie had ever experienced in her life. She always scheduled her life, other than when she first met Ted, making lists and goals with little time for spontaneous moments. She vowed to live what remained of her life in exactly this way, avoiding deadlines and enjoying every moment of the journey along the way. The three ladies, along with the pets, grew closer every day, making the time in the Southwind even more enjoyable.

After Anna Marie and Granny Rose resolved their differences, there were very few conflicts that caused any disagreements amongst them. If one wanted to do something different than the others, they stopped, giving each person time to enjoy the chosen activity while the other two read, walked, or just enjoyed sitting in the sun. Sometimes they'd all participate in the activity chosen by one of them and, therefore, kept trying new things along the way.

At any moment, one of the ladies sang or hummed a song and if the other two knew the song, each joined in. Anna Marie could not remember a time in her life when music was so spontaneous or joyful. Even the pets rocked to the music or listened aptly when the ladies sang. Occasionally, Anna Marie whistled with Granny Rose accompanying her as they tried to teach Christa the skill of whistling a tune. Anna Marie thought about her mother's dire forecast for whistling and thought if she had known this was the bad end, she would have whistled more often throughout her life.

Anna Marie was surprised to discover how knowledgeable Granny Rose was about nature, especially the cycles of the moon and stars. Granny Rose talked for hours at night as they observed the sky above them. Anna Marie never realized how much there was to know about the sky or the moon with the fundamental connection to women's history, traditions, and symbolism.

After Granny Rose and Christa fell asleep at night, Anna Marie sat for another hour or more thinking about the women who came before her, imagining those women learning about the moon from their mothers and grandmothers.

Many of those thoughts she added to her journal that was given to her by Erin. She felt saddened that this had not been part of her childhood lessons or something she had been able to pass on to her own daughters. She was glad that she now had the opportunity to learn these significant but hidden fragments of women's history. She was determined to share this information with her daughters and granddaughter, hoping they were interested.

Each shared their deepest thoughts, desires, and fears without reservation or worry that it would somehow change the relationship. Anna Marie was amazed at the stories of Granny Rose's life, most of them about her childhood or years after her husband died. For some reason, Granny Rose shared very little of the middle part of her life, including talking about her sons. Occasionally, Granny Rose lost her train of thought or drifted off into a nap during the middle of the story, but in general, she seemed to grow healthier and more alert each day.

Anna Marie already thought ahead with sadness when she would lose this day-to-day closeness with these two women, an experience she had never had in her life before. Even her friendship with Diana had been tempered by the need to care for her family and the pace of their lives always interfering with any extensive time spent together.

The final day before reaching the foot of the Grand Tetons, where they had reserved a campsite for two weeks, they stopped in Cheyenne to wander the streets, shop, and have an extended lunch in one of the local steakhouses. It was late afternoon by the time they were on the road again. Anna Marie wanted to reach their next campsite before dark, as she still had not connected the utilities or prepared the campsite in the dark.

She hoped to dump the almost-full brown and black wastewater tanks, a task she never looked forward to, never quite mastering this dirty task. Fortunately for her, each time she had attempted to do this herself, another camper or worker at the campsite had stepped in and assisted her. Anna Marie wondered what it was about campers that they all seemed to be an automatic community no matter where she was. Maybe it was that they all knew how to make a home and community wherever they stopped for the night. They understood the attraction of the road and the need to occasionally put down roots.

She knew her foot was heavy on the accelerator but the road ahead dipped and straightened out with almost no other traffic to contend with. She became mesmerized by the pace of travel and the road she could see in the rear-view mirror as they rapidly left each mile behind.

Granny Rose and Christa played Rummy at the dining room table while the animals napped. Every so often, she heard a minor argument erupt as one of the ladies accused the other of cheating or changing the rules midstream. Occasionally, one of the animals woke up from her nap to change position or give a look to the noisy card-playing ladies to indicate in their own language to keep their voices lower. Anna Marie felt like all was right with her world and they would have smooth sailing into Jackson Hole.

She looked in the rear-view mirror, noticing red lights flashing behind her in the distance. She wondered if it was an emergency vehicle and instinctively slowed down to let the vehicle pass as it approached the Southwind. It was a police car, and it took Anna Marie a few minutes to realize that the driver angrily waved to her to pull over to stop.

Anna Marie slowly let off her foot from the accelerator, looking for a place where she could pull the Southwind off to the side. As there was no place immediately coming up and not wanting to anger the police officer further, she pulled off as far as she could and sat waiting for the police officer to approach.

She cautioned the two ladies, who looked up from their intense card game, "We may be in for some trouble. I've been pulled over by a police officer. Sit tight for a few minutes. I'm sure it's a mistake. We'll be on our way soon."

The animals felt the RV stop and woke up from their respective naps. Little Bear jumped from her perch and ran to the front of the Southwind to investigate what was happening. As she noticed that they were no longer moving, she jumped up on Anna Marie's lap to look for the cause of the stop. Maya followed close behind, moving Little Bear over so that she, too, could look out Anna Marie's window.

Circe squawked, "Trouble in the front! Trouble in the front!"

She flew up to the front to see what was happening as Christa and Granny Rose put their cards down on the table. They kept Circe out of her cage more often as she had proved to be a good traveler who usually did not wander around the Southwind when it was in motion. They had discussed that it was possible Circe had motion sickness and stayed still or slept during the ride to counter the movement of the RV.

For whatever reason, all three animals were excellent travelers, causing no disturbances while they were in transit. They also knew as soon as the Southwind stopped, they could move freely around the RV.

Anna Marie looked outside and down into the reddened face of a very angry police officer.

He growled, "You going to a fire, lady? I clocked you back there at 87. It took you awhile to see me you were going so fast. You easterners think you can come out here and drive our roads however you want!"

Circe shrieked in response to the police officer's questions, "Copper! Copper in the vicinity! Hide the drugs. Hide the drugs! Copper!"

Anna Marie looked impatiently at Circe and the other two sitting on her lap, asking them, "Could you please move over and give me some room? Circe, quiet down this minute."

All three ignored Anna Marie, each trying to put her two-sense in and edging as close to the window as they could without falling out as Circe repeated the warning of the "copper" over and over.

Christa waddled to the front of the RV while Granny Rose grabbed a broomstick and came forward, using the broomstick as a weapon, shouting, "I'll save you, Maria Anne. I won't let anyone harm you again. Hang in there, Maria Anne."

The "copper" looked even angrier, firmly cautioning Anna Marie, "Quiet them all down, lady. Tell them to back off before I take y'all to the jail for questioning. You may look like some harmless ladies but with those New York plates you could be transporting drugs across state lines. You could be terrorists in disguise."

Anna Marie assured him, "We are not drug dealers and we are certainly not disguised terrorists. We are just three ladies with our pets traveling to Jackson Hole. I admit that I may have been traveling a little fast. Your roads are very nicely designed, with so little traffic I forgot the speed limit. I didn't see one posted?"

Anna Marie hoped that a little flattery might appease him.

The police officer calmed down a little bit, despite Circe's background noise, and said, "Lady, even in Wyoming you can't drive an RV 87 miles an hour. Let me see your identification, driver's license, and registration for this vehicle."

Anna Marie responded, "I understand that officer and I do apologize," as she reached for her purse and tried to rummage through it to find the requested items.

As she attempted to find what the officer wanted she also tried to nonchalantly push the two animals out of her lap, and motion Granny Rose to the back of the Southwind while all purposefully ignoring her.

Anna Marie handed the requested items one at a time to the "copper" as he shifted impatiently from one foot to another.

After she handed him only her license, he asked, "Can't you

hurry this up a little, lady? You sure don't find things as fast as you drive. I don't know how you can drive with all this commotion. I'm sure we have a law on the books in Wyoming about all these animals moving freely about your RV the way they are."

The "copper" looked at each one of the occupants of the Southwind, inquiring, "Are all these animals and people yours? Maybe they had better show me identification, too, as they could be the terrorists you are transporting. We surely don't need your kind here in Wyoming."

Anna Marie handed him all three items.

He turned back to say, "I'm going to check your identification and see if you are wanted anyplace. In the meantime, get out the identification for everyone else you have aboard, including those you may be hiding, and any licenses you have for this herd of animals."

He was gone for a few minutes which felt like an eternity to the waiting Southwind occupants. In as calm a voice as possible, Anna Marie asked Christa and Granny Rose to get their identification. Granny Rose calmed down long enough to put down her broom and reluctantly walked back to the closet where she kept her bag of secret treasures. She came back with her tiny purse that held the largest objects imaginable in such a small container.

She pulled out a card that Anna Marie hoped was some form of identification. Anna Marie had tried to retrieve this magical purse for information on Granny Rose's identity when Granny Rose was sleeping, never finding her hiding place. She suspected the secret spot changed frequently, and Anna Marie wasn't able to correctly guess the last or next hiding places.

Christa only had her high school picture ID as identification. The three animals moved to the passenger seat now quietly watching the activity.

The police officer seemed to be on the phone for a long time and then came back to the Southwind carrying the papers Anna Marie had given him.

He said, "For some reason, lady, you check out with no warrants. I still think you and your gang are highly suspicious."

Anna Marie burst out laughing at the use of the word "gang" to describe her motley crew. The officer stood up on his tiptoes on the edge of the window, peering closely into Anna Marie's face, "You think this is funny, lady? You easterners think you can come here and make fun of us Westerners? Well, I guess I'll have to put you down for resisting cooperation. You can follow me to my station to settle your fine while I check out your trailer for drugs and terrorist paraphernalia. I hope I can trust you to follow me so that I don't have to shoot out your tires and have you towed for hundreds of dollars to the station?"

Anna Marie was very sorry she had laughed spontaneously but couldn't take it back now. She said, "I really am sorry. It sounded so funny to hear my family called a gang. I do have police officers in Georgia who can vouch for us if you'll just let me contact them. I'll pay whatever fine you want. It would be a great inconvenience to go to your station as we would not be able to get to Jackson Hole tonight. I'm expecting to meet more of my family there and reporters to interview us."

As soon as she said the last, she knew it had been a mistake.

He grumbled, "Just as I thought. The press following you for your criminal or terrorist activities, I'll bet. You should have considered the inconvenience before you drove so fast over our roads. Follow me. No funny business or you will be in worse shape than you already are. We have plenty of room at the jail for you to stay, including all these animals here."

He looked disdainfully at the animals, Christa, who was obviously pregnant, and Granny Rose, who had the broomstick back in her hand, ready to take this officer one-on-one.

Anna Marie reluctantly but obediently drove slowly behind the police officer in his cruiser. While he expected Anna Marie to hold to the unknown speed limit, the officer drove very fast, Anna Marie occasionally losing sight of him over a hill or around a curve. She hoped he would not consider her uncooperative, tempting him to shoot out her tires because she couldn't keep up. She concluded that this police officer was not very stable, enjoying the power he felt he had over these "Easterners." She expected they would be able to reach the Sergeants quickly, resolve the misunderstanding, and be on their way before nightfall.

She thought, "Even if we hook up in the dark, we should know enough how to do this so it shouldn't be a problem. We could use the propane tank and generator until morning if we don't make it to the campgrounds."

She continued to hope for the best and cautioned herself to show as much respect as possible, especially not to laugh again as she had the first time, even though she still laughed silently over the "Southwind Gang."

At the station, the police officer directed her to place the animals on their leashes or in their cage. As they followed his directions with the pets, he then motioned abruptly for the three ladies to follow him into the police station, leaving the animals in the home. It was a cool day, so Anna Marie opened a few windows to let in ventilation for the waiting pets. She wanted to ask the officer if she could take them into the jail with the ladies but the expression on his face told her not to even try.

The town police station was on a four-corners with stop signs rather than a stoplight, unpaved roads from three of the directions, a seven/eleven convenience store, ranchers supply store, saloon, and a doctor's office. Two ramshackle buildings on both sides of the jail may have been residences or could have been abandoned buildings. The police station looked like it could fall down any minute. Despite the number of buildings, the streets were eerily vacant.

As they entered the doorway the ladies noticed various creepy-crawly things wriggle across to the corners of the small room. Anna Marie tried to hold her breath so that she did not breathe in all the years of odors from fear, evil, and sadness accumulated in the jail. She found she had no choice but to breathe in the nauseating smells. Always sensitive to smells, she had an instantaneous headache. Christa was very pale and obviously attempting to hold down her nausea. Granny Rose appeared dazed.

Anna Marie felt instantly dirty, hoping the fine would be given to them quickly, paid, and on their way to Jackson Hole. She wondered where all the room was the police officer had bragged about, as she noticed only one tiny jail cell. She hoped that would not be their home for the night. She also worried about the police officer handling her pets, wishing she could have brought them into the jail to keep them safe. While Little Bear had a wonderful temperament, Anna Marie worried about what would happen if she felt threatened or thought Maya or Circe were being endangered.

Looking around the town, she wondered if this was a legitimate police station or renegades that had decided to deputize themselves. As the day wore on, this thought became a more serious concern, with Anna Marie increasingly fearful for all their safety. She attempted to appear calm so as not to alarm the other two ladies.

Another man in a disheveled uniform and smelling of his personal years of accumulation of sweat sat at the desk. He grunted when they came through the door and was directed by the police officer from hell to put the three ladies in the cell while he looked over their vehicle for drug and terrorist paraphernalia. The word vehicle was said as Midwesterners and southerners pronounced the word with a different emphasis on syllables than spoken by easterners.

The dirty younger officer said, "What do we have here, Dad? A group of criminals or another group of Easterners who have disrespected us? I guess that's the same thing." "

"Dad" answered, "Sonny, never you mind. This is my bust. You just keep them here until I return. Don't let them escape."

Anna Marie wondered where to or how they could escape. She looked over at Christa, who was becoming increasingly paler as the men talked. Granny Rose had a look of total confusion on her face.

Anna Marie quietly reassured both, "As soon as they find we have nothing, or we can contact the Sergeants in Georgia, they'll let us go. We'll be on our way. Just cooperate and we'll be fine."

Anna Marie wished she felt as confident as her words.

As Anna Marie spoke, the dirty-looking younger man eyed Christa up and down. He approached her, towering over her as Christa attempted to pull away from him as his smells took over the space around her.

He laughed at her reluctance to be close to him, "Think you're too good for me? We'll see about that. You'll be begging for my help before long, missy! A few hours in that cage and you'll come begging me for help! You are a little thing. We don't see many like you around here. Looks like some other man had you first. I don't mind that, makes you more tasty to me. Means you're experienced in giving men pleasure."

He licked his lips, already picturing sex with Christa.

He looked over to the man he called Dad, who wrote something on a pad on the desk near the door.

He asked his father, "Do you think I could keep her? She is a pretty one."

"Officer Dad" growled and said, "You keep your hands off the ladies, even the young, pretty one. One more report on you and you'll lose your officer stripes. We don't want to draw any more attention from the state or feds to our town police force."

As he spoke, Anna Marie edged closer to Christa, placing her hand on her arm to reassure her she would let nothing happen. Anna Marie was glad she had carried her purse inside with the cell phone as she realized these men would likely never call the Sergeants in Georgia or give her the one phone call they were legally entitled to use.

Before Officer Dad left the room to examine the Southwind, Anna Marie asked him, "Aren't we allowed at least one phone call?"

He just chuckled, "Liberal easterners," and walked out of the jail.

Anna Marie could feel something shaking. She looked at Granny Rose, seeing her holding herself, shaking with tears rolling down her face. Anna Marie moved between Christa and Granny Rose, placing her arm over the shoulders of both.

She gently whispered, as much to soothe her as the other two, "We're going to be okay. As soon as I can, I'll call the Sergeants. They'll get us out of this place. We'll stay together and take care of each other."

Anna Marie pulled both closer, relieved to see less shaking from Granny Rose.

Granny Rose whimpered, "I don't want to let them hurt you again, Marie Anne. It's my fault I didn't stop them before."

Christa straightened up, immediately looking more mature and confident, "Together we'll be fine. We won't let these men, masquerading as police officers hurt us. I am worried about Little Bear, Maya, and Circe, though. Let me see what I can do."

Anna Marie watched Christa with pride as she left their side, approaching the younger police officer wiping snot from his nose. He looked up with amazement from his paperwork. Despite his previous bravado, he was shocked that a woman as pretty as Christa would come near him.

Christa said in the sexiest voice Anna Marie had ever heard her use, "Maybe you can help us, handsome? I've been thinking about what you said. Our pets are not used to being alone in the RV this long. I would surely appreciate your talking with the big guy to let them in here with us while you check us out. Surely two men as tough as you can't be afraid of little women like us. I'd be eternally grateful to you. I'd make it worth your while."

Christa brushed the man's arm, flashing her blue eyes at him. Anna Marie wondered how she kept a straight face or was able to breathe near the disgusting man.

It was obvious Christa charmed him. He was overwhelmed by her attempt to be flirtatious.

He assured them, "Don't you ladies worry about a thing. I'll talk to my dad. Now you just go over to that cell like I asked so I can lock you up and go find my dad."

He motioned them over to the cell using a gun that looked dangerous due to lack of care and knowledge of how to use it safely. Anna Marie assumed he was showing off for Christa as he winked at Christa, a hard feat for him given that one eye was so scarred it looked like it was eternally open. His eyes also appeared to focus on different directions so that the effect of winking was to make the eyes look like they were swirling in his head.

Anna Marie winced as he locked the rusted cell door. The three ladies huddled together in a corner of the cell, using each other for warmth and comfort. Anna Marie waited for the outside door to the jail to shut and then she quickly reached for her purse, that miraculously, the men had allowed her to keep. It could be these men did not know about the cell phone invention.

She turned on the phone, pushing the speed dial number for the Georgia Sergeants, hoping at least one of them was on duty that day. The switchboard operator told her to hold while she looked to see if either of the Sergeants was on duty while Anna Marie held her breath, hoping for the best. She tried hard not to let her fear take control of her.

A female voice came on the other end, "Can I help you? This is Rome Day in our town and all our officers are pretty busy with crowd control."

Anna Marie cringed at the thought that she would not be able to talk with at least one of the Sergeants immediately.

She responded, "This is kind of an emergency. I'm with a Southwind RV, and we've been mistakenly arrested in Wyoming."

Before Anna Marie could explain any further, the voice on the other end excitedly responded, "You must be Anna Marie! Are Christa, Granny Rose, and Little Bear right there with you? I'm so excited to meet you, even if only over the phone. The Georges have done nothing but talk about you all the time. The newspaper article about you all was wonderful. I wish I could be as brave as you are."

Anna Marie said, "I'm not feeling particularly brave right this moment. I'm stuck inside a jail that I am not even sure is an official police station. The officers do not seem to be mentally stable. They have a personal vendetta against anyone from the east and are searching through my Southwind right now, looking for drugs and terrorists with my animals inside. I'm afraid for their safety. That's why I'm looking for the Sergeant Georges to see if they can help get us out of this mess. I asked the men who arrested us to call your station, but the men have ignored my request. One of the officers has made some advances towards Christa. Can you please find a way to help us?"

Anna Marie tried to hold back tears or display her fear too obviously so that she did not frighten the other two ladies any further.

The voice on the other end responded, "My name is Sandra Cass. I don't think I can find either one of the Sergeants in this mess today, but I have worked here since both Sergeants were still in diapers. I know the ropes and I'll figure out a way to get you out of that jail. We have friends and contacts all over the country. I'm usually the one that talks to the other stations, so I'll get one of my lady friends at a station near you to figure out what we can do. Just sit tight and stay safe!"

Anna Marie answered. "Can you be quick about it? I don't trust these men and I don't know how safe I can keep us."

She added, "It is nice to meet you. I really do appreciate anything you can do for us. We'll be indebted to you."

Sandra Cass responded, "It's what we women do for each other. The men think they take care of us and all the problems, but it's the other way around. Give me your cell phone number again and I'll try to call you back. Even if I don't get you, I'll find a way to get you out. Watch out for an older woman on a mission. And they thought I should retire a few years ago!"

Anna Marie thanked Sandra again, reluctantly pressing the off button, feeling like she had lost their last lifeline.

Anna Marie thought for a minute as she noticed Christa and

Granny Rose quietly holding each other. She pressed another speed dial number, glad that she had left the number on her speed dial despite thinking she no longer wanted the contact.

A voice answered on the second ring, "Walter here. What can I do for you?"

Anna Marie almost cried with relief at hearing the cheerful, now familiar voice. She answered, "Walter, it's Anna Marie."

There was silence on the other end, and then, "Speak up. I can't hear you."

Anna Marie hoped her cell phone was not losing its charge and repeated her greeting loudly.

Walter responded, whispering into the phone, "Ah, Anna Marie, you've caught me at kind of a bad time. My wife is here. She still doesn't know about us. Things are so good between us that I don't want her to find out about our affair. I think she would not be too happy if she found out that my recent skills in bed are because of you."

Anna Marie ignored the comments of their brief coupling.

She said forcefully, "Walter, I really need your help. We are in a jail in Wyoming, falsely accused of being terrorists or drug dealers. Please, can you find a way to help us? I'm scared, especially for the safety of my pets, as these officers don't seem right. There is something strange about all of this. One of the officers has made some advances towards Christa. I'm worried about what he might do to her. Please, Walter. Your wife doesn't need to know about our business and if anyone can help, you can."

Anna Marie thought adding some flattery might do the trick and it did.

Walter sounded very confident as he spoke.

Anna Marie could picture him puffing up his chest as he answered her, "Harry, you just give me the information and I'll take care of it right away. My best friend at the senior center is a retired NY State Police Officer. I'm sure he still has some contacts."

Anna Marie was confused for a minute and then realized that

Walter's wife was within hearing distance. She gave Walter as detailed information as she could as to where they were located, describing the town, how she had driven to the area, and the police officers.

Walter answered, "I have it all down Harry, along with your cell phone number. I'll call back when I know something but we'll get you out of there so you can finish up your fishing trip. Excuse me a moment."

She heard Walter explain to his wife in the background, "Honey, it's my friend Harry from my days of working in City Hall. He's been drinking and landed in a Wyoming jail for causing disturbance in the campground. You probably don't remember me talking about him, but he was a good friend at work. He needs my help now. It will take me a little while and then we can go shopping for the new couch. Just give me a minute sweetheart."

Anna Marie listened to the endearments and thought about Ted. Tears came to her eyes as she brushed them away, needing Ted now more than ever. She silently begged Ted to help the Southwind Gang. For the first time on this trip, she regretted leaving home and wished for the safety of her own bed.

Walter interrupted her thoughts of Ted and home, "Harry just stay calm and don't cause any more trouble. I'll have you out in a jiffy. Get back to you soon."

Walter hung up, Anna Marie feeling like another lifeline was lost. She worried about the cell phone battery, so she shut the phone off for a brief period to let it rest. She moved closer to Christa and Granny Rose, who quietly rocked each other. Both were in a daze that seemed to take them out of the cell into safer places or times.

Anna Marie thought of one last possible source for help and turned the phone back on. The connection was very poor with considerable static but after a few rings she heard her son Erin's voice on his answer machine. She had hoped he might be preparing for his families' trip out West in a few days to join the Southwind travelers and have taken the day off. Erin, so interested in his mother's adventures, had rented a small motor home for his family.

She left a very softly spoken message, explaining where they were and the predicament, they were in. She asked him to help in any way he could if he got the message in time. As she hung up the phone, deeply disappointed, she wondered, in time for what? A small tear rolled down her cheek as she thought how she had let everyone in the Southwind down, especially the pets who she had no way of protecting them from the crazy acting men.

The minutes ticked by on the clock in the office as they wondered what was taking the police officers so long, worrying about the safety of the animals. The door opened after an eternity, which was probably closer to thirty minutes, as the younger police officer led two anxious looking pets and carried a cage with a squawking bird.

He approached the cell peering at Christa as he growled, "You had better appreciate all I've done for you as I really upset my father. I expect payment in full, sooner rather than later. I'll leave these pets here as an exchange. You can come with me behind the office in the alley."

He placed the leads and cage on the dirty floor as he found the key to open the lock. Christa looked at Anna Marie in sheer panic, afraid of the unspoken promises this officer perceived due to him, but not willing to give up the animals now safely in their protection. Each of the animals looked upset but obviously physically unharmed.

Anna Marie stepped in front of Christa when Police Officer Junior opened the jail cell, as she also reached for the cage and the two leads. Little Bear and Maya rushed to Anna Marie's side.

Circe exclaimed, "Anna Marie. Missed you! Bad men! Smelly..."

The police officer attempted to move Anna Marie aside as he said, "I don't have much time. My father is almost done going through the RV. I want the reward this pretty lady promised me."

Anna Marie said to him soothingly, "You certainly deserve your reward. The only problem is my daughter has a major infectious disease. The last man she was with lost part of his scrotum from the infection. He talks in a high voice now. She should have told you about the disease before promising you anything. Such a good-looking strong young man as you and so obviously virile wouldn't want to risk his manhood for a few moments of pleasure. I'm sure you have no problems finding willing women."

Anna Marie winked and pulled the officer to one side, wishing she could immediately wash her hands after touching him. She thought the smell of him would stay with her forever.

She whispered in his ear, "The last man told me it wasn't worth it anyway. She's not very good. She doesn't take after her mother. Now, I can give you pleasures you wouldn't soon forget as could my mother here. She taught me in some threesomes over the years. Though I think my daughter inherited the disease from us, as I've heard some rumors about men we've been with together. They're probably only rumors and we're worth the risk, believe me!"

The officer looked with disgust at Anna Marie moving swiftly back from her, afraid of instantaneous contamination. Granny Rose, more alert and suspecting what Anna Marie was doing, sidled over to the officer. Anna Marie was amazed at how ugly she had been able to make herself appear, gaining years and wrinkles in just a few minutes. As she thought about it, Granny Rose seemed to be able to take on different personas and appearances fitting different occasions. She was able to do that in what seemed to be the blink of an eye.

Granny Rose grabbed the younger police officer's sleeve and said, "Can I rub anything for you? My daughter and I usually charge a high price for a threesome but you're so good-looking, we'll consider it a gift from you to us. We haven't had anyone like you in a long time." Granny Rose licked her lips wiggling her hips as she pleaded, "Let an old lady show you real tricks of the trade!"

Granny Rose attempted to grab the officer's crotch as he pulled back from her and placed his hand over his mouth to stop him from throwing up. He ran out of the cell, forgetting to lock the door as he ran.

Granny Rose cackled after him, "You don't know what you are missing, sonny boy—the ride of your life with my daughter and me!"

The officer ran out of the jail, letting the outside door slam behind him. The keys, hanging out of his pocket, fell to the floor as he exited, but he was so fearful that Granny might try to tackle him he didn't stop to pick up the keys.

Granny Rose shook her head as she pondered, "I never used to get this reaction from men."

Thinking quickly, Anna Marie ran to the door locking it using the deadbolt so that neither officer could get back inside easily. She picked up the keys off the floor. She breathed a sigh of relief for one moment, beginning to think of possible consequences such as the officers shooting the lock off from outside the building or breaking in the one dirty window to get back inside. She hoped she had a few minutes to talk over what to do next. She turned back to Christa and Granny Rose who were laughing so hard that tears streaked down their faces.

In between spurts of laughter, Granny Rose said, "I wish I had a video camera. That is one of the funniest things I have seen in a long time. It's a shame that boy doesn't know what he could be missing. I've introduced a few young men to good sex in my time."

In that brief period, Granny Rose had made herself look respectable and less disheveled. Anna Marie shook her head at the apparently easy transformations, wondering where her ability to do that came from or was it only her own imagination.

Anna Marie cautioned the two laughing ladies, "We're not out of this mess yet so we need to think out what we should do next. His daddy is not going to be happy with him or us."

The two ladies sobered up quickly, realizing they were not totally out of danger yet.

Christa suggested, "Two of us should try to put furniture over the window and doorway. One of us should investigate if there are any other exits out of this place. Police officer Jr. mentioned a back alley so there must be some way to it without going outside."

Christa shivered at the thought of what she might have had to do in that back alley.

Granny Rose immediately began looking for a back door exit, while Anna Marie and Christa moved the desk in front of the door. They also set the table up on its' side placing that in front of the window, knowing these were only temporary stop gap measures.

Anna Marie didn't want to think about the possibility that these men could be real police officers. They could be in for even bigger trouble for trying to escape. But her instincts told her they needed to be away from these men, then worry about the consequences after they were free.

Granny Rose called from the back, "I've found an exit. I don't know where it goes or if they will be smart enough to block it. They may not even realize that we have control of the station now. I suspect the younger one has not told his father yet what happened and may still be sick someplace."

She shook her head in astonishment, repeating her previous comment, "I never used to cause that reaction in men."

She came out of her thoughts and said, "I think we should try to make a run for it."

Anna Marie looked around at her Southwind Gang and wondered what kind of run they could make with two elderly women, a pregnant woman, and the three animals.

She hesitated for a minute and then quietly directed, "Christa, you take Maya, Granny Rose Little Bear, and I'll carry Circe. We need to be very quiet. One of us needs to take the lead in determining where it is safe to go after we leave this jail."

Granny Rose told them, "I spent lots of years hiding from one of my husbands, who occasionally threatened to kill me or worse, figuring out places where he couldn't find me. I'll take the lead."

She pointed to a large scar on her arm that Anna Marie had wondered about.

The three ladies and their pets walked to the back door with Granny Rose in the front. Even as short as all three were, they needed to duck down to go through the door. Anna Marie brought up the rear, quietly shutting the door behind her as the three ladies tried to get their bearings.

The "back alley" was obviously where garbage was kept, and it was apparent there were no regular pickups for garbage. Anna Marie recognized many of the smells from within the jail and wondered about the history of the years of accumulation of smells that were inside and outside the jail. She didn't want to think about what might be in the piles of debris or what would have happened if Christa had to keep her promise to Police Officer Junior.

Granny Rose motioned for the ladies to stay put and handed Little Bear to Christa. The animals, including Circe, were surprisingly silent. They too sensed the need to escape and the gravity of the situation. Granny Rose approached the fence enclosing the back alleyway, climbing silently onto an overflowing garbage can. She found a way to grab onto the fence, peering over the top. She looked around for a few minutes and then climbed quietly back down.

Not saying anything to the others, she walked around the alleyway, sometimes climbing up where she could. She carefully examined the back of the building behind the jail. After a few minutes she motioned for the rest to follow her.

She indicated what looked like a cellar window and said, "I think this is our best option, though I don't know what may be in the cellar. The fence borders the street. I can see some movement and the Southwind, so I think that is where the two police officers are. I don't think they suspect anything yet. I bet sonny is still too embarrassed to tell his father."

Christa and Anna Marie looked hesitantly at the window and then around the rest of the back alley. While they were not anxious to enter the cellar they knew nothing about, at the same time they knew they had few other options, not wanting to go back into the jail. On the top of the building, Anna Marie noticed the Catbird, softly making a meowing sound that was now so familiar. Anna Marie knew it was a good omen and silently pointed out the Catbird to the other two ladies.

Granny Rose nodded and whispered, "I'll go first and scout it out. If it is safe, I will have you hand me the animals, and then each of you can climb in."

Anna Marie responded reluctantly, "Maybe I should be the one to go in and find out if it is safe?"

Granny Rose insisted, "No, I'm the smallest and the one who knows how to climb high walls. I'll be okay. If it's not safe, I'll come right back out. I promise you we'll be okay. I can just sense this is the right way to go. Our friend on the roof is telling us the same thing."

She slithered down through the window as the Southwind Gang waited silently, each deep in her own thoughts and anxiety. After what seemed a long time, they saw Granny Rose's wizened face in the window, motioning for them to hand the animals down to her. She nodded to say it was exactly as she thought and a good escape plan.

Silently, Anna Marie and Christa handed the pets to Granny Rose as Granny Rose settled each beside her while reaching for the next pet. The three animals stayed huddled at her side, looking to Granny Rose for directions and waiting for the rest of their family to join them.

Anna Marie motioned for Christa to go first helping her gently through the window with Granny Rose assisting her on the other side. Anna Marie followed Christa carefully through the window, trying not to think about her fear of the dark and unknown. She hoped this experience would cure her fear.

Once inside, Granny Rose gestured for everyone to follow her as she inched her way by the side of the wall, staying close to the dim light from the extremely dirty windows along the wall. They followed silently in a row, each touching the woman in front of her in a very slow-moving conga line. Anna Marie was relieved that the smells in the cellar were friendlier than the smells in the jail.

After a couple of minutes, they reached the end of the wall and could vaguely make out stairs in front of them. Granny Rose began climbing, with each following behind her. Anna Marie hoped that Granny Rose had some sense of where this came out in the street so that they did not end up face to face with one or both officers.

Granny Rose reached for the doorknob and found that it was locked or possibly jammed from years of disuse. She reached into her bra and pulled out what looked like a large safety pin. After a few minutes of working on the lock, the door swung reluctantly open, its hinges screeching complaint of the disturbance after years of rest.

Granny Rose said something that sounded like a rhyme and the door stopped screeching. She peeked around the outside of the door, motioned for them to wait while she looked around outside, and after the longest two minutes any of the waiting ladies could remember, came back inside.

She whispered, "I can see the side of the jail. I can't see the Southwind so I suspect this wall is not in the view of these disgusting men. I suggest instead of running away from the Southwind, we take them by surprise and take the Southwind back."

Anna Marie quickly exclaimed, "We could end up in jail for the rest of our lives or even worse, they could shoot us with those guns they carry around like little boys. I think we should find a building we can hide in until someone comes to rescue us."

They all hesitated for a few minutes, trying to decide which plan to follow or who would possibly be coming to rescue them when they heard loud shouting coming from the front of the jail. They could only pick up a few words but just enough to know that someone was very angry.

Anna Marie felt as though they were frozen in space with time at a standstill, until she heard sirens coming from a distance. She motioned to the other two ladies to listen.

Granny Rose said, "I can hear sirens coming from the West."

Christa corrected her, "No, Granny Rose, they're coming from the East. Maybe you should check your hearing aids."

Anna Marie listened for a few seconds and said, "You're both right. There are sirens coming from both directions."

She paused and then said, "I think I hear sirens coming from the North as well. Maybe there is something causing an echoing here so we can't really tell what direction they are coming from?"

The sirens became much louder. They realized that the sounds were coming from three different directions as well as different sources and were converging into the small town.

Anna Marie said, "I hope this is a good thing and that one of our pleas for help brought these sirens."

The sounds became so loud that the ladies gave up trying to talk to each other, waiting anxiously to see what happened next. The sirens rang as the vehicles came together in front of the building, almost simultaneously like the entrance to the town had been planned. The Southwind Gang heard doors slamming and yelling directions to come out of the RV with their hands in the air.

Anna Marie said to the others, "I think one of my calls must have gotten through. One of us should go to the front to see what is going on and let them know we are all safe. I think that should be me."

The other two nodded, perfectly happy to let Anna Marie investigate what was going on. They sat down on the steps of the building with the pets to wait for Anna Marie.

Anna Marie walked cautiously around to the front of the jail, hoping that she did not startle someone into shooting her. She peered around the side of the building to see a mass of men in uniforms, all arguing with each other with the two errant police officers in the middle of the circle of men. The two were obviously very shaken by the quantity of guns pointed at them as they held their hands timidly in the air.

Police Officer Senior attempted to ask what was going on but was quickly silenced by a one of the men in uniform while the others pointed their guns in the direction of the police officers as the officer surrounding the Southwind continued to argue with each other. Anna Marie could gather from the conversation that they were arguing over who had jurisdiction in that town and which one was the arresting authority. They were so deep in their argument that they did not notice Anna Marie or that Police Officer Junior was trying to inch off to crawl under the RV.

Anna Marie took a deep breath and then gave the loudest whistle she had ever produced in her life. The arguing men, Police Officer Junior, and the Police Officers in the middle all came to an immediate stop, turning to look for the cause of the loud, obnoxious sound.

Anna Marie held up her hand and hesitantly waved to the crowd of men quietly standing staring at her.

She said, "I think I and my friends are the reason you are all here. Was it Walter, the Georgia Sergeants, or my son, Erin that asked you to come and rescue us?"

Several of the men answered her at once. She heard answers of a reporter from the Tribune, the New York State Police, and Georgia Police.

Anna Marie held her hand up again and asked, "Could one of you answer at a time? It's hard to understand you all at once. You also almost lost Junior here as he's attempting to crawl under my Southwind."

The officers standing closest to Junior placed handcuffs on him attaching those to the side of the Southwind. A couple of other officers did the same thing for Senior. Junior obviously gave in to the inevitable and stood quietly listening, while Dad paced back and forth next to the Southwind, like a caged animal. Anna Marie hoped there would not be scratches on the side of her precious RV.

Anna Marie thought she might be adding to the confusion. She explained to the men, "I'm Anna Marie Golding with the Southwind. I was falsely arrested by these men here who refused to allow me even a phone call or to bring charges so we could be released. I was very fearful for our safety, which is why I called my friends and son for help. I assume that's why you are here and really appreciate it."

The tallest man standing in the center of the group of men, who apparently came from the north, stepped forward.

He took off his hat and said to Anna Marie, "I'm Captain Dan Grouper from the Wyoming State Police. My friend, Sandra Cass, called our station over an hour ago to tell us of your plight. Sorry we couldn't get here sooner. We've been watching these officers for six months now as we have had numerous complaints from tourists who have been stopped and arrested by them. Strangely enough, the complaints all seem to come from tourists with license plates from the east, especially New York so when Sandra called, we knew to take it seriously." A short, stocky man who came from the direction of the east stepped forward and said, "Nice to meet you. I'm Lieutenant Jack Daisy from the Cheyenne station of the Wyoming State Police. I received a call from my father in New York State who is a retired police officer about our need to rescue you from this duo here. Glad to be at your service."

A medium height woman stepped forward. Anna Marie hadn't noticed her with the group of men from the west before.

She explained, "I'm Captain Shirley Krupps. My roommate in college was your son's sister-in-law. She works for the Wyoming Tribune. She called me at Erin's request and that's why we're here to help you. Glad to see you. I hope that all the rest of your traveling companions are as safe as you are?"

Later, Anna Marie would have time to think about what a small world she lived in, that there would be so many connections to a place she had known little about. At that moment, she was relieved and grateful for the help all her calls had produced. She didn't know how she was going to be able to thank each one enough.

She responded to the last question, "Yes, the rest of my party is behind the jail. They are all safe. We escaped on our own but had no idea what to do next if all of you hadn't come to our rescue."

The northern police officer answered for all of them, "We're just glad to get in here in time before our state had a major embarrassment on our hands. We can't afford that. Who knows what would have happened with our Keystone Cops, here?" He glared at the two officers who stood with their mouths open, looking less confident than they had earlier.

He continued, "We need the tourist dollars. From what I understand, you ladies have become a little bit of celebrities in the south and northeast so if anything had happened to you there would have been hell to pay, especially with the potential for bad press."

He stopped to smile at the ladies reassuring them they would be taken care of through his smile.

"Let's get the rest of your party safely back on to the Southwind. We will draw straws to figure out which one of us will escort you to your campsite while we'll decide which one of our departments will arrest our wayward colleagues here. You're only a few hours away from the Grand Teton Mountains."

He pointed towards the distant seeming mountains. Anna Marie assumed they were the Grand Tetons. She breathed a sigh of relief they would be at the campsite soon, all the Southwind Gang safe and secure.

"With an escort you won't have to worry about the speed limit this time. Our renegade officers here will have some explaining to do and will not be in for an easy time of it. I suspect it will be a long time, if ever, before they can bother anyone else."

The Northern Police Officer puffed up his chest a tiny bit, looking to his audience for approval. Anna Marie was too exhausted to notice, and the other police officers turned away when he was done with his speech.

Anna Marie walked to the back of the jail quietly hugging the waiting Christa and Granny Rose before telling them, "Police are here from all three of the directions we mentioned to save us. One of them will escort us to the campsite tonight."

Both smiled, holding on to the pets with a strong grip, neither saying anything. They quietly followed Anna Marie. With little fanfare and much relief, Anna Marie brought her companions to the front of the jail and introduced them. She admitted absolute exhaustion to the police officers from the west that had drawn the privilege of escorting the Southwind.

One of the officers drove the RV, a long time RV user, while the rest of the passengers sat in a daze in the back. Captain Shirley rode with them in the back as cruisers led and followed the Southwind. She poured out glasses of ice water for each of the ladies, while also making sure the pets all had fresh water. No one said anything as the miles quickly passed by.

They were at the foot of the Grand Tetons and the reserved campsite in what felt like no time at all, especially after the long forever-lasting day they had all experienced. One of the officers was an experienced camper. He helped set up the Southwind and disengage the car from the Southwind for the ladies. Captain Shirley boiled tea water and prepared a very light supper. Each Southwind passenger was glad for the help, as they were exhausted from the day and just thankful to be safely together at the campsite. Anna Marie thanked each one of their helpers as they assured her, they would be back in the morning to check on the ladies, get some additional information regarding the crimes of the day, and give them the names of all of the officers who assisted at Anna Marie's request so they would be able to thank each one properly.

Before going to sleep that night, they all agreed a thank you party was in order, especially as Erin and his family would be joining them in just a few days along with Cynthia and Anita. The journalist from Georgia was also scheduled to fly in to do an interview of the Southwind Gang for her paper.

They all woke up late the next morning, relieved to come

out of their various dreams from the day before to realize all was once again well with their world. Anna Marie wondered how she would ever be able to feel safe around the police again, then thought of all the wonderful officers who had come to help them. After a quiet breakfast and a walk with Little Bear to learn some of their surroundings, Anna Marie made numerous calls to thank Sandra Cass, Erin, and Walter.

Each had been notified the day before about their safe arrival in the Grand Tetons and glad they could help. Anna Marie told each about their plans for a thank you party and asked those not already scheduled to come to Wyoming to join them if possible. Walter was extremely hesitant until Anna Marie assured him; he could bring his wife.

He responded, "I don't know how I could make you into Harry and explain everything, but I'll think about it and let you know. My wife is not very good with spontaneous adventures; she's not like you at all. I love her. I still wish she could be more like you when it comes to trying new things."

Each of the invitees said they would do what they could to join the party, leaving it up in the air if they were able to come. The ladies decided to plan for food and drinks for more than they originally planned instead of less. The leftovers could be shared with the rest of the campground or invite the rest of the campground to come to the party.

Later in the morning, a couple of officers from the escort party came to check on the Southwind Gang. Over coffee and freshly baked huckleberry muffins, a specialty of the region, the officers asked questions about the arrest, took down notes, and then gave the ladies an update over the process.

Before they left, they gave the ladies telephone and address information for the party. They assured them that as many as possible would be at the thank you party, planning to invite the officers and support staff who also made the rescue go down so quickly.

Anna Marie and Christa drove into Jackson Hole to buy

groceries and find party supplies including invitations. Both felt great relief at being able to do the everyday tasks that make up people's lives. Often these events are taken for granted until a crisis like the day before happens.

They all spent the next few days sending out invitations, making telephone calls, and preparing for the thank you party, which was quickly growing in size as they met new people in the campgrounds, receiving positive responses back for the party. Katy and her oldest daughter were also going to join them for a couple of days while Clint took care of the two children in his ongoing attempt to apologize for his affair.

Walter's wife wanted to go shopping in Albany with her friends so gave Walter full blessings to go out to "Harry's" for a few days of fishing. Anna Marie disliked this misrepresentation of Walter's, deciding not to take responsibility for it. She planned to make it very clear to Walter that they would never resume their very brief relationship beyond the comfortable friendship that had developed over the months between them.

Anna Marie reserved three cabins that were miraculously free for the arriving guests who were staying a few days. She wondered if the planets, moon, and stars were converging together to make this a party of a lifetime.

Everyone grew excited as the day for the party drew near, each contributing new ideas to add to the celebration. Anna Marie was kept busy picking up people at the airport and especially excited to meet Sandra Cass, who she liked immediately. She was even pleased to see Walter and to note he had lost a few pounds, though he was now wearing a very unattractive toupee at his wife's suggestion, carrying fishing apparatus, and looking like an L.L. Bean advertisement for older fishermen.

Anna Marie wondered how their night had occurred so naturally and beautifully. She was relieved that Walter had come out for the adventure, not looking for sex.

His first words off the plane to Anna Marie were, "Now Anna Marie, I know I look better than ever but you'll just have to keep your distance. Keep your hands at your side. I don't want to do anything that would hurt my wife or marriage. This was risky enough, so I hope we have a Harry here someplace who can talk to my wife and reassure her I'm here with the guys. She is extremely jealous of me these days."

Walter patted his head to indicate his new hairpiece, thinking it added to his sexual attraction.

Anna Marie hugged him as a friend and assured him, "Walter, as handsome as you are, I have gotten over you. I am only happy to see you as a friend. I'm sure we can find a Harry amongst the police officers who are coming to our party or somewhere in the campgrounds. If worse comes to worse, my son Erin can be Harry for a few minutes on the phone."

Anna Marie wanted to do everything possible to keep Walter's marriage intact as she did not want him seeking anything other than friendship from her.

Each of the arriving guests were settled easily by the campground crew, who were also invited and excited about the upcoming party. As there were limited available cabins the arriving ladies shared one cabin. The two Sergeant Georges were housed with Walter. It was especially exciting to meet the Sergeants in person even though they felt like long-lost friends. Neither looked like Anna Maria expected, still they were a welcome sight with friendly faces and obvious pleasure at being there.

Erin and his family arrived the day of the party. Anna Marie helped them set up their rented RV on their campsite, which was located relatively near the Southwind.

Erin exclaimed, "Mom, not only do you look beautiful, but you are also an expert at this. We might be tempted to buy a used one after this trip or maybe borrow the Southwind from you when you return home."

He asked hesitantly, "You are planning on returning home someday, aren't you?"

Anna Marie responded carefully, "I'm sure I will. I just don't know when or how long I am going to keep traveling. I'm having too much fun right now to think about ending this any time soon. Even my misadventure in Wyoming hasn't turned me away from the joys of traveling with my friends. I'm sure being on the road must get tiring at some point."

Anna Marie wondered when that would be or how this journey would end. She put that unhappy thought out of her mind for the moment.

The full moon rose early that night, long before the very vivid sunset, which colored the mountains a purple and red tint. The ladies turned on the twinkling white lights in the trees around them, adding to the light that would soon bathe them from the stars above.

People slowly arrived, bearing gifts of food and beverage, thus adding to the already overloaded tables. Anna Marie's grandchildren mixed in with some other children from the campgrounds, running in and out amongst the people. The pets observed the activities from a distance in the door of the Southwind, happy to be a part of the festivities even if from a short distance.

As the moon climbed high overhead, laughter and song rose to greet the moon. Anna Marie took some time to watch the party from a distance hugging herself over the richness of her life.

She whispered to the planet Venus, low in the sky, "Ted, I know you are watching this and have helped shape this night. Thank you, my love."

Anna Marie joined the various groups of people, making sure they were eating and taking time to thank each one for coming to their party. The magic of the night went on for many hours, until people drifted away, leaving the Southwind Gang to their dreams and the preparations for the next stage of their journey together.

In remembering tomorrow, today is the cost.
A memory borrowed from a past action since lost.
The highway screams how can you ignore me?
In this dream I am what makes you free.

–By permission of Vincent Bishop, author's son

Chapter Eight

Ma's Hilltop Café and Bar:
The stars in alignment

The Present, Higginsville, NY

Anna Marie woke up with a startle from her nap. Little Bear's nose was directly in front of her, informing Anna Marie that it was well past lunchtime and her pet family was hungry. Anna Marie quickly fed the three impatiently waiting pets, then put the teakettle on for a light lunch. She thought about how much her Southwind journey had changed her eating habits. She had been reminded that food was a celebration meant to be enjoyed without guilt during each meal. As a result, she had slowly lost weight, kept the weight off, and rarely felt deprived of food.

She wondered how her own struggles with food and her dieting over the years had contributed to Katy's problems with eating. Anna Marie was grateful that since Katy's trip to the Southwind and the subsequent rebuilding of Katy's life, Katy had found a way to come to grips with her Anorexia. Maybe she, too, had learned on that brief trip not to use food as self-punishment and to take joy out of food?

The teakettle boiled as she prepared a treat for herself. The wind increased outside, rain beating at the side of the house. Anna Marie heard branches scratching against the side of the house, causing some of the old shingles to loosen. She turned the radio on to listen to any storm warnings issued. As she slowly ate her lunch and drank her tea, she listened to the storm outside, transported back to the Southwind seven years before.

Seven years earlier, somewhere in Montana

It was raining cats and dogs, an expression that originated during times of thatched roofs when heavy rains brought burrowing animals pouring into the houses from rooftops. Anna Marie could barely see the road and knew she had no choice but to pull off at the next exit.

Of course, Murphy's Law always held true; this was the most rural exit she could have found, with no obvious services available at the exit. No signs had advertised this exit, but Anna Marie hoped they could find a small local service station or restaurant. They could wait it out in the motorhome, but the propane tank was low, and she had no idea how soon she would find a service station or campground to replenish the tank.

She was also concerned that she should park the Southwind on high ground, as she was unfamiliar with what streams might be in the area or low-lying roads that could easily flood.

Christa pointed out the handmade sign on the side of the road after they had turned off the expressway that read, *"Ma's Hilltop Café and Bar."*

Anna Marie asked Christa and Granny Rose, "Do you think a place called Ma's could be all that bad? It does say hilltop so it must be on higher ground than here."

They all agreed that it was worth a try since they had few other options other than cold food and flooding roads. Anna Marie headed down the isolated country road in the direction the sign indicated. A large dirt parking lot greeted them at the top of a small hill full of pickup trucks, relatively small tractor-trailers, and four-wheelers.

After placing food out for Little Bear and Maya, both

appearing content to stay sleeping through the downpour, and covering Circe's cage, the three rushed headlong through the rain to the old wooden door with another hand-printed sign.

Inside was a dimly lit room full of men in flannel shirts, despite the recent hot summer weather, and jeans or coveralls. A few belched loudly as they entered and there was the sound of a fart from across the room. All the men in the room turned to watch silently as the three women entered the room.

Anna Marie mumbled to herself loud enough for the other two to hear, "I am so glad that I have accomplished my goal number one after seeing this motley excuse for the opposite sex."

Christa asked her what she meant as Granny responded loudly at the same moment the jukebox in the corner shut off, "I think she's talking about sex, honey!"

A few of the eyes lit up in the room as fond, long forgotten memories were apparently renewed. One man in the very back of the room made an obscene gesture. Those closest to him laughed.

Quickly changing the subject, Anna Marie asked the men in the room, "Is Ma here?"

A man dirtier than the rest, wearing an apron that had not been described as white or clean in many years, stepped out from the back of a counter littered with crumbs, ketchup, and dirty plates.

"I'm Ma. Who's asking and why?" he said gruffly.

Anna Marie shakily answered, "We had to get off the expressway because of the heavy rain. Our propane tank is low. We thought your sign indicated you were a café as well as a bar?"

Someone else belched from across the room and another man laughed, "You can call it whatever you want, sweetheart. I hope you all have strong stomachs, bad eyesight, and poor smell."

A small wiry man dressed in clean clothes, for this group of men, with a bright red flannel shirt and jeans, weaseled his way to the table with a broad smile said, "I think we've hit pay dirt today! Don't mind these men. They've forgotten their manners.

We're pleased to have you join us for a bite to eat. Ma here is called that because he was once a sergeant in the army. He was a cook in the same army and was so miserable that the men called him Ma because he was the farthest thing from most of their mothers. It's what you easterners call an irony."

The man continued explaining, "Especially with his cooking that is still barely edible today! We all humor him by eating his food for various reasons such as starvation or someone's latest wife or girlfriend has left him for the mailman."

The man paused and then held his hand out to the middle of the table, hoping at least one of the women would be brave enough to take it.

He said, "I'm Harry Matter. Let me introduce you to some of my boys."

None of the women took his hand, though Granny Rose looked like she was just about to take it. Harry Matter turned to the rest of the room to make introductions, placing a name with each body and face.

Harry asked, "Your names are…?"

Anna Marie hesitated and then introduced each of them to the very dirty-looking, ragged group. She thought giving a name to each of them might make them more human to the men. She had once read that the best thing to do in a hostile situation was make yourself human to your aggressors, not that any of the men were being openly aggressive.

The room became a little less frightening as the minutes ticked by with no one assaulting them yet, so Anna Marie asked, "Are these all your sons, Harry?"

Harry nodded and then said, "Most of them. Some are son-in-laws or brother-in-laws. Except for Ma. I wouldn't want to be related to that son of a B. Unfortunately, I am. He was married to my sister many years ago. She left him two weeks after the wedding. None of us knows why but I bet it wasn't pretty. I don't even credit him with being my brother-in-law. Unfortunately, in this area of the country relationships like that stick like glue!"

"Could we possibly see a menu?" Christa asked shyly, her hunger overcoming her better judgment.

This question caused quite an outburst of laughter amongst the men.

One said from the corner, "Yeah Ma, give the ladies a menu! We'd like to see the menu, too!"

Ma responded, "There ain't no menu. Do you think this is one of those big city Bee-stroos or something? What I'm cooking today is what you get."

Christa, still thinking of the hunger pains she felt, became braver and asked, "And what is it you are cooking today?"

Harry answered, "It's probably some stew. We've found it is best not to ask what's in it."

Ma asked, "Do you want to eat or don't you?"

Anna Marie began to think that the crackers in the RV looked like a better choice than the options in this "bar and grill."

She couldn't figure out how they could tactfully get out of this and safely get back to the Southwind, so she nodded and answered, "Yes, we do want to eat" for all three of them.

It was still raining so hard she couldn't see outside the muddy windows, but they could hear it pounding on the tin roof. Anna Marie had no desire to go out to the motorhome in this downpour. A few areas of the room were leaking and there was a mouse in the corner shivering from the rain. Anna Marie hoped its relatives were not already in the "stew."

As if to confirm her decision to stay inside the bar being the right one, lightening split across the sky with no time difference from the strike or the thunder.

She heard someone murmur, "I hope that hit a tree rather than my truck."

While they had been talking, Granny Rose got up from her chair wandering around the room, looking each man in the face. Anna Marie was afraid she would upset one of the men. She noticed they each seemed to be accepting Granny Rose with good humor so she relaxed her concern, remembering her promise to take time before concluding these men were dangerous or bad. Granny Rose had moved throughout the room staring at every man, including Ma, leaving the man who introduced himself as Harry for last. She returned to the table and stood in front of Harry, staring into his eyes.

Suddenly, she said softly, "Harry-Jim-Bob."

Harry looked extremely surprised looking closely into Granny Rose's face.

Anna Marie corrected Granny Rose, "No, Granny Rose this is Harry, our new friend we have just met."

Granny Rose shook her head and repeated "Harry-Jim-Bob" over and over.

Anna Marie apologized to Harry for Granny Rose's mistake. Harry stopped her mid-sentence.

"No, I once was known as Harry-Jim-Bob. I was a three-instrument one-man band. Harry was the guitarist, Jim played the accordion, and Bob the harmonica of the group. I traveled all over Northeast Texas and parts of Louisiana. I was quite famous and in demand until I drafted myself into World War II. The casualties of war ended my days of playing. At least I came back alive."

Harry lifted up a the right arm with his left hand pointing out the hand no longer functioned.

He continued, "This was my playing hand. I couldn't even play one of my instruments, let alone three, after this was injured. The only good thing was I came home from the war before it killed me completely. I was able to do trucking after the war and that brought me to Montana. I've outlived two wives and have all this family around to show for my life. Not too bad a trade-off."

He looked somewhat proudly around the room.

Granny Rose still stared intently at Harry. She listened carefully to him, watching him display his arm to the ladies. Anna Marie tried to determine if this was a lucid moment or a moment of confusion for Granny. Anna Marie thought how most of Granny Rose's responses these days seemed to be very coherent and in fact, often gems of wisdom. She wondered if it was the hearing aids that she used on and off as she felt like it, or if they had just become accustomed to Granny Rose's strange behavior.

Harry stared back at Granny Rose; both were silent for minutes.

Harry said, "I'm curious. What did you say her name was?"

Anna Marie and Christa both said at the same time, "We call her Granny Rose."

Neither chose to explain any further. Harry hesitated a moment and then searched for change in his pocket. After finding a quarter, he walked across the room and looked at the Juke Box for a few minutes, placing the quarter in the slot and made selections. In a couple of seconds, the music of often associated with striptease acts played on the Juke Box.

Granny Rose listened and then smiled. Slowly, she began to move to the rhythm of the music.

Anna Marie and Christa watched without suspecting what was going to happen next. Granny Rose moved faster and faster, increasingly sensuous in her movements to the music with an expression on her face that made her appear at least 20 years younger.

Before Anna Marie or Christa could stop her, she was in the middle of the room removing her sweater, all the men still while she remained moving seductively with the music. The room was totally quiet. Anna Marie suddenly realized what was about to happen and tried to move towards Granny to discourage her.

Harry put his arm gently on Anna Marie and softly said, "Leave her alone. Can't you see she is happy? This is right for her, something she is very familiar with, and takes her back to her youth. You'll understand soon."

Granny Rose saw Anna Marie attempting to stop her. She loudly ordered Anna Marie, "Maria Anna, I'm your mother. Leave me alone. I know what I am doing."

Anna Marie looked at Granny Rose realizing Harry was right.

Any interference from Anna Marie or a reminder that she was not Anna Marie's mother was likely to result in upsetting Granny Rose. This was obviously Granny Rose's decision to make. Anna Marie sat back down, in dread of the next few moments though not knowing what else to do.

Christa looked confusedly at Anna Marie following her lead of watching Granny Rose and not interfering with her.

As the men became aware of what was happening, they each began clapping to the music. The room became full of the sound of clapping with everyone in the room mesmerized by Granny's movements. Rhythmically, Granny Rose removed her blouse, shoes, slacks, and knee-high stockings. All in the room seemed to have forgotten Granny's age, caught up with the natural ease of Granny's movements.

Anna Marie noticed for the first time a bright blue pennant in the shape of a crescent moon on a gold chain Granny wore. Anna Marie tried to determine what the object was made of and guessed that it was turquoise. It was obviously displayed against Granny Rose's skin. Anna Marie wondered why she had not paid attention to the necklace before. She planned to ask Granny Rose about the pennant when she had a chance in the future if they survived this incident without getting raped, mugged, or attacked.

Granny now moved around the room with only her cotton underpants, still perfectly in tune with the music. The men watched her movements intently as they clapped in unison to the music, each mesmerized by her movements. Despite her age, she was extremely muscular, with very small breasts, and few wrinkles. Granny occasionally held her breasts erect to offer them as a gift to the men in the room.

The men watched as she approached each man. When she stood directly in front of one of the men, he reached into his pockets for a dollar bill or loose change. Unfortunately, several of the men only had loose change. The men placed their offerings into Granny's underpants. Granny kissed each one on the forehead in thanks as she continued to move to the music. After the kiss, each man's face shone, bestowed with a blessing from a beautiful, ageless woman.

She now had to hold her underpants up as the change began to weigh down her underpants. Ma, the last man before Granny Rose reached Harry, pulled a twenty-dollar bill out of his pocket and placed it reverently in Granny's underpants like making a spiritual offering. His face was transformed, enthralled by a miracle that had happened in front of his eyes. A few of the men wiped away tears, the rest of the men beamed or clapped harder.

Granny Rose approached Harry last just as the music was ending. She turned to the entire room and bowed to the room as it erupted into thunderous applause. Anna Marie and Christa had not moved since the beginning of Rose's intoxicating dancing. The two looked stunned, afraid to breathe or move as much from the shock of Granny Rose's beauty in dance as from the unusual circumstance they found themselves in on this very strange day.

Harry cheered and clapped along with the other men, his face a bright red and a smile almost broader than his face. As Granny came up from her bow, he approached her, hugging her tightly.

He exclaimed in awe, "This is the famous Rose of Aberdeen. I can't believe you have come back into my life!"

Harry squeezed Granny Rose tighter and tighter. Granny did not resist in the slightest as she returned his hug. Harry then removed his flannel shirt over his long-sleeved turtleneck sweater and helped Granny put the shirt on. The shirt fell far below her knees with plenty of room to spare.

Granny Rose coquettishly thanked "Harry-Jim-Bob" for his shirt, giving him a quick kiss on the cheeks and a flash of her still very clear blue eyes.

Harry helped her remove the money from Granny's underpants, until Anna Marie quickly stepped in, angrily stated, "I'll help her, Harry. She must return the money to each of the men."

Granny Rose stepped back and vehemently said to Anna Marie, "I don't think so. I earned that money fair and square. It's not yours to decide."

The men all nodded in agreement, mumbling yes like the sound of a British Parliament meeting. They turned their backs from the women, realizing that the dance was over, not wanting to take on Anna Marie, who looked particularly fearsome.

Harry yelled to Ma, "This deserves a celebration. Bring out a keg of beer and make sure you cook the best meal possible. Forget your stew. I'm paying for everyone. I hope you can all free up this afternoon."

As he spoke, another bolt of lightning lit up the outside sky followed by a crash of thunder. The men individually nodded, settling back into their chairs or corners of the room. Harry brought a fifty-dollar bill out of his pocket.

The men cheered. Granny Rose looked extremely pleased with herself. Ma grabbed the bill before Harry changed his mind, sprinted to the back of the café for a keg of beer.

After setting up the keg and pouring the first beer for himself, he rushed to the back to begin cooking. Anna Marie hoped for hamburgers and hot dogs that might be edible. Harry poured beer in paper cups for each of the ladies, though Christa refused the beer explaining she was pregnant, even though it should have been evident to Harry. Harry found a root beer in a bottle behind the bar for Christa, as Ma was busy cooking in the back.

Harry and the ladies sat back down at the table as the men poured themselves one beer after another. A party had quickly broken out with none of the men paying attention to the four at the table.

Harry quietly explained to Anna Marie and Christa, "This here is Rose of Aberdeen. She was the best stripper in New Orleans, known all over the region. I was fortunate to play many times just before her performance. In those days, Rose of Aberdeen was a friend to me. I thought of her as more than a friend, but I couldn't compete with her audience of admirers."

Harry stopped, appearing to be lost in the past and then continued, "She was wooed by famous or wealthy politicians, ranchers, and businessmen. We all loved her and any one of us would have been proud to have her as our wife or girlfriend. Look at her. She was just as beautiful then as she is now. I can't believe my luck in seeing her again after all these years. What more could a man ask for in life? Now, I could die a happy man."

Harry beamed from ear to ear. Anna Marie shook her head thinking about this strange turn of events. She knew she would need more time to untangle this new revelation about Granny Rose. She wondered if there would be more to come.

The party lasted through the afternoon. Anna Marie and Christa became comfortable enough to party along with the men including an impromptu conga dance, a roaring cheer for Rose of Aberdeen, and a cheer for Harry for paying for the afternoon with accompanying gulps of beer.

In one corner of the room a card game broke out. The men invited Anna Marie and Christa to join them in poker, explaining the rules of the game, assuming neither of the ladies had played before. Anna Marie's natural competitiveness broke out. She became totally absorbed in beating the men as a pile of pennies grew in front of both Christa and Anna Marie. Some of the men grumbled that the ladies had pretended they didn't know poker pulling a switch and bait on them. Anna Marie did not respond to the accusations as she knew them to be true.

The biggest loser of all grumbled good-naturedly, "This was a set-up, wasn't it? First you bring in your stripper to get us excited, have us plied with food and drink, and then pretend you know nothing about cards. You're winning the money back for Harry!"

Anna Marie laughed while Christa raked in her latest winnings.

During most of this time Granny Rose and Harry sat in the corner talking quietly. When Granny needed anything, Harry rose quickly to meet her every need. He looked like he was entertaining the most beautiful woman in the world, a look of pure pleasure and enjoyment on his face.

Occasionally, Anna Marie looked up from her poker game to make sure that Granny Rose was comfortable. Rose remained in Harry's flannel shirt, but since it looked so warm and covered Granny completely, Anna Marie didn't worry about asking her to change back into her own clothes. In fact, she was pleased that Granny remained dressed, not breaking out into another performance the rest of the afternoon. She was so relieved that she didn't want to break up the conversation possibly starting Granny Rose dancing, stripping, or some other outrageous action.

Anna Marie was surprised Granny Rose appeared to understand the conversation completely as it seemed the conversation with Harry was a two-sided conversation, two old friends catching up with their lives. Once again, Anna Marie wondered if Granny Rose really had dementia or if she chose not to understand when it was useful for her to pretend confusion.

While her conversations and understanding had improved remarkably after the hearing test and wearing the new aids, there were still days when Granny Rose seemed to make little sense or to be dazing off in a world of her own. She still made comments that were bewildering to Anna Marie and Christa. Today was a day she was not wearing the hearing aids and yet, seemed to clearly understand her conversation with Harry.

Anna Marie thought it was possible Harry was good at pretending that they were carrying on a normal conversation. She applauded him silently for the respect for Granny Rose he was demonstrating.

An hour after the performance, 'Mom' came out with platters of hamburgers, steaks, and hot dogs, opening bags of potato chips, Doritos, and salsa at the same time. The heated rolls were piled high adding to the tables feast. After depositing the first stack of food on the table, he went back into the kitchen for homemade macaroni salad and chili that were quite good. Everyone in the room, including the ladies, ate hungrily, enjoying an unexpected free meal.

After the meal, Ma poured strong delicious smelling coffee for everyone. Though the ladies rarely drank coffee, they each enjoyed a cup. Christa drank hers with half cream and half coffee. Anna Marie thought once again what a wonderful mother Christa was going to be, taking such care to assure the health of her coming baby.

The rain never let up throughout the day. It was becoming apparent to Anna Marie that they would have to stay parked in the parking lot for the night as the roads still looked unsafe for travel with almost no visibility. One of the men, John, offered to go to the next town to fill the propane tank and return the filled tank in the morning. Anna Marie took him up on his offer. Some of the men quietly left, Anna Marie assumed to rejoin their families or jobs. As very few of the men remained, except for two passed out in the corner, Anna Marie thought it was time for the ladies to go back to the Southwind.

Christa and Granny Rose quietly followed Anna Marie back to the RV. Anna Marie gave Little Bear a quick walk in the parking lot, feeding the three animals before everyone returned to their favorite napping places.

Before leaving the Café, Granny Rose whispered something to Harry, gave him a kiss on the cheek, and a strong hug that was returned enthusiastically by Harry. Anna Marie had picked up Granny Rose's clothes into a bundle, though Granny Rose clung to Harry's shirt indicating she was not going to give it back to Harry.

Harry shrugged, waving them out as he said goodnight.

After a light supper of crackers, rolls, and cheese, another quick walk for Little Bear, all the ladies settled down early for the night. The beer and activity caught up with Anna Marie as had the activity had also exhausted the now obviously pregnant Christa. Granny Rose was energized by the afternoon's events but went to bed along with the other two without protest. Anna Marie and Christa, along with the animals, slept through the night without waking up until the sun rose high in the sky.

Close to morning, the rain finally stopped. Little Bear woke Anna Marie up later than usual with her wet nose to let Anna Marie know she needed to go outside and was also hungry. Anna Marie stretched, quickly put on a raincoat over her jogging suit, taking Little Bear out for the requested walk.

On her way out she nudged Christa to wake up, noticing Granny Rose was curled up solidly under the covers next to Christa. She decided to let Granny Rose sleep a little bit longer as she must be extremely tired after the previous day's excitement and performance.

The day dawned a perfect sunny, crisp morning as is often the case after a heavy rainstorm. Anna Marie and Little Bear did a little longer walk than usual down the country road since Little Bear had so little exercise the day before. The birds celebrated the return of the sun by singing and flying around the two as they walked. Anna Marie felt like the world was currently picture perfect, somehow landing in a Disney movie.

She was amazed at the new unlikely friends she had made. Once again, she was reminded that initial appearances often hid the good character underneath. She had to keep reminding herself of this advice to herself so that she didn't miss out on meeting wonderful people and enjoying life to its fullest. She knew coming to quick conclusions about people had always been one of her flaws and was grateful for the opportunity to change that spontaneous reaction. She hoped this would be a lasting change for her, even with continual reminders.

They only had to travel a short distance this day to the next RV Park where they had made reservations. Anna Marie was grateful as they could all use a few days' rest. The area looked like a beautiful region to explore with their new friends giving them some personal tours of the surrounding countryside, as they had offered at the impromptu celebration the day before.

She was surprised Harry had said goodbye so quickly last night to Granny Rose. She thought he must have assumed they would stay in the area for a few more days. She still thought he might have wanted to prolong his goodbye to Granny Rose since he claimed she was the "love of a lifetime."

Anna Marie shook her head, amazed that Granny Rose had once been the Rose of Aberdeen. Yesterday's events were now such a blur she wondered if she had dreamt the whole event. In fact, as she thought about it, this whole trip was like a hazy gift with new adventures and friends every place she stopped. She hugged herself in gratitude for the Southwind and all that had been given to her because of her risk-taking.

She whispered to the pink and vibrant blue sky above, "Ted, you would be proud of me. You would have loved this trip yourself. I hope you are taking it with me from afar."

Then she reminded herself inwardly, "As long as he didn't observe the Walter affair." It was not her finest moment.

One of the birds overhead flew in closer to Anna Marie and Little Bear. Anna Marie suspected they were giving her a message that Ted was close overhead watching her and still loving her. She assured herself he would have ignored Walter entirely.

As Little Bear and she approached the parking lot, Christa came towards them.

Christa looked around nervously, "Granny Rose isn't with you? I thought she was as she got up long before I did. Where is she?"

Anna Marie looked puzzled, "I thought she was in bed with you still. It looked like she was sleeping so I didn't wake her when I woke you. Wasn't she still there?"

Christa shook her head and said, "No. Those were just pillows stuffed under the bed covers. She very carefully made sure we thought she was sleeping. Where could she be? I'm worried about her, Anna Marie. Did you notice she never returned Harry's shirt and he didn't ask for it. Isn't that kind of strange?"

As they talked, a door in the back of Ma's Café and bar opened. Two very tired but ecstatic looking people came out of the door, hand in hand. Both Anna Marie and Christa recognized with shock it was Granny Rose and Harry.

Harry looked down at his pants, quickly zipping them up, saying, "Oops!"

Granny Rose looked extremely ruffled. Anna Marie noticed that she still had on Harry's shirt. It had been buttoned up wrong exposing the top of one of Rose's tiny breasts. Little Bear wagged her tail, pulling Anna Marie towards Granny Rose. Granny Rose blushed like a young girl while Harry looked extremely pleased with himself.

Little Bear pulled Anna Marie, who could be surprisingly strong when the small dog desired. She and Christa stared with total shock at the couple. Both were relatively speechless since it was obvious what had happened—it seemed too unbelievable to even consider or put into words. Both Anna Marie and Christa knew there could be no other explanation, reluctantly trying to grasp the apparent situation but hoping for a different clarification than the obvious.

Little Bear ignored all the others, rubbing up against Granny Rose, very happy to see her. Little Bear looked at Granny Rose's companion, waiting for an introduction that usually ended with being told how cute she was or something else complimentary.

As Granny Rose reached down to hug Little Bear, Harry's shirt fell a little further down her shoulder revealing surprisingly young-looking skin.

Harry left their side and came over to Anna Marie.

He said, "Anna Marie, Rose and I have something to tell you."

He hesitated, obviously aware of the look of shock on both Anna Marie and Christa's faces and the total silence.

Then he took a deep breath, ignored the expressions on their face, and continued, "Rose and I are in love. We have decided with the little time either of us might have left we are going to marry. Rose has done me the honor of saying yes. We're not waiting another minute longer than necessary. We have decided to get married on Saturday. Rose can speak for herself, but both of us would be honored if you and Christa would give us away in marriage."

Harry looked extremely pleased and very shy, for the first time since they met him. Granny Rose nodded and beamed at Harry while she flirtatiously adjusted her shirt, covering her shoulder but still looking like a virgin who had just experienced her first pleasurable sexual experience.

Anna Marie uncharacteristically roughly handed Christa Little Bear's lead, yanking Harry away from Granny Rose.

She said harshly, "I need to speak to you Harry, right now!"

Anna Marie was so upset that she spoke loudly to Harry before they had walked more than a few feet away from the others. Her anger made her not care who heard her or how carefully she spoke to Harry.

She exclaimed, "What is wrong with you? Granny Rose is almost old enough to be your mother. This is the most disgusting thing I have ever seen. Do you think she has money or something? She is worth absolutely nothing. I've been supporting her all summer as we've tried to find her family."

A coughing fit stopped her for seconds. Ignoring her throat's discomfort, she continued. "If she ever had money as a dancer she certainly has never shown us any now. She is too old for you and too old to be getting married to a man she barely knows. She may have a living husband for all we know. What could you be thinking of, leading her on this way? She is already confused enough about who she is and where she belongs. I'm not even related to her, but she is so confused she insists that she's my mother."

Harry turned to Anna Marie, taking her firmly but gently by the shoulders.

He looked her straight in the eyes and asked, "First of all, keep your voice down so that you don't hurt Rose with your words."

He continued softly but forcefully, "Who do you think you are? You have no right to decide who can love or marry. Why do you think you can call our love "disgusting"? Our love and our decisions are our own business to call them what we prefer. We were including you because you are Rose's family, whether you want to claim her as your family or not. We didn't ask for permission from you. We were trying to include you in something important to us. I'm not looking for anything but love and some moments of happiness with Rose. That's more than any of us can ask out of life, money just gets in the way. We are adults who have the right to make whatever choices we want."

Harry stomped his foot as he said, "You have no right to try to take away our joy in finding each other after all these years."

Anna Marie responded bitterly, "But she is too old and probably has dementia. She can't make these kinds of decisions for herself. You don't even know her. Just because you obviously had sex last night doesn't mean that she has the capacity to decide to marry you. Why, you could even be accused of raping a woman who doesn't have the ability to consent. She probably has no idea what marrying you would mean or that she would be living with you on a permanent basis."

She hesitated, the added one more horrible thought, "I hope you didn't hurt her last night as she is very old to be having sex!"

Harry removed his hands from Anna Marie's shoulders, still speaking firmly, inches from Anna Marie's face, with no hesitation or apology.

"I know more about Rose than you ever will. I don't see an old person who is demented. I look at Rose of Aberdeen. That is what she will always be to me. That we loved each other last night has nothing to do with it and was far more than sex. How dare you try to take that away from us too, something that is meant for the joy of humans regardless of their ages? What we did last night is none of your business. It is certainly nothing illegal by the wildest stretch of the imagination."

Harry brushed off the sweat that had built up on his forehead.

He exclaimed, "Rose was able to teach me things last night that I couldn't even have dreamed about. She was certainly a very willing partner. We had a history together that we still share and understand. Maybe Rose gets confused occasionally. Who doesn't when we were younger or when we are older?

She is not confused over wanting to spend the rest of her life with me. Maybe because I see her as a beautiful, loving woman. You see her as a needy old lady that requires your care. You tell her what to think and do is the better life than the freedom of choice to live as she wants? Do you have the right to deny us our happiness, our life?"

Harry paused for a breath before continuing, "What gives you the right to take away Rose's happiness because it doesn't seem correct to you? I'm surprised that a daughter of Rose's would be so self-righteous. And if Rose thinks you are her daughter, there is a reason beyond dementia. You ought to be thrilled she thinks of you in that way."

Anna Marie protested, "I am not her daughter, just someone she chose to attach herself to when she wanted to run away from her sons. She thinks I'm her daughter and that shows you how demented she is. I've only known her a few months, yet she talks to people like she has known me all her life. I've grown to love her and feel responsible for her safety. I do not see Granny Rose, I mean Rose…"

She stopped and thought about Harry's hurtful words. Tears came to her eyes, shocked at her own ageism. She closed them so that Harry could not see her tears or her sudden realization of a truth she had left uncovered. She was immediately taken back thirty-five years to Ted and her standing in the living room of his parents' home.

In her memories, Ted's mother spoke loudly, "We don't approve of her. She is not good enough for you, Ted. After all we've done for you, this is what you do to us. She is just after your money. She's not of our religion or our background. How could you even consider marriage to this opportunist?"

Ted had responded that Anna Marie and he were getting married. His parents were either welcome to come to the wedding or they could choose to ignore his love by staying away from the most important celebration of his life. The young couple left the house with his mother crying in the living room, while his father sadly motioned for them to go. Neither had come to the wedding.

It was not until their first child, daughter Katy, was born that Ted's mother spoke to them. Over the years she had declared a truce with Anna Marie. Most of the time she spoke about Anna Marie like she was not in the room. She never let Anna Marie forget that she was not good enough for her Ted. Anna Marie often wondered how someone as kind as Ted could have come from such spiteful parents.

Anna Marie's thoughts moved ahead to Ted's funeral. His mother had arrived at the funeral late.

She immediately blamed Anna Marie for not giving her the right time and then said; "I knew all along you were no good for Ted. He killed himself trying to work to give you everything you wanted. I'm surprised that you are having church services for him since you couldn't be bothered to raise the children in a proper religion. I will make sure you never see any of our money. It's bad enough you have taken Ted's all these years."

This was said loudly, in front of Anna Marie's friends and her children. Thankfully, Diana had seen what was happening, tactfully leading Anna Marie away from Ted's mother while motioning to Erin to take his grandmother to another section of the room.

Harry touched Anna Marie's hand. She had been standing so still she frightened him.

He gently said, "Anna Marie, I only want to make Rose happy. Dreams of Rose of Aberdeen kept me alive in the foxholes in Germany. Even though we had only friendship between us over that year she touched my heart. I married too quickly; afraid I would not survive the war. When I returned injured from the war, I tried to find her to let her know that, but she had disappeared out of sight. I couldn't search any longer as it was not fair to my wife."

Harry clarified, "She tells me that she was married and left dancing in the club to have children and raise a family. She stayed in an abusive marriage to care for her children, some who did not survive long. Her husband, a mayor of the city of Fayetteville when she met him, turned out to be a scoundrel who rarely took care of his family. He never let Rose forget she was a stripper, beating her frequently. I think Rose learned to forget much about her life and live each day as she could. That may explain why she appears forgetful at times. I wouldn't be surprised if one or two of his sons takes after the old man, beating her for her Social Security check each month and what was left of the estate."

Harry looked pleadingly at Anna Marie, "For some unknown reason Rose was brought back into my life. I am going to make her happy for as long as we both live. I don't care how old she is or how forgetful, all I see is the Rose of Aberdeen who makes me feel young again. And something I can tell you, Maria Anne existed. I knew her and loved her. You should be pleased to be mistaken for her."

As Harry spoke, Anna Marie's cell phone rang. Anna Marie cursed herself for not shutting the phone off more frequently now that her family had adjusted to her trip. Though she was a little relieved for the interruption in the intense moment. She turned away from Harry and Granny Rose to take the call. The voice on the other end was Walter's.

He talked loudly, screaming across the miles, "Anna Marie! I'm glad I caught you at a good time. My wife left a few minutes ago for a shopping trip. We are planning one hell of an anniversary celebration for this weekend if you catch my drift."

Anna Marie could imagine Walter winking at her over the telephone line. She sniffed into the phone, walking further away from her waiting friends.

Walter paused briefly, obviously hearing Anna Marie's sniffing and asked, "Anna Marie, what's the matter? You're not still upset over our breaking up, are you? I thought we had resolved this issue."

Anna Marie laughed despite how upset she was with Harry and Granny Rose.

She responded, "No, Walter. It has nothing to do with you and your minute-by-minute descriptions of your love life. Granny Rose met someone here in Montana she knew in a previous life. He's quite a bit younger than her. To make a long story short, she thinks she's going to marry him and live happily ever after even though he is almost young enough to be her son."

There was silence on the other end as Walter took in Anna Marie's news.

He then asked, "And you are upset why?"

Anna Marie exclaimed, "Well, isn't it obvious? He's too young for her and it's just not right."

Walter said in a much quieter and more soothing voice, "It's not right by whose standards, Anna Marie? Yours, or the rest of the world's standards? Since when have you taken such a moral stance? I can remember a wonderful woman who changed my life because she lived the moment we were together. She didn't worry about what the world thought of our private time together."

"Anna Marie, it may be hard for you to accept, but you cannot control other people's lives," Walter stated firmly. "They will make their own decisions and own mistakes; all you can do is hope for the best and live fully along with them. At one time you would have asked the question, who is it hurting? If the answer is nobody, then it is not even an issue."

His tone changed and he continued speaking uncharacteristically in a soft voice, "From what you have told me of Granny Rose and the brief time I met her in Wyoming, I suspect she can take care of herself. At her age, she has the right to make decisions for herself. It only hurts you because you are letting it hurt you. Let it go and be happy when anyone can find love, even if only for a brief time. Answer this: Are you a little bit jealous because you hoped it would be you rather than Rose?"

Anna Marie was silent for a few seconds as she absorbed the surprising wisdom and criticism from Walter.

She softly asked Walter, "Can we talk tomorrow? I am thinking of what you just said. I need time to think it all through. Thank you, Walter. You really have turned out to be a good friend."

As she hung up the phone, she felt guilty for her immediate reaction, especially thinking about her own life and Ted's mother along with Walter's words.

The next thought that came to her was, "Granny Rose came into my life and now she will be leaving it."

Granny Rose, reading Anna Marie's mind, came over to Anna Marie, took her hand and drew her closer to her to give her a slight hug.

Reassuring her she said, "Maria Anne, I will always be a part of you as I was a part of you before we met. My path is meant to be with Harry now, for what remains of my life. Please don't be upset or cry. It was what was meant to happen and why I joined you on this trip. None of us knew this or expected me to rejoin the love of my life, but there it is. Sometimes life gives you gifts that more than make up for the difficult moments."

Granny Rose looked over to Harry and then back at Anna Marie.

"Harry's and my path are supposed to come together now at the end of our lives. You still have other adventures, people to meet, and time to learn about who you are. Someday you will understand that you are my daughter, as Christa is yours. We are all related with shared histories, even if they didn't occur in this generation or era. We all are from the same mother, all one. Me staying here while you go on doesn't change that. I love you, Maria Anna, and I always will."

Anna Marie hugged Granny Rose as if she never wanted to let her go. It felt so right. Maybe Granny Rose had been one of her mothers. At that moment, Anna Marie stopped questioning why Granny Rose insisted she was her mother, realizing it no longer mattered. What was important was the love and experiences they had shared in their brief shared respite of time.

Christa came over to the two women, placing her hands on each of the hugging women, all three crying from the emotions of loss and tremendous gain. Harry stood quietly to the side with his hands in his pockets, whistling a soft tune as he observed the beauty of the three women, the matriarch, the mother, and the young maid who was soon to become a mother herself.

Harry sighed at his good fortune in finding Rose of Aberdeen and the lovely women with her.

Finally, Anna Marie stopped crying. She looked at Granny Rose, motioning for Harry to join them.

"Tell me your plans and what you need us to do to help you. This is going to be a magical celebration. I want to help you make it special. I'm sorry for being so miserable about your happiness," she said.

Later that evening, while Granny Rose was still with Harry meeting some of his relatives and Christa was walking Little Bear, the phone rang. Anna Marie heard Sergeant George's voice and responded to his greeting with a gut feeling of bad news.

Sergeant George quickly confirmed her fears, "Anna Marie, I think we have good news, maybe not so good news. A couple of men came into the station this afternoon claiming they were Granny Rose's sons. I asked why it had taken so long to respond to our search. They indicated that the nursing home had told them Granny Rose was likely dead since it had been so long since she disappeared. According to the men, the nursing home was responsible for looking for her. At least that's the story they told me. I haven't confirmed it with the nursing home yet. I asked for proof that they were her sons. They had her birth certificate, pictures of someone who looks like Granny Rose, pictures of their families with Granny Rose, and some other personal items. From the Granny Rose I met, it looks to be the right person."

Anna Marie drew in a deep breath and said, "I'm not sure if this is good news or not, Sergeant G. Just this afternoon, Granny Rose informed me she is getting married to someone she knew years ago whom we happened to meet by accident in a bar because of a rainstorm. That may not sound like a good choice for us, but given the circumstances, the bar and cafe was the only safe choice we had at the time."

She paused while waiting for a response from Sergeant G. With no response coming soon, Anna Marie continued.

"The wedding is planned for next weekend. And strange as it seems, I think it is the right thing for her to do. You can't believe how happy she looks, as well as years younger. I've also been told there was major abuse of her by her husband and possibly sons. I'm afraid we would be opening her up to all kinds of problems. Why now?"

Sergeant George responded, "They mentioned they wanted to get to her as soon as possible as there were problems releasing the estate to them since they do not have proof she died. There was something about these boys I just didn't like. I'm giving you the information and you can do with it what you think is right. I told them it had been a long time since I heard from you and I didn't know if I could contact your traveling party. I told them I would get back to them if I was able to make contact. I am legally bound to be honest with them, so please don't tell me where you are. I should have already turned over your telephone number to them, but I wanted to talk to you first."

Anna Marie thought for a minute and said, "I need to talk this over with Granny Rose. It's her life and her decision. Can you give me until tomorrow to get back to you and tell you what to do?"

Sergeant George answered, "Of course. They've waited this long. They can wait another day. I hope you figure out the best thing for me to do without me violating my oath of office and still doing what is best for Granny Rose."

Anna Marie agreed with him, wishing him goodnight.

Christa entered the Southwind at that moment, noticing the look on Anna Marie's face. She asked, "You're not still upset over Granny Rose's marriage, are you?"

Anna Marie answered, "No, I just got off the phone with one of the Sergeant's George. The sons have turned up looking for Granny Rose, showing sudden concern. It appears they have not been able to legally get her estate. We need to go to

Granny Rose and see what she wants us to do. Sergeant George has given us until tomorrow to tell him if Granny Rose gives permission to release her telephone number to her sons. If we don't tell him to give them the number, he wants us to figure out how he can do this legally."

The night was misty and cool enough that both Christa and Anna Marie needed sweaters. They were uncharacteristically silent as they waited at the door to Harry's dark cabin for someone to answer their knock, each deep in her own thoughts. After a few minutes, a light came on. Harry came to the door, obviously having woken up from a deep sleep.

Anna Marie quickly said, "I'm sorry to bother you. We really need to talk with Granny Rose."

Harry asked, "You're not here to persuade her to leave me again. Because she's set on us marrying. There is nothing you can do to talk her out of it."

Anna Marie shook her head and said, "No, we just received a call from Sergeant George. Granny Rose's sons have turned up looking for her. I need to talk to her to help us figure out what we should do. Whatever we do, we can't put the Sergeant Georges at risk, as they have been helpful and good friends to us."

Harry agreed to wake up Granny Rose. He returned a few minutes later with a very tired and older-looking Granny Rose.

Granny Rose agitatedly said, "This had better be good, Maria Anne. I'm not as young as I used to be. All this sex with this wonderful man has worn me right out."

Anna Marie asked, proud for not even blushing over the reference to sex, "Can we talk to you alone for a few moments?"

Granny Rose responded, "Whatever you have to say, you can say it in front of Harry."

Harry, realizing how rude he and Granny Rose had been, invited Christa and Anna Marie inside. They refused the offer of coffee, quickly updating Granny Rose on the phone call from Sergeant George.

Granny Rose sat in silence for a few moments before responding.

She looked at Harry and said, "I will not return to my sons or allow them to find out where I am. They can rot in Hades before I make it easy for them to take my estate. I don't care about the estate, but I do care about them not being part of my life any longer. I left that part of my life behind when I found Marie Anne and Christa."

After a few seconds, she added, "And what is important to me is not part of that estate in Georgia, though I have ideas how to protect some of it. I'll take care of that part on my own."

She looked at Anna Marie and Christa, "What can I do to disappear forever from these men? I have a hard time remembering they are my flesh and blood. Sometimes children just go badly. I think they turned sour the day you left us, Maria Anne."

All were silent for a few minutes, trying to think of a way out that would not jeopardize the integrity of the two Sergeants.

Christa suggested, "What if you gave them proof of your demise? They'd have no reason to try to find you. We wouldn't have to tell the two Sergeants how we got the proof."

Harry chimed in, "I have a good friend who is the editor of the local paper. Could we have him publish a fake obituary in his newspaper and send that to the two Sergeants? That might be enough to give your sons what they want, which is the release of your estate to them. I also have a friend at the City Clerk's office. She might be able to give me a blank death certificate that I could give another friend to fill in."

He asked, "Since we're not doing this to gain anything for ourselves and we're really not hurting anyone, it's not wrong is it?"

The three ladies each responded that there was nothing wrong with what Harry suggested.

When Harry heard their response, he continued, "I don't think any of my friends would mind helping us out. I do have one concern, though. I don't think we should share our plans with the Sergeants. They should think it's legitimate or at least not know what we are doing. Can you do that, Maria Anne?"

Anna Marie noted that Harry already called her by the same name as Granny Rose did. Somehow, that reassured her of his love for Granny Rose rather than making her feel uncomfortable.

After a few seconds of thought, Anna Marie answered, "I need to think about how I can make this work and not look suspicious. I want to support Granny Rose in breaking off contact with her sons."

She turned to Harry, "Granny Rose is an adult who should be able to make her own decisions."

Harry winked at her and patted her arm.

The next morning Harry contacted his friends, beginning the process of paperwork to send to Georgia proving Granny Rose's death. He and Granny Rose spent a great deal of time figuring out the information that should be included in the obituary so it sounded realistic to her sons and the authorities in Georgia.

Anna Marie agonized over the best way to deal with their plans without lying to the Sergeants while she helped Granny Rose in her desire to have her sons believe she had died. Finally, she came up with a solution she felt worked for everyone but one that saddened her.

Later that morning she called the Sergeants.

After talking for a few minutes with Sandra Cass, she greeted Sergeant George and said, "We've come up with a solution. In a short while, we will be faxing some documents to you that you can share with Granny's sons. That should allow them to legally attain the estate. The fax machine will be from another state than the one we are currently in. I don't want to explain any more. I think you shouldn't contact me again so that you are left out of it. I will change my telephone number in the next day and will not contact you again by any private phone number, if at all. You will try to reach me on the number you have to verify the information but will not be able to reach me. As far as you know, the documents you receive are legal."

Anna Marie felt deeply saddened as she said, "It has been wonderful knowing you. I will miss our talks and keeping up with what is happening with your family. In the future, when I can contact you again, I will. But it may be a long time from now."

There was silence on the other end, then Sergeant George said, "I understand why you are doing this. I will miss you, too. You have added so much to our lives here, an extra spark that wasn't there before."

Anna Marie asked, "Can you tell me Granny Rose's last name? I don't even know that."

Sergeant George responded, "The son's last name is Lemier. They did mention that their mother might be going by another name. They also mentioned the name LaRoches or even Turtle. Possibly her maiden name? Or her name could be Mohawk from Upstate New York with a name like Turtle or one of the other Northeast tribes? I do know that is one of the matriarchal clans of the Mohawks."

Anna Marie wrote down the names to follow-up the with Granny Rose later.

Both Anna Marie and Sergeant George hung up the phone with sorrow, knowing they were doing the right thing for Granny Rose. Anna Marie regretted that the Sergeants would not be able to participate in the celebration of Granny Rose's wedding.

The preparation for the wedding proceeded smoothly with no glitches and lots of cooperation from Harry's friends, leaving Granny's new extended family time to plan the wedding celebration.

The Present, Higginsville, NY

Anna Marie had dozed off. The wet nose of Little Bear, along with Maya's tail, woke her as they both tried to take the largest portion of her lap. Anna Marie laughed at their antics. She thought sadly about all she had gained by knowing Granny Rose and all she had lost with her death.

Realizing she could now contact Georgia, she found her address book with Georgia Sergeant's information. She dialed the number, and an unknown voice answered the phone. She learned Sandra Cass had died in her bed after a long day at the office at the age of 86 and that one of the Sergeant Georges had retired.

Sergeant George the Second quickly came on the line when he heard it was Anna Marie, "Anna Marie, hardly a day has gone by that I haven't thought about you; I'm missing our talks."

Anna Marie told him of Granny Rose's death. They talked for several minutes, catching each other up on their lives and happy to talk again.

Sergeant George asked, after sharing with Anna Marie the death of his beloved wife the year before, "Anna Marie, you were such an example to me of someone who learned to go on with her life after losing her loved spouse of many years. Would you mind if I came up to visit you for a few weeks to think over what I want to do next with my life?"

Without hesitation, Anna Marie responded, "I would love to see you again and to have you visit me here."

Sergeant George was obviously pleased with her response.

He said, "I haven't taken time off in years and they owe me some vacation time. There is also a young officer here who is chomping at the bit for my job. I'm thinking it might be time to give it to him. I could stay in a hotel or the Southwind if you still have it. I've been dreaming you would contact me again and I could spend some time with you."

Sergeant George paused.

Anna Marie answered quickly, surprised at how her heart skipped a beat, "You can stay right here in one of my guest bedrooms. I have plenty of room. It will give us more time together. I haven't cooked for anyone for a while. It will be fun to spend some time with you while you decide what you want to do next. You'll have to wait until I come back from Louisiana on an errand. I promised to complete this task for Granny Rose, but any time after that would be fine."

They agreed to talk in a few days about the necessary arrangements and specifics. As soon as they hung up, Anna Marie searched for the paper on which she had written the name of Granny Rose and her sons. She knew she had left learning Granny Rose's name and the stories that came with the names for far too long, now being too late. Unless Harry knew the origin, she would likely never know Granny Rose's full story. Anna Marie was determined that after things settled down, she would research Granny Rose's story through others who knew her.

Anna Marie thought of the possibilities ahead, realizing she had been lonely for male companionship. While George was a few years younger, Granny Rose had set the example for that not being a problem.

Anna Marie wandered out to the front lawn where the Southwind still sat with a large 'For Sale' sign on the front windshield. She thought again about the adventures yet to come and then removed the sign, ripping it up and throwing it in the garbage. She knew the continual spiral of life and the connections she had made in the past were now coming back together in many ways to enrich her life even more than they did the first time they came into her life. She was thrilled about the possibilities ahead.

They move to the rhythm of the bells.
Two by two, united in the present and the past.
Water springs from the well as a gift that will forever last.
Tears no more as this day gives to night.
A celebration for embracing the light.

–By permission of Vincent Bishop, author's son

CHAPTER NINE

THE WEDDING: ANOTHER NEW MOON

The Present, Higginsville, NY

Anna Marie listened to the phone ringing in Montana, hoping to find Harry home. She had no idea of what plans he needed to make but she was sure that there must be some. On the seventh or eighth ring, a female voice answered the phone.

Anna Marie listened to the phone ringing in Montana, hoping to find Harry home. She had no idea what plans he needed to make but was sure there must be some. On the seventh or eighth ring, a female voice answered the phone.

Anna Marie identified herself and the person responded, "Yes, I'm Maude. I met you at Rose's and Harry's wedding. You probably don't remember me, but I remember you. He's not in right now. We expect him back in a few minutes. He's been at the funeral home with Reverend Sophia in town all morning, so it shouldn't be long. I'll have him call as soon as he gets back."

Anna Marie thanked her and hung up the phone. She could not picture the woman whose voice she had just heard, though immediately, visuals came to her mind of that magical wedding day in Montana.

Seven years earlier

Anna Marie studied the chosen wedding grove from the back, surrounded by large pines and singing birds. Anna Marie thought that from the looks of the grove, it had been used for many years for ceremonies with pathways long worn. The wedding was scheduled for precisely at sunset. Anna Marie took a deep breath, trying to relax until she was needed for useful tasks. She was sure she would be found when the need arose.

Christa was assisting Granny Rose with bathing, styling her hair, and adding the finishing touches to the wedding dress. Anna Marie was amazed at how much detailed planning they had achieved in such a short period of time. She thought of her own children's weddings with months of planning costing thousands of dollars.

She suspected this wedding cost less than two hundred dollars and probably would be remembered far longer than her children's weddings or any other wedding she had ever attended.

She wished her children were here to share in this magical night. Cynthia, Katy, and Anita had all been invited but were unable to come at such short notice. Erin had used his vacation time for the trip to the Grand Tetons and couldn't take another vacation so soon after that trip. He sent a bushel basket of apples, freshly harvested from New York, accompanied by Adirondack sharp cheese, fresh cider, and his best wishes for a beautiful wedding.

Once again, Anna Marie lamented that the Sergeant Georges, Sandra Cass, and their families could not be invited to the wedding. She silently sent a message to them to thank them all for their help along the Southwind Journey.

Three roads entered the grove from the South, East, and West. Guests arrived from all three directions, parking their cars on the roadsides. They all seemed to know exactly where to go as they followed the three separate, winding paths through the forest to the grove.

Anna Marie did not know that each path made exactly seven complete spirals before reaching the center of the grove. At the center of the grove was a spring; next to the spring stood a large circular shaped rock with a hole carved through the middle. The rock appeared worn down from the glacier that likely brought it to the grove thousands of years before or from years of use, as the top was almost perfectly flat. History books credited the movement of the rocks to glaciers, while natives of the region claimed the large rocks were moved by their ancient ancestors long before the glaciers were known to travel through the area.

On top of the flat surface was a cone-shaped candle; surrounding the candle were spiral patterns, seven stars, and a crescent carved into the rock. Also, on top of the flat surface were a chalice and a conch shell. Between the rock and spring, a crescent-shaped lyre was set up. Anna Marie assumed that someone would be playing the lyre as part of the ceremony.

Behind the rock and spring stood an old oak tree that Anna Marie estimated must be at least two hundred years old. Hanging from the tree were vines of wild grapes. Anna Marie could see bird nests at the highest limbs of the trees that looked like the eagle nests she was familiar with in the East along the Hudson River and parts of the Mohawk Valley. The eagles were returning in large numbers there.

The grove itself was large with over 200 hundred chairs set up and a curving aisle through the chairs. The chairs faced the spring with the rock next to it, which was to the north. The chairs were decorated with flowers gathered from the woods and roadsides. On each chair was a packet of seeds for the guest occupying that chair. Hundreds of old Baskets, old glass chipped vases, broken pottery, and vintage bottles were filled with an array of wildflowers, more beautiful than any professional florist's arrangements. Next to each flower arrangement was a sheave of wheat and rosemary, tied together with a bow made of purple ribbon.

Three lovely young girls in woven white dresses with hand-stitched flowers seated each guest. They handed each person a white lily as they sat down. Anna Marie wondered where they were able to find lilies this time of the year in this climate where they surely could not grow naturally. The aisle between the chairs was strewn with petals of flowers and reams of wheat and rosemary scattered amongst the flowers.

The front of the grove where the ceremony was to be held was covered with fresh pine needles and hundreds of white candles. The bubbling spring provided background music. As the grove began to fill with people, most spoke in hushed voices, and the spring could still be heard.

Along the sides of the grove were huge tables laden with every kind of food imaginable. Anna Marie could see bottles of wine and at least two kegs of beer. There was also a large punch bowl in the middle of one table. Anna Marie could make out bowls of nuts and what looked like round honey cakes, apple pies, plates of cookies in all shapes and colors, and bowls of what looked like golden apples.

One table was covered so that it was impossible to see what was on it. Anna Marie assumed that the table was full of hot items and looked forward to the unveiling. She had been told that all the ladies of the town and Harry's large extended family had been "cooking up a storm" since the announcement of the upcoming wedding. Anna Marie thought the glorious food must be the outcome.

While people were seated, members of the local press walked around the grove, taking pictures and talking with many of the guests. She noticed one reporter eyeing her and quickly moved away so that she could continue to observe the wonders of the grove and the guests who were congregating.

After most of the two hundred people invited to the wedding arrived, a large honey-colored woman in a long purple robe walked down the aisle to the front of the grove. Anna Marie knew this to be Reverend Sophia. Harry arranged for her to perform the wedding ceremony. Harry told them the Reverend had performed weddings and birth ceremonies for generations of his family.

Granny Rose, Anna Marie, and Christa invited Reverend Sophia to the Southwind for dinner two nights before to meet her and learn her story. The four became immediate friends, feeling like hey had known each other for a lifetime.

Harry left them alone claiming, "I think this is an evening for you women. I don't belong here."

He had been exactly right; leaving the women to an evening of shared storytelling was better than any bridal shower Anna Marie had ever attended in the East.

Reverend Sophia told them the story of how she came to be in Montana. She explained how when she was only in her teens, she married her husband, a dreamer who wanted to become a cowboy. He dragged her reluctantly across the country to this area of Montana for a job on a ranch where she became the cook. He was quite a womanizer, something she knew before the marriage, thinking that he would change with marriage.

He also liked using her as a punching bag after a few drinks on Friday after he was paid. One Friday night, he was a little rougher than usual, and Sophia ended up in the hospital due to multiple head wounds and broken ribs. The hospital Social Worker, Ellie, was a spiritual minister in her private life. She dispensed medical and spiritual healing to the young Sophia while she was in the hospital.

The Social Worker tended a small group of people who practiced Gnostic Christianity. When Sophia was released from the hospital, the group invited her to join them, advising her on how to confront her demons, with her husband at the top of the list.

Sophia followed their advice which was a combination of threats, spells, and firmness. Her husband became so afraid of her that he disappeared one night, running away from his very formidable wife. Sophia never heard from him again. She remained on the ranch as the cook and advisor to the ranch hands.

Eventually, she became the common law wife of one of the members of her spiritual group, with thirteen children as a result. The Social Worker mentored her, and when Sophia's friend died, Sophia became Reverend Sophia for the group that had now grown to hundreds. She was now teaching another young woman in her spiritual community to eventually take her place, although still loving her ministry as much as she had forty years ago when she began.

Reverend Sophia had a sense of humor that was remarkable making them laugh hysterically well into the night with her stories and jokes. Best of all, her laugh was a huge belly laugh where even if you found the story not very funny, you could not resist laughing with her.

Often throughout that delightful night, they were in tears from laughing so hard. Some of the jokes were so ribald that Anna Marie couldn't believe she was hearing them from the mellow-appearing Reverend. Granny Rose added some stories of her own, especially from her days of dancing—sometimes without clothes—that were equally as funny.

Reverend Sophia informed Granny with a wink and said, "Usually, this is the night I give sexual tips for the soon-to-be-wed couple. I think you could probably give me some tips."

Anna Marie knew she would never forget that night, thinking of it as a bequest of new friendship and celebration. She was grateful for this once in a lifetime evening amongst new friends.

Four massive grey wolfhounds surrounded the Reverend making a circle walking down the aisle with the Reverend in the center. The dogs walking in step with Reverend Sophia, blew out large sighs, drawing the attention of the hushed crowd.

The dark, ruby red robe Reverend Sophia wore today was hand-stitched in gold thread with figures of birds, snakes, and spiral patterns. Over the robe she wore a delicate net of gold thread. As she entered the grove, all eyes in the area watched her with stunned silence, the only noise in the distant surrounding forest, the bubbling spring, the sighs of the dogs, and the sound of rustling from Reverend Sophia's robe. Even the birds were now voluntarily hushed, watching from trees above.

Sophia's hair was plaited in cornrows with golden decorations, and over her hair was a shimmering white see-through silk headdress. On her feet were golden sandals that sparkled as she walked. Carrying a carved oak stick in one hand and a golden purse in the other, Reverend Sophia looked majestic. When she came to the front of the grove, the four tall female hounds arranged themselves on each side of her and together they approached the large glacial stone.

At the stone, Sophia bowed to the rock, emptying the contents of the purse onto the stone. Anna Marie could see incense, a pestle with a mortar, and what looked like a mixture of herbs. Each dog now placed herself on the four sides of the large stone table, looking out to east and west, respectively.

Anna Marie shook her head, amazed that this could be happening in Montana of all the places in the world! She felt like she had been transported to another place and time. While the last-minute arriving guests were being seated, the regal black lady lit every candle around the stone along with the incense.

From the sides of the glen, young girls lit the candles circling the grove so that it appeared to be in flickering ephemeral light as dusk fell over the area. The smell of cedar, rosemary, cinnamon, wheat, and sage permeated the grove. As the summer day began to cool, mist rose from the spring and the surrounding area where Anna Marie suspected there must be other springs similar to this one.

People talked in hushed tones with even the children in attendance appearing to understand this solemn and magical moment. Most watched the woman at the front in awe; some of the older women brushed away tears of joy. Anna Marie tried to hold back her own tears so that she could get through the walk up the aisle and the ceremony. Granny Rose had asked her to escort her down the aisle to Harry.

Anna Marie noticed Christa gesturing to her from the edge of the grove.

She walked over to Christa who exclaimed, "You will not believe how beautiful Granny Rose looks. If I didn't know her, I wouldn't think she was a day over 50. Come and see. Actually, we do not know her real age; we are always guessing."

Granny Rose paced back and forth next to one of Harry's son's car. She was dressed in a long red silken skirt and a white sequined blouse. Christa had helped Granny Rose pick out her new outfit for which Harry had more than willingly paid. Christa curled Granny Rose's hair piling the soft, grey silken hair on top of her head in lovely curls. Granny Rose carried a large straw hat at her side decorated in multi-colored roses.

When Granny Rose saw Anna Marie, she hugged her, being careful not to squash the roses on the hat, nervously sharing with them, "I'm really scared. I didn't bargain for all these people and this huge ceremony at my age. I'm so glad both of you are with me."

Anna Marie hugged her back responding, "Don't worry! You are going to be the most beautiful bride they have ever seen in this part of the country."

Anna Marie wiped away a few tears continuing, "Christa and I feel like we will be losing a family member and our travel partner. I don't know how to continue without you. We are thrilled for you that you are back with a love of your life. And we will always be here for you when you need us."

Christa kissed Granny Rose on both cheeks as she said, "We have something for you."

She handed Granny Rose two packages and an envelope. The first package was a cell phone.

As she opened this package Anna Marie explained, "This is for you to contact us at any time day or night for whatever reason you need us. We know you love and trust Harry. The phone makes us feel better. It helps us feel connected to you regardless of where we are or you are."

The next package was a small, multi-colored woven lap robe.

Anna Marie said, "This is all the squares I have woven since we have been together. I hope you will use it often and will think of Christa and me when you use it."

Granny Rose opened the envelope last. It was a card with water-colored flowers, signed by Christa inside with a note, 'If the baby is a girl I am going to name her Maria Anne so that I think of you and Anna Marie all the time. I'm hoping with all my heart that she is a girl.' Granny hugged both again and thanked them for their gifts.

She then said, "I have something for both of you."

They looked surprised as she handed them each a small velvet pouch. Anna Marie took the pouch and loosened the strings to peer inside. She pulled out a small gold key with a card tied to it. On the card was the name of a bank and a 7-digit number.

Granny Rose explained, "This is a key to my safety deposit box in a town called Sumer, near New Orleans. There are some very special objects in there that I want you both to watch over after I am gone. Maria Anne, you will be the caretaker of these objects until you decide it is time for Christa or someone else to assume the responsibility. It can be at your death or sooner; whatever you decide is best for each of you and the care of the objects. Harry has already been told that you are the first to be notified when I die. You've made it even easier with your gift."

She touched the box with the cell phone.

She continued, "I want you both to go to Sumer and open that box now so you see what it is I am asking you to guard. It is my legacy to you, my daughter, and my lovely granddaughter. But it is more than a legacy; it is a responsibility to make sure the objects are handed down to each succeeding generation of women. This has been done for thousands of years and you cannot break the chain of care passed down to us from our ancestress."

Rose looked intently at Anna Marie and Christa, hoping they understood the importance of what she was telling them and gifting them with on this momentous day.

"It is essential that all our granddaughters and great-granddaughters know there were many remarkable women who came before them. These objects are symbols to the rich history of women. You will also need to choose one object to add to the others for the next generations. It's like a chain letter, only with our treasures from the past."

Anna Marie and Christa were stunned. They had both given up on correcting Granny Rose that they were not her daughter and granddaughter. They both now realized that they essentially were her relatives, however connections were defined. They had learned relations of the heart were as important or maybe more so than blood relationships.

Granny Rose said, "I really do know that Maria Anne you are not my birth daughter, and that Christa is not my birth granddaughter. But it was meant for all of us to come together at this time of our lives. In spirit, that is what you are and that makes the relationship to each other even stronger. That is why you both must go together to follow out my wishes for my box."

She sadly continued with her explanation, "My own daughter, Maria Anne, tried to run away with someone she loved. She disappeared and I never saw her again. I look for her everywhere I am, hoping she will return. You are both beautiful, inside, and out. You remind me of her. I wondered when she disappeared if she might have been pregnant. I may have grandchildren and great-grandchildren by her someplace in this world. She had help with the running away from my husband at the time and his sons. Or at least so I believe."

Granny Rose shook her head sadly, the memories of her past too painful to recall. She had spoken quickly to Anna Marie and Christa, maybe because of the waiting wedding guests or because it was too painful to dwell long on the memory.

She said, "I never got over the loss of my daughter. I never trusted my husband or the sons after that. I kept my distance from them. I left home because I overheard them talking about putting me in a nursing home. That's all I can tell you today. I want this day to be one of pure joy so enough of my long ago past."

She turned to Anna Marie, "For some reason you were brought back to me, in another body but the spirit of my daughter Maria Anne. Not only just you came back, but also the Granddaughter I wished for by her," indicating Christa.

She continued, "Now Christa will continue the generations with her daughter. That's how it is meant to be. You of all people Anna Marie, with your love for weaving, should understand there is a pattern of life woven for us that is eternally connected to the past and future generations. Both of you have always been part of my pattern of life, even if we don't remember which life or the details."

Harry and his brother Hank, who was his best man, approached the three women.

"Rose," he said, "It looks like everyone is here, they are all waiting for us."

Anna Marie and Christa each took an arm of Granny Rose's, walking back to the grove with the two men.

Christa stepped back to let Anna Marie walk Granny Rose down the aisle.

Granny Rose pulled her back stating, "No it is fitting that both of you walk me down the aisle."

As Harry and his brother approached the front of the grove by the spring, Reverend Sophia blew the conch shell, making an eerie and ancient sound. She called the ancient generations to join those present and witness this ceremony of love.

Once Harry and Hank were in place, Anna Marie and Christa slowly and gracefully walked Granny Rose down the aisle. At the opening to the spring, where Harry stood, Anna Marie gave Harry Granny Rose's hand.

Reverend Sophia had instructed all of them that they were to do what felt right during the ceremony. She felt there was no need to practice what would intuitively come to them during the occasion.

Anna Marie had initially felt anxious over these directions, remembering the many hours of practice for her daughter Katy's wedding, but the surroundings of the grove calmed her nerves. She settled into the moment, not thinking ahead to anything but the next step and how that step fit into the beauty unfolding before her.

She thought of her other two children. Her youngest daughter Cynthia was not allowed to legally marry her lifelong partner, Anita. She hoped this fundamental human right would be allowed in the not-too-distant future for all who desired to legally and publicly connect with their desired partner. Listening to the debates on legalizing had become a very personal and unexpected concern for Anna Marie.

Reverend Sophia laid her hand on Anna Marie's arm reassuring her, "Don't worry. It will be beautiful and will come from all our hearts. There is no such thing as 'should' when we do what is directly from our heart and soul."

Despite all intentions, Anna Marie had drifted off to another time and place. She smiles at the Reverend to reassure her she was all right.

With everyone in place, the Reverend Sophia raised her hands over her head as all sat in hushed expectation.

She lowered her arms to reach out to those in the chairs, speaking in a powerful voice carrying across the grove, "We have come today to celebrate the union of Rose and Harry. They have found each other after many years and have chosen to share this moment with all of you. I can speak for those who love this couple. It is with great joy we receive you here and in joy we bring together Rose and Harry."

Reverend Sophia turned directly to Harry and Rose as she continued, "It is meant for humans to complement, to care for each other, and to live in harmony with each other. Rose and Harry will be our guideposts for leading our lives, for our joining together with those around us to celebrate the sacred union of two people coming together and sharing that coming together with their chosen community."

All eyes and ears were on Reverend Sophia. As she spoke the crescent moon rose slowly and gracefully over her head beside the evening star, Venus. Around the outside of the grove, it was darkening, providing a veil, making those in the grove feel cocooned in a world shared in this moment only by those present.

Reverend Sophia continued, "Some may say that it is foolish for Rose and Harry to join in this sacred, ancient rite due to their age. But who are we to decide who can or should participate in this ceremony of joining. We are meant to be with each other and are honored to share the joyous celebration of love with Rose and Harry."

Anna Marie immediately thought of Cynthia and Anita. She determined to talk them into a ceremony in Montana with Reverend Sophia. Though she listened intently to Reverend Sophia; she also mentally planned a lovely ceremony for her daughter.

Reverend Sophia spoke powerfully, "Most of our ancient stories share commonalities of coupling, loss, and then regeneration of life. This ceremony tells us that all is possible if we love each other and care for each other while we carefully watch the bounties that Mother Nature provides for us. We are meant to be caregivers of each other and the earth."

As she spoke, Reverend Sophia motioned all the wedding party, including Anna Marie and Christa to come forward to the spring on the side of the rock. She quietly asked each to wash his or her hands in the spring water. Each did reverently, mesmerized by Reverend Sophia, the people surrounding them, and this night of magical celebration.

She then picked up a tablet laid on the rock and said, "I will now read to you a passage from an ancient poet of Sumer. This poet reminds us that there is always a time of loss, poverty, and starvation that comes to us when we forget to honor the nature around us."

Reverend Sophia read from the tablet as all listened without moving. Those in attendance listened in hushed awe to what was strange but melodic poetry.

The poem seemed to go deep to the recesses of Anna Marie's mind. She knew she would remember where she had experienced this before if she just thought hard enough.

Reverend Sophia concluded the poem with, "Our ancient ancestors understood the importance of the union of people to each other, not just for procreating children, but for the abundance of all to help feed, clothe, and shelter their community. Today's ceremony should remind us to continuously support others who complement each other to come together in a sacred coupling. For as our ancients knew in their wisdom, the fertility of the land and animals depends on our love and care for each other, not just the act of sexuality itself. We are all meant to be caregivers. A society that forgets that will soon dissolve in despair."

Reverend Sophia beckoned to the young girls who had passed out the flowers and now stood to the side with trays of chalices. The young girls came forward. Anna Marie watching from the side, wondered why everyone seemed to be moving in a magical, slow motion with time standing still.

Reverend Sophia poured a red beverage from a huge pitcher that never seemed to empty, into each chalice. As each girl's chalice filled with the liquid, they passed them out among the crowd, returning for other trays of chalices until everyone in the grove had a chalice in hand. No one drank from the chalices, waiting expectantly for something to happen that would indicate it was the right time for each to drink together in a communal celebration of love and hope.

Anna Marie noticed when it was Christa's turn, a purple liquid was substituted for the alcoholic beverage that was given to other adults. The children were given the same drink as Christa. She felt it was remarkable the attention paid to the safety of Christa and her future daughter.

When all were served, Reverend Sophia raised the chalice in front of her encouragingly, "Let us share of the fluid of life together to honor this moment and these two people who we have come to love."

Each person in the grove raised their chalice to their lips, drinking the liquid of life and love. Anna Marie felt the fluid run down the back of her throat, aware as the fluid flowed down her esophagus to her stomach, literally able to visualize the path. The liquid was warm and sweet with a consistency of honey. Anna Marie wondered what it could be. She knew in this group of people and from Reverend Sophia, whatever it was it was something good, meant for sharing in this manner.

Around her others finished their drinks, many in the audience pausing to take in their surroundings. The mist hung lower over the grove, shrouding the people in the grove from any harm on that night. As Anna Marie looked at Harry and Rose, she viewed a beautiful, ageless couple in love.

She wondered if she was hallucinating as a golden glow rose from the ground and at the foot of the trees at the edge of the forest. The trees overhead seemed to be filled with the stars from the sky, blinking on and off in commemoration of the moment.

She had rarely felt so lighthearted in her life or this happy. The only times in her life that came close to this feeling of pure joy and communal sharing were her own wedding and the birth of each of her children. She wished she knew what was in this cup, if the liquid contributed to this well-being, so that she could take this feeling with her for other times in her life. Though, she also instinctively knew it was only possible to have this kind of sensation a few times in a lifetime. Too much joy could be just as painful as too little.

Reverend Sophia spoke again now that all finished their drinks. Her voice came to Anna Marie from a long distance away even though Reverend Sophia stood very close. The everyday words seemed to have a musical rhythm, nothing ordinary allowed on this evening.

Reverend Sophia placed her wooden cane that had been leaning against the rock on the ground, directing the couple, "Please, jump over the stick together to symbolize your union we are all participating in tonight. For this rite is almost as ancient as the moon above, the joining of two people in love, viewed by their friends and family."

Granny Rose and Harry held hands tightly, jumping over the wooden cane in perfect unison with each other. On the other side, Harry grabbed Rose of Aberdeen, giving her a kiss that was reminiscent of a young man. The kiss lasted for many minutes. The crowd sighed with envy, remembrance of their own or other weddings, and in thankfulness for this shared moment.

After the kiss, Reverend Sophia picked up the wooden stick, joyfully holding it over her head. A spontaneous applause and cheering erupted from the crowd. Anna Marie whistled louder than she ever had in her life.

Reverend Sophia said to the jubilant crowd, "Let us all join our hands together in dance and song."

She took Rose's hand in her right hand while Rose imitated her action with Harry. The three of them walked together to join hands with others. All around Anna Marie, people clasped their hands, joining the crowd in unison. Anna Marie reached out on her other side to join Christa and Harry's brother to the lengthening snake like line.

Soon the entire congregation was joined in a long line with Rose of Aberdeen, Harry-Jim-Bob and Reverend Sophia leading the way through the winding paths around the grove and tables laden with food and drink. Reverend Sophia sang a strange, melodic song that others joined in to sing with her.

Anna Marie called it singing in her mind, but the language was a language she had never heard before. Anna Marie joined in, not knowing where her knowledge of the strange language or tune came from.

Someone had brought a flute. Eerie flute sounds followed the group as the two lines wound through the grove of trees and then back to the stone in the center of the grove. Many people skipped or swayed to the flute music as they made their way three times through the paths, recalling ancient natural rhythms they left had behind in childhood or with their ancestors.

The candles gave enough light for everyone to see. A flickering glow added to whatever had been in the chalice to create an ephemeral, magical evening.

At the end of the third swing through the grove, Reverend Sophia dropped her hands from Rose.

She loudly proclaimed, "Now let's eat and drink to celebrate tonight and this new union of Rose and Harry!"

The crowd roared back, stepping towards the tables where additional young girls now waited to serve the food and drink. The covers were removed from the hidden tables to display trays of meats and fish of every variety or kind.

The centerpiece of the largest table was a roasted pig that took up most of the table. Two of Harry's sons stepped forward to carve the pig while people piled their plates high with the delicacies. The air smelled of a mixture of foods, herbs, burning candles, and honey.

Anna Marie piled her plate as high as she could carry, wandering amongst the crowd greeting people she had met previously or making new friends. All seemed to know her treating her like royalty, appearing pleased to be meeting her in person. Reverend Sophia was soon at her side and the two of them walked amongst the crowd, taking turns retrieving food from the tables.

Anna Marie ate ravenously, never seeming to be filled, even as she continued to consume plate after plate of strange and unique delicacies from all four corners of the world. Anna Marie had never been great at carrying or balancing food while walking but on this night she was able to eat, move about amongst the people, and never spill a drop. She imagined ancient magical fairies that filled the grove, holding her food while she moved.

After several plates of food, Anna Marie and Reverend

Sophia drank wine using the goblets from the ceremony. Any time their goblets were close to empty, someone filled the goblet from silver pitchers that also appeared to be bottomless. Anna Marie thought for a fleeting moment that she would regret all this indulgence in the morning. When she awoke the next morning, she felt surprisingly refreshed instead of the "morning after" feeling she had in the rare past when she had eaten and drunk to this extent. The magic of the night stayed with her for many days to come.

The evening ended slowly with people gradually drifting away to their homes. At midnight Rose and Harry said goodbye to the remaining guests, as he laughingly carried the tired Rose to the car that had been driven to the center of the grove. The car was decorated with flowers and streamers. They drove to a neighboring resort town where they planned to stay for two days for a brief honeymoon.

Anna Marie did not remember how she and Christa came to be in the Southwind in the morning. She assumed one of Harry's family must have driven them back as very early in the morning, she heard the Jaguar being parked outside. Anna Marie fell back into a deep sleep, dreaming of Ted.

The Present, Higginsville, NY

The phone rang. It was Harry, explaining again that the funeral would be held later after the tasks requested were completed. Granny Rose wanted Christa and Maria Anne to go directly to Sumer as you did shortly after our wedding rather than come to Montana for the first remembrance ceremony.

After some discussion, Anna Marie agreed that would be best, indicating to Harry, "If you change your mind and need us, we'll be there. We could change our plans as we do want to support you, too. You have become part of our extended family."

Harry responded, "I believe it is important we follow Rose's last wishes to the T. It was what she wanted and obviously she has reasons. Maybe you could come out and visit me after the funeral. I am sure the LaRoches' will inform us what to do next. You take care of whatever you need to in Sumer. I have my family here to take care of me now. Rose is watching me from a short distance above. I can feel her presence all the time."

Anna Marie said, "That's strange, Harry. I can too. Not only that but I had a dream last night that she and Ted, my husband, met and are both watching over me together. Unfortunately, in my dream the two of them shared every funny story they had about me. Not all of them were complimentary. I do think they are together as that is something they would both do even if I requested they not share the uncomplimentary stories."

Rather than displaying her raw emotions to Harry, she ended the call explaining, "I have to make all the final arrangements here to make sure my menagerie will be cared for while I am gone. I love you, Harry. Thanks for all you've done for Granny Rose and me."

It was obvious that Harry had begun to cry because he sniffled, "You ladies don't know how much you've brought into my life. Rose was a gift intended for me. I cherished every moment. There is nothing that I have done; it is what you have given to me."

Anna Marie thought with regret about her original reaction to Harry, especially her violent objection to Harry and Granny Rose's marriage. She couldn't take back what had already happened but vowed to do everything she could to help Harry through his loss and to follow Granny Rose's directions exactly.

Anna Marie said as she hung up the phone, "Take good care, Harry."

Hanging up her landline, Anna Marie contemplated what object she would add to the mysterious box in Sumer. She hoped in the future she would be able to choose just the right object.

Yesterday unearthed will change where she sits.
Shadows form in the light.
Perspective gained in a laughing fit,
She has reclaimed a second sight.

–By permission of Vincent Bishop, author's son

CHAPTER TEN

LEAVING: THE CONTINUING CYCLES OF THE MOON

The Present

Needing fresh air and exercise, Anna Marie took Little Bear to the town park for her walk. While it was cool and breezy, it felt good to be out in the air to clear the "cobwebs from her brain." She needed time to take in the telephone calls from Harry to process Granny Rose's death. If all happened smoothly, tomorrow, she and Christa would be in Louisiana viewing the contents of the mysterious security box.

She was anxious about her trip, yet excited to see Christa again, along with seeing the insides of the strange box she had thought about over the past seven years. Occasionally, during phone calls or visits with Granny Rose, Anna Marie learned little bits and pieces about the objects in the security deposit box, usually with directions from Granny Rose as to where to learn about each object. Anna Marie had taken careful notes over the years. She hoped to be able match the items in the box to her list and to understand why she had been assigned this task.

Little Bear did her usual sniffing of every blade of grass. Their walk was slow along the meandering park trails, though each enjoying the moments of quiet. Tears came to Anna Marie's eyes as she noticed a Catbird following along the trail. Memories of the trip on the Southwind with Granny Rose and Christa came back as they had been coming to her so vividly since Harry notified her of Granny Rose's death.

Suddenly, she stopped dead in her tracks with Little Bear looking at her confused at the sudden stop. Anna Marie stared at the Catbird, thinking how much the bird resembled the traveling companion that seemed to turn up frequently on her first Southwind trip. In various locations on their journey, especially in times when she needed support the most, the Catbird appeared.

The bird now overhead made meowing sounds as she flitted back and forth from tree to tree trying to catch their attention. When Little Bear noticed the Catbird, the gentle dog jumped up and down in excitement, greeting a long-lost friend. Anna Marie realized that she had rarely seen a Catbird since her first journey on the Southwind and wondered if she had stopped looking once she returned home.

Little Bear appeared to nod to the Catbird in recognition of the bird. Once the bird realized she had their attention she landed on a branch overhead of the two, making repetitive cooing sounds. Anna Marie felt like the bird was trying to soothe her. She wondered to herself if the bird knew Granny Rose died.

Then an even stranger thought came to her. Could this now be the spirit of Granny Rose? She decided this was what she wanted to believe; since it didn't hurt anyone else, why not?

Anna Marie bowed her head to the bird and voiced a "thank you."

The same deep, sinking feeling of loss she had when she lost her partner Ted accompanied Anna Marie since she had received the first phone call. Somehow this bird brought her the essence of Granny Rose, reminding Anna Marie that memories never die.

Anna Marie thought, "Maybe all our spirits remain in another living creature after each person dies. I wonder what creature my soul would choose to be in. Or maybe our spirits are in everything that was connected to us during our lives?"

Anna Marie decided that she would add a carved Catbird to the box, since this seemed to be an ongoing part of her connection to the Southwind and Granny Rose.

These thoughts were healing to Anna Marie. She planned to tell Christa about the bird and her beliefs about the connection to Granny Rose. She thought back to another time when she had to say goodbye to Granny Rose, with even then birds helped her through that difficult morning…

Seven years earlier

The morning dawned with mist rising over the mountains in the distance. Anna Marie and Christa had decided that today was the day they needed to leave Granny Rose. They were afraid they would be tempted to stay with her forever if they didn't say goodbye soon. They had enjoyed the 2 days after Granny Rose and Harry returned from their honeymoon as well as the days of rest in between. She and Christa helped Rose decorate her new mobile home, spending time with Harry's very large extended family, and exploring the beautiful mountains of the region.

The break had helped calm their roller coaster of emotions over the past few weeks to prepare for the next part of their journey. They had put their leaving off for as long as they could. It was now time for them to continue their journey while Granny Rose led her new life without them.

Christa grew larger by the day—her due date was growing close. Christa's mother anxiously waited for her return and for her first grandchild to arrive soon, though Christa herself was not as anxious to leave Anna Marie or Granny Rose. Both Anna Marie and Christa had places they wanted to visit along the way before Christa was delivered home to her family.

The three women had been dreading this day but knew it was inevitable from the moment that Harry-Jim-Bob had told them he and Rose were marrying.

Anna Marie also sensed that she was coming close to the last part of her own personal journey, though she was going to do everything possible to prolong it for as long as she could. She was afraid that once she returned home she would lose her newfound energy, friends, and independence. While she missed her home, seeing her grandchildren, children and Diana frequently, she was afraid that once home she would resume her patterns of grief and lack of interest in new things, making her feel much older than she was.

Somehow this journey had helped her connect back to Ted and to understand that Ted would always be with her but in a different way. She was afraid that seeing her house would bring back all the intense pain she had been feeling for far too long.

After Ted's death, she had wondered what it meant to be a widow. She asked people when she should remove her wedding rings. Often they changed the subject, afraid to answer her question or believing intense pain could be contagious. She continued to wear the rings all the years since Ted's death, even after her quick romance with Walter, a term she liked better than other alternatives.

Now she had mentally redesigned the rings to have the rings melted down for her in a design to give to the local jewelry store at home. The spiral pattern she had selected to wear on a gold chain necklace seemed to suit this new phase of her life, while still honoring Ted's memory.

This journey forced her to continually change routines, become accustomed to making new friends, celebrate events as often as possible, and seek new challenges every day. Once back at home, she feared the return to housecleaning, cards at the senior center, and quiet evenings without companionship would absorb her back into a boring routine.

Anna Marie thought about how few of her evenings had been quiet or lonely on this trip. While thoughts of Ted never left her, they were peaceful thoughts of a life once lived with a kind and gentle man. She knew the challenge was going to be to avoid falling back into those old patterns. She also had no idea how to say goodbye to this wonderful time of her life as goodbyes had always been extremely difficult for her.

Granny Rose came to have breakfast with the Southwind Travelers one last time, as they had said their goodbyes to everyone else the night before. It was fitting that the three ladies and the animals should be together one last time. They ate quietly, each lost in their own thoughts of loss, changes, and renewal.

Christa and Granny Rose took one last walk together with Little Bear while Anna Marie checked out the Southwind to make sure all the hookups were disconnected, the slide outs back in, and everything safely in its place for traveling. Maya and Circe sadly watched Anna Marie, sensing there was going to be a permanent change. Circe made little cooing sounds that could be her form of crying. Maya rubbed up against Anna Marie as she left the inside of the Southwind.

Tears rolled down Anna Marie's face as she tightened the connections to the tow bar pulling the Jaguar, straightening the luggage underneath to make sure nothing moved in travel. They had removed Granny Rose's few items, including her rocking chair, so she could have memories from the Southwind close by.

Anna Marie thought how strange it was that the Southwind felt empty, when only a short while ago adding Granny Rose had made her feel like the RV was overcrowded with too many creatures for such a small living space. Anna Marie thought about how the perception of the amount of space was directly related to how you felt about the people, pets, and objects occupying those spaces.

Harry and his brothers connected the Jaguar on the tow bar last night even though the ladies had protested they were perfectly capable of doing it themselves.

Harry clarified to the ladies, "Enjoy the help while you have it. You will have plenty of opportunities to do it yourselves."

When Harry left he committed to Anna Marie and Christa, "I will take care of Rose as though she were a precious gem. She will want for nothing, and I will do everything I can to make her happy. You are always welcome to visit. Maybe we can come visit you when you return home?"

Anna Marie and Christa had come to love Harry and his family; especially as they could see the respect and affection they all had for Granny Rose. They knew Granny Rose would be well cared for in her new community. They also knew that Reverend Sophia would watch over Granny Rose and be a great friend for Granny Rose. She had already asked Granny Rose to assist with community ceremonies. The two ladies were already inseparable.

Anna Marie hugged Granny Rose, "Granny Rose, I don't know how we are going to go on without you. We both know it is time to move on. If you ever need either one of us, contact us and we will be there immediately. We will take care of your gifts and make sure that we do what you have asked us to do. We, of course hope that is a long time away."

Granny Rose responded, "I'm in my nineties. I have only a little time left. It is only through death and loss that we are all regenerated again. I will always be there with you just as all our ancestors before us are there with us. You will have to look for me harder to find me in the everyday things around you. The instructions that you need for the security box in Sumer will come to you from an unexpected place."

Anna Marie looked confused and asked Granny Rose, "But give me some idea where I need to look or who I should go to for the information. I want to do my best to care for your box when it is time. I can't do that without direction."

Granny Rose patted Anna Marie, answering her in Rose evasive style, "You will do what is exactly right or I would not have entrusted it to you and then Christa, who will do the same. Be patient, you will come to learn what to do with the contents of the box. Life has patterns that come together. Do you think our meeting is chance"?

Rose shook her head, disappointed Anna Marie still did not understand, "We were destined to meet thousands of years ago;

you were selected to be the next caretaker of the box after me that many eons ago. Who knows for how long you will watch over it. You are needed for a time that has been predetermined. Patterns will come together when it is your turn. And for a brief while I will be here to help answer some of your questions to start you on this next journey of discovery. I love you Maria Anne!"

Anna Marie thought about how much Granny Rose had changed in their too brief time together or at least her perception of Granny Rose's capabilities. Their roles had changed drastically, with Granny Rose becoming the teacher and Anna Marie the student. She remembered an old Chinese proverb 'When the student is ready, the teacher will come." Maybe reversing roles worked the same way.

Anna Marie wondered how many older people were thought to have dementia when they were either depressed, had hearing impairments like Granny Rose, or were just a little different from everyone else around them because they no longer feared being who they wanted to be.

She also thought about how much she had grown to love this diminutive woman and how she wished she had a lifetime to learn from her instead of only a few remaining years. Those years would be at a distance.

She responded to Granny Rose with a heartfelt statement, "I love you, too!"

They hugged as a truck came down the road. Anna Marie recognized it as Harry-Jim-Bob's knowing it was time for the final goodbye. They all hugged each other quickly and gently one last time. Granny Rose gave Little Bear a hug, and patted Maya and Circe, who were sitting at the door, one last time before getting in the truck, waving an energetic goodbye.

She sat up very straight, looking queenly as Harry-Jim-Bob started the engine, driving away from the campsite. Anna Marie and Christa watched as the red truck drove off. They could see the dust from the truck for a long time after they could no longer see the vehicle itself. Neither said anything. Both got into the

Southwind with the animals as Anna Marie started the engine. She put her head down on the steering wheel for a minute to try to regain her composure before driving. Christa was lost in her own sense of loss.

The three pets were lined up on the couch, each extremely quiet, grieving Granny Rose's leaving them for her new life. Circe, sitting between Little Bear and Maya, had her head tucked under her wing making sounds that resembled the crying of humans.

They drove out of the campground in unusual quiet except for the sounds coming from Circe. At the end of the road to the campground, Anna Marie pulled off to the side.

She said to Christa, "I'm sorry Christa. I'm crying so hard I can't see the road in front of me. I need to get out and calm myself for a minute so that I am safe to drive again."

Christa indicated she would get out with her. They stood looking over a field, neither saying anything nor making any sound until Christa excitedly pointed to the end of the field.

She exclaimed, "Look Anna Marie!"

Christa pointed to a flock of white pelicans that had begun their daily ascent. One pelican rose at a time, in a long, slow spiral pattern until he or she had reached the height for flight. Each pelican that had risen before the others waited in a holding pattern, circling around overhead in a pre-agreed upon flight pattern.

Christa and Anna Marie watched in amazement for over forty minutes as each white pelican took his or her turn to join the others using the same slow, spiral pathway while catching the wind drafts upwards. The wind from the plains lent an eerie background sound to the surreal scene, all seeming to fit perfectly into this day for goodbyes. Anna Marie thought with amazement how much the pattern of the pelicans looked like the necklace she had mentally designed that morning.

As the last white pelican joined the others, the group took off in a V pattern both ladies had seen with Canadian geese. Neither had known this was also a pattern for white pelicans. As the white V flew off into the distance, a Catbird called to them from a tree nearby, looking amazingly like their friend that kept returning to them throughout their trip.

Anna Marie said, "Look, there is another Catbird or maybe the same one following us. She does appear at the most opportune moments. I wonder if we will ever see her again or if she will stay here with Granny Rose. I don't know exactly what this all means but we were meant to see this today to help us through our loss of Granny Rose. I think we just had a special moment. Granny Rose is going to be fine and so are we."

Christa nodded.

Both ladies peacefully climbed back into the Southwind with Christa taking her place as map-reader. Maya, Circe, and Little Bear returned to their favorite riding places as Anna Marie negotiated the curves to the major highway. The picture of the rising white pelicans and the Catbird calling from a tree nearby stayed vividly in their mind for the rest of the day.

They stopped for the night at a campsite at the foot of a mountain in Western Montana, very close to the Idaho border. The day had been so emotionally draining that after settling at the campsite and eating a light dinner, all the occupants fell asleep early.

Anna Marie hoped that this feeling of loss and ending, the very feeling she had tried to leave behind in New York, would not last for the rest of their journey. She thought that rather than leaving the feeling behind, she should think of the losses as adding to her knowledge gains.

The next morning was foggy and unsafe for driving through the mountain passes. Anna Marie and Christa decided to sleep in and stay an extra night at this campsite. The animals seemed relieved at this decision as well. All fell back asleep, catching up on many hours of lost sleep or sleeping to avoid reality.

The fog never lifted, with the day remaining gloomy and unusually subdued sounds around them. Christa, Little Bear, and Anna Marie took a leisurely hike after a relaxing breakfast and tea through the trails around the campsite. They were careful to stay close to the campground trails due to the fog and lack of familiarity with the area.

Once they heard rustling in the woods near their campsite. Both ladies tensed up to the sound, afraid there could be bears searching for some unattended food. The gloomy day turned gloomier.

The Southwind passengers stayed inside working on their weaving and needlework while the pets slept off and on. After a very light supper and tea, they again went to sleep early hoping the weather would break so they could leave this campground.

In the morning, Christa was the first up. Little Bear begged her for her early morning walk. Christa opened the door to a strange silence to find a foot of snow piled in front of their RV. In the night, the ladies had turned on the heat, never realizing it was snowing outside.

Even Little Bear didn't protest the quick walk, especially after she and Christa observed very large tracks in the snow circling the Southwind. It looked like someone, or something, had been looking into the Southwind while the occupants slept. It started to snow again, small flakes turning to large heavy flakes, as Christa and Little Bear entered their home.

The ladies stayed in the Southwind the entire day again.

Once Anna Marie tried to leave to walk or drive to the office to reserve another night. She was stopped by gales of wind and snow blowing in gusts around her feet. She knew the Jaguar would not do well in these road conditions so she returned to the warmth of the RV making the correct assumption she could pay the next day. She doubted anyone could even get to their space for the upcoming night.

This time she observed large foot or paw-prints around the north side of the Southwind and tried not to think about the creature that made those prints. She sent a silent prayer to Granny Rose to help guard them and then called the real person.

Granny Rose answered the phone after several rings, sounding very tired. Anna Marie explained where they were and the size of the prints in the snow. Granny Rose talked to Harry, who was more familiar with the mountains in the region.

They advised their friends to remain inside for the rest of the day until the storm subsided. Harry knew of no wild animals that could break into the Southwind or had he heard of any dangerous person in the area.

Harry indicated that he would check it out with his brother-in-law, the police chief in town, and get back to them with any information he learned. Anna Marie missed being able to call the Georgia Sergeants to ask them for any information they could find out.

The Southwind occupants spent the rest of the day dozing, reading, listening to the weather channel on the radio, and eating light meals together. Toward dusk there was a loud pounding on the door. Both ladies went to the door together, armed with a broom and dust mop respectively. They peered through the window to see a park employee standing in the cold wind, blowing on his hands to keep them warm.

Anna Marie opened the door a crack, greeting the man standing at the door. He showed his park identification badge, so taking a risk Anna Marie asked him in for tea or hot chocolate. Little Bear uncharacteristically growled at the ranger, as Anna Marie silenced her. Circe spit at the man. Maya stood protectively in front of Anna Marie.

Anna Marie wondered if the animals were responding to severe weather conditions or the man himself.

Ignoring the upset animals, the ranger gratefully accepted the offer of hot chocolate and some cinnamon cookies left over from the wedding. Nostalgically, Anna Marie thought about the wonderful muffins with unknown ingredients that Granny Rose used to have ready for company. She realized there would be many more occasions that would remind her of Granny Rose.

Christa and Anna Marie sat down for hot chocolate with Paul White, the name on his tag, as he gave them an update on the storm. Anna Marie thought that Mr. White must have lost a significant amount of weight since the picture was taken.

Mr. White described the current weather condition, "All of the roads in the surrounding area are closed. We are expecting this storm to last at least another day. You need to sit tight until it is over, and the roads are open. We have snowmobiles that we can use to check on you. We'll check a few times a day. Give me a list of any essentials you need, and I'll bring them back to you in the morning."

Mr. White wanted to know if they had a cell phone and a way to contact the office if there were an emergency, which they assured him they did with so far good reception. As he looked around the Southwind, he reached over to pat Anna Marie on the hand. Anna Marie instinctively pulled back, then regretted her automatic response wondering why she did not want him to touch her.

He appeared to ignore her reaction, apparently used to women responding to him this way, and said, "You ladies have it mighty nice here. I'm sure you'll be just fine. Are there the two of you here alone?"

Christa, who had been very quiet during the conversation between Mr. White and Anna Marie, answered quickly, "We have a very large dog in the bathroom we don't let out when strangers are here because he is so vicious. He's very well trained and will break through that door if we give him the order. If you listen, you can hear him breathing on the other side of the door."

Anna Marie found Christa so believable she thought she could hear actual breathing. Little Bear, sitting to the side, watched Mr. White intently. When Little Bear heard Christa's response to Mr. White, she ran to the bathroom in clear understanding of Christa, scratching and whining at the door.

Christa continued, playing into Little Bear's behavior, "When Little Bear doesn't like someone, as apparently she doesn't like you, Mr. White, she looks to Big Bear to take care of that person."

She called Little Bear to come back to her, explaining to Mr.

White, "Big Bear could break down the door if she wanted. Little Bear helps moderate her. You probably want to make this quick, Mr. White."

Anna Marie looked at Christa, trying to hide her astonishment but not contradicting Christa.

Mr. White looked very nervous as he said, "Yes, well, I'll be getting on my way here so I can tell the other campers about the storm. Uh, I'll be happy to get supplies for you but I'm a little short on cash... Even a credit card number will be fine."

Anna Marie hesitated and then responded, "We are well stocked for now and could go many days with what we have. I appreciate the offer but we're fine."

Mr. White shook his head, saying, "You're ungrateful for my offer. You will most likely regret it."

He then tried to explain, "I mean, with the storm and all. You ladies could be sitting here a long time and will need my help."

Reluctantly, Mr. White stood up.

As Mr. White prepared to leave the RV, Anna Marie asked him, "Are there any bears in this area? We have had very large paw prints around our motorhome."

Mr. White thought for a minute and then responded, "Ordinarily, I could reassure you that there are no bears in this park. However, in the past couple of weeks there have been reports of a large female bear with young cubs. That's very unusual this time of the year and not normal for this park at all. The bears tend to be back further in the woods. They do not like to be around the campers any more than campers want to be around them. I would stay put. Do not wander very far from the RV when you need to walk your dogs."

Mr. White waved to them as he boarded the park snowmobile. The buzzing of the snowmobile lasted a long time, becoming a soft whine in the distance. The animals immediately let down their guard.

A few minutes later the phone rang. It was Harry-Jim-Bob.

He told the ladies, "My brother-in-law has informed me of

a breakout in the state prison located about 25 miles from the RV Park. I would guess that since you can't travel, the escaped prisoner can't either. In any case, be very careful. If you need anything, ring us and we'll try to get help there. Don't let any strangers in and be wary."

Anna Marie asked for any descriptions that were available, which Harry-Jim-Bob did not have. She relayed their discomfort with Mr. White's visit.

Harry-Jim-Bob responded, "I think I will have my brother-in-law call the sheriff in that area to keep a watch over you just to be on the safe side. Rose sends her love. She's concerned about you, as is Reverend Sophia. Those two are doing what they do to send you protection. I have no idea what that is. I'm probably better off not knowing."

Harry chuckled with obvious great love for Granny Rose and fondness for the Reverend.

Anna Marie said to Christa, "He didn't reassure me any. I guess we have little choice than to wait it out. I think both of us should walk Little Bear and not go any further than right outside the RV. She'll have to be content with the short walks."

They went out with Little Bear twice that evening, with very little protest from Little Bear over the brief walks. Little Bear also seemed to sense the possible danger right outside the Southwind.

On the last walk of the night, they noticed that the prints now went all the way around the campsite. They also noticed a yellow territorial marking surrounding the Southwind. None of the occupants slept well that night. The Southwind shook from the blizzard condition winds howling like a living creature in pain. Anna Marie hoped it was the wind and not some poor distressed living thing.

The morning was not any clearer, with high winds and snow still falling. Anna Marie and Christa became increasingly anxious to continue their journey. The pets also looked as though they'd had enough of the enforced rest, wanting to resume their previous pattern of the days. The tracks and the yellow marks in the snow looked recently refreshed, a thought that frightened the two ladies. The roads were still impassable.

They wondered if the storm would ever stop before the following spring. Anna Marie could picture her delivering Christa's baby in this isolation. She tried to hold back the anxiety that began to mount as she looked at Christa's large, protruding stomach. They checked through their supplies finding there were still plenty of staples, many left over from the wedding. With their store of dried herbs, they could make a variety of meals while they were stranded in the snowstorm.

Anna Marie, thinking about what Granny Rose might have done if she was with them, took the last remaining clove of garlic, hanging it in a small cloth bag over the door. Christa watched her quietly, not saying anything and desiring any means of protection available.

They heard the loud sound of a snowmobile approaching. Both ladies took a deep breath before looking out the window over the sink. It was Mr. White dressed in the same clothes they had seen him in the day before. Anna Marie opened the door enough to peer out at him. She kept the latch on the door. The animals and Christa lined up behind her.

She greeted Mr. White, "We didn't expect you back so soon. Surely there are other campers that need your attention more than us?"

As Mr. White came closer, Anna Marie noticed an odor of alcohol and vomit.

He growled as he ordered, "Let me inside. We need to talk."

Anna Marie responded, "Mr. White, I'm afraid Big Bear would be very upset if you came inside in your current condition."

Mr. White pulled out a gun from his pants and shakily demanded, "The hell with Big Bear. I can take care of him in a minute. If you ladies want to remain alive, you had best let me in immediately. In fact, I want all of you out of that RV now. I'll give you two seconds to get your coats and a blanket, shoes on your feet if you don't have them on already. That's what a good person I am. Bring the other animals out with you and I'll take care of the big one."

Christa and Anna Marie hesitated only a second. They figured they would be better off taking care of the real animals and themselves, rather than worrying about an imaginary beast. Mr. White looked angry enough to shoot out the door and the windows any minute if they didn't comply.

They quickly grabbed a few blankets and sweaters for each of them as well as a couple of warm sweaters to wrap the animals. They all rushed out of the Southwind. Anna Marie hurriedly tried to put the cell phone into her pocket. Mr. White grabbed it as they walked by him before she was successful.

He motioned them over to the side of a small spring cautioning them, "Don't move from there or I'll shoot all of you. Where are the keys to this wreck?"

Anna Marie indicated they were in the ignition, trying not to pay attention to the insult to their home.

Mr. White shouted, "All of you on the ground and don't move."

Anna Marie placed one of the blankets on the ground at the foot of a large pine tree. All five huddled together in the smallest ball possible.

Within minutes, Mr. White was back outside, screaming at Anna Marie, "Get back in here old lady! I need you to show me how to turn this thing on."

He waved the gun at again as Anna Marie walked to the RV, feeling like she was deserting a friend, even if it appeared to be an inanimate vehicle.

Mr. White shouted at the others, "Don't try anything funny or I'll shoot your old lady here, then you'll be next."

For some reason Anna Marie found him comical, almost a stereotype of a criminal. She restrained laughing remembering how much trouble her laughter had gotten them into in Wyoming. She kept her face as stoic as possible as she followed him.

A picture formed in her mind of Mr. White making the yellow

territorial marks around the Southwind, causing the laughter to want to bubble to the surface. A sub-conscious part of her also understood the potential for harm to them all, helping her suppress the sound. Instead of laughter, Anna Marie spontaneously and quietly whistled a song that came to her from her past.

As Anna Marie entered the Southwind, the door to the bathroom shook, causing the rest of the RV to shudder.

Mr. White pushed Anna Marie to the driver's seat and said, "Never mind calling your dog on me. I'll get back to him in a minute and take care of that problem. This thing wouldn't even turn over for me so you must have a code you use to start it. Do it now."

Anna Marie tried to explain that until the slides were in and the lifts off the ground, the motor would not start.

Impatiently Mr. White screamed at her, "Don't give me any nonsense. Just start this thing now."

As he talked the bathroom door shook harder, so hard Anna Marie thought it would come off its hinges.

Anna Marie pressed the button to raise the lifts. Mr. White leaned over her shoulder, the smell of alcohol, vomit, and disease so strong that Anna Marie had to stop to cover her mouth not to be nauseated. Mr. White slapped her across her head with the hand not holding the gun, hard enough to knock her back into the seat.

She tried to steady herself, as the Southwind shook violently, pleading, "Please Mr. White, I can't do this with you hitting me or standing so close. Please stand back."

Mr. White gestured to hit her again and then thought twice about it as he moved slightly away from her.

Anna Marie, thinking quickly, suggested to him, "Mr. White, over the door is the panel. If you could step over there I could tell you the next button to push before I have raised the lifts. To start my Southwind you have to go through all the steps I have mentioned. It will not start unless you do."

Paul White appeared to hesitate, then reluctantly followed

her directions.

As White approached the panel in the middle of the motorhome the door to the bathroom shook even harder, he growled, "Hurry up! What switches do I need to push? I want to get the hell out of here after I take care of that beast back there."

Anna Marie indicated the correct button to move the back and front slides in. She instructed White to the first and then the second buttons once the front lift moved to inside of the motorhome. She had to stop White before the second control button as a suitcase lay in the middle of the passage in the bedroom blocking the back slide from moving further. Thankfully, Mr. White listened to her instructions, finally following as directed.

After both of the slides were in, Anna Marie informed Mr. White he needed to come to the front of the RV to start the control to the balancing lifts. She showed him the control and instructed him, "Turn the motorhome on before you use the lift control. Wait until the lifts are fully up. When the sound stops there will be a beep. After that you can place the transmission into reverse so you can back out into the street."

She wondered how she was able to remain calm as in a few minutes her beloved Southwind could be moving down the street with this horrible man driving it away.

Before she finished her thought, the door to the bathroom flew open, and a ball of light rushed down the aisle of the Southwind. Mr. White's eyes appeared to be larger than the rest of his face—he clearly registered fear. He climbed out of the driver's seat and moved towards the door. But as he stepped closer to the door, he tripped over the top step, falling down the steps with a scream, using language Anna Marie had never heard before in that exact combination.

Mr. White, even though injured from the fall, stood up quickly, running towards the snowmobile. At the same time, the ball of light followed him down the steps and out the door to the snowmobile. White frantically tried to start the snowmobile, the motor turning over after the third try. The motor sputtered until it gained energy, taking off with Mr. White driving erratically. The snowmobile careened down the almost visible line of the road with the bright light following close behind. White's screams mixed with the whine of the snowmobile.

Anna Marie followed down the steps, in a daze watching the scene in front of her. Seconds after the snowmobile disappeared with the frightened driver, three figures walked out of the woods, turning to the bundle huddled under the tree.

Anna Marie realized it was a mother bear and her two cubs. All three looked hungry and ragged. They turned away from the Southwind and the group waiting outside for Mr. White to disappear, moving slowly back into the words.

Anna Marie moved to the tree to help her Southwind companions, the clouds clearing overhead to show the first sunlight in days. Without knowing how, she was sure that the three bears, the yellow marks around the Southwind—which she now thought of as protective marks—and the scaring away of Mr. White were all connected with the sun appearing overhead.

After helping Christa and the pets inside where it was warm, Anna Marie looked for any food she thought would satisfy the bears.

"Regulations be darned, I am feeding these bears to thank them."

She found frozen berries in the freezer and a large honey jar. She placed them in a bio-degradable container that would make it easy for the bears to get the food. Anna Marie placed it near where she had last seen the bears.

Amazingly after days of grey and fog, the sun now shone in full force. The wind had cleared the fluffy snow to the sides of the road, creating a pathway out of the campsite.

Once Anna Marie was back inside the Southwind, she mentioned this to Christa, who replied, "If the road looks at all passable, let's get out of here. I've had enough of this place, even if we only get a few miles into Idaho before stopping later."

Anna Marie prepared the Southwind for travel. The brief

time this took allowed more of the snow to melt. She was able to drive the Southwind out of the campsite to the entrance with no difficulty at all.

As she approached the entrance to the park, she noticed numerous police cars surrounding a snowmobile. It was Mr. White, who appeared to be begging the police officer to take him in.

Anna Marie rolled down the window hearing him say, "Please take me back to prison. It's much safer there than out in this crazy world. You have some strange things happening in your park. There is one strange old lady who seems to be the boss."

Anna Marie tried to ask the Park attendant about paying for the additional nights they had camped. The Park attendant ignored her request, waving them out the gate impatiently, obviously caught up in the scene in front of him. Anna Marie decided to call the park later to make her payment, gratefully driving out of the park away from Mr. White and whatever else lurked there. As she drove down the road to the main highway, she noticed three bears standing beside the woods, watching the vehicle with its occupants leave the park.

She silently pointed them out to Christa, who nodded and said, "I think they are watching out for us. I believe Granny Rose and Reverend Sophia are behind our protection, but who knows how, and they'll never admit it if we ask them. For the first time, I'm looking forward to going home."

The Present, Higginsville, NY

Anna Marie looked with appreciation at her faithful companion, Little Bear. She was glad Little Bear was aging so well and could remain by her side. Anna Marie knew it was time to return to the house from their walk and finish packing for the journey to Sumer.

As they ambled back to the house, she thought about the total of her life. She appreciated how rich her experiences had been, especially during her Southwind journey. Even the bad experiences, such as with Mr. White, had helped her grow in confidence in her own abilities and understand that there was always a magic to life—if one is willing to help make it happen.

Anna Marie suspected that bears were frequently part of her personal magic, even if this one bear was tiny with a pug body. Little Bear rubbed against her leg, seeming to understand her thoughts and in apparent agreement.

Then, a tune came to her: 'Bears and Catbirds, oh, my!' It was a take-off from "The Wizard of Oz" which had always played on TV over the Easter holidays throughout her childhood. She chuckled as she thought of the playground after they returned from Easter vacation, where they created their own yellow brick road singing to their walk. It was amazing to her that she didn't know at the time that the author of *The Wizard of Oz*, L. Frank Baum and his mother-in-law Matilda Joslyn Gage, lived only 15 miles from her childhood home.

Over the next years, Anna Marie attempted to make Granny Rose or Reverend Sophia confess to involvement in the Mr. White episode. But Granny Rose always changed the topic to something totally unrelated, and Anna Marie knew she would never have an explanation for what happened that day. Still, she knew it didn't really matter. Life should always have unexplained events if they turn out as well as her own misadventures.

Anna Marie whistled as she walked back to the house with Little Bear moving puppy-like at her side.

"Nowhere in history do we find a beginning, but always a continuation...How then shall we understand the end, if the beginning remains a mystery?"

—J.J. Bachofen

CHAPTER ELEVEN

CHRISTA RETURNS HOME: THE WANING AND WAXING MOONS

The Present

Anna Marie checked again to reassure her that her luggage was packed with everything she needed for the next days of her journey. It was still warm in Louisiana, though she had packed a sweater just in case planning to carry a heavy jacket on the plane where it always felt cold to Anna Marie.

She smoothed over her wrinkled khaki pants thinking even her journey of discovery had not made her neater. Ted always laughed when she bought white as stains and wrinkles found her wherever she went. Once she had attended an organizational training session to teach her how to get rid of her clutter and disorganization.

She left the session after an hour, telling Ted when she returned home "it's the clutter of my life I like best."

He hugged her, laughed, and agreed that he couldn't imagine her without stains or the clutter of her memories around her.

Little Bear, Circe, and Maya had been safely delivered to Katy and Clint's house with her grandchildren so excited about babysitting that no one seemed to notice when she left. Hopefully, they would keep the three pets too busy to remember Anna Marie was not there or to wonder why she had not taken them with her as she usually did. She thought about what gifts her pets were for her and was glad that despite being seven years older than their first Southwind Journey, each remained healthy and active.

She looked outside her side window to see the Southwind safely parked beside her garage. Walter had tried to get her to sell the RV back to him after her return from the West. She resisted the temptation, knowing that the Southwind needed to be part of her life for at least a little while longer. Extensive repairs to the 1998 Southwind now made her once again question her decision to keep it, though she decided to wait until her return from Louisiana.

She thought about the possibility of taking a long weekend trip with Sergeant George when he visited her after her return from Louisiana and what fun that would be. She was amazed how young all of this made her feel. She could never really get a grasp on her actual age as the years had accumulated much faster than she felt.

Once again, she was reminded how much she missed having someone to share with her day-to-day life, to talk about the small daily happenings that make up one's life. Her children were too busy and her card partners at the Senior Center were not that interested as it often mirrored their own dull experiences.

She had presented slides to her friends at the Senior Center after her return home the first time. That had been the full extent of her sharing the trip with her friends. The frequent phone calls to Granny Rose and Christa, along with the occasional visits with each had been the best opportunities she had for reliving some of her Southwind experiences.

Later trips with the Southwind had been fun, though none of them matched her first journey. She knew that she rediscovered herself on her first trip to learn the essence of who she was. She had needed to do that to regain her life and energy. She also re-created herself into a person that was different than Ted's wife, one who could build a life on her own.

During her first journey she made a point not to read

newspapers or listen to the news. Before her journey she found herself watching the daily news, as she and Ted had done during their marriage. She knew she absorbed too much of the pain in the world. Every time the president declared war or bombed another country, a hurricane hit an area of the US, or another politician was indicted for stealing from his constituents while cutting benefits to the elderly or poor, she absorbed the pain and anguish as though she solely could resolve the problems.

While she had returned to being a news addict, the time she spent focused on what was in front of her in her own life helped her reestablish her own equilibrium. As a result, she understood that it was the daily small things in life that most affected each woman's moods and feelings. She also understood she had to take quiet time away from the world and the news every day.

She had rented the Southwind to Walter and his wife the summer after her first journey with the RV, but that had been a mistake as Walter had described in vivid detail his sexual escapades with his wife in Anna Marie's Southwind upon their return.

When he returned to her the Southwind, she immediately went shopping for new sheets, towels, and even a new rug since Walter had described one night on her rug that created too many unwanted visions. Walter continued to share this personal information with Anna Marie, despite her protests every time the topic was brought up. Fortunately, his wife never learned of their brief relationship or his frequent private conversations with Anna Marie. She wondered about Walter's newfound sex life with his wife if it was reality or imagination due to hopeful thinking.

She didn't know why she had allowed Walter to share his intimate information no one else had told her, not even Ted. She suspected he had wanted her to think that he was sexually active, maybe to make her jealous or to give a spark to his own sad life. Possibly his stories had given her a vicarious feeling of sex and adventure, even if untrue.

Regardless, his death last year had been a surprising loss in her life as she missed the unexpected phone calls at inopportune moments. The losses in old age were the hardest part of aging as far as Anna Marie was concerned as they were accumulative. She was appreciative of learning the importance of the balance of gains with losses and inspired to seek them out.

She never met Walter's wife and did not have contact with her after his death. She had observed a wedding announcement in the paper of Walter's wife and Iggy, the president of Walter's Senior Center. She wondered at the time if that relationship had really ended even after Walter's wife returned to him or if she had returned to Walter because he had more substantial pensions and investments than Iggy.

She would never know the true story, thinking it best to let Walter's memory live in peace by believing the stories and remembering the good characteristics of Walter, hidden behind an obnoxious exterior. He had reminded her that she could physically love again if she chose. He had also reminded her of the strange chemistry that often existed between men and women, with each interrelationship uniquely beautiful if chosen by both but not always love.

Anna Marie looked at her turquoise banded watch, purchased on her first western journey in the Southwind, noting she had another hour before Erin would arrive to take her to the airport. She sat out on her front porch with her bags beside her thinking back to her and Christa's arrival in Portland, Oregon.

Seven years earlier

Anna Marie drove the RV carefully in the heavy fog and traffic. In another hour, according to Christa, they would be in Portland. Anna Marie glanced at the now very pregnant young lady beside her who looked extremely tense as she clung to Little Bear sleeping on her lap. Anna Marie thought she saw her brushing tears away and knew that she was close to tears herself.

Their long journey and adventure would soon be coming to an end, nothing would be quite the same again. Both tried to hang on to these last moments they were sharing. Anna Marie agreed to stay for a few days knowing that would only postpone the agony of saying goodbye. She planned to take the southern route home to miss the early snow, a lesson learned from their Western Montana adventure. She planned to be home by Thanksgiving. The Southern Route ahead did not excite her as she would be seeing new places alone without Christa or Granny Rose.

The animals were quiet. Anna Marie was grateful that at least she would not be saying goodbye to them. She had enough goodbyes in the past few weeks to last her a lifetime.

They would have waylaid Christa's return home as they both were still enjoying the exploring of new places. Christa had not been feeling well in the past few days. Anna Marie feared her birth would be soon, remembering first time mothers were often at risk of an early birth. Anna Marie felt Christa should see her mother's doctor at least once before the birth. She did not want her to have the baby in some strange hospital along the way.

They had visited clinics as they traveled to Portland, including one in Harry-Jim-Bob's town. Each assured Christa that the baby was developing fine, appearing healthy. Maybe if Granny Rose had still been with them they could have delivered the baby themselves. Anna Marie was too unsure of her own midwife skills, wanting nothing to go wrong for Christa or the new life soon to join them.

Anna Marie also thought Christa's mother should be there to share in the birth of her first grandchild, as Christa's mother so desperately wanted to do. Maybe her mother was trying to make up for the years of neglect while trying to humor Christa's Stepdad. Anna Marie thought how each woman as a mother tried to do the best she could. She had never heard any mother say that as a mother she had done everything right.

She thought, "Maybe in a society that did not really value

motherhood, children, or women. Women were set up for failure in the role from the beginning to the end?"

Christa left the passenger's seat, gently setting Little Bear down on the seat, walking carefully back to the bathroom. Maya, sitting on the dashboard in front of Christa, watched Christa with anxiety, then followed her to the back of the Southwind.

Anna Marie anxiously asked her, "Christa, do you feel alright? You look a little peaked."

Christa answered her, "I just need to use the bathroom again. I'll be okay."

About ten minutes later Christa came back to the front, anxiously expressing her concerns, "Anna Marie, I've been feeling strange all morning and last night. There is water all over the bathroom. I don't have the energy to clean it up and I have the worst cramps I have ever had in my life. What's going on?"

She looked at Anna Marie who had pulled over into the right lane, searching frantically for the next exit or rest stop. She guessed from her own birth experiences what was likely happening to Christa.

Anna Marie said as calmly as she could, "Christa, honey, go back to the couch and sit with your feet up. How far apart are the cramps you are feeling?"

Christa answered, "I haven't counted the time in between. It started out hours apart, then about 30 minutes apart and now there is very little time in between each cramp with almost no relief from the pain."

Anna Marie sighed, wishing Christa had told her this before this moment. There was nothing she could do now about this lack of sharing of such essential information, so she worked at remaining calm. She mentally thought it was time to go to plan B, which meant finding the nearest hospital or emergency room and calling Christa's parents from there. She didn't think there would be any time for a homecoming before the baby came.

She also thought about her long-ago written list for this journey from another lifetime; experiencing a baby born on her

Southwind had never been added to that list. Distributing her remaining personal cards to hospital staff had also not been part of her original plan.

At the next exit there was a hospital sign with directions to turn right at the first light. She asked Christa, "Are you familiar with where we are now? Are we very close to your home?"

Christa looked out the window from the couch where she sat with her feet up as Anna Marie had suggested.

She answered, "Not really, other than I know we are close to Portland. I can't tell you how close. Did you see a name on the exit?"

Anna Marie said, "I was so busy looking for a hospital sign that I didn't notice the name of the town or the exit."

Anna Marie hesitated, not wanting to frighten Christa, and then said, "I'm turning here. We're going to the emergency room at the hospital. I think you may not be very far away from having the baby."

Christa spoke, sounding frightened, "I thought maybe that might be what was happening to me. But I'm not supposed to be due for a couple of weeks yet. I was hoping to be home for at least a few days so that I could set up a nursery for the baby in my old room."

Anna Marie responded, trying to sound calm, "Babies don't wait for convenient times to come. We were never sure of your due date since we were guessing when you became pregnant. It could be a false alarm, but I don't think so. My experience with my own children makes me think you are less than an hour away from giving birth. We don't want to take any chances. For my eldest daughter Katy, I just got to the hospital when I had her in the Emergency Room." Christa, in a wavering voice said, "Anna Marie, I'm afraid."

Anna Marie reassured her, "That's natural, honey. All first-time mothers are afraid and even mothers who have had several children. But once you see your baby you will forget all your pain and fear. I promise you; it will be okay."

Christa asked, "Suppose I don't? Suppose I don't love my baby like everyone says I automatically do? Maybe all I will remember is the pain of birth? It's not as though I loved the father or have a great future for my baby right now. Suppose she resents me for bringing her into the world without a father, a nice home, or a future? Or maybe I'll be giving her my handicap. I don't want her to live with being disabled and people looking at her funny like they do with me sometimes."

Anna Marie softly answered Christa, "I think life is like a big puzzle that falls into place as you live it. You will learn to love your baby for the baby's sake, not the father's. There will be days you can't imagine life without her and other days you wish you could go back to the time before being a parent. It will all work out."

She glanced sideways at Christa, giving her a sympathetic but encouraging smile. Or at least Anna Marie hoped that's what her facial expression looked like to Christa.

Anna Marie reassured her, "You will find a way to make a life for you and your baby. You have your parents. You can always come out to stay with me if you want to go back to school. I'd love to have you stay with me. I know your mother is hoping you will go to college and is willing to help you. She will love your baby too, especially as this baby is her first grandchild. There is nothing like that thrill, a child of your own having a child of her or his own. You'll see it will all work out. Granny Rose and I will be there to help whenever we can or when you need us the most."

Anna Marie added much more forcefully than she felt at that moment, "Everything will be okay including this birth. If she does have a handicap, which most likely she won't, you will know what to do to help her grow into all she can be. I've never noticed that you are disabled or different. You are beautiful to me. You will love your daughter as she is and as she becomes more of who she wants to be. There is always a pain that you feel for your children because you want what is best for them. That is not always what happens in their lives. But somehow they find their own life and live through their own pains, disappointments, and successes."

Anna Marie knew she was rambling on with her own thoughts, possibly not even making much sense to Christa. At least her voice seemed to be calming Christa.

There was a moment of silence, then Anna Marie added to her previous comment, "People who look at you differently have their own problems. I think they are afraid that somehow any differences will be contagious. People who are disabled are important to help us all think about what is significant in life."

Anna Marie recalled, "When I was a Special Education Assistant, I learned far more of what was valuable in life than the children ever learned from me. There was one little boy who had been severely abused and lived in a foster home. He was always so excited to see me. He gave me the biggest smile every day making me feel wonderful about myself and the world. Sometimes in my worst moments, I picture him smiling, thinking how he showed me there was so much good in the world."

Christa asked, "Whatever happened to that little boy?"

Anna Marie responded, with a sigh of deep regret, "He grew up to go to war and was killed fighting a battle over oil in another part of the world. No one ever knew how far he had come in his life or how difficult it was for him to achieve all that he had. He came to visit me just before he went to war. He hoped that he would use his military benefits to go to school to become a special education teacher. Instead, he has been lost to the world and all the difference he could have made."

After a pause to reflect on what Anna Marie said, Christa whispered, "I wish Granny Rose could be here with me along with you and my mother. I'd feel as though I had all the support I needed then. Do you think Harry-Jim-Bob will drive Granny Rose out to see my baby and me?"

Anna Rose smiled and answered, "Without a doubt, honey. As soon as we call and let them know. Granny Rose will be here as quickly as Harry can bring her. But I do agree with you, I wish Granny Rose were with us right this moment."

Anna Marie pulled off the expressway slowing to turn right at the green light. She attempted to stay calm, concentrating on the road to deliver Christa to the door of the emergency room safely. At the end of the long street, she saw a sign indicating "St. Rose's Hospital" with an arrow to turn right. She thought the name of the hospital was a good omen and her anxiety level dropped a little bit.

Anna Marie advised Christa, "The hospital is St. Rose's Hospital. That's a good sign. We'll be there in a few minutes. As soon as we have someone examine you I will call your parents to let them know you are here. I'll also call Granny Rose and let her know where we are."

Christa made the sound of a cry, "Anna Marie, I hope it's real soon as I'm in terrible pain It's not letting up at all. I don't want my baby to be hurt."

Her voice trailed off as another wave of pain overwhelmed her.

She panted loudly, small cries of pain coming from her reluctantly. Tears rolled down her cheeks as she held her large, expanded abdomen trying to stop the pain by touch or to stop the birth from happening by pressure and sheer will until help arrived.

Anna Marie parked sideways in the driveway by the emergency room exit, careful not to get too close to any of the parked cars. She recalled Walter's story he had told her during their driving lessons of making a turn to a gas pump with the Southwind, hitting a parked car on the side. The car had thousands of dollars worth of damage and the Southwind lost its rear bumper. Anna Marie was glad she had so far avoided that on this trip. She continued to keep herself calm during this latest emergency so that all of them, including the Southwind remained undamaged.

Christa cried, "Anna Marie, get me help please. I don't think I can get up without losing the baby. I feel pounds of pressure and I'm afraid I can't stand up. Please help me! I feel like I am going to pee my pants, only much worse than that!"

Maya and Little Bear both stood beside Christa watching her with frightened expressions. Little Bear whimpered and Maya meowed. Circe remained uncharacteristically quiet, not wanting to add to the stress of the moment.

Anna Marie shut off the motor home instructing Christa, "Put your feet up on the pillow. I'll try flagging someone down outside and then help you with your clothes."

Anna Marie opened the door of the Southwind peeking anxiously outside. She saw an older couple enter a car outside the emergency room. She yelled to them but neither seemed to hear her as they closed the doors behind them. They drove off like someone being pursued. Anna Marie did observe the woman in the passenger seat looking back at them. On the rear bumper of their car was a bumper sticker "Stop the killing of babies. End Abortion Now!"

Anna Marie noticed a young girl carrying a paper bag full of books. She motioned to the young girl who looked at Anna Marie suspiciously.

Anna Marie said to her, "Please, help my friend. She is going to have a baby any minute. I can't leave her to get help from the hospital. I'll stay with her if you go inside for a doctor or nurse to come out here quickly. Tell them a first-time mother is about to have a baby in a motor home in the parking lot."

The young girl nodded, rushing inside the doors to the emergency room while Christa screamed for Anna Marie, "Anna Marie, please help me. I think I'm going to have the baby now."

Christa began repeating some unknown rhythmic sounds, in an apparent effort to calm herself and help the baby.

Anna Marie rushed back to the bathroom. She carefully washed her hands, grabbed a couple of clean towels, and then returned to Christa. She asked Christa to prop pillows behind her so that she could partially sit up. She helped her remove her underpants, which were now soaking wet with a pink fluid. As calmly as possible she asked Christa to breathe deeply in rhythm with the pain.

She instructed the soon to be mother, "Christa, go to the white pelicans. Watch each one fly overhead to join the others. Breathe in rhythm to their spiral circles thinking of yourself flying with them in the same pattern. Whenever you feel a sharp pain, instead of fighting the pain, go with it as though flying with the pelicans. Help Mother Nature deliver your new daughter to us. We can do this just like trillions or more of women before us have given life. I'm here with you; we'll do this together."

Anna Marie did not know if the words were to soothe Christa or herself. Anna Marie hummed a childhood lullaby as she arranged the towels while grabbing a blanket from the cupboard overhead, for once glad the Southwind was so compact that everything needed was close by. Like Christa, she comforted herself by flowing with the rhythm of birth, placing herself overhead as an observer and a participant.

Christa did as Anna Marie instructed, appearing a little calmer. Anna Marie gently pulled up Christa's maternity blouse stroking Christa's belly in a circular pattern, wondering where the help was from the hospital. She didn't realize how shy the young girl was she sent inside for help.

The little girl silently and politely waited in line for her turn at the desk in the emergency room behind a line of people with their own emergencies. Anna Marie had not understood the red tape each waiting person had to complete before the hospital could provide any services. Unaware of the delay, Anna Marie focused on the world within their vehicle, softly soothing Christa. She repeated the guidance of the pelicans gently repeating the pelican's ascent.

At first Christa calmed down until she jerked and screamed, "Anna Marie I can't wait any longer. I can feel the baby pushing hard. I can't stop the pushing."

Anna Marie softly responded, "Don't try to stop the baby honey, work with her. Let her come. I'm here to help you. You'll both be fine."

The more frightened Christa became, the calmer Anna Marie

grew. From somewhere deep inside Anna Marie felt very calm and sure of herself. She felt all her female ancestors before her were standing at her side to help with the delivery of this next generation of woman.

Anna Marie repeated over and over, "its okay honey, think of the pelicans" as she gently stroked Christa's stomach and instructed Christa to open her legs as far apart as she could.

She asked her to pull herself up further on the couch with her behind hanging off the end, thus letting gravity work with the birth, placing clean towels underneath Christa.

Anna Marie could see a small head appear with the next strong contraction as Christa cried louder, "Please, stop the pain and make my baby come. Please let my baby be okay. Help me Anna Marie!"

Anna Marie continued to reassure her as she wiped some sweat from Christa's face with one towel, then gently suggested, "With the next contraction honey, push as hard as you can. I'll help your baby come to this life where her family is waiting to welcome her. We can't wait for help. We can do it together."

At that, Christa gave a large cry pushing with as much force as she had left in her. Anna Marie encouragingly said, "The head is coming through. We just need one more push and she'll be here with us. You're doing great honey."

Anna Marie repeated her calm directions over and over. In between she hummed her lullaby, wanting the new baby to come into the world to the sound of the peaceful lullaby. She wondered if it was possible that there was some ancient memory for all women about giving birth and if the more "advanced" medical technology became the more that memory was disguised.

Christa pushed with all her might as the next contraction followed immediately after the previous contraction. Anna Marie pushed down gently on Christa's stomach and continued the rubbing movement, instinctively knowing what to do with every stage of the birth. She massaged Christa's stomach, whispering words of encouragement. It would only be afterwards that she would wonder how she was able to remain so calm during the birth. With Christa's pushing down and Anna Marie's help, on the next contraction the baby came easily through the birth canal.

Anna Marie held onto the baby, gently holding the head as she said, "She's three fourths of the way here. Just one more push and she'll be all the way out."

Anna Marie had forgotten about the young girl she had sent inside for help who was now next in line and waiting patiently for the receptionist to call on her. She and Christa, along with their pets, remained absorbed in this life-giving activity with the world stopped at the Southwind's doors.

With one last push, the soon to be named Maria Anne was out of her mother and in the arms of Anna Marie. The umbilical cord remained attached to her mother. Anna Marie wiped away some of the blood with the clean towel and gently slapped the baby to be sure she was breathing.

Maria Anne screamed loudly at the intrusion on her body. Anna Marie thought that this new person already had an amazing life force. Anna Marie left the umbilical cord attached as she placed the baby on her mother's stomach and hugged the baby along with her mother.

She said to Christa, "Here is your lovely Maria Anne. You do have to push another time or two to bring out the after birth. Then you'll be done. Wonderful job, honey! You were a natural."

Anna Marie kissed the baby on the forehead. She encouraged Christa to give one more push. With the last push the afterbirth came out with the baby. Anna Marie sat on the floor, relieved at the baby's healthy cries and that the birth was over. Without touching the cord or the afterbirth, Anna Marie gently cleaned the tiny girl as best as she could with the materials she had available.

She sat on the floor, unsure what to do next and exhausted from all the energy she had put into Maria Anne's birth. Anna Marie listened for sounds outside for help with the last steps of the birth. Hearing none, she sat observing the beauty of the mother and child, amazed at her own participation in this miraculous event.

Christa held her baby, crying with relief over the end of the pain and the apparent good health of the infant.

She exclaimed to Anna Marie as the tears from Christa fell onto Maria Anne, "She is so beautiful. I never knew she would be so beautiful."

Maria Anne routed for Christa's breast. Christa helped her find the nipple. Instead of crying, loud sucking noises were heard in the Southwind as all the passengers looked on in amazement at the new life that had so suddenly joined them. The animals appeared to realize a miracle had just happened in front of them. Even Circe looked happy, sitting quietly at peace.

The little girl inside directed the receptionist to where she had seen the lady with the motor home with an expectant mother on board.

She shyly said, "The lady said someone was giving birth right now. That was awhile ago while I waited in the long line."

The receptionist called one of the nurses in the back, "Mary, can you go see what's going on outside? This young lady says there is a mother ready to give birth in an RV in the parking lot. Just go and check. I'm sure it's a false alarm but just to be on the safe side."

The receptionist turned to the little girl and said, "You do know that it is very bad to lie?" The little girl nodded shyly, even more frightened now as Nurse Mary Faye walked outside to see the Southwind in the Emergency Room parking lot.

She walked to the door of the motor home and called in, "Hello. Is anyone there?"

The little girl followed along behind her, still clinging to her bag of books, wondering what would happen next on this very unusual day. She couldn't wait to tell her mother about this exciting moment on her way home from school.

Anna Marie heard the voice at the door and said, "Come in, the door is open. Christa has already had her baby, but I need help with the afterbirth and cutting the umbilical cord."

The nurse rushed in and said, "Oh my god! The little girl was not lying."

Maria Anne, happy to be in the world with her mother and Anna Marie but upset her breastfeeding was disturbed, whimpered softly.

The nurse approached Christa, "You look like you have delivered a healthy baby girl."

The nurse then turned to Anna Marie ordering her, "Go inside and get a couple more nurses to help me!"

Christa loudly protested, "No. I want Anna Marie here with me. She's helped me so far. I need her here."

The nurse nodded and shouted out to the little girl standing hesitantly outside, "Please go and tell the lady you talked to before that there is a birth in the parking lot and I need a couple of nurses to help me along with supplies."

The little girl walked swiftly into the Emergency Room; this time determined not to stand in the already growing long line again.

She approached the head of the line, said "Excuse me" to the first person in line, then louder and more forcefully than she had ever spoken before in her life related the message from the nurse.

The lady at the desk hesitated for a minute before calling on a pager for more help in the parking lot. Immediately, there were more staff than could fit into the Southwind standing outside the Southwind, including a receptionist responsible for paperwork to make sure no one received health care without paying for it.

An argument broke out as to who should go onto the Southwind first, until Nurse Faye solved the issue by pointing to two nurses. She asked the rest to wait outside until the emergency was over.

The nurses attempted to move Anna Marie out of the way. Anna Marie complied, wanting the afterbirth removed and the baby cleaned so that there was less risk of infection.

The older nurse performed this service, while clucking, "How could anyone today not know enough to get to the hospital in time? What a shame this is, placing the mother and baby at risk instead of having this baby in the hospital as she should have!"

She looked glaringly at Anna Marie, obviously accusing Anna Marie of intentionally causing this birth to happen at this time before entering the hospital for help. She continued to shake her head at the potential horror of this birth.

Anna Marie remained quiet, content to observe the care provided by the nurses and marveling in the splendor of Christa and Maria Anne. She recalled her own children's and grandchildren's birth. She thought what a miracle newborn life was, especially for her when the baby is born accidentally aboard the Southwind. Now that Christa and the baby were fine, it somehow seemed fitting that the birth took place in the Southwind rather than in a sterile hospital setting with strangers.

Noticing Christa was comfortable with all the attention to her and her newborn, Anna Marie brought her cell phone and Little Bear outside, after settling Maya and Circe in their tiny houses.

She first called Christa's mother and then Granny Rose. Christa's mother was not happy she had missed the birth, though relieved both mother and daughter were safely cared for by the hospital nurses. She assured Anna Marie she would be there in less than 30 minutes as she was familiar with the location of the hospital.

Anna Marie's next call was to Granny Rose, who answered on the second ring, exclaiming before Anna Marie spoke, "Give me the directions. I want to see my Maria Anne. Harry and I will be out by tomorrow evening."

Anna Marie shook her head, amazed at this diminutive but powerful and mysterious woman.

She ended the call as simultaneously the phone rang shrilly. Anna Marie thought it was likely Walter as this was exactly the time-of-day Walter often chose to call. She answered the phone, expecting to hear Walter's voice but instead heard the shrill voice of her mother-in-law.

Her mother-in-law shouted into the phone, "You didn't even have the decency to tell me you were traipsing off across the county leaving your poor children alone to face who knows what tragedy. I would have spent the summer up there with them had I known. My beloved Ted just fresh in his grave and you're off meeting men and who knows what else. You're probably looking for a replacement for Ted so you can kill him off too."

Anna Marie took a deep breath, silently said a few calming words, and then responded, "Why Harriet, it is so nice to hear your voice. This is really a bad time. In fact, any time will be a bad time in the future unless you start talking to me respectfully. I've done nothing to deserve this tone from you. I will no longer tolerate it. Call me when you've thought about it and want to have a reasonable relationship."

She pressed the end call button, forcing herself to breathe again while remaining calm. She was proud of herself for doing something she should have done years ago. She finally understood only she could control her response to such abuse. She talked to Ted silently, telling him that she was sorry they both had not done this sooner. She imagined hearing Ted sigh, then applauding her action. At least now she was not hurting anyone except possibly herself. Not her mother-in-law though she might have to find someone else to take her anger out on and Anna Marie hoped it would not be one of her own children or Grandchildren.

Christa's mother arrived shortly after the last phone call. The hospital staff pulled her aside to complete all the necessary paperwork, giving her no time to spend with her new granddaughter. As they tried to move Christa and the baby into the hospital, Christa loudly protested, calling her mother and Anna Marie to her side.

She explained, "I had this baby safely in the Southwind. I want to go home to my own house now. There is no reason for me to stay here as Mom and you, Anna Marie, can do everything for me that I need. I do not want to be in a strange room without you both. I don't want to start my baby's life here. Do you both understand?"

Christa's Mom, Gail, looked to Anna Marie for her advice.

Anna Marie thought a minute, answering, "Can you contact your family doctor to ask him or her to meet us here? I think if we know there is someone close who could help it would be alright."

Gail nodded using Anna Marie's cell phone to call home for the HMO's number and then to call the HMO.

After a brief conversation, Christa's mom came back to explain, "They don't see any problem with it if we understand that we take full responsibility for our decision. I personally think they are happy not to have to pay for a night in the hospital for the baby and Christa."

She turned to Christa and asked, "Are you sure you feel okay and are up to this?"

Christa nodded, too full of relief to say anything more.

The rest of the early evening was spent with telephone calls and arrangements for Christa and the baby to return home. Christa insisted on arriving home in the Southwind with the baby held snuggly in her arms. She was tired and pleased to have others to take over arrangements. The doctor from the HMO visited Christa and the Baby in the Southwind, providing suggestions and medicines to help ease Christa's pain after birth.

Maria Anne began life with much life force but also be easily appeased by cuddling, feeding, and changing. Anna Marie and Gail took turns holding the baby while Christa washed up and changed, coming back to the baby with much more enthusiasm. Anna Marie prepared her bedroom for Christa and the baby during the move aboard the Southwind.

The hospital staff checked out Christa and the baby one more time with only one nurse making noises about the "irresponsible decisions these people continue to make." The rest looked excited to be part of an unusual and healthy birth.

The little girl, Missy, who had tried to help in the emergency had been sent on her way home, after many hugs and kisses as well as contact information so that Christa could send thank you flowers and candy to her. Christa would never know that those flowers would be dried and kept by the little girl all her life, even as she became a grandmother and great grandmother. It would be her reminder of her first participation in the miracle of creation.

As the Southwind pulled out of the parking lot, followed by Gail and Christa's stepfather, Tim, who had joined them reluctantly after his work, 13 of the hospital staff lined up and waved them goodbye along with well-wishes. The sun had long since set, the quarter moon slowly rising in the sky.

Within the hour, they arrived at Christa's parents' house. Christa and Maria Anne rushed to their room as the evening grew late. Anna Marie was glad that this had to be done quickly and with little fanfare as the symbolism of Christa leaving the Southwind would have been too much for her otherwise. The nurse practitioner from the HMO arrived to examine Christa and the baby again to be sure they were okay and understood how to care for both.

Anna Marie walked Little Bear, feeding all three animals as well as cleaning the Southwind so as to be out of the way of all of the confusion. Later, Gail thanked Anna Marie for her consideration allowing her to become the primary Grandmother rather than Anna Marie.

That evening Anna Marie and her remaining companions fell asleep into a deep sleep with Anna Marie dreaming of Ted, Christa, Maria Anne as a teenager, and Granny Rose who tried to tell Anna Marie something that she could not understand. As she attempted to hear Granny Rose, Maya and Little Bear stirred in their sleep, chasing something in their dreams they could not reach. Anna Marie woke the next morning feeling achier than she had been in years, and with a sense that all was not right with her world.

Shortly after fixing herself and her pets a small breakfast, the phone rang. It was her mother-in-law, sobbing into the phone.

She said, "Anna Marie, please don't hang up. I had some bad news yesterday that I'm going to need a triple bypass. I don't have anyone here to be with me. I would like you to come with Katy or Erin. They've scheduled it for next week. I need to give them a health care proxy. I know that I haven't always been kind to you. I also know that you would see that the doctors take care of me. I am sorry for all our misunderstandings."

She paused, waiting for Anna Marie to respond.

After a long awkward silence, Anna Marie said, "I don't quite know what to say. You do know that I am out here in Oregon. It would take me several days to get back to New York and then down to New Jersey. When is it scheduled next week?"

"It's scheduled for Friday, so you have almost two weeks. I know I am asking a lot from you."

Again, there was an awkward pause.

Anna Marie thought and then said, "I'll call Cynthia first and see if she is available. I'm not sure if Katy can get away or Erin but Cynthia is most likely to be able to leave her job."

Anna Marie knew she was really pushing the button by suggesting Cynthia, but she firmly believed that good things should come from bad moments. She also wanted to see how badly her mother-in-law wanted her there. She wanted to mend as many broken fences as possible.

Her mother-in-law responded, "Yes, that would be alright. I haven't seen Cynthia in a long time. She would be a great support for you during this difficult time with me."

Anna Marie would have laughed if the moment wasn't so serious and her mother-in-law obviously trying very hard to be nice.

Instead, she said, "I'll call and see what arrangements I can make. Maybe Erin would be able to come out and drive back with me so I could drive longer days."

Anna Marie was able to reach Erin, who had some important business meetings to attend that were essential to his job. He apologized offering to cancel them.

Anna Marie did not want to hurt his promotional opportunities, so she assured him, "I'll be able to find one of my friends to come back with me. Don't worry. I just thought it would be nice to spend a few days together. We'll do that in the future. Give my love to everyone."

After hanging up the phone, she called Diana who answered on the second ring. After updating Diana about Christa and the baby, she explained the mother-in-law's situation. She asked Diana, "Would you fly out here and drive back with me? I would love to spend the time with you. It would help relieve me so that I could do some 10-hour days of driving?"

Diana answered, "I would love to come but I don't think I could drive that big thing. It terrifies me. If you just want the company I would be happy to join you."

Anna Marie agreed that the company was what she most needed adding, "I have missed you. It would be a perfect ending to this journey for you to be here with me. It would help me transition back to my life."

Anna Marie heard some sniffles on the other end.

Diana said, "I was afraid I had lost you, that you would never come home again. Or if you came home you would be so changed that our friendship would never be the same."

Anna Marie exclaimed, "Diana, you will never stop being my closest friend. I have changed. My change does not affect our friendship. It only makes it even more important. Christa once told me of a Native American legend in which every new friendship is thought to multiply the previous by seven. That's what has happened to us; with so many times seven I can't count them all."

The next day Gail drove Anna Marie to meet Diana at the Portland airport. Both were overwhelmed with emotion holding each other quietly as they cried.

Back at Christa's house, they spent the day with the baby and preparing the Southwind for its journey home. Cynthia had agreed to meet Anna Marie in New York to drive to New Jersey for her grandmother's surgery with her mother. She was a little surprised her grandmother would allow her to be there but was more than willing to help her mother out as she knew her relationship with her mother-in-law had always been very difficult. Anna Marie marveled once again at the compassion of her middle child.

The tearful goodbyes to Christa and the baby were said that night so Anna Marie and Diana could leave very early in the morning without disturbing the family. The baby woke at 5 am after her first night of sleeping straight through most of the night. Christa and Maria Anne waved the ladies farewell, everyone else in the house sound asleep.

The days returning to New York passed quickly with Diana and Anna Marie talking the entire time, catching up on each other's lives. Anna Marie told Diana about her brief affair with Walter and the follow-up phone calls, the first person she had ever told. She knew Diana would understand and she did. Diana laughed when she heard the details of the timing of the phone calls.

The arrival at her house was anti-climatic. Katy spent the day before she returned cleaning the house to welcome Anna Marie home. The house smelled of herbs as they entered the door. On the hallway table was a lovely flower arrangement with a large 'welcome home' balloon in the center of the arrangement.

Maya and Circe examined their new home, quickly finding what would be their favorite spots, Maya in a sunny window and Circe in the middle of the kitchen. Little Bear explored every nook and corner to see if anything had changed or if there were new smells she needed to investigate. Finding none, she fell asleep on her couch in her own old favorite place.

Anna Marie was glad that she had arranged for mail forwarding to different post offices during her journey so that she did not have boxes of mail waiting for her, something she always found discouraging after a trip. When it sat there in a pile it often felt as if real life did not allow time out for reflection or quiet. She learned on this trip that it was essential in the healing process to take time to face grief, build new ways of contentment, and to learn about who she wanted to become.

The Present

Anna Marie jerked into full consciousness as she heard Erin's car in the driveway. She thought of all that had happened since her return home from her first journey with the Southwind. Her mother-in-law had been very civil to Cynthia and Anna Maria, apparently grateful for their support. Harriet Golding survived the surgery dying nine months later from complications of infection caused by the surgery.

She changed her Will before dying, splitting most of her estate between Erin and Katy. She left a small leather suitcase to Cynthia with instructions to share this with Anna Marie at the right time.

That right time was recently, when Cynthia explained the contents over the phone, "It is full of old letters from friends in Louisiana and some from Sumer, Louisiana. Mom, isn't Sumer, Louisiana where you are going this week at Granny Rose's request to view a box? Isn't it strange these papers turn up at the same time you were asked to take care of a box? It must be the same box. I wonder how Grandma Golding could have been connected to Sumer, Louisiana."

Anna Marie assured her daughter that this was no stranger than other experiences related to Granny Rose and the Southwind. She then asked her daughter for more details.

"Apparently, my three times Great Grandmother on Dad's side of his family was one of the keepers of the box in the early 1900s. Somehow the papers were separated from the box. It appears the families involved had an argument. They never returned the papers to the other branch of the family."

Thinking of the significance of this information given to

Cynthia by Anna Marie's mother-in-law she wondered how she could learn more. Maybe she wasn't descended from Granny Rose's family, instead it was Ted and their children. It reminded her how much her mother-in-law did not trust her or want her in the family. She felt a little piece of a large puzzle fall into place.

Cynthia continued, "The family knew the documents were important. They were handed down to the wives of each of the Golding sons on the first wedding anniversary, the anniversary for paper gifts. My ancestors understood the significance of the information on those papers. Grandma Harriet told me in her papers she 'forgot' to give them to you, asking me to pass them along to you. I'm sending the package of papers to you. I will insure them to make sure they are protected. I haven't read them as I felt they were meant only for you. I hope you will share the information with me."

Anna Marie realized this was the unexpected help Granny Rose had described. Did she know how close their relationship was through marriage or were their other connections. She enjoyed detective stories, looking forward to solving this one. A shiver shot through her, telling her the investigative phase would be more than she expected. Was this information connected to people she had already met or was there more to come?

Anna Marie looked at her watch noting Erin was later than he expected. To ease her mind, she thought back over how much had changed and what had stayed the same after her Southwind first journey.

Diana married a gentleman she had met while Anna Marie was in Oregon visiting Christa and Maria Anne. Anna Marie became part of their threesome for occasional dinners out, similar to Diana's role when Ted was live. She now understood how Diana had felt all those years with her and Ted. While she was happy for Diana it was hard to see the affection they had for each other and the secret looks between them, the same kind she had often shared with Ted. The friendship with the couple was worth it for the slight awkwardness.

Katy and her husband stayed together over the past 7 years. Katy had gone on for another master's degree, this time in women's studies. She now worked for a consulting company producing educational textbooks to make sure women and women's history were included in the books traveling frequently conducting research. Anna Marie suspected there were times that Katy paid back her husband by having brief affairs on the road. They never spoke of it but there were signs that Anna Marie could not miss. She chose to accept Katy's decisions while staying out of that part of her life. It helped that her grandchildren appeared to be well adjusted and happy with their lives.

Cynthia remained with Anita. They had been persuaded by Anna Marie to go out to Montana for a ceremony with Reverend Sophia. While the ceremony was small, it had been lovely shared by their closest family and friends.

After they returned from Montana, the two of them took in foster children needing good homes. The Boston adoption system had still not advanced enough to allow adoption by couples of the same sex. Occasionally, they brought the foster children out to visit Anna Marie. It was apparent that the couple was providing a loving, safe environment for children who came from neglected and abusive backgrounds.

Erin continued to remind Anna Marie of Ted as he was protective of his mother every chance he got, Anna Marie hoped his wife did not mind this attention to her. He did receive his promotion at the newspaper but quit the newspaper a year after the promotion. He and his wife developed an antique business with at least half the sales conducted on E-Bay. In addition, he published his first novel the previous spring with moderate success and was writing his second novel. He had also begun a book of poetry with Anna Marie awed by his talent and sensitivity.

Late at night she carried on her conversations with Ted. She imagined him agreeing with her over the wonder of these children they had created together. She had also begun to write herself, joining a writing group, realizing that some of Erin's talent was inherited from his mother.

Anna Marie returned to the senior center, and for a short period of time felt like she was quickly being sucked back into the previous rhythm of life before the Southwind. One day she received a letter from an organization of motorhome owners. She jumped at the chance to join this group. They did frequent long weekend trips together with two cross country trips in a caravan.

She also joined another couple she developed a close friendship with for two winter months in a motor home park in Florida. She found the park to be welcoming and was instantly a member of the community. Diana and her husband or one of her children with their families came to visit her in Florida for short vacations.

She traveled out on her own to Montana and Oregon to spend time with Granny Rose and Harry-Jim-Bob, then on to visit Christa and the baby. Christa completed her GED and then attended college the next semester, achieving both a bachelor's degree and a master's degree in three years. A couple of times Maria Anne returned to New York with Anna Marie to give Christa time for school and Maria Anne time with Anna Marie. Maria Anne had become as precious to Anna Marie as her own grandchildren with Maria Anne calling her "Grandmother Anna, my New York grandmother."

Life had been very good over the seven years from her first journey with the Southwind. As Erin grabbed her suitcase waiting by the door, she silently said goodbye for a brief time to her house. She also sent a thank you to the goddesses who had given her all the gifts of the past years. She wondered what this next journey would bring as she stepped into Erin's car, and he closed the door behind her.

The Present: Louisiana

As she rode to the airport, Anna Marie thought how far her life had come and how many people she added to her family of loved ones. She also thought of all those she had lost in the past few years. She realized that it was the accumulation of all those people that made her who she was.

The day before Anna Marie left for Sumer she had received the package from Cynthia with the papers from her Grandmother Golding.

The brief note from Cynthia read, "Grandma Golding gave me these in her will as I told you after the will was read. She said I could make of them what I wanted. She had received them from her grandmother. She had always felt they were a burden and was happy to pass them on to me. I think these papers will help you on your journey to Sumer. At first I was resentful this is all I got from Grandma Golding. Now I suspect this was the best inheritance of all. All my love, Cynthia."

In her brief look at the papers, she thought there might be some connection of this information to the box she was on her way to view. She thought about Granny Rose's comment that she would get help from an unexpected source. She certainly had not expected that source would be in her own family. Especially not her mother-in-law who seemed the farthest removed from Granny Rose than anyone else she had known in her lifetime.

She brought these papers with her to read on the plane and to show Christa. She suspected there were many years ahead trying to understand the connections and understanding of the information. She was now even more anxious to reach Sumer and observe this mysterious box.

She had found a professional carver in the Syracuse area who was currently searching for ancient Rosewood on E-Bay to carve her Catbird for the mysterious box. She had given him very small dimensions. He was excited about the challenge. Anna Marie knew she had selected the right object and the right carver, looking forward to the completion of the carving.

The plane trip was uneventful and remarkably on time. She had a few minutes in the coffee shop in the New Orleans airport for a café au lait before meeting Christa's and Maria Anne's plane. She had read through some of the hundreds of pages of writings on the plane.

Christa's plane was also on time. Soon she was hugging Christa, exclaiming over how much Maria Anne had grown since the last time she had seen them both.

Maria Anne hugged Anna Marie and said, "I've missed you Grandma Anna. I'm glad Mom let me come with both of you."

Christa waited for her bags while Anna Marie arranged for the rental car. Soon they were on the highway to Sumer, Louisiana.

Christa and Anna Marie reminisced as they drove to Sumer. They caught up on what was happening in their lives. The rhythm of the car quickly put little Maria Anne to sleep.

They continued talking, acknowledging how much they would miss Granny Rose, even though they knew she would be with them forever, just in another place they could not see. They wondered what they would find in the security box at the bank.

When they arrived in Sumer, they searched for the Bed and Breakfast, 'The Ancient Rose', where they had reservations for the night. Anna Marie's travel agent had suggested this Bed and Breakfast at the recommendations of one of the women in her agency. Anna Marie had thought the name was another good omen.

It was a lovely old house on the main street of the town. Sybil, a lady who was probably as old as Granny Rose met them at the door. They quickly settled their bags in their separate rooms, selected their dinner menu from the options given by their landlady, and were given directions to the bank where the security box was located.

Maria Anne had already met Sybil's great-grandchildren who were staying with their great-grandmother during their school break. Sybil suggested Maria Anne stay with her and her great-grandchildren while Anna Marie and Christa conducted their "errand at the bank." Maria Anne begged them to let her stay with the other children. After a brief discussion, Christa decided it was probably best for her to stay back and play.

Christa could also sense that no harm would come to Maria Anne under the watchful and loving eyes of Sybil.

Christa said, "Since we don't know exactly what we are going to find or how long this is going to take, it makes sense for Maria Anne to stay here and play. If you don't mind one more child with you…?"

Sybil assured her, "The more the merrier. This will give you ladies more time for your task. I love children around me. That doesn't happen often enough these days. I have some great gardening projects they are going to help me with, then we are going to make homemade ice cream. Mother Rose would also be pleased for me to get to know Maria Anne!"

The children cheered and jumped up and down with excitement as they heard about their afternoon ahead. The children excitedly pulled Maria Anne out the door to show her the swing hanging in the old oak tree before they began their gardening tasks.

It took Anna Marie a few seconds to realize who "Mother Rose" was and to understand that Sybil had a powerful connection to her. She shook her head in amazement.

Anna Marie and Christa left Maria Anne on her way out to the swing with the other children. She was already naturally directing the other children as to who could do what tasks.

Christa, observing her lovely daughter, shook her head and said, "I don't know where she gets it from. I was always shy as a child. Maybe it was the time spent with you and Granny Rose? I don't think it's genetic."

Christa hesitated and then asked shyly, "Did you notice Sybil referred to Granny Rose as 'Mother Rose?' That's strange in that Sybil looks older than Granny Rose was when she died. She also referred to her in the present tense, as though she is still living."

Anna Marie nodded and shrugged her shoulder to indicate that there was much that was strange about Sybil, Granny Rose, and this journey at the request of Granny Rose.

Within a half hour, they found the bank, provided the needed identification to get access to the security deposit box, and were in the basement area of the bank. The banker, Mr. Avebury, an elderly gentleman dressed in an expensive pin striped three-piece suit, left them in the basement. He explained how to open the box, pointing to a long table in the room where they could lay out the contents of the box.

He asked before leaving them alone, "Do you think you will be renewing the security deposit box for the next year?"

Anna Marie told him, "We don't know at this point. But that's a decision we will talk about later and get back to you when we decide. We are not really sure of what is expected of us yet."

He nodded and said, "Whatever you decide. You may want to know that this security box has been here for five generations, since the bank was opened in the 1800s. There has been the same security box with different sponsors from various countries of the world over all those years so you may consider leaving it here with us. We seem to be well suited to the storage of these items. You'll find this is a beautiful area of the country to visit. Keeping it here will give you opportunities to do that."

Mr. Avebury paused, lost in recent memories, "The last time Rose was here was early this year. She told us at that time that would be her last visit. She said to expect the two of you the next time the box was opened. That was when she signed everything over to your name, Mrs. Golding. No one has been here since Rose. I have looked forward to meeting you both."

Anna Marie asked, "Has it always been signed over to someone else in this way?"

He said, "I looked this up before you came because I was

interested in history, too. Rose is the only caregiver I have ever known. According to our records from my father, grandfather, great-grandfather, and great-great grandfather, yes. In the 1800s it looks as though the contents were shipped from Switzerland at the request of the Egyptian keeper. It is usually signed over before the woman dies. It has been women from different areas of the world. In the late 1800s, a woman who lived in France maintained it until she turned it over to a woman who lived in Boston. Then a local Creole woman was responsible. You are the first woman from New York that I know about."

He paused as they absorbed the information.

He instructed them, "If you have any other questions or need further help, I'll be in my office upstairs. I do have some interesting documentation upstairs concerning the keepers of the deposit box that you may want copies of before you leave Sumer. Just use that phone on the wall to ring for help. Here is my card if you should want to contact me at home to come back in. I imagine it will take you a few days to comprehend everything that is in the security box."

Anna Marie thanked him and turned back to the area of the security boxes.

She said to Christa, "Well here goes. I'm anxious to see the insides but also frightened of what we might find. It already feels like a huge responsibility, without even knowing what is inside. I have my notes from Granny Rose's directions over the years but if you don't mind, for the first time I would just like to view the objects. Then we can decide how we want to match the notes to the objects and what we want to do next."

Christa indicated agreement to Anna Marie's suggestion.

They carefully took out the numbered 1649 security safety deposit box, placing it on the table in front of them.

Anna Marie said to Christa, "Isn't it strange that Granny Rose was here early this year. She never mentioned it to either of us. Yet we had to be on her mind when she was here."

Christa said, "The whole thing is strange. I trust Granny Rose, this is obviously something very important to her."

Anna Marie placed the golden key inside the lock and turned. The box lid sprung open. Both ladies stepped back from the table almost expecting Granny Rose's spirit to come out of the box. Anna Marie reached over and carefully opened the lid further as they looked at the carefully wrapped items in the box.

Christa asked, "How do we want to open these? Any ideas...?"

Anna Marie answered, "I think we just use our instincts. Obviously Granny Rose believed that we would do the right thing."

Anna Marie reached in and took out a rolled parchment paper, wrapped in gold string. She said to Christa, "Maybe this will have some explanation or directions. Let's start with this."

Anna Marie untied the string and unrolled the multi-sheets of parchment paper. The paper was obviously hundreds of years old and likely very rare. Anna Marie wondered how it had stayed in this condition for so long.

The top of the first sheet had a date of May 1, 1675 written in calligraphy. Next to the date were a woman's name and a reference to an address that looked like Egypt or someplace in the Near East.

Anna Marie said, "Do you believe what good condition this is in if this means the date on the paper was the date the note was written? And look, there are women's names following the first name with date intervals of about thirty to forty years in between. There is one here that is only five years, but the others are close to the same amount of time."

Christa looked intently, then turned to the next sheet of paper, the sheet after that, and to the last sheet where she exclaimed, "Look Anna Marie. Here is the last submission. It has your name and the date of two days ago."

Anna Marie looked at the paper with a puzzled expression.

She said, "How can that be? That was the date Granny Rose died but Mr. Avebury said that Granny Rose was here months ago. He said that was the last time anyone opened this box.

Either he's mistaken or Granny Rose knew the exact date that she was going to die!"

Anna Marie shook her head in confusion. "

This gets stranger and stranger. Let's see what else is in here. We'll study that sheet for names. Maybe we can do some Internet searches to see if we can find anything out about the names of the women when we have more time. At least we have access to information through the internet that the other keepers of the box did not have."

Christa agreed.

Anna Marie indicated for her to open the next object, which was a sterling silver cup engraved with a crescent moon and a snake for a handle. There were v or triangular shapes all around the cup with initials G.A.I.A. engraved on the top part of the cup. Neither could guess the meaning of the engravings or the age of the cup.

Christa said, "Don't you think that cup is at least as old as the paper?"

Anna Marie replied, "I suspect even older. And I'm wondering if that reference to a bank in Egypt may be to sheets of paper with names even older than the 1600s. Maybe there are other objects that go with these items? Granny Rose never mentioned traveling outside the US but then there is so much about Granny Rose that we don't know or will never know."

The next object they unwrapped was a carved ivory statue that looked like a pregnant woman with no arms or legs. The bottom of the statue was pointed with no distinct feet.

Anna Marie asked Christa, "Can you guess the age of this? And have you ever seen anything like this?"

Christa responded, "No. It looks to be at least hundreds of years old. I wish I knew more about how to date objects, as I would guess that they are thousands of years old. But why would it be in this security box instead of in a museum?"

Anna Marie said, "I don't know but I'm beginning to think that all the objects in here are of museum quality with inestimable value. For that alone I can see why Granny Rose valued them and wanted them safe. But there must be some reason they are all together in this box and some reason that Granny Rose had them. It looks like there have been women caretakers of these objects for at least hundreds of years. When we were in Montana, I wondered who Granny Rose was. There was just something very strange about her immediate connection with Reverend Sophia as well as her apparent knowledge of the rituals that were part of her wedding."

Christa and Anna Marie looked at the remaining objects in the security box.

Christa said, "There is something else that is very strange about all this. This security box looks small and yet there are still many more objects left to open than you would expect to find in a box this size. It is as though it is a box used by a magician with a false bottom, yet I can feel the top and bottom so there can't be a false bottom."

Anna Marie nodded and took out the next object, even more confused than when they had first arrived.

She unwrapped what appeared to be a sterling silver mirror. The glass of the mirror was wavy, like waves of shimmering water. The silver was not tarnished, dolphins engraved on the handle of the mirror.

Anna Marie exclaimed, "This looks like something that could have been made in ancient Greece. Maybe there are modern day artisans that have created reproductions that look extremely realistic."

"Or maybe," Christa said, "These are the real thing?"

Christa unwrapped the next object, "This looks like antlers from an ancient reindeer or horned animal that might not even exist today? What do you think these markings are all around the antlers?"

Anna Marie said, "I don't know. I've seen something like this in a textbook. That object was found at a site near Stonehenge. It was thought to be an ancient calendar using the moon and women's cycles to mark the passing of time."

She counted the rows of markings, each distinctly separate from the others and said, "There are thirteen different sections of markings."

The next objects were a sea shell with engravings of fish, a set of thirteen very tiny golden bees on what looked like a pure gold bracelet, a small piece of wood covered in carved snakes encircling the wood, a gold circle pin with a lapis stone in it's center, a porous looking black rock that reminded Anna Marie of a meteorite, a tiny clay vessel with engravings of a pig with a butterfly on the end of the nose, a golden bee on a jar of pure golden honey, a ring of a blue material the ladies suspected could be turquoise, and a sheaf of wheat made out of sterling silver.

They were unable to guess the meaning of each object and became more frustrated as the afternoon wore on. They reached for the last object, which was a carved alabaster dove.

Anna Marie said, "These are some of the most beautiful objects I have ever seen. But after looking at each of these, I am even more puzzled as to why Granny Rose wants me to have them or to make the decision to pass them down to you. I don't know about you Christa, but I am emotionally drained and hungry."

Anna Marie brushed her hair away from her eyes in obvious exhaustion.

She suggested, "How about if we go back to the Inn? I had thought we would take the objects in the box with us. I suspect we could not buy insurance for these objects that would be even close to their inestimable value. I don't want to take the chance of any one of them being lost. We'll make a list and go back and talk about what we should do next. I also think I want to buy a digital camera to take pictures of all the objects in the box, including the lists."

Christa agreed, quickly summarizing the objects as best she could in her daily notebook. As they left the bank, the banker handed them the information he had promised them.

When they arrived back to the Inn the children were all quietly eating homemade ice cream, looking tired from the gardening activities. Sybil asked the ladies if they would like some ice cream.

When they said yes, Sybil suggested, "I am going to lay the children down for a nap and then we can talk. How about if you go out into the garden and I'll join you after the children are nestled in their beds?"

Both Anna Marie and Christa were relieved as Sybil poured them sun brewed iced tea sweetened with honey. She dished out the ice cream in crystal that could have been hundreds of years old.

Anna Marie asked, "No paper dishes and plastic spoons, even for the children?"

Sybil answered as she left the room to take care of the children, "Half the enjoyment of food is the appearance. The other half is the preparation and anticipation. Paper plates and plastic would destroy the pleasure. Why do that just to save one broken glass or dish? I find that children respect that. I never have any broken dishes. I think they love coming to visit me because I trust them to understand the value of the objects I give them, making them feel valued."

Anna Marie and Christa walked with their snacks to the garden Sybil had indicated.

Christa exclaimed, "This is beautiful. I feel like I am back in one of the old plantations. Look, there's the Mississippi in the distance. I didn't realize we were so close to the river."

Anna Marie responded, "This is peaceful and restful here. Just what I needed after this afternoon's increasing unanswered questions. I feel even more confused now than I did before we opened the box."

Sybil came up from behind, commenting, "Puzzled by all the objects you found in the security box? That's normal for your first time or two viewing the box."

Anna Marie turned quickly, shocked, "How did you know about

the box. We never said anything to you about why we were here."

Sybil answered, "Because for many generations, including when my great-grandmother was the innkeeper, the women who are the guardians of that box stay here. Rose and I were very close friends as were her predecessor, Brigit O'Connor. My grandmother first told me of the box, the objects in it, and about our responsibility to care for the caregivers of the box."

Anna Marie, now even more puzzled asked, "But how can that be? My travel agent suggested we stay here. This wasn't Granny Rose's idea as she really gave us very little direction."

Sybil chuckled and said, "Rose didn't have to give you any direction. This is where generations of caregivers stay. You would have been guided to do the same. It's the spiral of life that many women are never even aware exists yet surrounds each woman throughout her life. While it appears to be a choice for you, it really was predestined that you would stay with me. It is partly because I can help waylay some of your frustrations and lack of knowledge. It's also because this is a place of peace and understanding cycles."

Both Christa and Anna Marie looked confused.

A gentle breeze blew making the afternoon heat in the garden very comfortable. Anna Marie did not know how to answer Sybil, so she looked around the garden while trying to get her thoughts together to speak to them out loud later. The garden was abundant with every color and kind of plant native to this region. There were some plants that were not considered native like a bamboo tree thriving alongside native plants.

Bees were busy in the heat of the afternoon flying from flower to flower to gather as much nectar as possible from each plant, the plant chosen for that days' collection consistent. Birds chirped overhead, even in the heat, the sound of a Catbird joining the cacophony of sound.

She thought, "Maybe it is a mockingbird common in the South and it is only coincidence?"

Anna Marie turned to Sybil, "What can you tell us to help us understand the objects in the box?"

Sybil answered as she pulled out a leather-bound journal, "It is what I can give you. This is a journal with a list of resources. You are not expected to understand the objects anymore than the women who came before you did in the beginning. You are expected to learn and over time, understand the ancient meaning of these objects as well as their connection to the history of women. You are the preserver of the information. Your role will become clearer as time goes on and The Others will come to assist you in understanding."

Sybil motioned to Christa as she said, "As you learn you will guide Christa to learn after you if she is willing and if she is the next logical chosen one. It is rare that the successor is chosen at the same time as the Guardian. Obviously, Granny Rose thought you would be the next logical Guardian. The Others will understand your own choices Christa. I suggest you both learn it together at the beginning so that Christa is better prepared than you are Anna Marie to assume this heady responsibility, should she so choose. Most of The Guardians spend many years preparing and start out as one of the family."

Looking to Anna Marie, Sybil paused to note her reaction. She noticed that both ladies were listening to her intently with obvious interest.

She continued, "Part of the responsibility is learning this history and carrying it on so that other women after us will understand their own rich heritage. You will be given a journal when The Others determine you are ready for that next step in your discovery. It is planned you will meet others who once took this journey or who have clues for you to learn the pathway forward. In this way we will pass the information on orally, in writing, and through these precious objects, as women have done for thousands of years before us. It is a great responsibility but also a great honor to have been chosen. Only women who are capable of this honor are chosen."

She paused to watch a great heron overhead on her daily

feeding at the river as Sybil assured them, "Rose obviously had great faith in your integrity and commitment to your promise to her. Rose was one of the best caregivers we have ever had. Her decision to give it to you next can only mean that she thinks you can carry on as she has done."

Anna Marie shook her head, "I don't understand how she could think I am capable of this task or have enough time left to understand all of the implications of these precious objects. We only spent the one summer together and a few days after that every year with ongoing correspondence in between but not about the security box. We talked about it so rarely I thought she had forgotten she had assigned that to me after her death. It is not as though she could observe me for lengths of time to make her decision. She made the decision on the day she married, or even before that day."

Sybil sighed and patted Anna Marie's arm, "Do you think your journey when you met Rose and spent time together was chance? Do you also think that really was the only time or life that you knew each other? Rose has known you for thousands of years, as she has known you Christa. You have known her in other bodies and spaces. The pattern of who cares for our history is a spiral pattern that keeps returning to those spirits who have best cared for these objects in the past. Rely on your instinct to learn. Go back to your sub-conscious to return to what you already know. Trust yourself and trust Rose."

Anna Marie felt an immense sense of peace as she listened to Sybil's words. She knew that everything that Sybil had said was true. She was only expected to return to what she had already known and to try to pass that knowledge on to others. That sense of harmony and understanding carried with her throughout the evening. The evening itself was restful with an early dinner and after dinner drinks on the veranda in the twilight overlooking the flow of the river beyond, a tributary meandering into the nearby great Mississippi.

Later that night, Anna Marie woke up to a sound coming from outside, the eerie echo of a voice calling her. She dressed quickly and walked out into the beautiful night, the chirping of the peeper frogs in the background and the crescent moon shining overhead. The moon brought remembrance to her heart, as she thought of the lessons about the moon and sky from Granny Rose. For the first time, she understood the difference between thinking with the heart rather than the mind.

Rustling grew louder behind her. She turned to see Christa coming toward her, both aware they had been called here for a reason. Christa approached Anna Marie, placing her arm around her shoulders as they both silently watched the moon climb over the cupola of the mansion.

Christa whispered, excitedly, "Anna Marie do you see Granny Rose's face in the window?"

Anna Marie answered, "Yes. But I also see the thousands of women's faces behind her. Granny Rose is with her family of women. She is telling us that someday we will join her, too." They watched quietly as one by one the women walked past the window to wave to the two women below who waved back each time. The very last vision to leave the window was Granny Rose who waved and threw a kiss to the two women.

She mouthed the words, "We have a Southwind here waiting for you when you are ready. Ted will be able to join you next time. Enjoy your lives and teach other women our story."

The vision of Granny Rose faded. The two women watched in silence as the crescent moon continued to move across the sky, in its never-ending cycle of life and renewal.

Author's Notes

I originally published *Whistling Up The Wind* in 2007. Back then, I imagined I'd complete the second book in the series within a short period of time. Fifteen years later, with the second book still in the development stage, I attended a small Writer's Retreat in Southern France organized and presented by author Kathleen McGowan and the Publisher of Flower of Life Press, Astara J. Ashley.

I was re-energized by the opportunity for support for publishing, printing, and marketing my work. The agreement was for me to accomplish what had seemed impossible over the past years—publish book two, *Following the Cycles of the Moon*, and book three, *Gazing at the Stars,* as well as republish book one, *Whistling Up the Southwind* (formerly titled *Whistling Up the Wind)* in one year, each as part of my "Women with Wisdom" Series.

I was determined to complete this challenge to give voice and presence to older women, remind readers of the importance of women's friendships supporting each other, and help restore ancient women's history in subtle ways through a modern-day story. Interweaving the social issues challenging women today was necessary and fun.

While the books are fiction, I did extensive research to ensure that the stories could have happened to my characters. I tweaked locations and changed around some dates that do not impact the stories to make a better flow for readers. I hope that you enjoy the stories as modern-day events, become curious about the women's history in the hidden layers of the story, and become a critical questioner, asking the tough questions about why women's history has been suppressed and what you can do to bring light forward.

Thank you for taking the time to read my books and for sharing them with others. I hope to meet you someday to learn about your history. Take joy in your days and your reading.

—*Mary Kathleen McKenna*

References and Readings on Ancient Women's History

I have enclosed the following list of readings in the hopes that you will want to explore the rich but hidden history of women. Granny Rose and Anna Marie would have encouraged you to do that. This can be your gift to each of them. This is only a very brief list. There are thousands of resources available that can take each one of you a lifetime to discover.

Armstrong, Karen (1987). *The Gospel according to Woman: Christianity's creation of the sex war in the West.* New York: Anchor Press/Doubleday.

Baring, Anne & Cashford, Jule (1991). *The Myth of the Goddess: Evolution of an Image.* Viking Arhana.

Begg, Ean (1985). *The Cult of the Black Virgin.* London: Arkana.

Bochofen, J. (1967, translation from original 1800s writings). *Myth, Religion, and Mother Right.* Princeton University Press.

Campbell, Joseph (1959). *The Masks of God: Primitive Mythology.* New York: The Viking Press.

Dames, Michael (1976). *The Silbury Treasure: The Great Goddess rediscovered.* London: Thames & Hudson.

Engelsman, Joan (1973). *The Feminine Dimension of the Divine.* Philadelphia: The Westminster Press.

Frederick, Paul (1979). *The Meaning of Aphrodite.* Chicago: The University of Chicago Press.

Goldenberg, N. (1979). *Changing of the gods: Feminism and the end of Traditional Religions.* Boston: Beacon Press.

Harding, M. Esther (1955). *Woman's Mysteries: Ancient and Modern: A psychological interpretation of the feminine principle as portrayed in Myth, Story, and Dreams.* Los Angeles: Pantheon Books, Inc.

Iglehart, Hallie (1983). *Womanspirit: A guide to women's wisdom.* San Francisco: Harper & Row, Publishers.

Johnson, Buffie (1988). *Lady of the Beasts: Ancient Images of the Goddess and Her Sacred Animals.* San Francisco: Harper & Row.

Ochshorn, Judith (1981). *The Female Experience and the nature of the divine.* Bloomington: Indiana University Press.

Olson, Carl (Ed.) (1983). *The book of the Goddess Past and Present: An Introduction to Her Religion.* New York: Crossroad.

Pagels, Elaine (1979). *The Gnostic Gospels.* New York: Random House.

Paris, Ginetter (1986). *Pagan Meditations: The World of Aphrodite, Artemis, and Hestia.* Dallas: Spring Publications, Inc.

Patai, Raphael (1990). *The Hebrew Goddess.* Detroit: Wayne State University Press.

Reed, E. (1975). *Woman's Evolution from Matriarchal Clan to Patriarchal Family.* New York: Pathfinder press, Inc.

Rowbathom, Sheila (1973). *Hidden from History: Red iscovering Women in History from the 17th Century to the Present.* New York: Random House.

Rush, Anne Kent (1976). *Moon, Moon.* Random House/Moon Books.

Shlaim, Leonard (1998). *The Alphabet versus the Goddess: The Conflict Between Word and Image.* New York: Arkana.

Stone, Merlin (1976). *When God Was a Woman.* New York: The Dial Press.

Stone, Merlin (1990). *Ancient Mirrors of Womanhood.* Boston: Beacon Press.

Tanner, N. (1981). *On Becoming Human.* London: Cambridge University Press.

Warner, Marina (1976). *Alone of All Her Sex: The Myth and Cult of the Virgin Mary.* New York: Alfred A Knopf.

About the Author

Mary Kathleen McKenna, aka Kathie Bishop, Ph.D., began her journey researching women's history and advocating for women's rights in her teens. She remains a lifelong feminist, actively seeking out women's stories, in particular, ancient women's history (no, women did not sit in caves by the fire while the men hunted, fished, created tools, and found resources to bring home to their  families as current written history would like us to believe).

Adopted before she was born, Mary Kathleen sought her biological connection to the past and at the same time, searched for hidden history which often turned out to be hidden in plain sight. Expecting to take about six months, Mary Kathleen has found that thirty years later, she is still uncovering that history and applying that knowledge to her writing. While her writing is fictional, the stories are always thoroughly researched. They are written in layers with characters from the present who also seek their past history, often uncovering surprising information in mysterious ways.

Ms. Mckenna lives in central New York at the foot of the Adirondack Mountains where the snow can sometimes reach the second story windows in the winter. Her second, much warmer home near Tampa, Florida is where she spends most of the winter. She lives with her beloved husband Ron and her cherished pet family. She has two adult children Vincent Eric (poem author) and Katrina Anne.

Contact the author at **www.MaryKathleenMcKenna.com** or email **bisbur1@earthlink.com.**

About the Poet

Vincent Bishop aka Vincent Pirillo is the son of the author, Mary Kathleen McKenna. Vincent has been writing poems and studying esoteric ideas since very early in his life. Besides the continuation of his life-long studies on the hidden past, his hobbies include music and its importance to solving social inequities, as well as rescuing cats.

As a proud mother, Mary Kathleen wanted the world to experience his work. She shares, "Vincent has taught me so much, as many of the historical and esoteric beliefs he studied long before I knew they existed, helped me move to deeper levels of understanding."

When Vincent was eight years old, his mother and stepfather accused him of plagiarizing his poems, finding it difficult to believe that a boy of his age could write the very advanced thoughts presented in his poetry. They did exercises with him to prove his authorship by giving him topics and asking him to write a poem about it right in front of them, and the products proved that he was the sole/soul (pun intended) author of his poetry.

Vincent was first published at age ten in a poetry anthology, and is now thrilled to partner with his mother on *Whistling Up the Southwind.*

Mary Kathleen is awestruck by his poetry and hopes that you, too, will enjoy the depth of his writing and appreciate his ancient soul.

Vincent currently works in data management and resides in central New York.

He can be reached at **www.marykathleenmckenna.com.**

FLOWER *of* LIFE PRESS

floweroflifepress.com